RECLAIMING THE SPY

AGENTS OF ESPIONAGE
BOOK TWO

LORRI DUDLEY

WILD HEART
BOOKS

In loving memory of my dad.
You sat in the front row and mouthed the lyrics to my vocal solos.
You came to all my long dance recitals.
And you read all my romance novels, even though you prefer
action/suspense.
I love you and miss you.

PROLOGUE

*L*aurel House, Worcestershire, England 1807

Abigail Hartington Emerson's new husband scooped her into his strong arms. Her petticoats flounced and her feet dangled in the air. Nicholas faltered a step, and she shrieked, digging her nails into the thick wool of his overcoat. "I love you, Nicholas Emerson, but it's bad portent to drop your new wife, especially before you cross the threshold."

The glint in those mischievous hazel eyes revealed he was teasing her by pretending to trip. "I'm not going to let you fall. In fact, now that I've made you mine, my plan is to never let you out of my arms."

She clung to his shoulders, buried her face in his neck, and breathed in his woodsy scent of newly cut cedar. The vibrations of Nick's husky laughter tickled her nose. She lifted her head but didn't relax her grip.

"Welcome to Laurel House, Mrs. Abigail Emerson." Nicholas raised his gaze to the rustic, two-story stone home that stretched along the bulrushes. Ivy climbed the exterior as if wrapping the house in a leafy embrace, and the primrose in full bloom burst with cheery color from each window box.

"Do you hear that?" He tilted his ear up.

Abby stilled but only heard a distant woodlark song.

"It's the sound of our future children playing."

"Truly?"

"I hear them as clearly as the clock tower."

"I do hope you're being prophetic and that I didn't marry a man who's as mad as a hatter."

A crooked smile graced his lips.

His breath mingled with hers, tickling her mouth and cheeks.

"Either way, I don't care. As long as you're mine." Public affection was considered improper, but on impulse she pressed her lips to his, savoring their velvety feel and his strong arms.

His mouth moved on hers with a slow, tantalizing kiss — just a taste of what the next forty or more years would hold.

The front door swung open.

Abby tore away with a gasp.

Mrs. Smith, the housekeeper, stepped aside and held the door to allow the newlyweds passage.

Heat spread through Abby's cheeks quicker than a house fire. When was she going to learn to control her whims? She avoided the woman's gaze as Nick's swept her across the entranceway into the open foyer.

The setting sun spilled its golden rays through the mullioned window, illuminating the large bouquet of red roses, most likely freshly cut from his mother's rose garden, that graced the pedestal table.

Her new home. Her grip on the lapel of his coat tightened. The reality of this momentous day sank in. She was Laurel Manor's new mistress.

Would she make a good wife? Would she please her new husband?

Nick's eyes sparked. He held her gaze while he addressed Mrs. Smith. "You may attend to your duties."

With a knowing smile, the woman bobbed a curtsy. The massive ring of keys at her hip jingled with her steps as she departed.

Nick held Abby tight and kicked the door shut with his heel. He leaned his forehead against hers and whispered, "I love you, Abigail Emerson."

She savored his possessive tone as much as she relished the sound of her new name. Her fingers slid over his collar and rubbed little circles along his neck.

A proud roar rumbled in his chest, and he mounted the stairs.

Abby tucked in her legs beneath her thick layers of petticoats. She laughed and squeezed him tight.

He stopped at the entrance of the bedchamber that adjoined his and slowly released her.

She melted down his body like a pat of butter on warm bread. When her slippers touched the floor, he crushed her to him.

He smelled heavenly—masculine and woodsy, comforting and breathtaking at the same time.

With a force of will, she disentangled her arms from around his neck.

"This will be your room."

She turned and gasped at the chamber decorated beautifully in rich, creamy ivory and gold fabrics. "It's lovely."

Her eyes settled on the large canopy bed in the center—the marriage bed—and her stomach fluttered.

He pointed to the right. "Over there is the adjoining door to my chamber. I'll give you ten minutes."

He scooted her in the direction of her lady's maid waiting in the corner. "Go and get yourself ready."

~

*N*icholas Emerson closed the door and strode into his stately room, loosening his cravat in front of the freestanding looking glass. By Jove, was this how Wellington felt after winning the Battle of Trafalgar? No longer would Nicholas be remembered as the crossed-eyed kid. His eye had straightened out as he'd grown. His clumsiness had faded, his investments in shipping had paid handsomely, and he'd just married his childhood friend—the loveliest lady in the Midlands. They'd discussed building a home, and he planned to build her a mansion to rival the grandest in all of Altonwood. He'd already spoken to his banker about purchasing land. The only thing he didn't hold was a title, and he had a plan laid out to accomplish that feat too. Abby wouldn't sacrifice her place in society by marrying him as his mother had when she married his father of a lower social class. By gaining a title, he'd ensure Abby walked among society where she belonged instead of merely reading about it in letters from her friends and family.

"May I help you with your dressing robe?" his valet asked.

Nicholas waved him off. "That will be all. I will dress myself this evening."

"Master Emerson, an important missive arrived for you earlier." His valet placed it in the silver tray on the bureau. "It has the king's seal on it. I thought perhaps you'd want to read it straight away."

"Splendid, Wesley. Good night."

He glanced at the adjoining door. Had he told her ten minutes? He should have said five. Even then, it would be an arduous five minutes knowing Abby prepared herself for their wedding night in the next room. He itched to run his fingers through her glossy black hair, free it from its coiffure and see it frame her wholesome, heart-shaped face. He'd swim in those crystal-blue eyes that glittered with laughter. It was her smile, however, that left him feeling like he could conquer the world. He'd often conned Stephen Hartington, her twin brother, for supper invitations just to watch Abby smile from across the table.

Nicholas picked up the envelope from the silver tray, needing a distraction, and turned it over. It indeed held the king's emblem. He broke the wax seal with a quick swipe of his letter opener, pulled out the paper, and unfolded it. He scanned the contents and stumbled back, dropping onto the edge of the bed's feather mattress. Gripping the page closer, he reread the entire letter carefully, hoping the second reading would reveal a different result.

In a daze, he neatly refolded the page and placed it back in the tray. Nicholas squeezed his eyes closed and rubbed his temples.

Blast it all, he didn't expect to receive a summons to report for military duty for another month or so. He hadn't even been married a full day yet. What was he going to tell Abby? He'd been too rash that night he'd bought his commission, too distraught by the thought of losing her to a titled gentleman. She'd proved a thousand times over she didn't care about such things, but that night, something within him had snapped. He'd made a desperate decision.

And now came the price.

CHAPTER 1

*S*nuggled in a wing-back chair next to her mother-in-law's sickbed, Abby steadied the open Bible in her lap, her legs tucked underneath a blanket to ward off the chill. The thick velvet curtains were pulled back to allow in afternoon sunlight, but the weather had turned, bringing an early frost. A fire popped in the hearth, working to combat the cold, while outside the leaves swirled in the brisk breeze, a final dance of vibrant autumn colors.

Mama Em, as Abby fondly called her mother-in-law, lay abed, her head and shoulders propped into a reclined position with pillows and the covers drawn up to her chest. A wheezy rattle sounded with each intake of breath, and Abby fought the urge to cough for her. Abby read aloud from the book of Isaiah. She paused between verses.

Her mother-in-law feebly smiled. "You know I care for you deeply." Mama Em's voice sounded weak, but her rheumy eyes shone brightly.

Abby placed the book in her lap. "As I care for you."

"You are the daughter I never had." A cough forced its way through. "I have cherished every moment we've shared. Nicholas's final present to me was you. My only regret is that you have wasted so many years taking care of an old lady." She paused and another wheeze rattled. "You will be well provided for when I'm gone. Promise me you will move on. Fall in love again and live your life."

Abby's lips wobbled as she fought to keep her smile. "No one can take Nicholas's place."

"Promise me you'll try."

Abby relented when Mama Em struggled to rise. "I promise."

Mama Em relaxed back onto her pillow. Despite her labored breathing and frail state, love illuminated her face.

Cold prickles raised the fine hairs on Abby's arm. Abby wasn't ready to lose her mother-in-law and friend—her last connection to Nick. Seeking comfort for herself and a diversion for Mama Em, Abby flipped the page of a well-worn Bible and continued reading.

"Abby, do you see him?" The strained lines in Mama Em's face softened.

Only the two of them were in the room, and other than a bird swooping past, nothing in the window scenery had changed. Abby pushed the blanket aside and knelt by the bed. She scooped her mother-in-law's wrinkled hand into her own and rubbed it to warm the woman's chilled bones. "See who?"

"The man outside the window standing under the willow tree. Sweetheart, look at him. He has the most wonderful eyes you've ever seen, so loving and caring." Her eyes widened. "Could it be?"

A swift wind swayed and bent the tree branches together, but there was no sign of a man.

"My sweet Jesus." A tear slipped down Mama Em's cheek. "He's beautiful, so beautiful."

Her eyes fluttered closed, and the pink of her skin faded to a gray pallor.

Abby jumped to her feet. Her heart pounded against the strings of her corset as she hovered over Mama Em.

God, please don't let her die.

She put her ear above Mama Em's mouth. Hearing the gentle inhale and exhale of breath, she sagged with relief.

Mama Em opened her eyes, but they glazed over as if peering into another realm. "There it is again." Mama Em moved her index finger, bouncing along to an imaginary rhythm.

The wind rattled the glass pane, and a chill slid across Abby's shoulders.

"Wonderous music." Mama Em paused to catch her breath. "Like bells ringing ... not bells—voices, tenors and sopranos ... a grand chorus." She sighed. "It's glorious."

Her eyes glazed over, and Abby's heart pressed against the top of her rib cage. "Mama Em, I shall summon Mrs. Smith. Don't go to sleep. I'll return straight away."

Abby released her mother-in-law's hand and slipped silently into the hall. Once the door clicked closed, she gathered her skirts and ran. "Mrs. Smith!"

The housekeeper stepped out of the larder with a bit of flour dusting her nose.

"Come quickly. It's Mama Em."

Her face paled. "Oh, dear." She instructed the scullery maid to send for the physician and rushed alongside Abby to Mama Em's room.

The two women crouched on opposite sides of the bed.

Mama Em's eyes shone clear and alert and danced with life as they had over ten years before. "Oh look, it's Henry." She waved her frail hand to her invisible husband, who had been gone a decade. Her face animated, her expression changing to one of childlike glee. "And Mama and Papa ... Hello ..."

Abby's tears overflowed, running down her cheeks and splashing on the bodice of her dress. She choked back a sob. *Don't leave me*, she wanted to cry. *I can't lose you too.*

Her mother-in-law's chest rose and fell at a slow but even pace compared to her earlier labored breathing. A peaceful expression softened her features, reminding Abby of the vivacious woman who'd taught Abby how to manage Laurel House's staff and shared stories of Nicholas's childhood. Her strong spirit had pulled Abby from her grief over Nick's disappearance ten years ago.

"How lovely to see everyone." Mama Em peered straight ahead, and her gaze drifted along the empty back wall as if scanning a crowd. "I've missed you all."

Silence filled the room, broken by a loud pop from the fire that startled Abby.

Mama Em's eyelids softly fluttered closed, and she muttered, "But where is Nicholas?"

Abby's mouth opened in a silent gasp.

A deep rush of air passed between Mama Em's lips, and the tension left her body.

"Mama Em?" A harsh sob tore from Abby's throat.

"She's gone, m'lady. Gone to kingdom come." Mrs. Smith pulled the covers over Mama Em's face. "Her spirit is in heaven. God rest her soul."

Mrs. Smith patted Abby's shoulder. "I'll give you some time alone." She slipped quietly from the room.

Abby buried her face into the coverlet and wept.

~

*A*bby struggled to breathe against the vice of grief squeezing her chest. She stood, with hymnal in hand, choking out the words in the first pew. Mama Em's still form rested in the highly polished coffin in the nave of the same rustic church in which Abby and Nick had been married. The coffin had a surreal aura. Mama Em appeared like herself, but her body lay like a porcelain doll—a beautiful shell whose spirit had streamed into heaven. *She's with Jesus.* The hot pressure of a fresh bout of tears threatened to erupt, but Abby gulped it back.

The tears weren't for Mama Em. They were selfish tears. Her mother-in-law was her only remaining link to Nick. Abby twisted the gold wedding band on her left hand. Even though he'd been missing for ten years, presumed a casualty of the Napoleonic war, she couldn't bear to remove the ring. If she still wore it, then maybe he'd come back.

A choked sob gargled in her throat. Who was she fooling? Nick was dead. He wasn't coming back. She'd tried to accept it over the years, but her heart refused. She'd tried to believe it for her mother and Mama Em's sakes, but Mama Em's last moment in life haunted her thoughts.

What did it mean? *Mama Em saw Jesus, but she didn't see Nick.*

Was he still alive somewhere, trapped in some French prison? Or had he not been admitted into heaven and now spent eternity in ...? She couldn't bear to finish the thought. The song ended while Abby sent a quick prayer for her husband's soul. Nick had attended church every Sunday with his mother. He'd bowed his head in prayer at family meals. Abby had assumed he'd had a relationship with their Heavenly Father when she'd married him, but had he really?

Despite the recent unseasonably warm weather shift, a shudder ran through her body. She shifted in the family pew. A familiar restlessness itched her fingers and toes and Abby prayed again for God to take away her unsettled spirit, but it continued to plague her. She concentrated on keeping her back straight and remaining still to honor Mama Em.

The vicar stood in front of his congregation, preaching his sentiments for the deceased. Sniffles sounded throughout the room. Abby glanced back at the seats filled with family, friends, and neighbors, and the many tears shed, evidenced by the flutter of white handkerchiefs. The congregants offered her sympathetic looks and smiles of encouragement. She offered a weak smile before turning back to face the vicar.

The rusty hinges of the old church door creaked. Abby wiped her lace handkerchief under her eyes and nose before glancing over her shoulder. The back door of the small church peeked open a crack, just enough to let a single person pass through. The tenebrous silhouette of a lone man dressed in mourning blacks entered. A slight limp threw off the stranger's furtive gate. His shoulders were hunched, but she guessed him to be almost six feet tall. He removed his beaver hat, revealing tousled dark hair much longer than what would be considered stylish.

The sexton opened a pew door and gestured a silent invitation for the latecomer to sit, and he slid into a seat in the back pew.

An influx in the vicar's volume drew Abby's attention back to the open casket. Pushing past the pain piercing her heart, she willed herself to stay strong and not give in to the sob clogging her throat. She fought to take her mind off the past, but it was a day for remembering and saying goodbye. Now that Mama Em was gone, Abby was in a free fall. Maybe it was past time for her to let go. Helpless to prevent it, her thoughts drifted to her wedding day.

Nick had burst into her parents' drawing room because she'd taken too long in arriving at the church.

A dreary rain had made certain roads in Altonwood impassable and delayed her twin brother, Stephen, and her extended family's arrival. She sat in the middle of the floor, wilted flowers drooping in her hand. The gown, which her neighbor, Lady Etheridge, complained made Abby's complexion sallow, pooled around her. Tears streamed down her cheeks much like they did now.

Nick had pulled her to her feet, wrapped her in his strong embrace, and whispered in her ear. *My beautiful darling, all I need is you and the vicar. The rest is pomp and circumstance.*

Her fears and disappointment had melted away, and the next thing she knew he stood smiling at her in front of the altar professing to love her until "death do us part."

Death.

The vicar's undulating voice brought Abby's attention back to the present. "We're but a breath, a wisp of smoke, a gentle breeze passing through on our way to eternity."

The ceremony ended, and the mourners proceeded to the family cemetery plot in the far corner of the churchyard. Bright sun warmed Abby's face but not her spirits.

Guests dressed in mourning clothes formed dark shadows against the background of the church's honey-colored limestone. A shift in the breeze drifted the familiar aroma of cedar her way. The scent always reminded her of Nick. She breathed it in and glanced about with the irrational notion she might see him.

Lady Etheridge lowered her parasol, and Abby caught a glimpse of the mysterious stranger who'd slipped in late.

Offset from the group gathering around the gravesite, he stood in the background. His high collar points covered most of his cheeks, and the brim of his beaver hat hung low over his face, hiding his features.

She felt his stare, but from under the shadow of his hat brim, she couldn't be certain.

The dark figure tipped his hat before roaming among the headstones.

Who was he? A friend of the family? A distant relative? An old Eton chum of Nick's? Why was he lurking on the edge of the crowd and not interacting with anyone? She followed him with her gaze, catching a quick peek of him over the shoulder of Lord McAllister, who was conversing with Mama.

Abby's scalp tingled, and she stepped in the stranger's direction. Why did this enigmatic man with his large frame and long hair cause her heart to quicken its pace?

"Lady Abigail." Lord McAllister gripped her hand. His smooth skin stretched over high cheekbones, and his light eyes conveyed his sorrow. "My deepest sympathies for your loss. If I may be of service in any way, please don't hesitate to ask."

"Thank you." She forced a weak smile.

Mama touched Abby's lower back and guided her to the grave. Lord McAllister hovered near her elbow.

Headstones dotted the lush grass landscape. Their tilted moss-covered shapes begged not to be forgotten.

The vicar spoke concluding remarks before the pallbearers lowered the casket into the ground. The first thud of dirt echoed off the casket's lid, and it reverberated within Abby's heart like a chapter of her life slamming closed.

There hadn't been a casket at Nicholas's funeral, never a body to bury, but now hearing the soft earth being cast down, Abby felt the finality of it all.

They are not coming back. He is never coming back.

A breeze rustled the leaves and lifted the loose strands that had escaped her coiffure. Abby raised her chin and blinked back tears.

Her blurred gaze locked on the stranger. The air quivered with tension between them before he turned away, edging the crowd's perimeter.

She turned to ask her mother whether she'd recognized

him, but Mama was engaged with guests bestowing their regards.

One after another, neighbors grasped Abby's hands and offered their deepest sympathy, and she found herself entwined in an overwhelming display of heartfelt compassion. She waited for the man in black to approach and offer his sentiments, hoping to find out his connection, but instead she caught the swirl of his cape just before he disappeared into the woods.

∾

*T*hree days later, Abby was still caught up in a dizzying whirlwind of callers paying their respects. Pies and breads poured in as townsfolk showed their love in the only way they knew, through food. She didn't have the heart to eat but thanked everyone with a wholehearted smile she hoped demonstrated her appreciation.

As the sun sank below the horizon and the last guest was ushered out, Abby slumped into a low-backed armchair. After days of hosting—standing, conversing, and pouring her guests' tea—her legs ached to her bones. It had been helpful to stay busy, but now as she sank her weary muscles into the chair, she once again fought the urge to cry.

"I had no idea how many people were touched by Mama Em." Abby rested her arms on the wooden armrests, not caring if it appeared unladylike.

Mama passed her a cup of steaming tea. "Mrs. Emerson was well loved by all." She ran her fingers down her daughter's hairline, tucking a stray strand behind her ear. "You represented the family wonderfully, but I know it's taken a toll on you."

Her mama sat in an adjacent chair, and they sipped their tea in companionable silence until Mama spoke again. "Abby darling, now that Mrs. Emerson has gone to be with the Lord, it's time for you to remarry."

Abby's grip on the cup handle tightened.

"There is still a chance for you to enjoy the season. You are not yet on the shelf at seven and twenty. You've mourned your husband and cared for his mother, and now it's time to think about your future and setting up a nursery." Mama folded her hands. "In the eyes of the crown, you are free to marry. I realize this is difficult to hear, and I should have pressed you on this a few years ago, but you are clinging to a fantasy. Nicholas is gone. It's time for you to consider your future. I've talked it over with Stephen, and he agrees."

A pinprick of betrayal jabbed at Abby's heart. Stephen was her twin and had been Nick's best friend. He should understand her and, above all, be on her side. But now, Stephen had Katherine and little Benjamin. They were his priority.

"Stephen and I want you to be happy. You've always dreamed of having children, and it's not too late. I had you and Stephen in my thirties."

Abby put down her cup. Children would be wonderful, but she envisioned them with Nick's eyes and thick hair.

"Lord McAllister asks about you whenever given the chance. I think you should make it known that you are accepting suitors."

A heaviness weighted Abby.

Maybe her mother-in-law, mother, and brother were right. But Lord McAllister? She'd only held hospitable fondness for the man. She wet her lips and forced her voice to remain level. "I shall consider it."

CHAPTER 2

*A*bby gripped the railing and pulled her tired body on unsteady legs up the stairs to her bedchamber at Laurel House, where a maid assisted her in readying for bed. She sat in front of the mirror and grimaced at the sight of her ragged face. Her normally vibrant blue eyes had paled to a dull gray and were still puffy from crying. She pinched her cheeks to restore their color, but they merely turned splotchy. Hopefully, a good night's sleep would restore her glow.

She picked up a brush and pulled it through her hair until it crackled from static. The monotonous motion soothed her and provided a chance to sort through her day before considering the possibilities of tomorrow.

Grief left ugly scars, trying its best to pull her into despair. She fought to keep her optimism, as she had done for the last decade. Mama Em's voice echoed in her ears. *Things will get better. You will get through this. Just keep breathing.*

Abby set down the brush and knelt beside her bed in prayer, spilling her fears to God out of habit, but was God even listening? If He cared, would she still be going through this? Wouldn't He have done something to help Nick or Mama Em?

When she finished, she climbed into bed. The cool fabric encased her like a healing balm for her weary limbs. With a deep exhale, she released the tension of the day and sank into the soft surface, but sleep wouldn't come.

It wasn't fear for her future that plagued her. It was the past. Mama Em's last moments played over and over in her mind, keeping the much-needed sleep from her grasp. She flopped onto her back and debated ringing for a servant to bring her a cup of warm milk, but she was too exhausted to rise and tug the bell pull. Eventually, she stared at the ceiling and created shapes out of the moonlit shadows cast there. Over and over, the same thought returned.

Mama Em hadn't seen Nick in heaven.

Abby flipped over and pressed the pillow around her head as if it could block her mind from running scenarios. She'd become an expert at thinking "what if," but it never solved anything.

What if she never slept again?

"Harrumph!" she grunted under the pillow.

Nick was dead. All her life she'd been impulsive. Yet in this, she stubbornly clung onto hope, as if her wanting it with all her heart would be enough to bring him back.

"I love you, Nicholas Emerson." She whispered the words into the fabric of her pillow, but the darkness held no response.

With a resigned numbness, she slid the gold band off her ring finger and set it on the nightstand.

~

*A*bby had no idea how long she'd slept when she sat up in bed. *What was that?* Her breath froze in her chest, and her heart thundered a wild pace. She glanced about in the darkness, but the new moon cast no light. She felt frantically for the tinderbox and candle she'd left on her bedside table.

A low tortured moan sounded again, but this time it gradually built into a toe-curling scream before it died.

She struggled with shaking fingers to light the char cloth and candle wick. A spark ignited into a small flame. The glow permeated the darkness, filling her room with soft light. The tightness in her shoulders relaxed.

No monsters hid in the shadows, and she exhaled to calm her thumping heart. She pulled back the covers, slowly lowered her feet to the cold floor, and padded to the window. She peered into the moonlit night. Tree branches hung over the yard, casting crisscrossed silhouettes on the grass, but the only sign of life was the occasional cricket's chirp.

She must have been deep in a nightmare. With a yawn, she stretched her arms over her head, then crept to her door. She opened it and peeked out. Surely, if the strange wail were real, it would have woken Mrs. Smith or the servants.

An eerie stillness hung over the house. Abby wandered back to bed. Funny that she couldn't remember what she'd been dreaming about.

The tormented moan started again.

She dashed back to the window to determine where the cry emanated from. The anguished noise sent an icy chill up her back and raised fine hair along her neck. Was the sound coming from the woods behind Laurel House?

A stray animal of some sort, no doubt. Abby wiggled out a shiver, shaking her shoulders, and drew the sash closed. She crawled back under the warmth of the covers, pulling them up to her chin, and lay there listening, but the sound didn't repeat itself. Eventually, she blew out her candle.

*N*icholas awoke drenched in sweat, kneeling atop the bed. He clutched his rifle to his shoulder with one hand while the finger of his opposite hand poised over the trigger. Screams and gunfire echoed through his mind, distorting dreams from reality. He shook his head to clear it, attempting to distinguish what was real in the darkness. Each rapid intake of breath stretched his nostrils, and he forced his breathing to slow. His heart raced like a thousand galloping hooves. He willed his fingers to slide down the cool steel of his weapon and lean it against the wall.

Shrouded in darkness, he rummaged around for the bedclothes and discovered them twisted and knotted like a rope. Other parts were torn as if he'd tried to rip the mattress in two. Exhausted, he collapsed back onto the bed and ran a hand over his face. His nightmare slowly dissipated as the demons in his mind hissed like water thrown on a fire until the comforting blanket of silence finally surrounded him.

He expelled a long, shaky breath and forced his mind to think. Rough wooden slats on the walls confirmed his location. The old wood cutter's cottage. Close to home, at least as close to Laurel House as he could get without arousing suspicion.

Sitting on the bed, he stared out the nearest window, searching for any sign of the dawning sun. Nothing. Sleep had eluded Nicholas for years. Working for the Foreign Office and now England's Home Office, he'd learned to live on a few irregular hours of rest here and there. He should be used to the night terrors, but the more he tried to hide them or control them, the worse they became.

How long could he keep being an agent before one of his episodes got him killed or blew the operation? He was navigating treacherous waters. Of course, he should have known coming home would rehash old memories and emotions, some he wished to bury and others he'd been forced to. It had been a good run, though, a whole sennight since his last nightmare.

Nicholas rubbed the back of his neck, his hand running over the twisted flesh of the burns that men and women alike turned from with a look of disgust. He donned a shirt, pulling it over his head and adjusting the cravat and collars to hide his deformity. He lit a candle, picked up his pocket watch, and flipped it open. Quarter past two. Three and a half hours of sleep. It was enough. He closed his watch, donned his breeches and boots, and reached for his hunting rifle, then thought better of it. He ought not to wake the neighboring tenants and cause a disturbance at this early hour. He grabbed his bow and quiver instead and strode out the door into the crisp night air.

~

"Did you hear all the racket, Lady Abigail?" Mr. Kroger, Altonwood's shopkeeper, filled Abby's basket with items. His bushy eyebrows wiggled his excitement. "I bet me right arm it was a werewolf."

He pushed the basket over the counter in her direction. "Made my hair stand up on end, it did."

Last night had been the first in several weeks since she'd heard the eerie wailing sound. Nervous fear pricked at her, but she shrugged it away.

"I'm not the only one concerned about ye livin' by yerself in Laurel House."

Other people's ridiculous imaginations wouldn't deter her. Some silly night noises wouldn't scare her into packing her things and moving back home with her mother, brother, and his family. The only blessing about being a widow was being allowed a smidgen of independence.

"I'm not alone. There are servants. Besides, I'm enjoying my freedom." How easily the words rolled off her tongue. If only they were true. She would heed her mama's advice and accept Lord McAllister's intentions, but how would she force her heart to let go of Nick's memory? How could she love another as she had Nick? She longed for a baby to hold and love, but she'd never have children with a memory.

"It sounds beastly." He leaned toward her over the counter. "Half-human like."

"Mr. Kroger, you're going to cause an uproar with your nonsense talk. I'm quite certain it was merely a lost or wounded animal."

"Or a werewolf."

"There hasn't been a wolf sighting in England since the reign of King Henry the VI."

"I didn't say a wolf. I said a *werewolf*." He crossed his arms and leaned his hip against the counter. "The whole town's talking about it. The women folk are in quite a hullabaloo, and the men are planning to set up a huntin' party to catch the beast."

She fought to keep her expression impassive at such a ridiculous notion. "May I have those licorice whips also?"

Mr. Kroger opened the candy jar, pulled out the licorice, and wrapped it neatly in paper before adding it to her basket. "Are yer plans to call upon those wee kids at the orphanage?"

"Indeed, I've some fun activities arranged for them today."

"You have a good heart, Lady Abigail. God will surely bless you for your kindness."

Abby thanked him and passed him a shilling for her purchase. With a polite farewell, she left the shop and strode along the cobbled stone road toward the orphanage.

God will surely bless you for your kindness. God may have blessed her in the past, but for the last decade, He'd remained silent. She'd prayed and prayed for Nick to come home. When Nick first went missing, she'd believed with her whole heart that, since she'd prayed for his protection, no weapon forged against him would prevail. A year had passed, and she'd obstinately refused to relinquish the hope that Nick would be found alive and well and return to her with open arms. But then a year turned into three, then five, then ten. Her prayers for Nick had been met with nothing but silence.

Abby sighed. She didn't understand God's will. Her faith wavered periodically, but Mama Em had been the tree that kept Abby firmly rooted. That tree, however, had returned to the earth. Now, it was Mama Em's words that kept Abby from teetering over the edge into hopelessness. *"Bring your questions to God. He can handle them."*

So Abby sought Him. She poured out her heart, asking God for wisdom to make hard decisions, and if she was to move on from Nick, to please take away the lonely ache that shadowed her. He hadn't answered her prayers, but she hoped maybe He was listening.

A bell jingled as the door to the milliner's shop opened, and Lady Etheridge swept outside with footmen in tow, one carrying several hat boxes and the other snapping open her parasol and holding it over her head.

Abby searched for a back ally in which to hide.

"Lady Abigail."

Ugh. Too late. Abby forced a smile. "Good morning, Lady Etheridge."

The corners of the woman's pursed lips turned down. "Your mother-in-law hasn't been in the ground for a full week and you're out socializing." She clucked her tongue. "How disgraceful."

"I'm helping at the orphanage, not socializing." Abby struggled to keep her smile from turning into a smirk.

"I'm glad I ran into you on your way over and not upon your return. Those children carry hordes of diseases, you know." Her nose wrinkled. "I daresay you should keep your distance or send your maid in your stead."

Abby snorted. "But then I would miss out on the blessing of helping others."

"It's unladylike to blow air through your nose in such a manner. Mrs. Emerson would be ashamed." Lady Etheridge cleared her throat. "However, to your credit, you honored her well during the ceremony and following days."

"She deserved such a lovely tribute."

"Indeed." Lady Etheridge blinked twice.

Was she blinking back tears? It was so rare for Lady Etheridge to show any emotion that it caught Abby off guard. A moment of silence passed between them until Lady Etheridge sniffed. "If you can help the orphans then I expect you to still join me for your regular visit, since it's good for my health."

Without even waiting for a response, Lady Etheridge marched past her toward Mr. Kroger's shop. The shop keeper darted inside and attempted to flip the open sign.

"I see you Mr. Kroger," Lady Etheridge's voice rang. "Don't even think of closing up shop."

Abby chuckled to herself before veering off the road and up the brick walkway to the orphanage. The two-story thatched-roof manor rang with the chorus of children's voices repeating back their lessons. She stopped in front of the thick oak door archway and recited her favorite Bible verse from the book of Romans. *Nothing can separate us from the love of Jesus Christ.* God was with her. Nothing could separate her from Him. Still, why didn't He answer her? Why was He silent?

God, are you listening?

She raised the oversize brass handle attached to the thick oak panels and knocked.

Squeals of delight from the children rang out, followed by a harsh commanding voice, then utter silence.

The door opened, and the sour-faced Miss Quiller stood in the archway, blocking Abby's view of the children.

"You are early, Lady Abigail. We were not expecting your arrival until half past." Miss Quiller's stern expression appeared even more austere with her gray hair pulled back into a tight bun. Her practical dress buttoned tightly up to her chin elongated her neck.

Abby flashed her a broad smile. "Good afternoon, Miss Quiller."

Miss Quiller clasped her hands tightly in front of her and stepped aside to let Abby pass.

"The bit of warm weather pleases you. Your cheeks are rosy, and your eyes are sparkling." Someday, Abby would crack the woman's tough exterior.

Miss Quiller turned, and Abby followed her into the school room.

"My color is high, Lady Abigail"—her tone hissed over her shoulder—"since I have found it necessary to impose a sterner approach with the children. Left to their own devices, they will turn into wild rogues and molls, pilfering and thieving the countryside." She spun around to face them and shouted, "The whole lot of them."

The children jumped, straightening their backs and pinching their lips closed.

"Young master Willowby." The stern woman's words pierced the silence. "You will remain standing there, with your nose facing the corner, for the rest of the day because of your insolence."

Even with his head down, Abby recognized Samuel, who probably hadn't seen ten summers yet. He stood proudly erect as he faced the wall and, to the passing eye, appeared unaffected by Miss Quiller's punishment. Except, the staccato rise and fall of his chest revealed the boy fought to control his emotions.

She'd had much of the same spirit growing up. Lady Etheridge's venomous tongue had often leveled Abby with a good set-down.

"Lady Abigail Hartington," Lady Etheridge would say in her haughty tone as she peered down her nose at Abby, "ladies of the highest quality would *never* be caught climbing trees. You do your mother and your family name a grave dishonor by behaving in such an unladylike fashion. It's no wonder your parents stay so secluded. Those of highborn status call upon the country folk to ensure the town is meeting expectations. *Your* parents only venture out on Sundays to attend church. They're embarrassed to show their faces." She assessed Abby with a critical glare. "I daresay, that's entirely your fault."

Lady Etheridge had continued on for minutes at a time delivering her lecture, reminding Abby of every past infraction. Meanwhile, Abby stood, straight and tall, absorbing her verbal tirade without emotion. However, Lady Etheridge's words cut deep, and shame flooded old wounds, adding to Abby's pain.

As soon as Lady Etheridge moved on, commending herself for the great service she'd done with her constructive criticism, Abby faced the wall, unable to bottle her emotion. To the occasional passerby, she appeared as if nothing were the matter. But those who looked closely noticed the tracks of tears and her shuddered intakes of breath.

The reverend, Mr. Cantor, peeked his head into the room, bringing Abby's thoughts back to the present. His friendly face outlined by his thick beard contrasted with his somber vicar's clothing. He'd yet to marry, but could she envision a life with the vicar? They'd have children of their own, and she could be a fulltime mama to the orphans. She peered at the vicar's wiry frame and tried to summon a smidgeon of what she'd felt for Nick.

Nothing. Well, it was a thought.

Upon spying Abby, the vicar grinned, his eyes forming

half-moons with deep crow's feet on either side. "Good morning, Lady Abigail. Splendid to see you on this fine day." He clapped his hands. "All right, foundlings, your Bible studies are over for the morning. Enjoy your free time with Lady Abigail."

The children cheered.

He quieted them with a look. "The noontime meal is in forty minutes sharp. Afterward you are to report to the far field for chores."

The reverend turned, and the children followed his lead, filing out of the schoolroom like little soldiers under Miss Quiller's watchful eye.

Abby held back, watching through the window. Once the children's feet touched the courtyard, they ran, laughing and behaving like children again.

"I shall go and oversee food preparations." Miss Quiller paused before exiting the schoolroom. "I trust you won't get the children all wound up before their noontime meal?"

Abby politely curtsied. "Indeed, I will do my best to unwind them, Miss Quiller."

Miss Quiller's eyebrows snapped together at her glib remark. "Very well, then." She turned on her heel and left the room.

In the corner, Samuel's hands remained clasped behind his back.

On impulse, Abby reached into her basket and withdrew two licorice whips. She crept over and placed them into his hands.

Startled, he turned and glanced at the candy in his palm, then back up. "Lady Abigail."

She quickly put a finger to her lips to silence him. If Miss Quiller found out, she could prohibit Abby from visiting again. "I know we don't all fit Miss Quiller's standards," she whispered, "but you have God-given abilities, Samuel, that Miss

Quiller doesn't understand. Just remember, you are uniquely and wonderfully made."

The boy's bright expression warmed her like a sunbeam on a cold day. Humming a cheerful tune and swinging her basket, she strode into the grassy courtyard.

Children squealed as she engaged them in a game of keep-away. Shrieks of laughter echoed off the stone building when she was tagged *it*. A little while later, exhausted and out of breath, she sat on a small bench to rest a moment before she placed her basket in her lap. From inside she pulled out scraps of cloth, some tin soldiers the blacksmith casted, and her art supplies. She showed the girls how to create dolls with cloth and string, while the boys painted uniforms on the soldiers.

Abby checked the watch pinned to her cloak. Five more minutes until Miss Quiller would call the children inside, and they would be forced to behave like adults for the rest of the day. She dug deep inside her basket and pulled out her surprise, the licorice.

The children's eyes widened, and their mouths formed into tight little *O*'s. Some licked their lips.

"I have a licorice piece for everyone. However, there is one condition. You mustn't let Miss Quiller know I spoiled your meal, so you must eat every single bite. Is that agreeable?"

The children nodded simultaneously, never taking their eyes off the candy.

"All right, then, one for each of you." She hid her amusement while the children ate. Some savored the candy while others gobbled it up, immediately asking for more.

"Time to line up," Miss Quiller's brusque voice rang from the parish doorway.

The children obeyed, stiff as the tin soldiers the boys had painted.

Abby followed the children inside where Mr. Cantor sat in a quiet corner, already enjoying his noontime meal. She stopped next to his table, and they chatted amicably about the school and the latest law the Whig party brought before the House of Commons. The reverend glanced at the time on his pocket watch. "My dear, I've kept you overly long. You're excused to sup before the food grows cold."

Abby grabbed a wooden bowl from the stack and peered into the first of two pots of stew available. One pot looked as if the children had scraped the sides clean. The other stood over half full but emitted a distasteful odor.

The last time she'd eaten yesterday's soup, she'd suffered indigestion for the remainder of the day. It might be best to skip a meal.

Small fingers touched her hand. A wee, little girl named Hannah peered up at her. Hannah was small for her age, almost doll-like due to her big saucer eyes and porcelain skin.

"Lady Abigail," she begged, "please don't eat the soup from that pot. You may have mine instead."

Abby's heart clenched as the child held her bowl out. "That is very kind, but you need food to grow big and strong. I'm sure the soup is fine. I'm not very particular."

Hannah appeared unconvinced, still holding her bowl out.

Abby scooped herself a large portion.

The little girl's eyes widened. "I don't mind, really. Lydia will share hers with me."

"That won't do. You eat your own. I will manage."

Hannah turned back toward her table but hesitated. She glanced over her shoulder. Abby ate a bite of the soup and swallowed it. "See, it's good. Delightfully so."

Hannah nodded before sitting and eating her own like a good girl.

Risking a little indigestion to see Hannah eat was worth it, but Abby only swallowed bites while Hannah was looking. The rest she left to be taken away by the children assigned to cleanup duty.

CHAPTER 3

A few hours later, Abby helped the young girls pick beans in the orphanage's large garden while the boys harvested wheat in the field. These were daily chores for the children, since growing their own crops and selling the surplus in town was one of the ways the orphanage sustained itself.

Her stomach rumbled.

Lydia, one of the older girls who worked beside Abby, stood. "Lady Abigail, please tell me you didn't eat yesterday's soup."

Abby forced a smile. "Do not fret." She hadn't eaten much, but the sour taste still lingered. "It's merely a little indigestion."

Lydia flashed her a sidelong glance, then set back to work.

As the day lengthened, Abby tried to ignore her tummy's rumblings so the children wouldn't worry, but the sounds grew atrocious, and the pangs of queasiness intensified. Excusing herself, she shuffled over to the reverend.

"I beg your pardon, Mr. Cantor, but I'm afraid I'm not feeling at all well. I'm going to have to return home a trifle early."

Beads of sweat broke across her forehead, and she pressed her hand over her lips to fight the nausea.

He scrutinized her pale expression. "Go on, my dear. You've been a great help. I hope you didn't catch anything from the children. They are rife with illness and disease." He patted Abby's shoulder. "We will keep you in our evening prayers."

Abby had barely stepped past the hedgerow boundary before she purged the contents of her stomach into a nearby dog rose bush.

She wiped her mouth with the cloth that covered her basket. She should have required Polly, her lady's maid, to accompany her. Although Polly, with her weak stomach and sensitive nose, would have been useless in this situation. She was a sweet and efficient companion, but she wouldn't be any help in the current situation.

Phaetons, gigs, and mule-drawn carts cluttered the narrow main street. People milled about. Abby stepped in that direction but hesitated. She didn't want to make a spectacle of herself, which she would surely do if she cast up her accounts again. Or even worse if she retched in someone's carriage as they drove her home. Trying to control her rolling tummy was like trying to stop the waves of the seas, so she turned and stumbled down the narrow, dirt path leading into the woods.

Her lips trembled in an effort to keep her food down. She could only walk a few yards before her stomach cramped. It protested with the vigor of a lion's roar, and she emptied its contents, again, into the nearby underbrush. Shuddering and weak from the exertion, Abby veered off the path into the woods, hoping to shorten the route home. If she could just make it to the Laurel House, then Mrs. Smith would tend to her, and if necessary, fetch the physician.

Except Mrs. Smith had left this morning to assist her daughter with the delivery of her first child and would be away until the end of the month. Abby moaned and sagged against a tree.

Should she attempt to walk to Willowstone Manor? Mama or Katherine, her sister-in-law, would care for her there. Abby's stomach rolled, and she bent, wrapping her arms around her midsection. Willowstone was even farther than Laurel House. She wouldn't make it in her weakened condition. Another wave of nausea racked her body, knocking her to her hands and knees in the dirt.

"God," she prayed, "please get me home." She grasped a tree branch and struggled to pull herself up. Her wooziness distorted her vision, and to compound her confusion, she couldn't find a single familiar landmark. She forced her legs to continue to move in the direction she thought was right, but her body felt like an overripe pumpkin turning to mush. Twice she fell to her knees fighting dizziness. Thorns and briars pulled at her skirts' fine bombazine, but she didn't care. At this point, even death seemed comforting.

Her hands shook, and her teeth chattered.

"Not again," she whispered.

Another spasm of nausea jerked her body, and she tried to grip a sturdy oak for support, but her aim was off, and she fell. Her hair caught in a branch. With a good yank, she freed herself, sending pins flying in every direction, but the effort threw her off-balance. The fallen leaves and moist dirt broke her fall and filled her nostrils with their earthy aroma.

Helpless tears streamed down her face. *God, please help me.* She attempted to crawl, but her skirts hindered her progress. Another painful wave racked her body, but there was nothing left in her stomach. She cried for help, but it came out as a garbled moan.

She crumpled into a ball.

The moist autumn leaves clung to her skin and clothes. Her hair dangled in her face. Darkness blackened the edges of her periphery as if she'd fallen down a deep rabbit hole. The last of her energy ebbed away, and she rolled onto her back and stared up blankly at the treetops shivering in the breeze. Her eyelids fluttered as she succumbed to the sickness. Blackness swept over her.

~

*N*icholas finished his hunt and headed toward the woodcutter's cottage. He inhaled, filling his lungs with the rich, fall air, heavy with the smell of leaves and burning wood. During the war, his soul had craved the sanctuary of the Midlands, with its lush rolling hills and dense pockets of forest. He'd graced the opulent ballrooms of Napoleon's Chateau de Fontainebleau, paced alongside King George III as he ranted on his terrace at Windsor, and witnessed firsthand the politics and betrayal that permeated both rulers' lives. But here in Altonwood, things were different, simpler. Although he could never again be a part of this unaffected fragment of society, he could enjoy its peaceful sanctuary like a ghost haunting its grounds.

A deer walked onto the path and stopped to munch on undergrowth. Nicholas reached back to pull an arrow from the quiver but froze. He'd already gathered enough food to last a week—three ducks, two quail, and two rabbits—all of which were wrapped carefully and stuffed into his sack. He could add the doe to his list of accomplishments, but the meat might go to waste. He lowered his bow and jostled the heavy pack on his shoulder.

She looked directly at him and flicked her ear before darting off into the woods. He took it as a wink of gratitude.

Despite his limp, he silently picked his way through the woods. He refused to let his injury affect his work, and occasionally, his strong-willed nature worked to his advantage.

Though it had been his stubborn streak that had earned him the injury in the first place. Today was turning out to be a good day. His leg wasn't paining him overly much, and the short midday nap he'd slipped in while sitting against a thick oak tree buoyed his spirits. Rested and renewed, he envisioned the delicious supper he'd eat tonight and licked his lips.

It had been several years since the last time he'd received a respite between assignments from the War Department's Home Office. He was grateful for this break, which allowed him a sennight to mourn the loss of his mother alone.

A missive arrived late yesterday at the cottage, since he'd left the Home Office with a forwarding address and specific directions for when they needed to reach him. The letter informed him of a meeting with his handler tomorrow evening at the *Swan and Plough* tavern. He was to be assigned to gather intelligence on a local countess whose life was in danger. There must be some sort of mix up because the only countess local to Altonwood was Lady Etheridge. He snorted. The entire town either feared or hated Lady Etheridge. A list of suspects would be longer than his arm. He'd have to wait until tomorrow to hear more.

It had been the second time His Majesty's messenger had been late. The first tardiness had been in getting him the message about his mother's failing health while he was on assignment in India. Nicholas had forced the ship captain to sail through wretched storms, at one point considering rowing to shore if it would have gotten him to his mother's side faster.

But in the end, it wasn't enough. Nicholas had returned to Altonwood in time to pay his final respects at his mother's funeral. He'd lashed out at his handler, Lieutenant Sparks. All his anger and frustration wouldn't undo the fact that he hadn't been there to comfort his mother at the end. He would have found a way to sneak in without anyone's awareness to look upon her face and have her look upon his one last time. He made the best of the remainder of his break to ensure the family's accounts were in order. Other than the War Department, his solicitor was the only person who knew Nicholas Emerson still lived, and it was necessary to keep it that way. The solicitor also acted as his informant, apprising him of Abby's needs, whereabouts, and happenings.

A whimper stopped Nicholas short.

His mind flashed to a memory of tent flaps slapping in the wind and the moans of the injured men. He swallowed the bile that rose in his throat and exhaled to calm his nervous mind. *Keep it together, soldier.*

The whimper had sounded human, and duty called him to inspect the grounds and lend aid if needed.

His training took over as his ears strained to pinpoint the direction the noise had come from, and he slipped into the shadow of a large pine tree. He slid an arrow out of his pack and notched it to his bow. His muscles resisted the tension of the string as he waited for the sound to repeat itself. Even his breathing shallowed and became inaudible as the minutes ticked by in silence.

A weak cry resonated on his left about sixty paces away. Definitely human, and by the pitch, injured. Vivid images flashed in his mind, fatally wounded men strewn about the battlefield crying out, reaching for him. The stench of death hung thick in the air. He could almost smell the blood and musket fire.

Nicholas shook his head to clear his mind. He scanned the trees and underbrush. One couldn't be too careful. Foul play may be involved, and a disturbed individual could be lurking. Careful not to snap any twigs, he shifted from one tree to another and stilled when the low moan sounded again. Closer this time. He grabbed a stick, pushed aside the undergrowth.

A woman's dress draped against the earth and brush.

Nicholas stepped in for a better look, and his heart slammed into his throat.

There, among the leaves and moss, lay Abby.

He stowed his bow and arrow and knelt in the grass beside her. He felt her neck for a pulse and sagged with relief when it vibrated his fingertips. His hands shook as he inspected her body for sign of injury. He found none, but her gray-green pallor flipped his stomach.

Her dark hair, black mourning dress, and pale skin contrasted against the vibrant yellow, orange, and gold hues of the fallen leaves.

He yanked a handkerchief out of his pocket and dabbed the sweat from her brow. His fingers trailed down her slender jawline.

She moaned and curled toward his hand onto her side. Was she ill? It was the only explanation. Yet from his hidden blind, he'd spied her that morning leaving Laurel House and appearing healthy. Nicholas rubbed his hands over his face. He had to do something, but he couldn't be recognized.

She whimpered, and a spasm shook her body. *God, don't let anything happen to Abby.*

Did God even care?

Please, not Abby.

CHAPTER 4

$\mathcal{N}$icholas scooped Abby into his arms and cradled her head against his chest.

She felt lighter and more delicate compared to the vivacious woman he'd married ten years before, but even in sickness, her beauty surpassed that of other women.

He pulled a leaf from her thick hair, which rippled like satin over her shoulders. Her full lips were now pale, but he remembered how they'd shown red, contrasting with her smooth alabaster skin. Long thick lashes curled against her cheeks, and Nicholas knew they hid the most spectacular crystal blue eyes, which glittered when she laughed and flashed when angry.

In his youth, he'd resolved to keep her in one of those states at all times. Her smile could bring a grown man to his knees, and he was no exception. She was excitable and perpetually in motion, but when she was angry, she was a passionate, fiery goddess determined to rain down justice.

Nicholas cradled Abby closer as he tromped through the familiar wooded trails of his childhood. How many nights he'd lain awake on the dirt ground, in foreign emissaries' mansions, or in French prisons dreaming of holding her again. Now that she was in his arms, would he be able to let her go? He remembered standing on his bed clutching his rifle, sweat dripping off his brow, and the sounds of enemy troops fading like ghosts as his nightmare receded. He must let her go, for her own safety. But not right now. He'd savor this moment, cherish the feel of her in his arms, and pretend that this was his life.

The early autumn breeze showered leaves down around them. Laurel House peeked through the trees in the distance. He shifted her weight so he could leap over a trickling brook, and she let out a soft moan.

"We're almost there, sweetheart," he whispered.

Nicholas would sacrifice everything to be with her again, but the war had changed him. Abby deserved better than to have a flawed, deformed husband whose mental state was tenuous at best. He never knew when a noise or flash would trigger an episode. It would only be a matter of time before he'd suffer the same fate as King George III and be pressed into seclusion, or worse, locked up in Bedlam as a sideshow for the entertainment of mocking onlookers. He'd once seen sanitorium workers dragging away his unwilling fellow comrade who'd had similar nightmares. Nicholas lived with the fear they'd come for him next and worked to hide his attacks.

Due to lack of sleep and increase in the frequency of his nightmares, the lines of reality had begun to blur with his past. *By Jove*, he'd woken this morning with a gun in his hands. What if Abby had been there? No, he couldn't let anything happen to her. She was better off without him. The Nick she'd married died in the war, and it was best for her to remarry.

If she would. From what he'd observed, her stubbornness hadn't lessened over the years. So far, she'd refused to consider the offers for her hand. If she had remarried, then he would have moved on. Instead, he was constantly drawn to her, seeking any opportunity to see her, smell her, dance with her in secret at a masquerade. She was the reason he'd chosen to take up residence in the abandoned woodcutter's cottage. He drew comfort knowing Abby was nearby.

Pathetic. He was pitiful. Ten years ago, this life would have been incomprehensible, but he'd been headstrong and naive to the horrors of war. Now, his episodes forced him into seclusion, to live like a hermit and spy on his own wife like some wretched stalker. Fortunately, he was a good spy. He'd been trained by the best.

His knack for espionage came in handy as he turned the latch on the back door and slid quietly into the dim house. He'd witnessed Mrs. Smith's trunks being loaded into a wagon this morning, so he knew she was away. He didn't like the idea of Abby being alone with so few servants.

Just one more assignment, and he'd have enough funds to complete the house he was secretly building for her. Then, if she wished, she would be able to live in the grand home they'd dreamed of someday building, not the meager house he'd grown up in. Of course, when she remarried, she'd move into her new husband's home, but it could be her summer mansion in the cooler climate of Northern Scarcliffe.

His chest tightened as it often did when he thought of not being part of Abby's future, but she deserved a better life than being married to a man like him. His eyes adjusted to the candlelit hallway, and he mounted the stairs as he had on their wedding day. Her laughter back then had filled the air until he'd thought his heart would burst with all the love he'd felt for her. He closed his eyes and gripped her tighter. Now his heart might burst from the pain of regret.

He moved to her bedchamber and hovered outside the half-open doorway, listening and scanning for servants. All clear. The scent of lilac flowed over him, and he inhaled a deep breath.

He stepped into the room. This was where Abby slept.

She stirred in his arms. Awash in nostalgia, he closed his eyes and remembered the feel of holding her close, her scent of warm sunshine and lilac soap. He pulled her closer, nestling his cheek on the top of her head. Her hair still smelled of sunshine and lilac soap. She moaned softly and turned in his arms.

A gasp sounded as a connecting door opened. A maid jumped. The muff she'd been mending dropping to the floor with a soft thud. "Lady Abigail!"

"Your mistress is ill." The best way to keep a servant from asking questions was to speak to them with authority. Nicholas lifted his chin and used a harsh, aloof manner, adding a touch of disdain. "Stop dawdling and help me get her into bed."

The willowy maid rushed to pull back the covers, and Nicholas slid Abby between the cool sheets. As the woman tucked the covers over Abby's sleeping form, she sniffed and drew back gagging.

"You are no use to your mistress if you retch upon the both of us." He waved her away. "Run and fetch the physician. I will tend to her."

The willowy maid hesitated, crinkling her apron between her fingers. "Who are you?"

"A relative." The partial falsehood fell easily from his lips. He'd work it into an alibi later. "Hurry!" The boom of his voice reverberated off the walls. "There is no time to waste."

Abby sat up so fast that her head nearly collided with his. Waves of dry heaving erupted from deep within her, almost sending her over the side of the bed with the intensity of each spasm. Thankfully her stomach had already emptied.

The maid dashed out the door in a flurry of skirts, taking the only candle with her, but the glow of the fading evening light was enough for him to see to move around. Nicholas held her with one arm and pulled her hair back away from her face with his other hand. All the while, he shushed her and whispered, "Everything's going to be all right. Just keep breathing."

After the wave passed, she collapsed and closed her eyes. His heart twisted, wishing he could take this illness from her. He tucked her in again and smoothed out her hair, unable to pull his eyes from her heart-shaped face.

Her lids fluttered open, and he froze. She stared directly at him, his face mere inches from hers. Did she recognize him in the darkness?

"Nick?" Her voice was weak and scratchy. "Is it you?"

He remained still, not even breathing.

"I'm dead, aren't I?" Her dry lips barely parted to get the words out.

He couldn't help it. A smile tugged at the corners of his lips. "Mama Em didn't see you, but I knew you'd be in heaven."

She closed her eyes and moaned, then curled onto her side. For a moment, she was still, and he assumed she'd fallen back asleep.

He moved to stand.

Her fingers tugged on the sleeve of his jacket. "Nick, I hurt. Why do I hurt?"

Abby struggled to open her heavy eyelids and when she did her gaze was filled with such concern that his heart twisted. "It's a mistake. I've got to get you out." She squeezed the fabric of his sleeve and tugged him closer. "We've got to pray. Pray to Jesus like Mama Em said. He's the..." Her head sank deeper into the pillow. "The only one who can rescue..." Her voice trailed off, and her eyes shut.

He loosened her fingers and tucked her arm under the covers. Even in her weakened state, she was still full of spirit. He brushed a kiss on her forehead and whispered, "You are not dead. Only ill. I've sent for the physician. Don't worry, love, in the meantime, I'll take care of you."

He waited by her side as she drifted back into a fitful sleep.

When the door creaked open downstairs, Nicholas slipped from the room. He stopped at the hall mirror to brush his hair

forward over his eyes and tugged his collar points higher until
his face was mostly shadowed. He descended the stairs to speak
with the doctor. The man needed to hear of the state in which
he found her but the explanation must be simple to not draw
suspicion.

~

*N*icholas paced outside the door, waiting for the
physician to finish examining Abby. What was
taking the man so long? Was her illness serious? This new
doctor had taken over the town's practice after Nicholas left for
war. Thankfully, Dr. Cox wouldn't recognize him, but was he
reputable? Should Nicholas have Barnsby, the groomsman, ride
to London to fetch a better physician? *If anything happens to
Abby...* Nicholas was about to barge in and demand answers
when the door opened, and the doctor quietly slipped out.

Nicholas searched the doctor's face. "How fairs Lady
Abigail?"

"She'll be fine. I'm afraid some bad soup poisoned her
system, and she became dehydrated from all the sun and
vomiting."

"Bad soup?" Nicholas eyed the physician skeptically.

"I was able to rouse her, and she told me it all started after
she'd eaten some of 'yesterday's soup,' as she called it, when she
assisted up at the orphanage. If she can keep down the fluids I
gave her, she will be on her way to recovery. I have another
appointment I must attend to, but I can send for her mother."

Nicholas shook his head. "No need. I can stop there on my
way home."

"See that her maid has her drink at least one full cup of tea
or water. If she resists or stays asleep, prop her head up and run
some ice chips across her lips. It's fortunate you came across
her when you did, Mr. ...?"

"Thank you, doctor. It's a relief to know Lady Abigail will be all right." He put a stack of coins into the doctor's hand, walked him downstairs, and ushered him to the door.

The physician paused just outside and eyed Nicholas warily. "Are you the game keeper? Is that how you came across Lady Abigail in the woods?"

"Out hunting." Best to let the good physician believe what made sense.

"I'd hate to think of what could have happened to a lone woman in the woods at night." Dr. Cox opened his mouth as if to say something more, but he shook his head and murmured, "It's not for me to judge."

Nicholas bade the doctor good evening and shut the door.

To be safe, he forced a semiconscious Abby to drink not merely one cup of tea, but three. Even when he ran ice chips over her lips, she went through the motions, never fully awakening. There was nothing left for him to do but wait and check in on her progress.

He instructed the maid to resume her position in the corner chair. "I'll leave with you half of my hunting yield, but I'll need to prep it in your kitchen. Find me if Lady Abigail has another episode."

The maid hesitated.

"I'm the Hartingtons' relative here on a hunting trip. Lady Felton offered for me to hunt on the Hartington's land but didn't get her son or daughter's permission. There is some tension between our families, and I'd prefer not to start any infighting." Nicholas slipped the maid a few extra coins. "For your trouble. I'd appreciate if my visit wasn't mentioned."

She peered at her mistress with a worried look,

"I only want what's best for her." He jerked his thumb in the direction of the door. "I'll stay awhile downstairs in case you or she need me, but I'll be gone before morning light."

The girl nodded and he left the room.

He strode to the kitchen and pulled the fresh game out of his sack and the pockets of his hunting coat. He laid the rabbits, quail, and ducks carefully on the counter. After unwrapping each one, he got to work skinning and preparing the meat. Some he skewered and roasted on a spit over the large kitchen fireplace. The rest he re-wrapped and placed in the bottom of the larder for safe overnight storage. He cleaned the kitchen with the precision of a watchmaker and placed everything back into its proper place. Except for the lingering smell of roasted quail, he'd left no trace.

Nicholas pulled the cooked meat off the fire and carried his plate into the drawing room. He sat near the hearth and its dwindling embers and picked the meat off the bone with his fingers. He'd been away from society for too long and had become accustomed to living a paltry existence. His lack of propriety, however, didn't extend to forgetting a napkin, which he pulled over his lap and, after his small feast, used to wipe his face and hands.

A stillness settled over the house except for the crackle of the fire. Laurel House appeared in good repair. The informant Nicholas paid to check on the house and Abby had written as much, but Nicholas found comfort in seeing it for himself. Abby had resided at Laurel House since his mother's passing. Through his connections within the king's court, he'd secretly passed the entailment so the house could remain in her possession. A small suggestion to his mother's solicitor was all it took to obtain her concession. Mama even believed it to be her idea.

Even though Nicholas couldn't be with Abby, he could still provide for her. She now had her own house and a nice stipend. Abby's wise intuition posed a challenge for him, but he had his solicitor make it appear as if the money he supplied was the accrued interest on the Emerson family investments.

Nicholas figured he'd stay the night to ensure Abby's health and then slip out quietly before dawn. With his belly full and the warmth of the fire making him groggy, Nicholas stretched out in the chair, his thoughts drifting to Abby and how to ensure she made the best life for herself—he choked back the familiar ache that seized his chest, because her life had to be without him.

CHAPTER 5

*N*icholas jerked awake. The fire had dwindled in the hearth, and he lay sprawled in a chair in front of it. Mopping his forehead with his sleeve, he worked at slowing his rapid heartbeat. He knew this place. *Home. Laurel House.*

Abby was upstairs. He stilled, listening. Nothing. He flipped open his pocket watch. It was a quarter past four in the morning. He heaved himself out of the chair but winced when he put too much weight on his stiff leg.

Nicholas tidied up, ensuring there would not be any evidence of his presence. He pulled on his overcoat, retrieved a couple of the wrapped game from the larder, and put them in an orderly pile on the hearth next to his quiver and arrows. With one last glance around, he slipped up the stairs and pushed open the door to Abby's room. The maid snored softly from her sprawled position in the low back chair.

He told himself he was checking on Abby's well-being, but it was more than that.

He needed to see her, to be close to her, one last time.

Moonlight spilled in through the open window, illuminating her small form. She lay on her side with her knees pulled up and her hands tucked under her pillow. Her long silken hair splayed over the sheets. She looked peaceful. Nicholas crouched next to her and tried to memorize each feature, her long dark lashes, her full rosy lips, her delicately winged brows. His heart squeezed as if in a vice. If only things had turned out differently. If only he hadn't been so foolhardy. He could have been happy and whole. He could have been lying with Abby, curled against her side, not haunting her home like a specter. He held up his hand and lightly stroked her hair, sleek and soft, and he trailed his fingers down her warm cheek.

She sighed softly—the sweetest sound he'd heard in a long time.

Unable to control his impulse, he leaned in and gently placed his lips on hers in a feathery kiss.

Abby sat straight up in bed like a sprung mousetrap. "Is someone there?"

Nicholas dropped to the floor and pinned himself under the bed as far as he could squeeze. He lay there, unmoving in the shadows, barely breathing.

The maid stirred and shifted in her chair but within seconds resumed her snoring. Between her heavy breaths, he could hear the swish of Abby's hair as she looked about.

Minutes passed.

With a sigh, Abby pulled the covers up, and the bed shook as she wriggled under the sheets.

He waited in the dark, listening to her inhale and exhale until her breathing slowed and deepened. His own lungs cried for a deeper breath, and his legs ached from their cramped position. He ignored the pain.

She'd certainly fallen back asleep by now, but he waited for another ten minutes to be safe. Silent as a shadow, Nicholas crept out of the room, down the stairs, and out the kitchen door.

Pinks, yellows, and reds streaked the sky as dawn blossomed in the east. Nicholas picked his way down the dirt path littered with orange and yellow foliage. The scent of musty leaves and rain hung in the air, mingling with the aroma of burning wood as servants lit their fireplaces to prepare for the day. Sturdy tree trunks stood like black stripes against the colorful background.

When the door to the abandoned woodcutter's cottage creaked open, Nicholas grabbed an oiled rag. It was ingrained into his nature to silence anything that could notify anyone of his presence. It might make the difference between life and death.

It was past time he left his life of espionage and found another occupation. He could be a farmer or fisherman or some other isolated form of employment. His night terrors and constant lack of sleep were driving him mad and affecting his work. Lieutenant Sparks hadn't been pleased when Nicholas informed his handler he'd only do one more assignment, but if Nicholas frightened people or harmed someone, he would land in jail, get himself killed—or even worse thrown in Bedlam—as his friend Aaron had been.

A shiver ran through Nicholas, and he glanced about the small cottage, ensuring nothing had been disturbed in his absence. The room still held its original coat of dust and cobwebs. He swept the floor, but only to remove footprints. No one would believe anyone resided in this place unless they actually observed him here. He kicked off his boots and threw himself onto the bed, crossing his bad leg over his good ankle and lacing his fingers behind his head. Cracks of light peered in through the loose boards in the rafters.

He'd seen Abby. He'd held her in his arms, felt her warm skin against his own. It had been wonderful, and Nicholas replayed the events, savoring each moment, trying to sear it into his brain forever.

He chuckled when he thought of her sitting up in bed asking, "Is someone there?" She was like a princess who could only be awakened by love's kiss. However, he wasn't prince charming—at least not anymore. He envisioned himself ten years ago as a healthy, virile youth riding off like a knight in shining armor on a quest to grant his lover's every desire. Cupid's arrow had certainly hit its target as far as Abby was concerned.

My bow.

Blast. He'd left not only his bow and arrows sitting next to the hearth but also the roasted game. What had he been thinking?

In the war, such a novice mistake of leaving evidence behind would have blown his cover, compromised the mission and likely gotten him killed. Cursing himself for his stupidity, he stood and reasoned through his options.

He flipped open his pocket watch. Half past seven. There was still time to sneak back and collect his things before she stirred. He donned his boots and trotted back to Laurel House for the second time.

~

*A*bby awoke with cracked lips and a dry tongue, feeling as if she'd eaten sawdust. Her head throbbed and her muscles ached, especially around her middle. She rolled onto her back with a whimper. She should have heeded the children's warnings and skipped the bad soup. Her stomach groaned in protest, repulsed by the mere thought of food. Abby licked her lips, but her tongue stuck.

Liquids. An entire pot of tea.

"Good morning, milady." Polly bobbed a curtsy. Dark smudges underlined her eyes, deepened by her pale skin.

Abby's lips stuck to her teeth as she murmured a response.

She slid her feet over the side of the bed and stood on legs as sturdy as wet noodles. Her hand gripped the side table to steady herself until her balance solidified.

Polly scurried to her side.

"I feel dreadful. I must have been sick as a horse, and you, poor thing, look like you hardly slept." Abby attempted to smooth the wrinkles from her black mourning gown. It was the same dress she'd donned yesterday to wear to the orphanage. She must have fallen asleep without changing.

"Sorry, milady," Polly's throat convulsed, and her cheeks puffed as she fought against the urge to gag. "It's my sensitive nose. You were too ill for me to undress yesterday."

Abby waved Polly farther back lest she cast up her accounts. "It's about time I donned some fresh clothes." Abby shook out the wrinkles in her gown and noticed leaves stuck in the folds. "Good heavens."

A hazy recollection of yesterday chronicled in her mind. She'd become ill in the woods, struggled to stay on her feet, but she couldn't remember returning to Laurel House.

"How did I make it home?" She must have crawled back half conscious. It would explain how her dress had become so filthy.

"A relative found you in the woods and carried you."

"My brother?"

"No, milady. A cousin perhaps? He made it sound as if he was visiting."

Cousin? She had only one cousin on her mother's side, and he lived in Cornwall. Polly must have misunderstood. "Did he leave a card or give his name."

Polly hesitated, and her gaze dropped to her hands. "No, milady."

Pity. Manners and good character required she thank the man, but how could she if she didn't know his identity. Abby stretched her arms behind her head and unhooked the shell buttons. "You're going to have to hold your nose and handle the ones I can't reach. I can do the rest. If you become ill, I daresay I'll relapse, and that won't do for either of us." Polly assisted her. "Why don't you run put on a pot of tea and heat some water,"—Abby grimaced at the slight whiff of sour vomit— "because I can't stand my own smell."

Polly exited the room and Abby called after her, "Please hurry with the tea, I'm parched."

Still weary from her sickness, Abby paused throughout the process to rest. She rinsed her face, neck, and hands with the cool water left in the wash basin. Forgoing her stays, Abby selected and donned a simple dark muslin frock with few ties and arranged her hair, pulling it back in a simple chignon.

What was taking Polly so long? Still parched, the dirty water remaining in the basin even seemed appealing, but Abby held out against the temptation. She cleared her scratchy throat and rose, determined to discover what was amiss.

The stairs loomed before her, and she wavered at the top, gripping the railing for support. If she hadn't been so thirsty, she would have climbed back into bed, wrapped herself in a cocoon of blankets, and hibernated until next week. Instead, she carefully descended the stairs and padded into the kitchen.

At the sight of her mistress, Polly twisted a dishcloth in her hands, tears brimming in her eyes. "Milady, I beg your forgiveness. The scullery maid overslept without Mrs. Smith here to wake her. She just now brought up the coal and lit the stove. I've retrieved the tea caddy and put on a pot, but it will take some time to heat."

"Very well. Do oversee her lighting the fireplaces, would you?"

"Yes, milady." She bobbed a curtsy and left the kitchen.

Abby pulled a cup down from the pantry and peered out the window. The milkman's bottles sat in their usual drop off place by the door. She let out a pathetic whoop of joy, retrieved the bottles, and after shaking one, poured a glass. She gulped it down, and the refreshing liquid quenched her dry mouth and throat, restoring her equilibrium.

With renewed energy, she selected a tea and carefully packed the leaves. The milk tasted wonderful, but her morning didn't start without tea.

Still weak, Abby slunk down in a nearby chair to wait for the water to heat. The sun from the window warmed her skin. Closing her eyes, she conjured back the dreams that had infiltrated her sleep. In the most vivid of them, Nick had come to her rescue. His familiar scent of earthy cedar had surrounded her. She'd imagined his fingers in her hair, his lips descending on hers in a soft feathery kiss. But when she reached out, he was gone.

A shadow passed over the room. The hairs on her arms rose with a sudden chill. Drawn out of her revelry, Abby opened her eyes and caught a reflected silhouette in the copper pot hanging from the ceiling rack. A man, cast in shadow because of the light behind him, peered through the kitchen window.

She blinked, and he disappeared. It was probably Barnsby. She chided herself for being so jumpy.

But Tuesday was the groomsmen's day off, and he always visited his brother.

If the man hadn't been Barnsby, then who lurked outside Laurel House? The stranger who lied to her maid claiming to be a relative? Why would a good Samaritan tell a falsehood about his identity? Had he held an underhanded alternative? Had he scoped out the house and returned to rob them or worse?

Fear tingled her fingers and toes. She slid to the ground and crawled behind the dropped leaf of the prep table. Her eyes scoured the room for a weapon to defend herself.

The butcher's block.

She reached over the edge of the counter and pulled out a

carver's knife. Pinning herself up against the lowered drop leaf side of the prep table, she grasped the handle in front of her so tightly that her fingers ached.

Metal slid against metal as the latch lifted, and the door hinges creaked open. Only a thieving draw-latch looking to filch candlesticks and silverware would take such liberties as to enter a woman's house without knocking.

She bit her bottom lip to keep from crying out. She wanted to peek, but what if he spotted her?

Was he here to steal? Or was it something more sinister he wanted? Panic brought the taste of acid to her mouth. She leaned down and peered underneath the table.

She swallowed a scream, catching sight of the intruder's polished boots on the opposite side. If he stepped around the table, she'd be in plain view. Should she yell to draw Polly's attention? Would that put her maid in danger?

Abby crawled on sweaty palms to the far corner of the long prep table. Her knee caught on her skirt, and the knife in her hand struck the floor with a clink.

Had her folly been heard? She held her breath and looked beneath the table again.

The boots were no longer in sight.

Her gaze shifted, searching her periphery for movement. How had he disappeared? Where did he go? The feeling of being watched sent a fresh wave of panic over her. She gritted her teeth to keep them from rattling and remained completely still.

Minutes ticked by. Perhaps the sound of the knife had scared the intruder off. Or was he wandering the house? She should warn the servants. Mustering her courage, she clutched the weapon close to her chest and raised to peek over the tabletop.

No trace of him.

She cautiously stood, glancing left and right. Nothing. Her shoulders relaxed.

An ear-piercing whistle from the tea kettle reverberated throughout the room, startling a scream from her lips. She spun, slicing through the air with the knife until it connected with flesh.

A man grunted in pain.

Strong arms caught her, pinning her forearms to her side.

Abby screamed. The broad chest of her attacker shadowed the daylight. She squeezed her eyes shut, cringing at what may come next and praying to God for mercy.

A gloved hand grabbed hers in a vice grip and pried the knife from her fingers.

Abby's eyes opened as her weapon slid across the wooden floor with a loud clatter. She released a second shrill scream and tried to run only to struggle against restraining arms.

"Enough! Abby, it's me."

She gasped, and her hands dropped to her sides.

"Nicholas?"

CHAPTER 6

"**N**ick!" Abby flung herself against his broad chest and wrapped her arms around him.

"You're alive. Oh, Nick. I knew you weren't dead." Her arms moved up and down his back to reassure herself he was real.

Tears of joy wet her cheeks. She couldn't seem to stop repeating his name. Years of heartache melted as warmth spread through every part of her body in thousands of tiny bursts of gratitude.

"Thank you, Lord." she choked out, clinging to him, afraid if she let go, she'd awake and realize it all a dream. She blinked away the blur of tears and looked up into his beloved face.

A more mature and brawnier Nick peered down at her. His once light skin was tanned. Loose, dark waves of hair, longer than he used to keep it, hung in his face, which was once soft with youth but now held sharp lines and angles. An outsider wouldn't recognize him, but the spark in his eyes could only belong to her beloved Nick.

Footsteps thundered down the stairs, and Polly, with the scullery maid in tow, rounded the corner into the kitchen and skidded to a halt. "Milady, we heard your scream all the way from the other end of the house." The maid's gaze flicked from her to Nick, her eyes rounding.

Abby waved them away. "I was startled. Everything is fine." *More than fine. Splendidly marvelous.* "Give us a moment." She dismissed them and turned her attention to what she prayed wasn't a hallucination.

"Nick." She touched his face and the warmth of his skin. "Please tell me this isn't a dream."

Though she clung to him, his arms weren't wrapped around her. A twinge of alarm clouded her happiness. He wasn't hugging her back. She pulled away and searched his handsome face. Something was wrong. His face turned slightly aside, but his gaze remained upon her.

She saw it then, his hazel eyes flashing with a deep, fathomless love he couldn't hide, along with something else ... pain.

The knife.

Her stomach rolled as she remembered the knife's sharp edge catching on flesh. She stepped back, keeping her eyes on his face.

Please God, let me be mistaken. Don't let him be injured.

Abby swallowed hard and forced her eyes to look down. Blood covered his torn coat sleeve. "Oh God, no." Acid rose in her throat.

Nick stood there, alive and breathing and holding his forearm as the red liquid oozed between his fingers. Precious blood splattered onto the pine floor.

"Oh, Nick." Her hand covered her mouth, and she stumbled back a step.

"It's merely a flesh wound, Abby. I'll live."

"I-I didn't know. I thought you were a thief... a brigand. I'm sorry. So very sorry." She rummaged through drawers, pulling out clean linens. She lent him a hand as he shrugged off his jacket and carefully rolled up his shirt sleeve to press a cloth to his open wound.

Brushing the tears from her face with the back of her hand, Abby sucked in a deep breath to compose herself. "Let me take a look at it."

He held his arm out, and Abby fought dizziness. She blotted at the long slice in his forearm, then applied pressure. It was deep enough to need stitches.

He leaned in until their foreheads practically touched and covered her hand with his.

Abby's heart doubled its rhythm. His caramel eyes held hers, and her mouth trembled. Nick was alive. *He's right here, looking at me.* She didn't want to pinch herself. She didn't want to wake from this dream and have him disappear. Her eyes burned until she blinked again.

He was still there, directly in front of her. His warmth radiated into her skin, and the evocative scent of cedar encircled her like heady incense.

She'd waited for this moment for ten years—dreamed of him returning home and pulling her into his arms. He'd tell her how much he'd missed her, and she'd utter over and over how much she loved him. They would kiss. He'd sweep her into his arms, and they would begin their life over.

Instead, she sobbed fat tears full of pent up loneliness and anguish. "Where have you been? I prayed for your return for so long."

She peered up into his beautiful face. A face she thought she'd never gaze upon again. He was still as handsome as ever. A ruggedness replaced the carefree supple boyishness of his youth. The sparkle of mischief in his green-gold eyes had crystallized into hardened granite. He seemed guarded, hard to read, but that was to be expected, right? Who knew what he'd endured on the battlefield?

"I'm here now." He gently tucked a strand of hair behind her ear.

The simple gesture, so familiar yet so foreign, sent tears

cascading down her cheeks once again. He cradled her head to his chest and stroked her hair. She clung to him as she wept until she felt Nick wince. She followed his gaze down to where her fingers clutched his arm.

"Oh, sorry." She let go and pushed back, embarrassed that she'd forgotten herself. Grabbing his good arm, she drew him into the sitting room.

"Are you limping?" Merciful heavens had the knife also swiped his leg? She stared at his breeches but saw no blood.

"It's a war injury."

"Does it pain you?" She gently pushed him into the chair in front of the hearth.

He rubbed the knee with his good hand. "Only now and then."

This was not the way it was supposed to be. In all her imagined happy endings, none of them included her mistaking him as an intruder and slicing him with a knife. She wiped away tears with her sleeve and, once again, examined the wound. "I'll need to send for the surgeon."

"No." His voice reverberated, flat but stern.

"But you need stitches."

Nicholas frowned at the wound. "Indeed."

She half stood. "Polly can fetch him. You keep pressure on the wound with the cloth while I ring for her."

He gripped her hand. "No doctors."

Abby's eyes widened. "I will not stand by and watch you bleed to death after praying for you to be alive all these years." She stomped her foot for extra emphasis.

His lips pinched as if holding back a smile. "I know what to do," he said. "You'll need to get the bottle of brandy mother kept for visitors and a needle and thread."

"What?" The cords of her neck strained as she swallowed. "The only experience I have is with a scraped or bruised knee. I'll ring for Polly."

This time, his smile broke free. "Your maid doesn't have the stomach for it. One look at my wound, and she'll fall into a dead faint. You can manage. You're not the squeamish type. Now run along and grab the items I requested."

He'd met her maid? Was he the man who found her in the woods?

~

*N*icholas sank into the horsehair chair and closed his eyes. He breathed in the nostalgic smell of lemon oil furniture polish. It was good to be home, but he couldn't shake the regret that gnawed at him.

He couldn't stay, but she'd seen him.

It had been a mistake to return. *Blast it all,* if his superiors saw how badly he'd blundered, he'd be the laughingstock of the Home Office. Nicholas always lost his head around Abby, and it appeared nothing had changed with the passing of time.

When he explained he had to leave again, she was not going to take it well. He wouldn't be surprised if she grabbed the knife and went for his heart.

Nicholas rubbed a hand down his face. He should never have returned. Why didn't he leave before she got a good look at him? His wound was long but not deep. He wouldn't have bled to death before finding someone to aid him. Selfishness was the painful answer. He'd jumped at the chance to see her again, pressing through the woods with swift steps, his heart thumping against his rib cage at the chance to glimpse her face one more time. He'd gotten cocky, drawing too near, inhaling her scent. Three steps to the salon doorway, and he'd have grabbed his bow and been gone, but then she turned.

By revealing himself, he'd ruined her chance to remarry. Abby deserved children and a husband who didn't have to watch his back lest he be carted off to an asylum and leave her in disgrace. She didn't merit a jaded aberration of a man with hideous scars. Their grotesque appearance always hovered in the background of his thoughts. On his right side, he looked like the same-old Nick, but his left side bared puckered and twisted flesh that crept above the neckline like spidery fingers. He had situated himself in the chair so Abby couldn't see them.

He adjusted the high points of his collar and cravat with his uninjured hand. The style afforded him the comfort of knowing his neck remained hidden from view. His hair, longer than the popular Grecian style, aided in covering the rest.

One look of repulsion in her eyes, and he'd never recover. *Devastated* wouldn't begin to describe the agony he'd feel. He'd seen it in the eyes of others, revulsion tinged with horrified curiosity. He couldn't survive Abby looking at him like that.

Nothing would have stopped the pre-war Nick from taking her in his arms, kissing her passionately, and reminding her once and for all that she was his. Instead, he'd stood there, holding his bleeding arm, trying not to drip blood on her gown.

Perhaps he should be grateful for the cut. It reminded him of who he was *now*, a tattered and torn shell of his former self.

Nicholas clenched his fist and pounded it on the chair's arm. Why hadn't she remarried? It would have alleviated the temptation to kiss her. He blamed the kiss for addling his wits and causing him to leave his bow behind, which was how he'd stumbled into this predicament.

After his falsified funeral six years before, she should have picked the best fop of London's gentry and lived in luxury, but she'd chosen to cloister herself with his mother in Laurel House. She could have sparkled like a jewel and set all of London on its ear, but instead, she had stashed herself away in this small town.

She returned with the brandy, a towel, and her sewing basket, complete with embroidery hoop.

"Is the plan to stitch a neat row of flowers into my arm, or maybe some fall leaves and ivy vines?"

She tilted her head.

Nicholas flicked his gaze to the embroidery hoop, and Abby let out a nervous laugh. "I grabbed everything. I wasn't quite certain what was needed."

By Jove, she looked amazing. Her face was still pale from yesterday's illness or maybe from the looming task ahead of her. But when she smiled, even a nervous smile, her eyes sparkled and lit up the room. He wasn't sure what was causing him more pain, his wound or the ache to dive his hands into her hair and kiss her breathless.

She carried over an oil lamp and placed it on the nearby side table, adjusting the shade just so. She pulled a small, tufted stool in front of his chair. With a flounce of skirts, she plopped down and scooted closer to get a better look at his arm. She accidentally brushed his leg, and a jolt ran through his body.

He clutched the armrest with his good hand so he wouldn't yank her into his arms and bury his self-loathing in the softness of her curves.

Blue eyes, the color of flowering Delphinium, peered up at him, "What now?"

Nicholas cleared his throat to regain his composure. Focusing on the task at hand, he pointed at the brandy. "Hand me that."

She did, and Nicholas poured the burning liquid over the wound. Abby blotted at the drips with the towel before it leaked onto the rug.

"Splendid, I'm ready."

Her eyes widened. "You want *me* to stitch you up?"

"Who else?" He arched an eyebrow.

"I thought you were going to do it."

"With one hand?"

"I didn't know *how* you were going to accomplish it, but I never thought you intended for me ..." Her face paled even further.

"I don't believe I can manage," she pleaded. "You need a surgeon."

"No."

Abby put her hands on her hips and shot him a stern look. "Truly, I think in this instance ..."

"I mean it, no surgeons."

"But I have no experience."

Abby set her jaw in that familiar stubborn way of hers. She wasn't going to back down, so he changed tactics.

"Well then, I shall have to make do. I figured time was of the essence. I'm feeling a little woozy. Might be the loss of blood. Weak, too, really weak. I suppose I'll just close my eyes for a bit." He pretended his lids were becoming heavy as if he were going to faint. "No time to lose."

"Fine." Abby's pitch rose to a squeak. "Tell me what I need to do."

His eyes fluttered back open. "Jolly good. Get the needle and thread and sew me back together."

"Sew your skin."

Nicholas gulped back his laughter. She looked positively green. "You can do this."

She nodded, more to herself than to him. Swallowing hard, she picked up the needle and threaded it with a good length of thread.

"Pinch the skin closed with one hand and stitch it with the other."

She inhaled a deep breath.

"Has your embroidery stitching improved in the last ten years?"

She shot him a madding look. "You know I don't have the patience for embroidery."

He chuckled. "I guess you'll have to practice on me."

"Stop funning me. This is no time to jest." She pulled his arm closer and pinched the wound closed.

The bleeding had already lessened. He blotted away any seeping blood with a cloth.

"Very well, then, I'm ready. This will hurt."

Nicholas braced himself as she poked him with the needle. He didn't wince, but his teeth clenched.

Abby paused and scanned his features.

Nicholas schooled his expression, and she continued.

Her hand shook, and little beads of perspiration formed on her forehead. Abby always had a kind heart, taking in stray animals and bandaging their wounds, making certain all children felt included. In their pretend childhood sword fights, Abby often felled her opponent and then apologized for knocking him to the ground.

Lost in thought, Nicholas forgot the task at hand. When Abby pierced his skin for a fourth time, he sucked in a sharp intake of air.

Abby froze, almost dropping the needle. "I'm hurting you. I should send for the surgeon. I can't do this."

"Since when have you ever given up?"

"Since I've had to sew flesh."

"It barely hurts. I was merely caught off guard."

She shot him a sideways look to communicate she didn't believe him.

"You're doing quite well. It will be over soon. Finish it, Abby. Do it for me." His voice was gentle but stern, but he couldn't stop the corners of his lips from curving when she sighed and returned to her task. He needed to get her talking, take her mind off what she was doing. He searched for a safe topic that wouldn't lead to questions he couldn't answer.

"How is Lady Awfulridge faring these days?" Might as well get the inside scoop before his assignment began. "Still as dreadful as ever? I swear she sought you out to give a good set down just so she could feel better."

Abby chuckled. "She's still known for her tongue-lashings. Last week, most of the shops in the area closed when her carriage approached, and the shopkeepers made themselves scarce. I had to come back the following day to complete my errands. It didn't deter Lady Etheridge, however. She remained in her carriage and waited until the particular storekeeper she needed to visit couldn't afford to lose any more business. Then, she rang a peel over him about his elongated break and how God despises laziness."

He grunted. "People still tolerate her impertinence? I figured by now someone would have set her in her place."

"Well ..." A nervous laugh escaped Abby's lips.

Nicholas smiled. "If there was ever someone to take on Lady Etheridge, it was you. I bet you gave her a good tongue lashing."

"Actually, it wasn't me. Lady Etheridge and I have come to a sort of truce. You see, her children gave her the ultimate set down."

"Really? They didn't even have a spine to hold themselves up. They cowered to their mother just like their father did."

"It's sad. Charlotte is married now and lives in the Leeward Islands, and Anthony was happy to get out from under his mother's rule as a sea captain. They rarely visit. Lord Etheridge became ill and died. Their children came to the funeral but departed too soon for Lady Etheridge's taste. She took to her bed, and no one checked on her or even visited except for the physician. With a little prompting from my mother, I called upon her, and as a means to stall, I even picked a few flowers on the way over. I expected to be berated with subtle insults. Instead, she delighted in seeing me. She even said she wished her children had turned out like me. I almost fainted dead away from shock."

Abby glanced up at Nicholas, her expressive blue eyes still

registering her disbelief and swimming with a thousand unasked questions, he wouldn't be able to answer. Her thumb kept stroking the inside of his wrist as if to ensure he wasn't a figment of her imagination or an apparition. The slight movement ignited a desire he'd long since exiled to the recesses of his being.

Her lips parted.

She probably had a plethora of questions that needed answering but he couldn't. He had to keep the conversation light and away from himself. He chuckled. "I can't conceive that sort of change within a dragon lady like Lady Etheridge."

"Don't move." She pierced his skin, but he no longer winced.

Abby had impeccable focus when she set her mind to a task. She continued with the story. "Lady Etheridge rambled on and on about how grateful she was for my family and for me. It was the strangest day ever. She asked me to come calling again the following day, and I did—merely out of curiosity. I figured her behavior had been a fluke or the effects of some elixir the physician prescribed. It wasn't. She was just as nice the second day. Don't get me wrong. She still has a sharp tongue, but now I can see the love behind it. And if she is too harsh, I tell her so, and she apologizes."

"Egad, that is something I must see to believe."

"I wouldn't have believed it unless I'd experienced it."

Abby paused from her task and bit her lip. A mist filled her eyes like rain clouds crossing the Northern moors. "Your mother—"

"I know." A lump rose in his throat, but he swallowed it down. "A special courier was sent to find me in the wilds of India. I left everything and traveled as fast as possible." His throat tightened and pain sliced his chest. "But not quick enough."

"She is greatly missed." Abby's voice caught and she blinked away tears.

He fought the burn of his own. "Indeed."

She held his gaze, and her fingers wrapped around his good hand.

He cleared his throat and changed the subject. "Tell me of your parents and Stephen."

Abby explained that her mother was well, but her father had passed on. Nicholas already knew this. At the time he'd been recovering from his wounds, but he'd worked over the lieutenant to have anonymous flowers delivered.

Her eyes sparkled as she spoke of her twin brother, who was now married to a wonderful woman named Katherine. They had one child, a boy named Benjamin. This, too, wasn't new information. Nicholas's informant reported back to him about every detail regarding her family, but he listened intently, enjoying the sound of her voice.

Despite the throbbing of his arm, it felt good to be touched. No one had touched him in a long time. He relaxed in his chair, enjoying Abby's nearness. *This is what my life could have been like.* One unwise choice had changed his course. He'd had everything he'd wanted right in front of him. The title he'd desperately fought for now held no appeal to him. Viscount of Scarcliffe. Although hard earned, it was a title he would never use. People with titles were recognized and sought after.

Nicholas had no choice but to hide.

Abby tied off the last stitch with a firm knot. "I think that does it."

A straight row of neat sutures lined his arm. "Nicely done."

Abby sagged with relief. "I'm glad to be finished with it." Her lips wobbled with a weak smile. "I have a newfound respect for surgeons."

An awkward silence grew between them. Abby chewed her

lip, and Nicholas could tell she was practically boiling over with questions.

"Nick, what happened? Where have you been? How come—?"

"Perhaps some tea first?"

Good manners must have overruled her curiosity because she stood and blurted out, "I apologize. I've been a wretched hostess...er, ah...wife."

Abby had sliced him with a knife, stitched him up, and *now* worried about being a proper hostess? Nicholas stifled his laughter but not his smile. It felt good. He hadn't smiled this much in ages.

"Would you care for scones? I can have some baked."

"I'm fine, thank you."

She rose and turned to leave. Nicholas stood also.

Abby stopped and glanced back at him with wonderment in her clear blue eyes. "Nick, I'm beyond delighted that you're home. I didn't want to... My heart refused to believe you were dead."

Abby stood within arm's reach, vulnerable and innocent. Her eager eyes pleaded for him to hold her. His fingers twitched to pull her into his embrace and promise her the world all over again. But he had nothing to offer.

He needed to evade her questions. The answers would cause her more pain.

"Where—?"

"God, how I've missed you." He opened his arms, seeking her embrace and hating that he was only making this harder on her and himself.

She stepped toward him and wound her arms behind his neck. Her eyelids fluttered closed. "I've missed you something fierce."

Her breath tickled his lips, and the sweet fragrance of lilac soap encircled him. Nicholas's resistance snapped. Logic screamed at him to leave. Run. Get out. But as if his body were being pulled by a magnetic force, he encircled her waist with his hands, and lowered his head.

"Why didn't—?"

He silenced her question with a kiss.

She tasted like fresh cream. Her body melted into his, and as their kiss deepened, the blood in his veins ignited like a kerosine fire. Ten years of pent-up passion culminated in the heat of one forbidden kiss.

She moaned, a soft purring sound.

His hands slid up her back and tangled in the silky tresses of her hair. He'd dreamed about this every night for ten years, but those dreams were nothing compared to the real thing. A part of him, one he'd thought long dead, resurrected. He was a conqueror, and she was his treasure. This warrior had battled long enough against his own dragons. Time was well overdue to reclaim the princess as his queen.

Her delicate hand slid up the lapel of his jacket, sending a tremor through his body. Her fingers moved to cup his face, and a crashing jolt of reality doused him like cold water.

He jerked away and grabbed her hand before she reached the telltale scars.

Her eyes shadowed, and she tried to step back, but Nicholas wasn't ready for the kiss to end. Instead, he kissed her fingers and the palm of her hand. She wavered, and her eyes fluttered closed. Her lips were red and swollen but he claimed them once more, savoring their soft sweetness. He trailed kisses down the line of her jaw and onto the delicate skin of her neck.

She tilted her head back and whispered, "I love you. I've never stopped loving you."

A bear-like growl escaped his throat, and he crushed her to him, his thin thread of control slipping.

A knock sounded at the front door.

Nicholas pushed Abby back to arm's length. She swayed

and clung to him, and he was pleased that she'd been as affected as he.

The knock sounded again, louder this time.

"I'll have Polly send them away." She stepped back and smoothed her dress. "One moment."

He met her eyes and forced his mind back to the present, to the truth. "I must go."

"You only just arrived." Her brow furrowed.

Nick locked her in his arms. "I'm sorry, Abby. I have to leave."

"I haven't brought your tea." As if he wanted tea. The way her eyes filled with tears and longing, it was clear she wasn't concerned about the beverage either.

"I have to go."

"Go where?"

"I can't explain, and you can't mention my return."

"I don't understand." Her voice hitched. "You're not staying?"

"Promise me." He infused his voice with sternness.

"What do you mean?"

"I need to leave."

"But you're coming back, aren't you?" Her eyes grew wild, her voice desperate.

"Pardon, milady." Polly hoovered in the doorway. "Dr. Cox is in the foyer."

"I must go," Nick said. "Swear the servants to secrecy. I'll slip them a bonus for sealed lips."

"You *are* coming back?" Her voice verged on the edge of hysterics. "Right?"

Her fingers dug into his upper arms, refusing to let him leave without dragging her along. "Tell me you're coming back."

Nicholas's gaze strayed to the door. His mind battled.

Walk away. Leave town. Forget your assignment.

Or stay.

He needed to think, weight his options, form a plan—get out before it was too late.

What she wanted, he couldn't give her. The husband she married died in battle, and only broken pieces remained—a dangerous mind and scarred body.

But he could return once, just to check on her before his next assignment.

"I promise."

Her eyes closed, and she sighed.

He let her go, and her hands limply fell to her sides. Pointing to the wrapped meat on the hearth, he said, "Put those on ice." He snatched up his bow and quiver and headed for the side door. "Go see to the doctor."

He exited his childhood home with Abby's baffled and torn expression haunting his conscience.

~

*A*bby didn't move until Nick had disappeared through the back door.

In a daze, she met Dr. Cox in the foyer and offered him tea. She absently answered the physician's questions regarding her well-being. He prescribed bedrest until her strength returned while her thoughts whirled about in her head like a spinning wheel.

Eventually, Dr. Cox bade her farewell, and she ascended the stairs to her room, where she quietly closed the door. Her knees buckled, unable to absorb the waves of emotion. She fell to her hands and knees. Joyful tears splattered onto the wooden floor. She rested her forehead on the smooth boards.

"Nick's alive. Thank you, God."

CHAPTER 7

A large bearded man with a brusque demeanor entered the tap room of the *Swan and Plough* Alehouse and stepped around a barmaid. He wandered to the far corner cloaked in shadows and slid into the empty seat of the dimly lit tavern. The man hacked out a rattling cough that he attempted to cover with his gloved hand.

Nicholas offered a handkerchief.

They made subtle eye contact before the lieutenant snatched it, wafting the tavern's stench of stale ale in Nicholas's direction. Lieutenant Sparks held it up to his mouth until his phlegm-rattling coughing fit subsided.

The man cleared his throat. "I'm not sure what's more dangerous, our operatives or working in that drafty old building."

"I'm surprised they let you out from behind that desk of yours."

"Indeed, but thank God for it."

"Jolly good to see you, Lieutenant."

"And you, Scar."

Typically, when Nicholas heard his nickname, it was tinged with fear or anxiety, but his superior from the Home Office always used it with pride. *Scar* was how Nicholas was known throughout the War Department. He held out his hand to Lieutenant Sparks, who grasped it with a firm grip.

"Dreadfully sorry to hear about your mother."

"Thank you." Nicholas was unable to mask the sorrow in his voice.

"I know you haven't had adequate time to mourn, but the department had one more assignment. I tried to make your last assignment easy, and you can stay where you are now."

Tempting as that was, it would be safer to hole up far away from Altonwood and probably the entire Cotswolds region. "Involving a viscountess? You don't mean Lady Etheridge."

"Indeed. Lady Amelia Sudham, Viscountess of Etheridge."

Nicholas shook his head and leaned back in his seat. "Surely, you jest?"

"I never fun about an operation." The lieutenant released a sigh. "Lady Etheridge can be a difficult woman."

"That's putting it nicely." Nicholas snorted.

"Some nodcock attempted to poison the old hag. Her dog was found dead after Lady Etheridge fed the dog her apple tart."

"I find that hard to believe." Nicholas rested his folded hands on the table.

"That someone tried to poison her?"

"No, that Lady Etheridge would find the charity in her heart to give away her food."

"This is not a laughing matter. An autopsy determined the cause of death was arsenic. She believes someone made an attempt on her life."

Sarcasm laced Nicholas's words. "Half the town would like to kill Lady Etheridge. The woman has a vile tongue and spites anyone she comes into contact with."

"If you need to bring in the entire town, so be it," Sparks said. "The killer must be stopped. Lady Etheridge not only has connections within the department but also has the ear of the king."

Sparks ran a finger under the collar of his shirt. "I don't need any of the higher ups breathing down my neck. The countess believes her husband's death may also have been foul play."

"The viscount died several years ago."

"Quite right. She believes an acquaintance or someone within her employ is responsible. She demands an operative go undercover as part of her staff to keep an eye on things."

"Lady Etheridge might recognize me."

The lieutenant leveled his gaze. "It's been ten years since she's seen you. You're not the scrawny green lad I initially recruited. Intelligence gathering under Napoleon's nose during times of war changes a man. It put meat on your bones, hardened the softness of youth out of your features, and don't forget your limp."

"How could I?"

He shrugged. "If you think she'll recognize you, go in disguise."

Nicholas raised a questioning eyebrow.

"I thought you'd thank me for making your last assignment simple."

"You haven't met Lady Etheridge, have you?"

Sparks's gaze dropped to the table and his voice lowered. "I'm asking you as a favor."

"By your reaction, I can tell you *have* met the delightful countess." Nicholas leaned forward. "I'm a little surprised you'd give me something so safe for my *last* assignment." Nicholas waited for Sparks to bristle, knowing his boss wanted him to stay on longer.

"Your wife was present moments before the poisoning."

LORRI DUDLEY

Nicholas jolted upright.

"Lady Etheridge has named her a suspect, but there is a chance that the food had been intended for Lady Abigail, and the servant mixed the plates."

Thunder and turf. Had someone tried to kill Abby? Was her recent illness a second attempt to poison her?

The lieutenant's face remained impassive. "Can I count on you?"

Nicholas issued a terse nod.

"Splendid. Here's the file." He pulled a roll of papers from his satchel and set them on the table. "Join her staff and report back any suspicious behavior."

"Abby being a suspect is ludicrous, but if she's in danger..." Nicholas slid the rolled paper off the table and tucked it into the lining of his cloak.

"Get me evidence, and we'll have the bloke dancing from the hangman's noose."

Nicholas stood, slightly dazed, and clapped Sparks on the shoulder. "Good to see you again, my friend. Are you headed back?"

"I think I might enjoy a mug of ale first." He held up his finger towards the barmaid, and she filled a mug for him. "Good to see you, too, Scar. Keep your eyes and ears open on this one."

"Don't I always?"

"That you do, my friend. I can always count on you."

Nicholas strode past the rowdy tavern patrons and exited the building. The cool night air helped him collect his racing thoughts. He needed a plan, a list of suspects, and a means to protect Abby.

The full moon cast shadows across his path as a groom walked toward him with the horse Nicholas had rented for the journey. The long ride back to the woodcutter's cottage meant he wouldn't sleep, but he was grateful for the time to think. Was Abby in danger? Who would want to harm her?

Nicholas grabbed the reins and pushed a farthing into the stable boy's hand. He kicked his bad leg up over his mount and slid into the saddle. Steering toward the proper direction, he spurred his mount down the road, back to the woodcutter's cottage—back to Abby.

The lieutenant's voice echoed in his head, *I can always count on you.* Failure wasn't an option. He must protect Abby at all costs, even if it meant trapping her within the sticky web of deceit that stretched around him.

∼

*A*bby paced the floor of the solarium in front of Polly, reviewing the events of this morning. She'd bathed and scrubbed her hair with fragrant soap, hoping to make a better smelling impression on Nick than she had that morning. The lilac scent she'd donned hovered in the air. Afterward, Polly had helped her dress in her best mourning gown, still honoring Mama Em, and brushed her hair until it shined.

"God *was* listening. He'd heard my most fervent prayers. My husband is alive." Abby paused and held out her arm. "Pinch me, Polly, I still can't truly believe I'm not dreaming."

Polly glanced at Abby's arm but made no move to pinch her. Instead, she looped the tread through her embroidery hoop in a monotonous rhythm. "Surely it is not a dream, for I am perfectly lucid."

Abby chuckled. God must have a sense of humor. "After all this time, it was a bowl of yesterday's soup that reunited Nick and me."

Polly paled at the mention of yesterday's ails. Her maid may be squeamish, but she could sit utterly content for hours, a feat

Abby could never attain. She'd also shown her loyalty to Abby throughout her seven years of service. Abby saw no reason to hide Nick's identity from her. Lord knows what the woman would think if she hadn't revealed that the man who entered her private chamber was, in fact, her husband. Abby still grimaced at what the good doctor must think.

During his visit, Dr. Cox had explained how a tall man with a slight limp—who never bothered to give his name—had sent for him. Dr. Cox peered at her from underneath his glasses and asked if the gentleman was still visiting.

Heat had filled her cheeks. "You misunderstand, he's my ..." Her voice had trailed off as Nick's words rang in her ears. *Don't mention my return.*

"He was just a kind soul who discovered me in poor health in the woods."

She was thankful Dr. Cox didn't ask any more questions.

For the rest of the morning, Abby floated on air. She had to bite her lip to keep from whooping with joy. Her fingertips tingled and her stomach floated as if she'd jumped a horse and remained suspended.

Nick was home.

Where had he been? Why hadn't he written to let her know he was alive? Refusing to let her spirits dampen, she pushed the thoughts aside. She'd been waiting for this day for so long, and she wanted to savor his return. All the unanswered questions would make her crazed and send her to Bedlam. Besides, she could ask him later. She paced the floor, unable to sit or to stand still. Her fingers itched to touch him. Her skin ached to be held. Her lips desired to be kissed once again.

She needed a distraction, so she directed Polly and Delia, the young scullery maid, to aid her in readying the house. The next few hours rushed by in a frenzy of activity. Abby tackled project after project and flittered from room to room making certain they were tidied and aired out. Everything must be suitable. When she finally stopped to take a breath, dirt and dust rimmed the bottom of her skirts. Cobwebs clung to her sleeves, and strands of hair stuck to the sweat on her face.

She sent Polly to deliver a scrawled note to Willowstone Manor. Abby typically dined with her family on Wednesday evenings, but she was not about to miss Nick's return.

The clock ticked as Abby sat, then paced, then sat, then paced again.

"We should bake." Abby spun to face her weary servants. "All his favorites—raspberry tarts, sweet breads, and plum pudding."

She scurried after the staff into the kitchen and set to work. A sweet and yeasty aroma filled the house as they finished their tasks and set the baked goods to cool. Her weary maids retired early for the night, and Abby returned to the drawing room.

The corners of her mouth stretched into a broad smile. Nick was coming home. The life she'd longed for was once again a possibility. It felt like a magic sleeping spell had been broken, and she'd awakened from a long, strange dream. Once again, she was a wife with a husband to care for, not just an empty house.

A dreamy sigh escaped her lips. God willing, they would fill this house with children. Oh, how she would love their children, little boys or girls with eyes that sparkled with mischief just like Nick's. On impulse, she grabbed a pillow and walked over to the mirror. Holding it up to her stomach, she envisioned a pregnancy. Her hands cradled the bulge that would be her stretched belly.

A knot formed in the pit of her stomach, and she tossed the pillow aside.

Where had he been for ten years? If he had been alive and well all that time, why hadn't he contacted her? Had he met someone else? She pictured an exotic French woman discovering him wounded and nursing him back to health.

Abby's knees threatened to give out, and she put a hand on the wall to steady herself. She shook her head to clear it. Wrestling with these thoughts would not get her answers.

Evening melted into night with still no sign of Nick. Abby sat by the fire, her eyelids drooping. The excitement of the day took its toll, and the rhythmic ticking of the hall clock lulled Abby into a deep sleep.

~

*A*bby awoke with a start to loud knocking. She rubbed her eyes with her fists to wipe the sleep from them and peered about the room, disoriented. Her neck ached from sleeping sitting up, and she twisted it from side to side to loosen the stiff muscles. Vague remembrances surfaced of Polly trying to wake her and her shooing her maid away.

Daylight peered in between the cracks in the heavy, woven drapes. She glanced at the wall clock. Quarter after ten. My word, she'd slept the morning away. The knock sounded again, and Abby jolted. *Nick!* Nicholas was at the door.

Torn between throwing herself into his arms and demanding an explanation for where he'd been the entire night, she didn't wait for Polly. Instead, she ran her hands down the bodice of her dress to smooth out the wrinkles, inhaled a deep breath, and threw it open. She stopped mid-motion, choice words for Nick dangling from her lips. Nick wasn't standing on the threshold.

She forced a wide grin, hiding her disappointment from her mother and sister-in-law, Katherine. Usually, she'd be delighted to see them, but she blinked away the prick of tears.

Why hadn't he returned?

"What a lovely surprise. Come in. I'll ring for tea."

Abby embraced her mother and Katherine and escorted

them into her favorite room, the solarium. She yanked the bell pull for Polly to prepare tea.

Wait until they heard the news. They would be ecstatic, but before she could get the words out, her mother's forehead wrinkled and her usual gentle expression darkened with concern.

"Why are you answering the door? You have plenty of means to hire more staff. Mrs. Smith would be horrified." Her mother's brows drew together. She untied the bow of her bonnet and removed it exposing her streaked white hair pulled back in a loose bun. "How are you faring, my dear? We received your note, but then Lady Etheridge mentioned the physician had paid you a visit."

Abby gritted her teeth. Lady Etheridge thrived on being the first to know everything. She also constantly summoned the physician for imaginary ailments just to prod him for news. How ironic that Abby had no memory of the doctor's first visit, but her entire family already knew about it.

Katherine's hands stilled. "Have you been ill?" She removed her poke bonnet and set it aside on the table. Spiral curls that had escaped her coiffure bounced and settled to frame her face.

"Your color seems high." Mama pressed a hand to Abby's cheek. "Do you have a fever? If so, you need to be in bed, young lady, not answering doors. Mrs. Smith's daughter picked a fine time to launch her child."

"Mama, it's not like she had any say in the matter."

"Truly, I worry about you."

Abby smiled. Despite her age, Lady Hartington could still be feisty, especially if one of her children was hurt or ill. Abby gestured for them to sit. They each took a chair. Abby fiddled with one of the chrysanthemums before sitting across from them. How should she tell them the wonderful news?

"Abby, dear, I hate to pester you." Her mother reached over and squeezed her hand. "But one could argue that it's time for you to hire some additional staff. Nicholas knew you loved him more than anything, darling. You don't have to keep a minimal staff to prove you never needed a title. He knows, sweetie. He is probably looking down from heaven and wishing you would stop this nonsense. At least hire back the staff the Emerson family used to keep."

"I'm not trying to prove anything..." Abby broke off at her mother's knowing look.

Perhaps there was a bit of truth in her mother's words. Was Abby trying to show she could live a common lifestyle, or was she punishing herself for Nick's death? It seemed silly to have a full staff for only her.

What did it matter? Nick was alive. She bit her lip to keep from smiling. The need to expend pent up energy tingled her limbs. To appease it, she leaned over to fix a drooping flower in the centerpiece, but it barely scratched the itch.

Mama and Katherine would probably faint dead away when they heard the news.

Surely Nick hadn't intended she keep his return secret from her family? She remembered his strange behavior before he left. He wouldn't keep such momentous news from them. They were his family too. She rang the bell pull for Polly to bring tea. "I have lovely news."

"Mrs. Smith's daughter had a healthy baby boy." Mama clasped her hands. "Lady Etheridge already told us."

"Oh." Abby nodded then shook her head, causing her visitors' brows to furrow. "That is delightful news, but it's not *my* delightful news."

Katherine's face brightened, her unruly curls bobbing on the top of her head as she straightened. "Did the orphanage receive a donation from a rich benefactor? Maybe they can finally put on that much needed addition."

"No, that's not it."

"Did Reverend Cantor hire another schoolmaster?" asked her mother.

Abby tapped her toes on the floor. "Much better—"

"Did Miss Quiller decide to retire?" Katherine giggled.

"No." Abby dug her fingernails into the armrests, her body threatening to explode.

Her mother and Katherine both opened their mouths to make another guess, but Abby raised her palms to stop them. "Let me speak."

They stared at her with wide-eyed anticipation, and their full attention gave Abby pause. Nick wasn't here yet. Maybe she should wait until he returned before she told them.

Don't be silly. She hadn't imagined it. He had been there, in this house, living and breathing. This time it wasn't a dream.

Abby filled her lungs with a deep breath. "Nicholas is alive."

Mama gasped and Katherine's eyes widened.

Mama recovered first. "Truly? Nicholas, alive. It's a miracle." She rose and fiercely hugged her daughter. When she released her, she kept Abby's hands in hers, squeezing them. "What an answer to prayer. God is faithful. It's like I told you, even when He's silent, He's working. Your husband is alive. Praise God."

Abby couldn't subdue her broad smile.

"How did you hear?" Mama asked. "Did you receive a letter?"

"Well, no."

"What happened to him?" Katherine asked. "Where has he been?"

"He...ah, I'm not completely certain."

Katherine leaned closer. "Is he hale?"

"I believe so." Heat rose to Abby's cheeks. She wasn't prepared for these questions. "He appeared to be."

"He was here. You saw him?" Katherine teetered on the edge of her chair. "Was he injured or captured by Napoleon's army?"

"I'm not entirely certain."

81

"What splendid news." Katherine clasped her hands to her chest and inhaled through a wide smile. "Tell us everything."

Abby gazed at the two most important women in her life. They were thrilled for her, and rightly so. They had prayed her through this. There were times when Abby hadn't been able to pray. It had been too painful, but Mama and Katherine had prayed in her stead.

"I came down for tea, and he was standing in the kitchen."

Katherine pressed her hands over her cheeks. "Oh, how wonderful. You must have been beside yourself with joy."

Abby smiled. "I was, sort of."

"Sort of?" Her mother's head drew back. "What do you mean?"

A nervous laugh escaped Abby's lips. "I didn't realize it was him at first."

"So he's changed?" Katherine's face pinched with concern. "He must have been a prisoner of war. Is his hair long and unkempt? Was he malnourished from being locked in some God-forsaken French dungeon?"

"No. Well, he has changed...matured." Abby shrugged. "He was only nineteen when he left. His hair is longer but stylishly so."

"You didn't recognize him because he looked older?"

"Well, no." She explained the events leading up to and including her slicing his arm.

"Egad." Her mother and Katherine came out of their seats.

"It was merely a flesh wound on his forearm."

They slowly sat back down. Her mother blinked a couple of times before asking. "Is that where he is now, with the surgeon?"

"Um, no."

"Where is he?"

"I'm not sure. He was adamant about not seeing a doctor, and after I sewed him up ..."

"Truly?" Katherine gaped at her sister-in-law. "You sewed a man's arm? I've never seen you take up a needle and thread. I didn't think you had the patience for it."

Abby laughed. "I don't."

"Where is he, now?" Mama asked.

Abby rose and fussed over the hibiscus plant. She released a deep breath. "I don't know. He merely said he had to go."

Concern lined their faces.

"He is coming back soon. He promised, and I believe him." She tried to recall his exact words. Did he tell her he'd be back soon, or did her mind just add in that part? She couldn't remember.

Katherine and Mama nodded as if waiting for her to offer more information.

When Abby didn't continue, there was a long pause. Her mother asked in a soft voice, "Did he say where he'd been all this time?"

She glanced between her mother and Katherine. "I was flustered, discovering him alive, and he was bleeding. I forgot to ask."

She tapped on the arm rest, then curled her fingers to stop the nervous habit. She'd wanted to ask Nick more questions, but stitching his arm absorbed a great deal of her concentration. Instead, they'd discussed her family and Lady Etheridge, *of all people*. Multitudes of questions plagued her, but she hadn't known he was going to leave again. Then he'd kissed her, and she'd never asked the most important one—*why?*

"He left in a bit of a hurry. He will be back, though. He gave his word."

Her mother offered an endearing smile. "I do not doubt you, sweetheart. I can't wait to see my son-in-law again. When will he return?"

Abby was torn between screaming and bawling like a child. She couldn't answer any of their questions. "I expect him any hour now." She walked toward the door. "In fact, I have a lot to prepare before he arrives." They followed her into the foyer. "I don't mean to rush you out. Thank you, truly, for calling." She opened the front door and held it for them. "We'll pay you a visit tomorrow."

Mama squeezed Abby's arm. "Dear, would you like me to stay and wait with you?"

Abby caught a flicker of concern in her mother's eyes, and a thread of doubt began to weave its web. What if he wasn't coming? What if this had all been a delusional dream brought on from her sickness? Had she imagined him here? He'd been so real. She'd touched him. She felt the strength of his arms encircling her.

It couldn't have been a dream. Could it?

"No, it's all right." She stepped back with a smile. "Thank you for offering. I'll be fine. Nicholas and I have a lot to talk about. We have ten years of catching up to do. Go and get some rest. We'll either come calling or send over a note tomorrow." She paused and stilled her mother with a hand on her shoulder. "I don't think Nicholas wants word to get out of his arrival yet. He's probably looking for some time to adapt and get reacquainted. If you could keep his return quiet for a bit. I would appreciate it."

Her mother flashed an understanding smile and patted her hand. They headed for the door, and Lady Hartington issued her daughter one last look. "I love you, darling."

Abby restrained herself from throwing her arms around her mother and pouring out all her doubts and fears. She was a grown woman now and needed to comport herself as such. Instead, she returned her smile. "I love you, too, Mama."

Waving goodbye, Abby yelled to their retreating forms, "Be certain to give Stephen and Benjamin my regards."

Abby closed the door and wandered over to the hearth. She curled up in a chair, slipped out of her slippers, and tucked her feet up underneath her skirts. The chair where she'd sewn up Nick's forearm yesterday stood across the room. The event was too real to have been a dream. Her dreams were never that vivid. As she shifted to stare into the fire, she could remember every word, every thought. The way he held her gaze and the little gold flecks in eyes, every change in his features. Except ... except now the memory was hazy.

CHAPTER 8

*a*bby awoke with a start. Her heart pounded wildly, and the small hairs on her arms stood on end. The fire had dwindled to mere embers and ashes. Moonlight spilled shadows across the floor.

Once again, she'd fallen asleep in the chair, and she winced at the stiff ache in her neck. Her ears strained over the thundering of her own heart, as she groped to turn up the oil lamp. What had awakened her?

She rolled the wick, and a warm glow illuminated the drawing room. The night air was still, almost too quiet. Not even the familiar chirping of crickets or croaking of frogs could be heard.

A wailing howl pierced the dead calm.

Her breath caught in her throat, and a chill slithered down her spine. It was the same haunting noise that had started the town chin-wagging about some werewolf creature.

Abby popped out of her chair with a gasp. The cry not only sounded human—it sounded like Nick.

It died away, but its eerie sound seemed to resonate in her heart. Was it truly him? She raced to the window and opened the sash. Her fingernails dug into the wooden sill as she held her breath waiting for the moan to repeat. Silence thickened the air, suffocating her. Her nerves stretched tight like the fabric over an embroidery hoop.

One cricket braved a test chirp, followed by another's reply. The chorus of familiar chirps picked up slowly and gradually grew louder until Abby tried shushing the insects so she could listen for another wail. Minutes ticked by. Her nervous fingers tapped out a piano concerto on the windowsill.

The howl didn't return.

Her mind whirled. Nick sounded close. Was he hurt or injured? It could be why he hadn't returned. What if he needed her help? How would she find him?

"Lord, help him."

A bellow ripped through the silvery night, ceasing the crickets' song again. Abby whirled and darted to where she'd left the oil lamp. She stilled for a moment and closed her eyes to determine the direction of the sound.

The forest. Grabbing her pelisse from off the peg in the front closet, she refused to think about the terrors of the night that might lay hidden deep in the woods. She didn't like bugs or snakes or other creepy crawlies, but the real threats were wild animals, hungry for a meal.

Abby considered waking the staff but thought better of it. Although she disapproved of servant gossip, she couldn't prevent it entirely, and her rushing out into the night to check on a noise she believed to be her husband would certainly feed the gossipmongers.

She must go. Nick might need her. He'd rescued her in the woods. She would do the same for him—anything to keep from losing him again. Swinging the door wide, she straightened her shoulders and held the lamp in front of her like a shield.

She thanked God for two fortunate boons. An earlier gale had brought in warmer weather than was typical in the fall.

And the moon was full, partially illuminating her surroundings and the path with its pale blue light.

She glanced back at the dark house and the town that lay behind it. The hour was late and very few candles remained lit in the townsfolks' windows. Holding the lamp above her head to light the way, she extended her other arm to feel for branches.

The wail echoed again, and she hurried in the general direction, praying to God to guide her steps.

The musty forest enveloped her like a veil. She grasped her pelisse tighter about her chest. The thin muslin material of her gown and her light stays did little to keep the cool night air out. Abby swallowed to maintain a sense of normalcy and quell the shaking in her legs. She wandered deeper into the forest. Minutes ticked past, five, ten, fifteen. Where could Nick be? How much further?

"Nick!" She didn't shout too loudly, but if he were close, he would hear.

There was no reply.

Without knowing which way to turn, which path to take, she was lost. She'd often traveled this pathway from Laurel House towards the Etheridge property and then on to Willowstone Manor, her childhood home, but now the darkness of the forest disoriented her, and everything appeared foreign.

Hounds barked in the distance. Whirling around, she searched for any sign of a cottage, candle in a window, or life of any sort. How far had she gone? How long had she wandered in the dark?

This had been a terrible idea. *God help me. I've gotten myself into a fine mess.* Why didn't she think this through? Instead, she'd jumped into action. *God, show me the way.* A Bible verse she'd memorized years ago to help overcome her fears came to her.

Thou shalt not be afraid for the terror by night; nor for the arrow that flieth by day;

"Psalm ninety-one," she whispered to the night air. "I will not be afraid. God is my refuge and fortress. His truth is my shield and strength." She peered into the darkness. "Did you hear that?" Her voice rang out. "I'm protected by the Lord God Almighty."

Abby listened as if expecting some response. The familiar nighttime sounds chirped about her. As her heartbeat slowed its pace, a calmness washed over her as if God's hand were on her.

There. The log. She knew that log. It had fallen a few years back during the storm. She inhaled a grateful breath of fresh night air and searched for other landmarks and familiar surroundings. The scent of burning wood drifted to her nostrils. A fire meant people. The old abandoned woodcutter's cottage couldn't be far from here.

As children, Nick and Stephen had pretended it was their clubhouse, and no girls were allowed, but she'd always managed to talk them into letting her join. Would Nick have taken refuge there? Where else would there be a fire?

God, be the light unto my steps. The smoky aroma grew stronger as she walked until the dark shape of the woodcutter's cottage came into view.

A jarring moan rang out. This time the sheer volume startled Abby nearly out of her skin. It was Nick. She knew it with all her heart. Abby ran the short distance to the door, and the wail intensified, then ceased altogether. What happened during the night that caused Nick to repeatedly cry out? She edged open the door and stepped in, half expecting to find Nick being tortured.

She held the oil lamp high.

Nick lay on a stuffed straw mattress with the bedclothes all rumpled and disheveled. He was sprawled out, face up, with one hand clutching the twisted sheets. He didn't appear injured or wounded, merely asleep.

Relief flooded Abby until her knees weakened. She put a hand on the wall to steady herself and crept closer to the bed. The soft soles of her slippers didn't make a sound. Beads of perspiration dotted his forehead, but when she dared to touch his face, it was cool. At least he wasn't feverish.

As if rejecting her mothering, he let out a deep grunt and turned onto his right side, taking the bedclothes with him.

Her heart ached for him. "Where have you been?" she whispered. "Why are you here? Why do you cry out at night?"

His brow furrowed as if he'd heard her, and she lightly brushed her fingertips over his forehead to erase the lines of tension. "What happened to you?"

She attempted to right the bed sheets and coverlet he'd twisted like ropes and longed to curl up under the covers next to him but hesitated. In their ten years of marriage, they'd slept in the same bed together only one night. Heat rushed into her cheeks at the intimacies they'd shared that night. Was it right for her to lay next to him? Did they need to reacquaint themselves again first?

Minutes ticked by as she stood alone next to a sleeping man. Not just any man. Nick was her husband. It was silly for her to be shy.

But ten years seemed like a lifetime, enough to create an ocean of differences between them. Would he still hold her hand when she grew fidgety? Did he still run his fingers through his hair when he was thinking? Would he still tease her with a lopsided grin? How had he ended up here?

The floor appeared swept and tidied. A large stack of neatly piled wood rested next to the fire. Embers glowed in the small fireplace. She quietly added another log, careful not to wake him. Nick's jacket hung on a peg next to the door beside his bow and arrow. There was no dresser, but a pile of men's clothes lay carefully folded on a low table in the corner.

Was he living here? The cottage didn't look homey, but if the items lying about were indeed Nick's, then he'd been here at least a few days, long enough to chop a good-sized pile of wood.

The kitchen was equipped with wooden shelves. Mason jars lined each one, neatly labeled with their contents. Had Nick always been so tidy? Strange, but she couldn't remember. He'd always appeared so nonchalant with his easygoing smile. She'd been the high spirited one, wound-up like a top.

Nick stirred, drawing her attention back to him. Sleep softened his features, and he appeared boyish, vulnerable. He was still dashingly handsome. Locks of thick brown hair curled on his forehead and added to the youthful effect. He whimpered and rolled back towards her. She leaned over and tucked a curl back behind his ear. The feel of his soft hair brought so many memories from when they were children, youths, and finally, adults who fell in love. So many things had changed, but his hair was just like she remembered.

He shifted again, and the tie of his nightshirt fell lose and the collar flapped open. Scars crisscrossed along his lower jaw and neck on his left side. Her lips trembled as she leaned in closer. Puckered skin twisted into thinly lined peaks and valleys led down his neck and disappeared underneath his linen nightshirt. How bad might the scarring be beneath?

Her hand shook as she lightly touched the wounded skin. She swallowed hard around the lump forming in her throat. *Oh God, what happened to him?* Her imagination couldn't comprehend the horrific pain he must have endured. She bit her lip to keep from crawling into his arms and crying out desperately for him to forgive her.

If only she hadn't been so foolish. A hundred times a day she wished she'd never made that ridiculous remark about

Nick not being titled. As punishment for her rash words, that night had seared into her memory. Spying the pain Nick endured for her thoughtlessness replayed the agony of her mistake all over again.

Abby had sipped her lukewarm lemonade as the violinists struck up another tune. Bits of conversation floated past her ears, and rich, velvety notes of the orchestra swirled around her. The ballroom sparkled with the light of a thousand candles and bloomed with color as elaborate gowns swept across the room in dizzying circles. She shifted her eyes away from *his* direction. Watching Nick engage other women would put a damper on her night, so she pulled her attention back to the group of friends gathered around her and Stephen.

Melinda Eyre grabbed her arm and whispered loudly into her ear, "Quick. Is my hair in place?"

Abby drew her attention from Stephen's conversation to look. Melinda's shiny blond curls were pinned perfectly in a neat coiffure arranged like a halo upon the crown of her head. "You look lovely."

"He's coming." Melinda lowered her eyes and furiously fluttered her fan.

"Who?"

Before Melinda could respond, another voice answered for her.

"Hartington." Nick's deep voice boomed behind her. "Good to see you, chap."

Startled, Abby dropped her fan. She groped the air, her fingers finally catching the errant object, only to realize it still looped her wrist.

When she peeked up, her gaze locked with Nick's.

"Lady Abigail, Miss Eyre." He smiled at each before turning to Stephen. "It's about time you arrived. I was busy making the acquaintance of the ladies, but don't worry, I put in a good word for you with Miss Calkins. She's a prime article and expects you to partner with her for a dance."

Stephen attempted to be nonchalant about gazing around the room, but Abby spied him shift his weight to his toes for an incline to get a better look at Miss Calkins.

"I can see you've created quite a stir," Stephen said to Nicholas.

Abby turned her head. Her brother was correct. Every lady in the room seemed to have eyes for Nicholas. Some batted their eyelashes, others whispered behind their fans to each other, giggling and casting looks of longing in his direction.

Melinda must have noticed it too, for her lips pinned together in a tight line.

Nicholas shrugged. "There is only one in whom I have an interest."

Abby peered around her brother. Which woman had caught Nicholas's eye?

A warm hand engulfed her fingers and gave a firm tug. She turned to find him raising her hand to kiss the back of it. As his lips gently brushed the thin satin of her glove, tingles spread up her arm. Sheer shock kept her from pulling away.

"And she is exquisite."

His warm gaze captured her own and held her there. She craved more, like some lovesick schoolgirl, but behind the rich green-gold flecks of his eyes, she spotted a mischievous glint. She'd seen that look before, possessive and sure of victory, just before Nicholas and Stephen had invaded her childhood tea party, taking her dolls as captives.

Abby snatched her hand away and stepped back. Heat flooded her face, and she glanced at Stephen to see if he noticed her embarrassment.

Stephen raised a warning eyebrow at his friend, who chuckled in return.

LORRI DUDLEY

"I will not stand here and listen to this flummery." Another wave of heat burned Abby's cheeks.

"It's the plain truth. You've grown into a beautiful woman, and Stephen knows it. Beaus are going to be knocking down his door to ask permission for your hand." He looked directly at Stephen. "I'm warning you now. I'll be the first in line."

Abby grunted. "Nic— Mr. Emerson," she corrected herself. "I'm not a wet goose who's going to believe all your gammon. I'm immune to your rakish ways and completely at a loss as to why you would even attempt to charm me. Other women may fall under your spell, but I know you too well. Don't think I've forgotten who tied my braids together and dangled worms in front of my face."

She put her fisted hands on her hips and turned to a stricken Melinda. "I'm going to go find our hostess."

Abby stepped back to search for Lady Helm, but stopped when she overheard her brother.

"Abby's got her own mind," Stephen said. "When she marries, she'll give some poor chap something to contend with. Be thankful it won't be you. If you recall, after you tied her braids, she retaliated by tying your boot laces together and throwing them up onto the highest branch of the old oak tree. You walked home in your bare feet that day."

Nicholas chuckled. "It still baffles me how she got them up that high."

"Excuse me." Abby pushed her way through the crush of guests. "Pardon me." She ignored the stab of pain as she stifled the tears of that little girl in braids, who'd dressed in her best gown to impress Nicholas that day. The knots he'd tied in her hair had easily been unwound, but her heart was another story. It had served him right to walk home barefooted.

After several quadrilles and a minuet, Abby ended her dance with her latest partner, a young baron who often got ahead of the steps, and spotted Nicholas in the corner. She'd

94

been aware of him all night—though she'd never admit it—as he'd danced with every woman in the room.

But now, he stood near the doors to the balcony and seemed to be watching her.

Heat flooded her cheeks, but she stared him down.

He inclined his head in a mock bow before returning his attention to the woman who hung on his arm like a wilted flower.

Abby smiled at her new dance partner, a fair-haired, well-dressed man of the dandy set. Once again, she was whisked across the dance floor, but as the dance came to an end, her thoughts drifted back to a pair of teasing hazel eyes.

Her partner returned her to a corner of the ballroom, where she noticed the women swarm about Nicholas like ants to jam. She lost him amidst the sea of pastel gowns and was about to seek out her next dance partner when she felt a light touch at her elbow.

"The next dance is mine." Nicholas's husky whisper tickled the hairs on the back of her neck and caused her to shiver.

Abby whirled around. "Mr. Emerson, what are you doing?"

"Asking for the next dance." He leaned against a column. The material of his jacket strained against his broad shoulders as he crossed his arms and flashed her a crooked grin. "I noticed your next dance isn't taken."

"It most certainly is." Abby pulled at the dance card attached to her wrist. "It's claimed by ..." A white gap between the listed names mocked her. Nicholas wouldn't let her refuse. He tucked her arm in his and escorted her onto the dance floor.

Reeling from the sudden change of events, Abby took her position, but instead of meeting his eyes, she stared at the front of his white cambric shirt. How had he noticed this dance had remained unclaimed? Had her brother put him up to this?

Her gaze slid past Nicholas's shoulder to where her brother stood in the corner surrounded by a group of women, his back toward the dancing. He wasn't even aware Nicholas had led her there.

Drawing her to his side, Nicholas escorted her around the floor with commanding grace. When the partners shifted, their fingers released at the last second. When she returned to his embrace, his powerful frame swooped her up as if she'd been away too long. Abby lost herself in the movement. Her heart melted each time his warm eyes captured hers.

She mentally scolded herself. Nicholas was like this with all women. He demanded their attention, like a packman selling his tonics. She wasn't fooled. *Don't be fooled.*

When the song ended, Nicholas tucked her arm, and they strolled around the outskirts of the promenade.

"Why didn't you believe my compliments earlier?" he asked.

"Because they were untrue."

"How so?"

She expelled a heavy sigh. "Look Nick…"

"Good, we're back to Nicholas. We've known each other too long to be formal." He flashed her a smile. "Besides, I like it when you say my name."

Abby shot him a sideways glance. "*Mr. Emerson*, I don't know whether you're merely trying to irritate my brother, or you think this is a game. I do know how you desire a challenge. You could have any woman here."

She waved a broad swipe across the room. "Any. But for some maddening reason, you enjoy teasing me. You're not truly interested in my hand."

"Where did you get that idea?" His gaze pierced hers.

"You've spent the last fifteen years tormenting me. That's not how one consorts with a lady in whom they have a romantic interest."

Nicholas shrugged one shoulder in mock resignation. "It's different now. You're older."

"Yes, and wiser—wise enough to know how courting is done."

Nicholas smiled, showing rows of perfectly even white teeth. "Maybe you could show me how courting is done? It appears I could use a lesson."

Abby wanted to pinch him for his sarcastic remark. "Nicholas, stop the pretense. Let's get back to our regular behavior, where you're my brother's closest friend, and I'm off limits."

"You won't take my suit seriously?"

She let out an inelegant snort. "Of course not."

"Why?" His eyebrows pulled together in a frown.

Because you're just teasing me like you used to do. Because I can't think clearly when you're around. Because I've secretly adored you for as long as I can remember, and I'm frightened you'll break my heart.

His eyes captured her gaze and held with an intensity that set her heart pounding. Could he see her longing? Would he hurt her now as he had before? Was he still waiting for her to answer?

All rational thought flew from her head like a startled flock of birds. Flustered, she spurted out the first thought that wouldn't reveal her true feelings. "Because ... because you're untitled."

Nicholas stiffened and drew back, but not before she saw pain flash in his eyes.

Her hands flew to cover her mouth, and the blood in her veins seemed to cease flowing. What had she done? She reached for Nick's arm, but he pulled away. "I-I didn't mean that. Please, let me explain."

He escorted her back to her brother.

The crowd of women parted to let Nicholas through. Her friends giggled and batted their eyes at him.

Nicholas bowed stiffly and wished the women good

evening. He clapped Stephen on the shoulder. "Good to see you again, my friend."

"Lady Abigail." He inclined his head to Abby with a curt nod, turned, and left.

Abby's reckless words had cost her dearly, but Nick even more so. The fresh pain of regret tore through her like a blunderbuss shot, leaving no part unscathed.

Nick wrestled in his sleep, and Abby was pulled back to the present. His moans increased in frequency and volume.

Abby whispered words of comfort in his ear. She grasped his hand in hers and rubbed her thumb against his palm, but his stirring turned to thrashing.

His fingers closed over hers in a tight grip that might have broken a bone. It required everything within her not to cry out, but just as quickly as it started, he released her.

She withdrew her hand and massaged the pain out with her fingers.

Nick sat up straight. Though his eyes were wide, he appeared to not see her. He released a terrifying scream that chilled Abby to the very core of her being.

She jumped back, stumbling over the nightstand, and pinned herself against the wall.

Nick's arms waved in the air as if swatting at bats.

Abby clasped a hand over her mouth to keep from screaming. She stood frozen, as Nick fought an imaginary foe, trapped in his nightmare.

His screams dwindled into muffled moans. He quieted but continued to stare at the wall. His eyes fluttered closed, and his body grew limp. He collapsed onto the pillow.

The only sound Abby heard was her own shuttered intake of breath.

What had just happened? She folded her shaking hands and clenched them tight, but it only transferred the trembles to her body. Her eyes never strayed from Nick as she prayed earnestly. Gigantic, hot tears rolled over her cheeks, leaving a salty trail and landing with a splash on the wooden floor. She prayed from her heart in her own words until the prayer no longer seemed to be her own but more like uttered groaning from a foreign tongue. She whispered until she ran out of air, then gasped in a large breath and continued. A restlessness swelled within her, so she stood and paced, praying over every square inch of the small dwelling.

Nick stirred.

Abby pulled a stool next to the bed and sat. She reached out, lightly resting her palms on his shoulders as she prayed.

He moaned and rolled to his side, away from her, but she moved her hand to his back. Nick rolled again.

Abby jerked away to keep her arm from being pinned beneath him.

His head tossed against the pillow, and his hands twisted the sheets into tight ropes, once more.

God, ease his torment. I don't know how to help him. Show me what I can do? How do I help erase his pain?

His thrashing grew worse, and his moaning began again.

In desperation, Abby jostled Nick's shoulders to wake him. She couldn't witness him battle his demons a second time. She leaned over him to try to rouse him, but his hand shot up and caught a fistful of her hair.

Pain burned her scalp. She grabbed his arm and tried to keep his hand from moving, to no avail. Her head throbbed. She prayed for release, but it converted into a squeak of pain.

Nick quieted. His fingers relaxed their grip and rubbed back and forth over her hair as a merchant might to test the quality of a fabric. He let out a grunt, and his arm relaxed against the mattress, taking her hair and head with it.

She winced, but his breath evened out, and he fell back into a deep sleep.

Abby slowly inched her head away, but her hair was twisted around his fingers, tangled in his firm grasp.

He continued to caress her hair between his thumb and index finger.

She reached around in an awkward attempt to pry his fingers away but gave up when her hands grew numb from the loss of circulation. She was trapped, her head pinned to the mattress, with no choice but to surrender to her situation. The rest of her body arched back onto the small stool next to the bed. What a predicament. Abby heaved a big sigh and nuzzled her head closer to his heart. Her body ached from the awkward position and exhaustion, but she listened to his heartbeat relax and thanked God for returning him.

CHAPTER 9

*N*icholas awoke to a bright light coming through his
lidded eyes. He squeezed them shut and wondered
who the devil was shining an oil lamp so close to his face. For a
moment, he thought he was back in the French prison camp,
the guards insisting on another round of questioning. No,
Napoleon had surrendered over a year before in a letter to the
Prince Regent. Nicholas had personally been assigned to
protect the carrier. Besides, the ground beneath him was too
soft and warm to be the prison camp, but it didn't explain the
strange silky fetter that bound his wrist and fingers. He rubbed
the texture with his thumb. His brain couldn't register the
material, but in an odd sort of way, he found it comforting.

Slowly he opened one eye. Sun streamed in through the
window, and he blinked in confusion. When was the last time
he awoke to daylight? He couldn't remember. His thumb auto-
matically stroked the silky treads. The odd sensation distracted
him from his thoughts, and he lifted his hand to see his
manacle.

His blood turned cold. It was a long thick lock of a woman's
hair that extended back to its owner. He shifted his eyes. There,

half on the bed, half off, was a woman with mahogany hair spilling over the mattress. He blinked to clear his mind of the French prison from his dream, but she was still there. Where was he? France, India...

Had he been drugged?

He made it a rule to never partake of spirits. In his line of work, he couldn't afford addled wits. If he'd been drugged, then maybe she had also been. He disentangled his fingers from the silky mass and eased off his side of the bed.

This must be some sort of trap. Was he on assignment? The echo of cannon fire and fading scent of smoke disoriented him. Was he dreaming? He rubbed his eyes. The hair had been real, and someone was still lying on his bed.

Was she alive?

At the sound of her soft rhythmic breathing, he released a rush of air.

His gaze skittered over the meagerly furnished cottage. He'd traveled home to England—to Altonwood. He walked around the bed.

The woman lay partially on the bed while remaining seated on a stool. She resembled Abby. Memories flooded back. He'd seen Abby—held her. He stepped closer and gently brushed her hair off her face for a better look.

It was Abby. What in heaven's name was she doing here?

He'd left her and met Lieutenant Sparks at the *Swan and Plough*. Only the lieutenant knew of his whereabouts, and Nicholas trusted his superior with his life.

How did she find him? Abby didn't know where he was staying. Had he slept walked and absconded with her in his dream state.

Thunder and Turf. Had he hurt her?

Her being here explained his nightmare, a woman had stood over him praying, and as she'd prayed, an angel had spilled forth water from heaven, dousing the flames that licked at his flesh. Abby's hair had flowed over his skin, soothing him with its touch. No one else had hair so soft. Even now, her familiar scent of lilac encircled the air around him like a halo.

He stared at her crumpled form with a furrowed brow. Her hands were tucked up under her head for a pillow. He couldn't leave her in such a pitiful state. She couldn't be comfortable sleeping in that position.

He scooped her up. The lower half of her body felt like ice. Her neck rolled to the side, and she winced in pain, releasing a faint groan. Thankfully, she hadn't awakened, giving him more time to consider what happened and what to say.

He laid her in the center of the bed, and she curled on her side. After untangling the mess of blankets, he pulled one up over her. She sighed a soft mew of contentment.

Heavens, she was beautiful.

Why was she here? He turned in a slow circle, but there was nothing to answer his question—no note, no packed bags, only Abby. What had brought her here?

What had she seen?

Usually, he was a light sleeper and woke to the slightest noise. However, once his body was deprived of sleep for four or five days, he'd often fall into a deep, fitful slumber which, he'd been told by other soldiers, was like watching a man battle the fires of hell.

His hand rose to the ties on his shirt. The top one had come undone, and the nightshirt flapped open, revealing the twisted skin beneath. He quickly retied it, clenching his teeth at the thought of her innocent eyes falling on the horror of his deformed body.

An inferno of heat rose from within. Why had she come here? Why didn't she wait for him to return? It was just like Abby to be impatient.

She'd probably become frustrated with waiting and sought him out. He should have gone directly back home after the meeting with the lieutenant, but his brain had switched to tactical mode in preparation for his next mission and confronting Lady Etheridge. Had Abby doubted his promise when he didn't return immediately. Could he blame her? His temper fizzled, evaporating like a drop of water on a hot stove.

Fear had kept him away after the war. He'd made excuse after excuse, but the truth was, he'd been afraid to come home. Afraid Abby would reject him when she saw his brokenness. Afraid he wouldn't be able to overcome his nightmares. Afraid he could hurt her.

The War Department labeled him gutsy and dauntless, but what valiant hero preferred to cower in the shadows than risk being rebuffed by the woman he loved?

Her reaction would be the same as anyone who discovered his secret. At first, Abby would be sympathetic, but soon he'd catch her staring when she thought he wouldn't notice. Disgust would set in. She'd slowly distance herself, but the final insult would be when she rejected his touch.

His exposed scars raised old hurts to the surface like burgeoning pustules. Her coming here—seeing his scars and witnessing his nightmare—had breached his carefully constructed walls, leaving him bare and vulnerable. He loathed what ultimately came next, the looks of pity, the sting of rejection, or worse fear. The fright in his comrade's eyes would forever haunt Nicholas when he awoke from his nightmare with his hands around the man's throat. The man kept silent about the incident but requested a transfer. From that moment on, Nicholas worked alone.

Even at the Home Office, people kept their distance from *Scar.* Outside the War Department, people didn't understand the horrors he'd witnessed and how they'd affected him. It was easier for them to lock away men like him than deal with the issues and their causes.

If the townsfolk or even his superiors put him in

Bedlam, he'd no longer be able to provide for Abby. She'd visit him like the rest of the madmen set behind bars like creatures in a zoo. She'd face scathing remarks about her marrying a lunatic. It would only take one incident for British officials to issue the command sending sanitarium workers to drag him away. He'd prefer to live as a recluse for the rest of his life than know Abby suffered more on his account.

But she'd discovered his hideout.

His fingers curled into fists at his sides. He'd leave before she woke up. Hole up somewhere else until he could finish the assignment. He grabbed his canvass bag and stuffed his belongings into it.

He'd promised her he'd return, was he going to break his word?

Abby stirred.

He froze, his hand half in the bag, while Abby yawned and stretched. He remained still and waited, willing her to roll over and go back to sleep. She moved onto her side facing him and snuggled deeper in the covers for warmth. He exhaled the breath he'd been holding.

Her eyes opened, and a shy smile spread across her lips. "Nick." She whispered his name in a raspy voice still thick with sleep.

His stomach turned a somersault.

Too late. Nicholas swallowed. "What are you doing here?" His gruff voice came out harsher than he'd intended.

Her smile faded, and she pushed herself up on her elbows. "I heard screaming in the night, and I knew. Somehow I knew it was you, so I followed your wailing here."

"You came alone?"

"Yes."

"You decided to stroll through the woods, in the middle of the night, by yourself?" He ran a hand over the top of his head.

"Anything could have happened to you. You could have fallen, gotten lost, or been eaten by wild animals."

Stepping forward, he held his hands up. Concern permeated his tone "Bandits and thieves camp in these woods. What if you'd stumbled upon the likes of them? You would have wished you'd been eaten by wild animals." He paused, pinning her to the bed with his glare.

Abby's blue eyes flashed, and she drew up onto her knees. He was momentarily stunned by the fiery goddess glaring back at him.

She pointed a slender index finger in his direction. "If you had come back like you promised you would, I wouldn't have needed to fumble through the woods late at night." Her mouth opened to say more, but instead, she exhaled. Her demeanor changed, and she peered up into his eyes with a softness that made Nicholas ache.

"I thought you were in pain and needed help." She radiated tenderness.

His screams traveled as far as the main house? Could the town hear him? He'd heard talk about a werewolf. Were his cries setting the town on edge? He swallowed. Blast. His time was limited. The wounded look in her eyes seared through his heart like a hot knife. *She saw his scars. It starts with pity.*

"I was so worried. I can't lose you again."

Blast it all.

"You can imagine my confusion when I found you here in the old woodcutter's cottage." Her delicate brows drew together, and she scooted closer. "Why are you here? Please tell me where you've been all this time."

Nicholas closed his eyes as his thoughts and emotions battled to hold their ground within his mind. "I've been at war."

"The war ended several years ago."

"Yes." His voice was flat, and he stared over her head out the window. He couldn't tell her what happened, not just because the retelling would horrify an innocent far removed from death and destruction, but because revisiting those memories could trigger one of his attacks.

"Why didn't you write to let me know you were alive?"

"I couldn't."

"You couldn't or wouldn't?"

He yearned to climb into bed beside her and unburden his soul from the terror, the pain, the suffering, beg her to make him whole again. He shifted and glanced towards the door. "I can't talk about it."

"Why not?"

"Go away, Abby." His painful words dislodged in a remorseful whisper. "It's best if I watch you from a distance."

"No."

He shouldn't have been surprised by her forceful answer, but it jarred him. It had been a long time since someone refused his direct order. If it had been anyone but Abby, Nicholas would have had him on the floor begging for his life.

Abby held her ground, but Nicholas didn't miss the trembling of her fingers.

She changed the subject, masking her worry with an overly bright smile. "I'm going to see to breaking our fast."

She pushed off the bed and strode towards the meager shelves.

"You know how to cook?" Genuine surprise tinged his voice. She shouldn't be doing menial tasks. He made a mental note to double her staff after he left.

"I've watched Mrs. Smith dozens of times."

As she poked through his supplies, he tried to ignore her rapid blinks as if fighting back tears. She pulled out oat flour and salted meat and started to prepare a meal.

Did he need to be so terse with her? His head screamed, yes, for her good, so she would realize he wasn't the man she married. But his heart begged to wrap her in his arms and confess his love, tell her his would fix this. Out of sheer will, he'd force away his nightmares and snap his broken mind back into place.

"Could you please re-light the fire so I can fry up a batch of oat cakes?"

Grateful to have something to do, Nicholas added a log to the dying embers. He stoked the fire into a flame and moved to sit near the barrel that served as a table. He stared out the window, but his mind was on Abby. He regarded her every move in his periphery, admiring the sway of her hips and the way she wrapped her hair around her finger as she waited in front of the hearth. Her gaze stayed on the flames. She avoided looking at him. He'd hurt her, and as much as he wanted to take back what he'd said, it was for the best. He needed to keep his distance. And she needed to keep hers.

It took all of his concentration to retain his self-control. He'd dreamt about her for so long. If she came within arm's reach, he could forget himself and sweep her into his arms, bury his face in her hair, and breathe in her scent as he'd done during their engagement party. That night, he had held himself like a king as he paraded her around the dance floor and she'd sparkled brighter than the chandelier ablaze with a hundred candles.

Abby flipped one of the oat cakes. It teetered on the lip of the pan and would have landed in the fire, but she nudged it back with a fork. Her free hand reached around her head and swept her heavy mane over her shoulder, giving him a view of the nape of her neck. It was torture to have her so close yet beyond his reach.

Even though her eyes were rimmed red, Abby composed herself before she brought the oat cakes and sliced meat to the makeshift table. She pulled up a stool, as he'd done, and sat, draping a dishcloth over her gown.

"Don't grimace"—she flashed a smile— "or you'll wound my tender feelings." She waited for him to take a bite.

Nicholas cut the biscuit-like cake with the side of his fork and ate a piece. He nodded. "Not bad." He took another bite. "Truly, it's quite good. You were funning me. You do know how to cook."

Abby twisted a corner of the dishcloth. "Mrs. Smith does tire of me peeking over her shoulder."

Nicholas chuckled. He knew how persistent Abby could be. He pitied Mrs. Smith and vowed to send her a bonus check at Christmas.

"Nick, I—"

He raised his palm to silence her. "There are some things I cannot talk about. I've lived a nightmare, but I'm trying to put it in the past." He rubbed his face. "There are things I've seen and done, things that have changed me."

"You have scars,"—she shrugged—"but you hide them well, and I'd prefer you alive with scars then a body in a grave."

For now. How could he explain? "It's more than physical scars. I'm ruined inside and out. Twisted up in here." He tapped his temple. "I'm not the man you married ten years ago. You're going to have to come to terms with that."

~

A long silence loomed between them. Abby wanted to grab his shoulders and shake him. How was she to come to terms with something he refused to share? He might not be the same person she'd married, but neither was she. Nick spoke as if they had no hope, as if the chasm between them was too wide to span, but they must try. For heaven's sake, she'd vowed to love him until death, and he miraculously sat before her alive and well. She prayed for God to make a way.

"I'm just grateful you're here. I begged God to bring you back to me, and He did. I will forever be thankful."

She leaned in closer. "You and I have both changed, but now we have the chance to start anew, to get to know each other, to begin again as husband and wife. We can restart the marriage we were deprived of ten years ago."

"You don't understand." Shaking his head, Nick put his fork down. "I need you to start a new life without me."

His eyes bored into hers, darkening with intensity. "Marry someone else. I'm not the husband you remember, and I never can be."

He might as well have crumpled her heart and discarded it like rubbish. The pain spread, permeating her entire body. "I can't marry someone else. I'm married to you."

"I'm dead, Abby." His eyes hardened into granite, exuding a force that stole the air from her lungs. "The entire world believes me dead. The crown has accepted my death certificate. There was a funeral. According to the crown, you are free to marry someone else."

Abby pushed away from the table and stood. Heat filled her face, and her voice surged in shrill, staccato bursts. "Are you mad? Listen to yourself. Have you ever heard anything so absurd?"

Leaning back in his chair, Nick pulled his leg up and crossed his ankle over his knee. "Yes, to the former. No to the latter."

His cheeky remark was kindling on the fire of her frustration. Pressure swelled in her chest ready to pop in a screaming rage.

She rose abruptly. "I stood in front of a priest and said my vows to *God* to love you and be your wife until death. I take that pledge seriously."

"That's just it. I don't want to be the cause of your death."

"Why would you think that?"

"You haven't seen the worst of my nightmares."

She shook her head. "You'd never hurt me."

"In my right mind, I wouldn't, but my mind's slipping. I can't control what I do when I'm under an attack." He rubbed the back of his neck. "Don't you remember the dreams for our future? You've always desired children and a family with a manor home in the country. It's not fair for that to be taken from you. You still have a chance to remarry. Everyone believes me dead."

"You haven't fooled God."

Nick's calm façade vanished. "God has forsaken me." He stood and leaned his palms on the table. "If God is a forgiving God, then He should understand."

Abby heard the pain in his voice and felt the words like a physical blow. Her anger escaped like the air out of a folding accordion. Nick was hurting, and she couldn't squelch the intense desire to mend that hurt.

"God hasn't deserted you." Her voice pleaded for under-standing. "It says in His word that He will never leave you or forsake you. I used to think God had forgotten me, but I grew to realize that He was by my side pulling me though. He's with you too."

She leaned towards him, but he stepped back, though the table still separated them. She ignored his rejection and the stab of pain in her gut it caused. "Sometimes our doubt keeps us from feeling His presence."

～

*N*icholas recognized the look in her eyes for what it was—pity. His stomach clenched. Pity was a harbinger of disgust.

She reached for him, but he jumped away. His chest tightened and couldn't catch his breath. Confound it. Not another attack. Not in front of Abby.

Cannon fire and the dull hum of round-shot threatened to swallow him.

A slick layer of sweat formed over his palms, and he wiped them on the sides of his trousers. His heart raced, pounding on his chest like a boxer thrashing his opponent.

"I have to go." He started for the door.

"Not again." She stomped her foot and followed him. "Last time you promised you would come back, but you didn't."

Nicholas stopped and turned in the doorway.

"I was going to." His voice was weak, and he barely heard himself over the roar of rushing blood in his ears. He was going to have an episode right here in front of Abby.

Was this how King George III began his lapse into madness? Nicholas pitied their dethroned king. He'd been present once when the king's fearsome excitement began. He ranted until the doctors rushed in, treating his majesty like a crazed animal, wrapping him in a winding sheet and stuffing a cloth into his mouth. Would Nicholas share the king's fate?

He rushed to get the words out. "I have work to do. I'll be back in a few hours."

"You'll give me your word?"

"Yes!"

He couldn't escape fast enough.

CHAPTER 10

*A*bby waited. Lord help her, she needed more patience. She paced to prevent becoming a quivering mass of nerves lying on the floor. She needed to do something to take her mind off Nick. Stopping mid-stride, she peered around the small, dilapidated room. Tidying up the cottage would keep her hands busy, but truthfully, she wasn't quite certain how to go about it. What would Mrs. Smith do? Abby tied a towel around her waist and started with the barrel table. Her original opinion that Nick was neat and clean changed after she began to scrub the layers of dirt off the table, cabinets, and shelves.

As her hands scrubbed top and bottom, her mind worked to disassemble the conundrum of Nick's strange behavior. She needed an objective approach to get him to see reason and resume the married life that the war had stolen from them. His return had been far from the passionate reunion of her dreams.

Instead of wrapping her in his arms and vowing to never leave her side again, he was distant and secretive. Silent tension crackled between them like the energy before a storm. His lackadaisical view of their marriage vows disturbed her deeply. How could she get him to see reason if he wouldn't talk to her?

She knew he'd suffered. She'd seen the scars. Unfortunately, he hadn't given her even a smidgen of information as to what happened while he was at war, so all she could do was speculate.

Two hours passed before Abby put away the broom and rag. She scrutinized the room. It almost appeared cozy. For the final touches, she moved a wooden chair near the hearth, tied back the moth-eaten drapes, and displayed some of the nicer dishes on the shelves. She hid the chipped spots by turning that section towards the wall. She even untied the towel from about her waist and draped it across the barrel for a tablecloth. Wiping her hands, she admired her work. The one-room cottage was small but almost felt like a home.

~

*N*icholas gritted his teeth as he lumbered back towards the woodcutter's cottage. His episode had passed as quickly as it had come, but he'd needed time to ebb his frustration. He'd observed the Etheridge property, watching the changing of shifts and tracking the timing of who came and left and by what means. His meeting with Lady Etheridge wasn't until tomorrow, but it didn't hurt to get advanced intelligence on his assignment. After that, he swung by the orphanage to speak to the reverend, Mr. Cantor. Nicholas couldn't find a link between the orphanage poisoning and the Etheridge poisoning. He documented a list of people who'd have access to Lady Etheridge's food—the cook, footmen, housekeeper, and butler. Arsenic poisonings typically were done by someone close to the victim. But who would have access to the poison? The physician, apothecary, gardener, rat catcher?

Much as he tried to focus, his thoughts kept drifting to Abby. He could still feel the silkiness of her hair in his fingers and smell the lingering aroma of lilac on his skin. He saw the clear blue of her eyes full of pity, and bile rose in his throat.

If Abby had only found herself another husband, he could live his life knowing Abby was happy without him. He wouldn't have to smother out the small ember of hope that ignited each time he saw her. He wouldn't have to muffle the small voice inside him that whispered *she's your wife. She needs you—and you need her.*

What else could he do? Resume their marriage? Fall deeper in love only to devastate her all over again when he was carted away permanently? People weren't released from Bedlam—at least none that he'd ever heard of. Nicholas shook his head, remembering the way her eyes had flashed like sunlight when she'd said, *well, you didn't fool God.*

By polite society's standards, Abby fidgeted too often and was a little too disarming, but he'd always admired her confidence. His wife knew who she was, and she didn't back down. That had been one of the many reasons he'd married her, but now it was his biggest obstacle.

Should he walk away from the assignment? Put as much distance as possible between Abby and himself? He had relatives who'd settled in America. Maybe an ocean's length would choke out his desire. Should he request Agent Warren to take his place? Nicholas shook his head. Warren was a good agent, but the man was a womanizer, and would another agent protect Abby as he would? The idea of not being there if the operation went south pricked his conscience.

He'd also given his word. The Home Office had been good to him. He must see this through. But he needed to set up boundaries, to protect her and not let her think the impossible possible. He also needed the proceeds he'd earn to put the finishing touches on her manor house. Once this assignment was over and the attempted murderer put away, he'd have plenty of money for Abby to live comfortably in accordance with her rank and the way she'd been raised. She wouldn't need him at all.

As he neared, a warmth emanated from the cottage. Merely knowing Abby was inside made the desolate place seem cheery. He'd hurt her feelings and owed her an apology. He also needed to disarm her.

An apology would throw Abby off balance. If she went on the defensive, she'd dig in her heels, and he'd have to fight all the harder to get her to see reason. Nicholas quickly rehearsed what he was going to say and stopped to pick a couple flowers to show his sincerity.

As he stepped over the threshold, he froze. The cottage that he'd intentionally left looking abandoned now appeared clean and cozy.

Abby stood next to the barrel-table beaming her brightest smile at him. The flowers slipped loosely from his fingers.

His gaze shifted over the neatly made bed, the scrubbed counters, and the pitcher in the center of the makeshift table. He scanned the perfectly tidy room. Gone was the unkempt, never-been-touched appearance. The layers of dust had been wiped away. The cobwebs swept from the ceiling. The room looked ... *lived in.*

Abby's smile faded. "Don't you like it?"

Nicholas closed his eyes, his careful control slipping as his head pounded. Abby hadn't known he needed the room to remain in its original state. He couldn't tell her cleaning the cottage could draw suspicion.

She'd complicated matters, but she couldn't possibly know that. As children they'd often peeked in the windows or snuck in for a look around. Passersby, cutting through the woods, would be curious to know who'd taken up residence. Gossip would spread and draw unwanted attention.

The throbbing in his head turned unbearable.

"I spent hours cleaning," she said.

He didn't respond as he stepped into the room. Instead, he focused on lowering his tight shoulders.

She frowned. "You're welcome."

"Thank you," he forced past tight lips.

Her shoulders slumped. "You're acting like you wanted layers of dirt and grime all over."

"You should have asked me first." Lieutenant Spark's voice barked in Nicholas's memory. *Never leave a trace of your presence. Might as well put a bullet in your back.*

Abby opened her palms. "I was trying to help."

The head throbbing resumed, making it hard to think clearly. "I don't want your help."

"You don't want my help, or you don't want me?"

Pain shot around the perimeter of Nicholas's skull the same as it had when the burning beam had collapsed and landed on him, temporarily robbing him of speech. The smell of smoke returned to his nostrils as real as if the cottage were on fire.

Abby's eyes filled with tears. They spilled over, leaving a trail through the soot smudged across her cheeks.

"Get out." She pointed at the door.

"I live here." He clenched his teeth, fighting to stay in the present. *Perdition.* He'd come back to apologize.

Abby's hands clenched into fists at her sides, and for a moment she stood stiff as an iron poker. "Fine." She brushed past him and headed out the door. "You win. Everyone wanted me to marry Lord McAllister anyway." She slammed it behind her with such force that the rafters shook.

Nicholas flinched and closed his eyes. Her words pierced him like a shot in the back. He waited for the screams, stench of smoke, and the crackle of fire to fade. This was not supposed to happen. He rubbed his temples with his index fingers. Abby was never supposed to have seen him alive. As he'd known would happen, his lack of self-control revealed his true nature and, within a few days, given her reason to hate him. She must

117

believe she'd married a complete cad. At least now she wouldn't be so opposed to remarrying.

The mere thought didn't console him. *Blasted McAllister, who'd been born with a title.* The idea of someone else touching Abby balled his hands into fists. *God help him.*

～

*T*ears blinded Abby as she half ran, half fumbled, her way back to Laurel House. Inside, she closed the door behind her and leaned against it for support. She released the torrent within until she could barely draw a ragged breath. She cried until her face felt raw and her chest ached.

Why was Nick acting like this? How bad could his nightmares be? Weren't they only bad dreams? Had she been so disillusioned ten years ago to have married someone without a heart? Or did the war change Nick so much that he no longer cared about anyone or anything? She stumbled up to her room and crawled into bed. Pulling the blankets up over her head, she curled into the fetal position.

"God," she prayed, "help me. I know it's a miracle that Nicholas is alive, but he's not Nick. He's changed. Nick loved me. He cared. Please, bring the old Nick back to life."

～

*N*icholas propped his elbows on the counter, keeping his head bent low and nursing a pint of ale at the *Swan and Plough* tavern. Maybe throwing himself into his work would take his mind off Abby. He listened to the gin-induced rambling of the men beside him.

"I thought I was seeing things," said a shabby gentleman slumped on a pub stool to Nicholas's right. "She was alone carrying a light like the goddess Persephone headed back to the underworld after a clandestine meeting with Adonis."

"On the edge of town, you say?" responded his equally foxed chum. "Lester, ol' chap, I'll be buggered if that ain't Laurel House and Lady Abigail out for a nighttime stroll."

Nicholas stiffened.

"That's the Emerson house." He elbowed the man he'd referred to as Lester in the ribs. "Think she's off on some clandestine visit? Must be meetn' a lover 'cause there's nothin' that direction but deep woods."

Nicholas's jaw tightened and his fingers curled into fists.

"Who is she?" The greasy haired Lester hiccupped and pounded his chest with his fist. "I've never heard of her."

"Ah, you poor bloke, I forgot you're not native to the area. She's the late earl's daughter, Lady Abigail Hartington."

"Pity." Lester frowned, and he slumped over the rim of his cup. "Someone so high in the instep would never have the likes of me."

Quite right, you sluggard.

"She used to be married. Her husband purchased a commission. Poor soldier never returned." The companion tossed back the rest of his ale.

"A widow?" Lester perked up. "A widow is another story. There's a different set of rules for a previously married woman whose known the love of a man."

Nicholas's fingers balled into a fist. *If he lays a finger on Abby...*

The man's friend burst out laughing and nudged Lester with his elbow. "Keep dreamin', ol' chap. I bet whores charge double when they see the likes of you."

Lester's eyes narrowed, and he cursed his friend and his lot in life under his breath.

"Frankly, I'm surprised to hear this tale. My wife knows all the gossip, and she hasn't mentioned a thing about Lady

Abigail. Honoria's tongue would probably walk right out of her mouth to get hold of this juicy tidbit."

Lester licked his lips. "The sight of that mysterious woman headed toward the woods the other night has stirred me up."

The barkeep tilted the bottle of gin, but the drinking companion set his hand over Lester's glass to keep him from pouring more liquor. "That's enough." He slapped Lester on the back. "Let's get a move on. We've got to be up at first light."

"Yeah, all right." Lester allowed his friend to aid him from the bar stool and stumbled a couple times on the way to the exit.

Nicholas eyed the barkeep. "Those two spoke of a friend of mine. Do I need to rearrange their faces?"

"Only if you're looking for a bit of sport." The barkeep snorted, and his shoulders shook in silent laughter. "Otherwise, I wouldn't bother. Lester Shue and his good chap Milo are harmless. The simpering fools won't remember the events of tonight. I can't complain because they're good customers. Downed a bottle each."

Reaching into his purse, Nicholas slid money across the bar top. "That should take care of it."

A greedy smile curved the barkeep's lips. "Thank you, sir. Come back any time. I'll start you a tab."

Nicholas nodded and flung his cape across his shoulders. He'd surveil those nodcocks and keep an eye on them. If they even glanced at Abby, they'd pay a hefty penance.

CHAPTER 11

hen Abby awoke, it was dark, and the moon shone brightly outside. She turned away from the window, curling tighter into the warmth of the blankets, and tried to go back to sleep. A niggling in the back of her mind caused her to toss in the bed, but she fought to block it out. She did not want to think about the past or the future. She sought the nothingness of sleep to ease the ache in her heart, but her spirit grew restless. Closing her eyes tightly, she willed herself to fall back asleep, and she'd almost succeeded when the howl pierced the night.

Abby groaned and pulled the covers over her head. She didn't want to hear the noise. She didn't want to remember, but it was too late. The wailing increased in intensity, and Abby knew Nick was in the throes of another nightmare. Despite her resolve not to care, a sob clogged her throat.

"God," she prayed, "I spoke irrationally yesterday. Help Nick, but I can't go to him again. It hurts too much. He's not the man I married."

The wailing stopped. Abby lay still when a clear thought awoke her spirit.

You held on for nearly a decade, and now *you're going to give up? After one argument?*

Her eyes sprung open, but she didn't move. She lay there listening for any sound, but there was nothing, only silence. The minutes ticked by, and her uneasiness intensified.

Throwing back the covers, Abby shot out of bed and scowled at the ceiling. "Fine." She slapped her palm onto her nightstand, scooped up her wedding band, and stuffed it back on her finger.

After donning her walking gown and tying her hair back with a ribbon, she headed into the woods. Unlike the last time, fear didn't overwhelm her. She stomped to the woodcutter's cottage, snapping twigs and crumpling leaves in her path.

When the groans began again, she gritted her teeth and walked faster. Entering the cottage, Abby noticed the crushed petals scattered on the floor near the entrance. She vaguely remembered Nick entering with flowers before her hurt at his ridiculous outrage had blinded her to everything else. Had those been meant for her?

She moved to the side of his bed and crossed her arms over her chest, but a tiny crack had opened in her wall of indignation. "Now what?" she asked God.

Nick tossed about, writhing under the sheets. He screamed like a man on fire. The cords on his neck protruded, straining against his skin. Abby's breath caught at his torturous mental battle. His eyes opened, and raw, wild fear shown there, panic like none she'd ever seen.

A startled cry escaped her lips, and icy chills raced up her spine. Nick's words echoed in her mind, *I can't control what I do when I'm under an attack.*

Should she be afraid for her life?

Lord, what should I do?

Nick stilled, and the boyishness returned to his face.

It was just a nightmare, *and just Nick.* Did he have these every night? A lump rose in her throat, and she pulled the blanket up over his body, but he threw it off again.

She shushed him and spoke soft words of encouragement like a mother would to a child. What had worked the night before? She scanned the room for anything that would help to calm him. Oddly enough, he'd settled down after he'd clung to her hair like a security blanket.

She untied the ribbon and let it cascade over her shoulders. Leaning over the bed, she folded her hands and prayed.

He grasped a handful of hair. She winced, but his moaning stopped.

She continued to pray.

He brought the fistful up to his face and nudged it with his nose. His violent gasps of air slowed and evened out. He curled onto his side, taking her hair along with him. She had no choice but to climb on top of the covers and lie beside him. As he settled, she dared to put her arms around him and snuggle next to his warmth.

"Lord, thank you for returning Nick to me," she whispered. "He's my husband and, if it's my turn to go to battle for him, I will."

~

*T*he metallic taste of his own blood mixed with the grit of dust in his mouth. Nicholas scrambled to right himself before anyone noticed him lying in the school yard.

A loud guffaw of laughter split the air, and a cold sweat broke out over his skin. A boy hovered above him with a malicious glint in his eyes. *Not Xavier.* Nicholas still had bruises from their last encounter.

"Cross-eyed Emerson just ate dirt. Well, I'll be buggered.

Look everybody. He's ripped his pants. Look there's blood running down his knee."

Other kids joined in the verbal thrashing—"Cyclops," "Freak," and "Misfit," they jeered, but Xavier's voice rang over them all. "Try to touch me, cross-eyes. C'mon, go ahead. Try." Xavier shoved him.

Nicholas gritted his teeth and thrust his hand out to push Xavier away, but unshed tears burned and blurred his vision.

Xavier jumped out of the way, dodging Nicholas's swipe.

"You missed. I'm over here."

Heat flooded into his cheeks, and his ears burned hot.

More kids gathered around to see the spectacle.

His hands balled into fists. With everything he had, he took another swing—and missed.

Xavier stuck his foot out.

Nicholas's body pitched forward. He struck the ground with full force, skidding across the dirt.

The circle of kids stepped back as Nicholas's hands and face slid into their shoes. Another burst of laughter spewed from the crowd.

Nicholas covered his ears with his hands to block out their loud cackling, but it morphed into the staccato beating sound of artillery fire. It pierced through the night air all around him.

Instead of dirt, his fingers dug into the painted French floor cloth. A shell burst high in the air, shattering the windows and casting an unnaturally white glow on the faces of the dead lying around him.

Smoke burned his lungs as yellow flames licked the walls of the French estate. Pandemonium broke loose. Men dressed in finery and woman in ball gowns screamed as fire danced around them. Several jumped through the gaping hole in the wall only to be sprayed by bullets from Royal troops.

The occasional shrill sound of projectiles flying overhead drowned out the constant drum of the round-shot.

Nicholas struggled to a crouched position behind a high-backed chair. He needed to think. He needed a way out that wouldn't get him shot. His heart beat like a caged bird.

Someone had botched the plan. They had attacked too soon. Now he was on the wrong side of the line dressed as a French messenger and under fire from his own troops.

A woman's tear-stained face obscured his view, and he drew back with a start. The woman couldn't have been more than three and twenty, not that much older than his own precious Abby. Even her hair was similar in color. Cameo drop earrings swung from her earlobes as she glanced about. There was a loud groan from above, and her gloved fingers clenched his forearm.

Nicholas glanced up to see a spray of sparks raining from the ceiling. The roof was on fire. Pulling the woman to her feet, he spoke in rapid French. "We must get out of here quickly, or we'll be trapped."

She pointed to the servant's entrance. Shrugging off his jacket, Nicholas held it above their heads to keep the flying ambers away as they ran through the back hall. The curtains burned like fiery waterfalls running up instead of down. Within ten yards stood an open doorway, the cool night air offering breath and life.

A thunderous crash shook the room, knocking Nicholas to the floor. Raging pain shot through his leg and midsection. A flaming weight immobilized him, squeezing the air from his chest.

He looked up, surprised to see night sky. The ceiling had collapsed, and he lay trapped under a beam. The putrid stench of his own burning skin filled his nostrils.

The woman's sharp cry drew his attention.

"Run!" he yelled, "Run!" He knew he'd said it in English, but pain fogged his mind.

Through the smoke, he saw the woman's face. A pair of

crystal blue eyes peered back at him. It wasn't a stranger. Abby's face appeared in the haze. She cried out to him with both hands extended. "Nick!" she screamed. "Help me!"

He struggled with all his might. How could Abby be in France? He didn't care, he had to get to her. Blackness threatened to overtake him. He fought to stay conscious. *God save her.* Suddenly, the weight of the beam was lifted from his chest. Strong arms encircled him, lifting. Protecting.

Nicholas didn't startle awake. Instead, an unfamiliar sense of calm surrounded him. He expected the feeling to dissipate as soon as he opened his eyes, so he kept them closed.

Early morning birds chirped outside of the woodcutter's cottage. As he sucked in a deep breath and flexed his feet, his leg barely pained him. Maybe it would be a good day. He remembered his meeting with Lady Etheridge and snorted.

Already a foul mood hovered over him like a black cloud. He turned to roll out of bed but caught on something. His eyes opened, and he stared at the streaks of early morning sun highlighting the wood grain on the wall. He'd slept until daybreak, again?

By Jove, no wonder he felt so good. He reached for his pocket watch, but his arm was tangled, and his upper torso felt wrapped in silken bedclothes.

Abby.

Her hair entangled his fingers and spilled across his chest beside one delicate arm and splayed fingers. Her thick eyelashes rested comfortably on the alabaster pillows of her cheeks. Her lips, rosy from sleep, were slightly parted, tempting Nicholas to brush them with a kiss. Before he relented, reality crashed upon him. *Blast!* What was she doing here again?

Gingerly he moved her arm and placed it by her side. Propping himself up on the pillow, he disentangled himself from her hair.

Abby stirred and opened her eyes. Her brow furrowed and, with a sleepy look, she blinked several times.

He studied her expression to catch any unguarded emotion while sleep still addled her wits.

She raised herself up on one elbow. Her hair cascaded onto his pillow. Tilting her head, she asked, "Since when did you start painting your hair?"

Nicholas's eyes narrowed. *What was she talking about?* Then he remembered. He'd dyed his hair charcoal black the night before to prepare for his visit with Lady Etheridge. He needed to disguise his appearance. With a shrug, he said, "Where I work, they require it."

"You're employed?" Her heart-shaped face lit up.

He gauged her expression. Would she think less of him if he'd fallen down society's ladder and now smelled of shop?

Abby sat up straight. "Where?" Her curiosity regarding the tiny glimpse into his current life showed on her face.

He had to think quickly about what to say. *Oh, by the way, I've taken up intelligence gathering.*

Or lose all his dignity and go with his cover. *Lady Etheridge hired me as her footman.* Peering into those pure blue eyes, he'd never been so tempted to throw away his mission and confess to espionage. But no, he'd be leaving as soon as the case was over, and the less she knew, the better.

"I thought you were angry with me?"

Abby arched one of her finely curved eyebrows. "I've decided to forgive you."

"Brilliant," he said in a slightly mocking tone, but relief unfolded deep within him.

"Indeed." Her generous smile emanated an infectious glow. Nicholas felt like he was staring into a campfire, enticed and unable to look away from the dancing heat. He couldn't resist smiling back, intoxicated by her nearness.

He captured an errant lock of her hair and wrapped it

around his fingers. The longing to touch her caused his skin to physically ache, but he couldn't trust himself. Her lilac scent surrounded him and clung to his skin. "It's hard to believe you're real. Magically, like a dream, you seem to appear each night."

She laughed. The musical sound caused his chest to swell and flood with a feeling of lightheartedness he hadn't felt in years.

"Someone must put a stop to all the commotion you make."

Nicholas let out a snort. If only he could. He'd scared off decorated soldiers with his haunted dreams. Only Abby was fearless enough to face the terrors he relived each night.

She ran her fingers through her long tresses, combing out the tangles. "You're very vocal in your dreams. Mr. Kroger believes you're a mythical werewolf, and the foolish rumor has spread around town. They've even started guarding the grave-yards at night."

"Why the graveyards?"

"Supposedly, werewolves eat the recently dead."

"What do they plan to do if they meet up with this supposed werewolf?" Shoot him? Send the sanitorium workers to cart him away?

"I believe the custom is to throw water on the beast to change it back to its human state."

"I hope they have proof it works, because otherwise, they're only going to irritate the poor beast."

"I'm not sure it works, but Mrs. Carlson gave Mr. O'Malley an earful when her husband came back from his shift soaked to the bone."

Nicholas raised a questioning eyebrow.

"Mr. Carlson had to—er—relieve himself. When he came back, Mr. O'Malley mistook the bushes shaking for the myste-rious werewolf and doused him with a bucket of cold water."

A low rumble erupted from deep within Nicholas. He

barely recognized the sound of his own laughter. Lying there looking at his beautiful wife, he felt young again, whole again. Every inch of his skin cried out wanting to feel her, hold her.

As if he'd willed her to it, Abby reached out. Her fingers hovered over his chest, but Nicholas drew back, afraid she'd feel the twisted, ugly scars on his chest beneath his thin nightshirt.

Her eyes widened, and her hand dropped back to her side. She stared at him with questions begging to be asked, but he turned away.

He craved her touch so acutely that his chest burned where her fingers would have fallen. He clenched his teeth to stifle the intense need. He hadn't been touched in years. He was a leper. Untouchable.

~

*A*bby jumped off the bed and shook the wrinkles out of her dress to dispel the charged atmosphere, even though she wanted to take an ax to the walls he'd placed between them. It was the third night in a row that she'd slept in her clothes. Polly likely wanted to box Abby's ears for all the extra work she'd created. It was going to take hours to get all the wrinkles out.

Nick lay on his back with his fingers laced behind his head. He appeared lost in thought as he stared at the ceiling. It was odd to see him with darker hair, and even odder still that his employer would require it.

She wanted to question him further, but something she'd seen behind those hard granite eyes reminded her of a timid animal ready to flee. She didn't want to scare him, knowing he could withdraw deeper into himself. Maybe if she treated him gently, the way one would tame a wild animal... If she continued to feed him, lure him in, and get him comfortable, then maybe, just maybe, he wouldn't run.

On that thought, she smiled sweetly and said, "Would you start the fire? I'll see to breaking our fast."

The old charming smile she remembered flashed over Nick's features. "I could go for some more of those oat cakes."

"Coming right up."

After getting a small fire started, he said, "I need to bring in more wood."

Abby watched as Nick strode into the brisk morning air. She couldn't resist peeking through the window as she pumped water into a kettle to go over the fire for tea.

He still walked with purpose, but a slight limp changed his gait. His confident stride was now measured. He gathered the wood into his arms, and Abby admired the smooth muscles of his back as the material of his shirt strained against them. Nick had been wiry as a youth, but now his muscles held raw power. His enhanced physique enticed her, but his dark menacing mood gave her pause. She thought about the nightmare he relived each night, and a spasm of shivers ran over her body. Whatever had happened, Nick was a survivor. If men were wolves, Nick would have been a werewolf.

He carried in the wood and stacked it beside the stone hearth.

Abby boiled water and made tea. While he drank it, she bustled around the kitchen area, making their meal.

Abby had to bite her tongue to hold back all the questions, but Nick seemed content to watch her in silence. She racked her brain for the right way to begin a discussion about the past.

"Why do you keep showing up here at night?"

His words startled her, but she settled herself while she placed an oat cake and some sliced meat in front of him. "I told you. You're keeping the town awake with your nightmares." She lifted her chin a notch. "My hair seems to have a calming effect on you."

Nick appeared to mull that over for a moment, then ate a bite of his breakfast. "I don't like the thought of you wandering about at night. You mustn't come here again. It's not safe."

She pulled out a chair and sat down across from him. "I'm sorry, but your ramblings would keep me up half the night."

"I forbid you to tramp about in the dark where any bridle cull could abduct you."

She noticed a muscle twitch in his jaw, and his lips compressed. Abby knew she was a hair's breadth away from inciting his anger. "There's an easy solution."

Nick remained stiff, his hazel eyes bored into hers. "Do explain." He leaned back in his chair and crossed his arms over his chest.

"You could sleep at Laurel House."

"It's not my home anymore. Laurel House is yours now."

"It's ours."

"No."

"Then I shall see you here."

"Abby." He didn't raise his voice, but there was an edge to it, warning her not to argue.

She ignored his tone. "Laurel House would be more convenient. If you're not comfortable, you can sleep downstairs. Besides, it's getting colder, and this shack is not going to keep the chill out like our house can."

"Your house."

"If you say no, I'm going to ask a thousand questions as to why you won't." She pointed the end of her fork in his direction. "Admit it, my logic is sound."

"I'm trying to protect you." A muscle twitched in his jaw.

"For ten years I've survived on my own." She sipped from her cup. "Besides, I've witnessed two nights of your nightmares without even a scratch." A little scalp pain but she wouldn't dare bring that up. "It seems prayer and the soothing touch of my hair might be the solution.

Hope flared in his eyes but he blinked and the darkness of doubts returned. A silence spread between them until he sighed. "Let me inform the staff. I want to ensure their confidentiality and keep gossip at bay."

Abby's mouth opened to protest, but she closed it, and fought back a victorious smile.

"I have some things I need to attend to today." Nick ate a bite of his oat cake. "What plans have you?"

"I shall visit the orphanage. They're probably wondering if I died."

"You almost did. Promise me you won't eat any soup."

Her stomach recoiled. "You have my word. I'm not certain I'll ever eat soup again."

His lips twitched with a smile, and he nodded. "Rightly so, I wouldn't blame you." After pushing back his chair, he stood and collected their empty plates. He took them to the wash bucket and scrubbed them clean.

Abby watched him work. She appreciated the gesture. Maybe some things hadn't changed about Nick. Most men would have left the dishes as woman's work, but Nick had always treated her like an equal. She smiled and took it as a sign that the old Nick was not completely lost.

After drying the dishes and stacking them neatly on the newly cleaned shelf, Nick folded the towel and turned to her. "I need to get to work, which will take me until nightfall. If you're stopping back by the house before going to the orphanage, I'll pack a change of clothes and send it with you."

She nodded but didn't trust herself to speak. She didn't want him to notice her tremble, so she clasped her hands behind her back. He was truly coming home. Abby pinched her lips together so she wouldn't smile when he passed her a canvass bag with a few of his personal items. As he bid her goodbye and headed out the door, she couldn't resist saying, "I'll see you at home."

Nick glanced back and dipped his head a single nod.

She vowed this move would be permanent.

CHAPTER 12

*N*icholas stood erect in front of Lady Etheridge to not break his cover if another servant entered the drawing room. She listed her expectations, and her skeptical eyes peered at him from beneath her purple turban as if gauging his reaction. He counted first to ten and then to one thousand, and his jaw ached from remaining clenched for so long. The stale air smelled of perfume and powder. Elaborate baroque period furniture cluttered the large sitting room, which was painted in creams with gold accents. Paintings of blue skies and fat baby cherubs decorated the walls from within their gilded frames. The only similarity between the cherubs and Lady Etheridge was their skill with arrows. The woman's tongue had the accuracy of a superb archer. Her sharp words never missed their target. He imagined her finding pleasure in reaching for the arrows, even giving them a slight twist before pulling them out.

"Obviously, my cooking staff, footmen, and handmaidens should be under the uttermost scrutiny. They have direct access to my food and easily could have added the arsenic that took the life of poor Poopsie." Lady Etheridge dabbed a handkerchief to the corner of her eyes in a dramatic display of sorrow.

"He was such a faithful pet, loyal to the bone. A better companion couldn't be found. I loved Poopsie like my own children." Her lips pursed. "Maybe more so, since they haven't visited."

She dabbed at another tear. "That takes them off the list of suspects. Whoever did this must have been at the house. My other regular visitors would be Dr. Cox and Lady Felton, but I usually do my visiting at her house, and her daughter, Lady Abigail Hartington or Emerson. I can't tell you why she still hangs onto the Emerson name. Mr. Emerson was not an advantageous match. I daresay he was handsome, but truthfully, if the boy had even an ounce of love for his wife, he wouldn't have purchased a commission, and he definitely wouldn't have done something so thoughtless as to get himself killed."

Waves of heat radiated beneath Nicholas's high-pointed collar, and he tucked his balled fists behind his back to relax, still maintaining a deadpan expression.

"You should especially keep an eye on Lady Abigail. She paid me a visit the morning Poopsie died and brought over an apple tart. I can't recall if she ate some herself, but I'd put a slice on my plate."

His jaw clenched. For her to hold insinuations against Abby was ridiculous. He considered Abby a saint for voluntarily visiting Lady Awfulridge on a regular basis.

He'd add Laurel House's staff to the list of suspects, but he'd known Mrs. Smith all his life and Polly seemed frightened of her own shadow, which basically left Delia the young scullery maid.

"And Lady Abigail is always up to something. Her fingers never stop moving, and she never sits still. Very improper, and I've lectured her on that fact repeatedly. Her fidgeting has always disturbed me. She's too headstrong for her own good, that one." Lady Etheridge paused to sip her tea and assess him.

He bit back his defense for Abby and forced a calm composure.

Putting down the teacup, she folded her hands in her lap. "Very well, then, you shall be stationed as my steward, and I will send Sanford to my sister's in the meantime—"

"I beg your pardon, but the role of steward won't do."

Lady Etheridge's eyebrows pulled up at the exact moment that her mouth turned down in a deep frown. It left Nicholas with the strange impression that her face engaged in its own tug-of-war match. "Why in heaven's name would you think that? The last thing I need at a time like this is some impertinent, know-it-all—"

"The steward hires and fires the staff. Do they not?"

"Of course."

"The staff will be less likely to confide in someone who has the power to dismiss them. I need a less threatening post—one the staff would consider as an ally—or at least not a threat. A position as a lower servant, specifically a footman, would work to the best advantage." His logic was sound, so he resisted a smug smile while Lady Etheridge struggled to come to the same conclusion.

Lady Etheridge's nostrils flared. She fanned herself. "That won't do."

"Why not?"

"I daresay you shouldn't be questioning me. However, this is your assignment. If you must know I ... ur ... I ..." She coughed into her hand.

Lady Etheridge was acting strangely, but why?

"It's your limp."

"I assure you, my limp will not hinder my duties." Nicholas spoke through tight lips.

"Is that so?" Lady Etheridge waved a gloved hand through the air. "Our footmen are busy, always scurrying about."

"As an undercover footman, I will do double duty with ease, madam." He leveled her with a stare to show his determination.

Lady Etheridge raised a haughty brow in his direction. "Agent Scar, you came highly recommended from the Home Office with the lieutenant's personal reference. I assume that makes you one of the best and most intelligent in your department?"

Nicholas narrowed his gaze. What was she up to? He issued a stiff nod.

"Then I know you will not waste my time or resources. Use the next two days to familiarize yourself with the position of footman. Report to my butler two days from now, and he will show you your duties. That is all, Agent Scar." She dismissed him.

With a slight bow, Nicholas left the room. His muscles ached from taxing his self-control to not tell that woman exactly what he thought of her. Blood surged through his veins. How dare she insult Abby? The caustic dowager wasn't even worth the dust on the bottom of Abby's kid boots. Now, he'd have to wait on Lady Etheridge as her hired hand. Lord, help him if he didn't poison her himself.

～

*B*ells jingled and Abby glanced up from the jars of preserves as Mr. Kroger's shop door opened. A man with black hair entered.

Nick? A spark lit in her chest but faded quickly. Even though the man's hair matched Nicholas's newly painted color, the man's ruddy face and long chin didn't resemble him. *Definitely not Nick.*

"I'll be right with you, gov'nor." Mr. Kroger packaged up the rest of the items Abby planned to take to the orphanage.

The man didn't reply but browsed the shelves, keeping his face down.

"The children will be delighted to see you." Mr. Kroger passed Abby the wrapped candy. "From what the reverend says, they watch eagerly for your visits."

Abby smiled, thinking of the youngsters. "I'm equally blessed to see them. The least I can do is show them a little of the same love the good Lord was gracious enough to give me."

"The reverend told me the children are under an early curfew for safety. Last night the men kept watch over our burial grounds." Mr. Kroger wiggled his eyebrows.

Was the man excited by the prospect of a beast in their midst?

"The werewolf couldn't get itself any fresh meat and howled to wake perdition. Hopefully, the beast will move along." Despite his words, Mr. Kroger's tone resonated with regret.

"Then we all can sleep better at night, and I'm thankful for that." Abby smiled at the fanciful man and slipped her package under her arm.

She strode towards the door, but as she turned to wave farewell, her bundle dropped with a thud.

The man with the ruddy face seemed to materialize out of thin air.

Abby reared back.

He bent to retrieve it and held the package out for her.

She put a hand to her chest and regained her composure. "Thank you, kind sir, for your trouble."

Abby reached for her bundle, but he held it for a prolonged moment before releasing it. His gaze roved over her like a painter's brush on a canvas, and Abby recoiled.

"My pleasure, madame." He tipped his hat, and his steely

gray eyes locked on hers. The awkwardness of the moment suspended time.

Mr. Kroger shuffled through a drawer as if unaware of his patrons.

"Thank you," Abby said again and stepped toward the door, but the man stood in her path.

Tiny broken red blood vessels outlined the corners of his nose. He continued his lewd stare until her palms perspired.

She cleared her throat and opened her mouth to demand he let her pass, but the man swept aside and held the door open.

"Good day, madame."

Abby hurried toward the orphanage, relieved to put the odd exchange behind her, and prayed she wouldn't run into him again. The feeling of unease dissipated as she greeted passing acquaintances.

"Abby? Oh, Abby." Katherine stood in front of the milliner's shop, on her tiptoes and waving to get Abby's attention. Her bonnet barely restrained the light brown curls attempting to break free of her coiffure.

Katherine paused for a carriage to pass, before scurring across the street, then fell into step next to Abby.

"There you are. I was just headed to purchase some trimmings for my latest bonnet, but I'm dying to know more about your happy reunion. I'm assuming you and Mr. Emerson have been spending time getting reacquainted?"

"Of course." Abby slowed her pace.

Katherine looked around. "Where is he now?"

"Oh, he has a few things to attend to." Abby shrugged and casually waved her hand.

"You're a lot calmer about this than I would be. I'm not sure I'd let Stephen out of my sight if he'd been gone ten years." Katherine nodded to a woman who passed and lowered her voice. "Your brother called upon you the other morning, but you weren't home."

"Polly mentioned it. I was with Nick."

"It's a miracle he's returned, an absolute miracle." Katherine leaned her head toward Abby until the brims of their bonnets touched. "I'm sure the two of you have had an awful lot of catching up to do."

"Quite."

"Has he told you what happened. Why it took so long to return?"

Abby dropped her gaze, observing the toe of her kid boot pop out from under the hem of her cambric skirt with each stride. "Not yet."

Katherine stopped and grabbed Abby's arm, halting her. "Something's wrong. This is not like you. Typically, you spill over with enthusiasm. Is something amiss?"

She couldn't keep anything from Katherine, but she appreciated her friend's concern. Abby pulled her over to sit on a bench.

"Nick has changed. Which would make sense, since it's been ten years. I know I've changed too, but that's what makes it so difficult. We're strangers. It's as if we must start all over again. I don't think he trusts me yet, not enough to let me know everything that transpired."

Abby sighed. "The old Nick used to be carefree and confident. The Nick who returned is cautious and reserved. He hasn't spoken of it yet, but I saw some of his scars. He's wounded physically, and ... and I believe emotionally too, but he won't tell me about it. I worry if I push him too hard, he'll disappear again."

Hearing her own words helped her accept their truth, and it frightened her to the core. "I can't lose him again," she whispered, wrapping her arms around her stomach.

A wrinkle formed on Katherine's forehead. "I'm so sorry."

She bit her bottom lip. "I assumed you'd have the joyful, romantic reunion that love stories are made of. Lord knows, you deserve it."

Abby tried to smile. "The reality is quite different from the fantasy. I still see glimpses of the old Nick, so I haven't lost hope."

"I'm sure with time—"

"It shall work out." Abby shook away the doubts and squeezed her friend's hand. "God has ways of turning these things around for His good." She nodded, more to convince herself than her friend. "He brought my husband back from the dead. I will be forever grateful."

"A miracle, truly, and you were so faithful in waiting. God shall bless you for that."

Abby shook her head. "There were times when I screamed and riled at God. Mama Em was the strong one, but she taught me God's ways are better than our ways."

"Mama Em was right." Katherine squeezed Abby's hand. "Be patient. God is working things out for your good."

"If there's one virtue I lack, it's patience." Abby checked the watch pinned to her jacket. "I'm going to be late to the orphanage. I must go or else I'll have to face Miss Quiller's stern look of disapproval." Abby pursed her lips and raised a haughty brow in what she hoped was a fair imitation of Ms. Quiller.

Katherine shivered. "You give me the vapors just thinking about facing that woman." She wrapped Abby in a hug. "I'll be praying for you and Mr. Emerson. As soon as he comes around, send for me immediately."

"Of course."

"Just remember"—Katherine smiled—"if God opens a door, no one can shut it. He brought your husband back, and He has a plan."

*N*icholas trailed Lady Etheridge's maid to the apothecary's shop. She looked both ways before entering, and he turned, lowering his gaze to the newspaper clutched in his hand. *Just a bloke catching the headlines on his way to work.* He'd wait until after she left to draw the information out of the apothecary as to her purchase and perhaps the maid's intent on what she'd be doing with the goods.

Nearby, a buxom servant beat a rug, leaning in such a way as to attract the attention of a costermonger selling fruit across the way.

The vendor didn't notice her. His bloodshot eyes told Nicholas he nursed a sore headache.

Mr. Kroger, however, did notice. He wiggled his bushy eyebrows and almost tripped over his broom.

Nicholas wore nondescript clothes that didn't draw attention and kept his collar high and his hat low. Even the heels of his boots barely clicked as they hit the cobblestone. While his appearance didn't turn anyone's head, he didn't miss a thing— not even the fellow he'd seen in the tavern lingering in the general store. The barkeep said the man's name was Lester Shue.

Perhaps it would be wise for him to station himself at Laurel House. While the woodcutter's cottage had offered a good surveillance point, it wasn't half as good as being inside the house, where he could protect Abby.

A young newsboy on the corner cried out the latest head-line and waved the front page of the paper in the air.

Nearby, a well-dressed gent in cream breeches and hessian boots had his nose stuck in his copy of *The Times* as a young bootblack hunched over, finishing up the final shine on the man's boots. The man passed the boy a half a penny. He then folded his paper, tucked it under his arm, and strode down the street.

The man passed two women sitting on a park bench, and Nicholas's heartbeat quickened from merely glimpsing Abby. Unlike himself, who faded into the background, Abby stood out like a lighthouse beacon welcoming ships to shore.

She hugged the other woman, Lady Katherine. The women smiled and waved goodbye. The freshness of Abby's grin stopped Nicholas mid-breath. She didn't hold back. She smiled with everything inside her, enough to make the tender shoots of crocuses bloom in the dead of winter.

He wished the smile had been for him. Then again, he'd wished a lot of things, that he hadn't enlisted, wasn't losing his mind, and didn't pose a threat to others during his episodes, especially to the people he loved.

He trailed her like a suspect, keeping close but never conspicuous. He noted the lightness in her step and the sway of her hips.

She waved and called out to passersby, happily greeting each one by name, sometimes asking after their families.

What for Nicholas would have been a brisk five-minute walk extended to fifteen for Abby, who stopped and said good morning to everyone she saw.

She was still very much a socialite. She blossomed around people, and they were attracted to her warmth like children to candy.

He used to be the same. He knew how to draw people in and make them feel singled out.

That was before. Things had changed. *He* had changed. The press of an invisible weight slumped his shoulders. Now, this was her world, one in which he no longer belonged.

Nicholas watched her knock on the thick oak door of the orphanage. The door swung open, and she disappeared into the dark entrance. A litany of children's cheers split the air. He knew how those children felt. He stuffed his hands into his pockets and stared at the gothic building. Its hard dark exterior contrasted with the happy voices within.

Nicholas peered up and down the dull gray street to ensure that Lester fellow he'd seen at the tavern moved along.

But no. The scoundrel stared at the orphanage door for a long moment before turning and loping away. Nicholas heaved in a big breath and released it with a sigh.

With Abby inside the orphanage, the commotion of downtown lost its appeal. She had taken all the freshness with her.

Several blocks away, Lady Etheridge stepped out of the milliner's shop. He'd recognize her purple turban anywhere. Her other footman followed, carrying an armload of hat boxes. A man in a tall beaver hat, sitting on a nearby bench folded his paper, rose, and fell into step behind her footman blocking Nicholas's view.

When he'd asked the details of her schedule for today, she told him she'd be visiting with Lady Felton. Had their plans changed? Or was Lady Etheridge becoming forgetful and showing her age? If it was the latter, then how accurate was the information she'd remembered from the poisoning?

Lady Etheridge's sharp tone split the air, but Nicholas couldn't make out her command. The beaver hat man waddled ahead and opened the door to a modiste. Lady Etheridge entered, but her footman moved along down the street, most likely to set the boxes in the carriage.

A cough drew Nicholas's attention back to the modiste. Lady Etheridge paused and exchanged words with the man holding the door before entering. Nicholas squinted trying to recognize the beaver hat man as the chap continued down the street.

It was probably coincidence, but the man's cough sounded like Lieutenant Sparks.

CHAPTER 13

$\mathcal{T}$he urge to fidget crawled like ants over Abby's skin as she stalked from room to room in Laurel House, chewing her bottom lip. Would Nick truly come home, or would he back out? Her insides jumbled like a ball of string after a cat had toyed with it.

She re-arranged the flowers, fluffed the pillows a third time, and checked on the evening meal until the cook chased her back into the drawing room.

Maybe she should go to the cottage? She removed her pelisse from the hook but hesitated.

What if he arrived here while she was there? She returned her jacket to the wooden peg and pressed her temples to keep from completely unraveling.

She strode through the dining room. The table was set for two, all ready for Nick. Movement outside the window drew Abby's attention.

Nick stood on the porch steps, one hand rubbing the back of his neck, the other poised to knock on the door.

Abby nodded to the maid-of-all-work. "I'll answer the door."

Helena bobbed a curtsy and left the room.

Abby folded her hands in front of her to keep them from shaking. Funny, Nick had been about to knock, but no sound followed. She leaned to the side for a better view out the window.

Nick paced on the brick walkway. Every so often, she caught parts of his mumbled phrases, "Terrible idea... mistake... can't stay." With each word, her stomach sank deeper, like a stone in murky water.

He was going to leave again.

He stormed all the way to the gate.

She drew in a ragged breath and held it, mentally willing him to stay. She could open the door and demand he come in. Or at least force him to tell her to her face. But no.

He needed to make this decision on his own.

He shook his head and reached for the latch.

Abby closed her eyes. The battle was over. She'd lost. She sagged against the door frame. The cool wood absorbed the heat from her face.

God has a plan, and He's in charge. He brought Nick back. He's not going to let him leave.

A resounding knock jerked her upright. Her fingers trembled as she reached for the door handle.

~

*N*icholas squared his shoulders as the door swung open.

Abby stood in the doorway, her glossy hair tied up in a loose chignon, the evening sun pooling in her bright blue eyes. She looked beautiful. Her dark lashes fluttered as she lifted her gaze to meet his. He read the imploring expression on her face and wondered how she knew his mind.

"Please," she said in a soft voice, "come in."

The urge to run caused him to glance one last time over his shoulder. But when Abby stepped back, it was like a shadow fell, and he could no longer feel the warmth of the sun. Sheer need drew him into the foyer. It wasn't desire but a basic human necessity God had placed in him.

Something deep inside Nicholas told him if he left, he would die in self-ordained isolation. If he stayed, Bedlam would be his fate and Abby's life ruined. But his heart pleaded for a chance. Maybe Abby could shine healing into his soul. In a dark and lonely world, Abby radiated hope. He longed to cling to it, but could he live with himself if the full embrace of his broken body, mind, and soul snuffed out her light? Hadn't he hurt her enough already?

Abby's lips curled into a shy smile, igniting a sparkle in her eyes.

His heart slammed into his ribcage, and a nervous smile twitched on his own lips. His carefully planned speech about why he had to leave crumbled like a sawdust toy left in the rain. He couldn't remember a single sentence.

They stood there smiling at each other like a young, courting couple.

Nicholas finally broke away and lowered his eyes, his grin broke into a chuckle. He ran a hand over the top of his head, then met Abby's gaze, still unsure what to say.

Her nervous laughter burst out, echoing off the walls. She stepped aside with an outstretched arm. "Welcome home."

Home is where you are.

As he followed her down the narrow hall, nostalgia washed over him. He breathed in the familiar earthy smell of his past mixed with the fragrant plants coming from the solarium. Burning wood from the hearth the residual sweet aroma of Bishop's bread, brought back memories of him and Stephen sneaking a roll or two and Mrs. Smith running them out of the kitchen as they laughed and hooted. Other than the soft shuffle

LORRI DUDLEY

of Abby's slippers and the clap of his boots, Laurel House stood quiet. His childhood home was missing something.

Children.

A stab of guilt struck him in the gut. In his dreams he'd always envisioned Laurel House filled with his and Abby's children.

"Dinner is waiting for us in the dining room." Abby paused and gestured for him to enter.

Nicholas raised his elbow for her to hold and steered them into the room. Steam rose from the bowls of stew and plated mutton with a side of peas. He pulled out a chair and assisted Abby, then took an adjoining seat.

"Do you normally sup at this time?"

"No." Abby gently unfolded her napkin and placed it on her lap. "I saw you outside the door and asked for the table to be made ready. Helena kept our meal in the warming trays until you arrived."

Nicholas snapped his napkin neatly in the air before placing it on his lap.

"You appeared to be debating something as you paced. I'm glad you worked it all out."

Nicholas's gaze flew to her face. "You saw that?"

"I heard something and looked out the window." Abby straightened the silverware.

Her nervousness tugged at his heart. He needed to say something to lighten the moment. "You always were a sneak. I still don't understand how you always knew where Stephen and I planned to go and begged to tag along."

"You had a loud whisper."

"Brat," he teased to evoke a response, but negated the sternness of his voice by curving one side of his mouth up into a half smile. His loud whispering, on occasion, had been intentional in hopes she would come along, but he wasn't about to admit it.

Abby raised her chin to a regal angle. "I'm not a brat."

He chuckled. "Remember the time you dumped an entire jar of pepper into my pudding?"

She placed her hands on either side of her plate and leaned forward. "You deserved that."

"In my delight for a delicious treat, I had gulped down a large spoonful. I almost choked to death. It took all my willpower not to spit it out across the table." Ignoring etiquette and resorting to childhood tactics, he tore off a piece of bread and tossed it at her.

She dodged, but not fast enough. The piece struck her on the shoulder.

"As I recall, you had invaded my tea party and swapped the tea for squeezed lemons." Abby loaded a spoonful of peas. "I'm still holding a grudge."

Nicholas flicked his gaze between her sassy determined face and her slender finger bending the silver piece back into a makeshift catapult. "What happened to propriety?"

"I dismissed the footmen. Polite society will never know." The spoon arched back.

"You wouldn't."

"I think you should apologize right now, or I shall not be held accountable for my actions."

"Let those peas fly"—Nicholas chose his weapon carefully, digging out a chunk of the mutton with gravy dripping heavily over the edge— "and neither shall I."

Her gaze fell on his artillery, and her smile broadened. "You wouldn't dare ..." But before she finished, her finger slipped, and peas soared across the table. Nicholas leaned left, deftly evading the small green missiles as they whizzed overhead. He pulled back the mutton catapult, ready to let it fly.

Abby's smile disappeared. "It slipped. I swear." Her wide eyes fixed on the gravy-sodden spoon. "Truly!"

Nicholas burst out laughing, putting down the fork with a clatter. Abby slumped back in her chair, holding a hand over her stomach. She joined in the laughter until tears squeezed out of the corners of her eyes. Once she caught her breath, she said, "I believe it's time for a truce."

~

*T*he rest of dinner was lovely. It felt to Abby as if the spell holding Nick captive had broken, and their relationship—their friendship—picked up where they'd left off ten years before. She and Nick spent hours seeking to top each other's stories of childhood mishaps.

Nick sipped from his cup. "Remember the time the groomsman put away the ladder and we were still on the stable roof?"

"You wanted to flag down the groom exercising a horse in the east field, but I thought it would be faster to jump onto the hay bales. We both jumped but rolled off the hay into the horses' water trough." Abby laughed until her stomach muscles ached. It was a healing balm to the years of hurt. The Nick she knew and loved had returned.

He cajoled her into conceding she truly had been a brat. However, she stipulated it was only to gain Stephen and Nick's attention, so she'd be included.

After dinner, they pulled a set of wing-backed chairs near the fire and played a game of cribbage. Despite losing several hands, Abby savored the time. Sitting across from Nick, she curled her legs beneath her and admired his skill. He outmaneuvered her as if calculating three plays ahead. Abby sat in awe, absently twisting a lock of hair around her finger.

"I've missed you." The statement was out of her lips before she could stop it.

Nick looked up from his cards. Silence lingered in the air, drawing out each second as if it were a lifetime. His gaze held hers and his eyes darkened. "Not a moment"—he spoke each word emphatically—"went by when I didn't think of you."

Abby forgot to breathe. Declarations of love and pleadings for him to stay sprang to her lips. But an inner voice told her to remain silent. *Let him speak.*

His gaze dropped to the table. "They didn't allow us any outside contact. I tried to write you, but the letters were confiscated."

He snorted. "I was able to persuade the mail carrier to slip me a few of your letters. I still have them. I could quote you every word, every..."

He stared at the fire. The flickering light accentuated the scars that crept from beneath his collar like wild vines climbing a tree trunk. "I just ... I never thought things would turn out the way they did. I was going to give you the world—a title, land, jewels, and furs, all on a silver platter." He peered down at his hands.

Her heart wept at the lines of pain etched in his face. She slid her hand across the table toward him. "I didn't want the world. I just wanted you." Her hand stopped a fraction of an inch from his. All he had to do was raise his fingers to brush hers. "And you're here now."

Hope flashed in his eyes, but his guarded look returned, shutting her out like a closed curtain. A long silence grew between them, but her gaze held his in a silent plea for answers. The hall clock chimed half past midnight.

Nick placed his cards on the table. "We'd best retire, or you'll sleep the day away tomorrow."

Slowly the implications of his words registered. He was going to stay.

Biting back a smile, Abby's head cocked to the side, "What makes you think I'm a late riser?"

"Truly? Oh, let's see." He raised both eyebrows. "I

remember your lingering in bed long after the sun was high in the sky."

"It was only one morning. And as I recall, it was you who'd kept me up the entire night."

As soon as the words left her mouth, a hot flush crept into her cheeks. Her reference to their wedding night lingered in the air between them.

Nick's eyes darkened to a stormy gray-green. Clearing his throat, he rose from his chair. "I'll escort you to your chamber."

Abby stood on shaky legs. As he guided her up the stairs, her skin tingled where his hand rested on her lower back.

He pushed her door open and remained there.

She stepped into the framed entranceway and paused, facing him.

With one hand resting on the knob, he peered down at her. "Good night, Abby." His husky timbre permeated her skin and lit embers within her stomach.

He hoovered closer, the heat of his body warming her.

Must we say good night? She wasn't bold enough to voice the words, but Abby tilted her head back further to better glimpse his face and pleaded with her eyes. Her gaze lingered on his lips, and her mouth softened, longing to feel the heat of his kiss. *Please ...*

~

*N*icholas watched her lick her bottom lip. His body ached to wrap her in his arms, dip his hands into her thick hair, and press her soft mouth to his. Her hand raised but his own shot up and grasped it before she cupped the left side of his face.

Abby gasped.

He released her hand, and it dropped back to her side. Better for her to be a little startled than horrified when she touched the twisted mass of skin that he hid beneath his high collar points.

With a nod and a gruff tone, he repeated, "Good night." He turned and marched into his former bedchamber.

He closed the door and leaned against it. Running his hands over his head, he grabbed a fistful of hair in each. This had been a mistake. The sweet torture of being near Abby physically pained him. Tonight, she'd made him feel like the old Nick was still alive. For a time, he'd forgotten about his scars and his nightmares, but he'd caught himself before sweeping her into his arms and carrying her over to the four-poster bed, beckoning in the background. The what-could-have-beens now carved out his heart like a river's current forging a new path.

His body ached in frustration. The remainder of the night would be agony, knowing she slept down the hall. He'd be lucky to get even an hour's worth of rest.

∼

*A*bby barely slept. Last night, without saying so, she'd welcomed Nick into her chamber, but he made it clear he didn't want to join her. She'd paced her room, trying to summon the nerve to go to Nick's chamber and crawl into bed next to her husband. But each time her hand touched the knob, she lost her nerve. Once the hall clock struck two, she climbed into bed and waited for his nightmares to start so she would have an excuse to rush to his side, but Laurel House remained still and quiet. She eventually fell into a fitful sleep, but awoke early, eager to see him again.

Only to be informed he'd left before dawn.

She needed advice, so she traipsed through the woods to Willowstone Manor.

Ivy vines climbed the picturesque Georgian manor house

that held fond childhood memories for Abby. Horses neighed and romped in the east meadow and the gardener stood on a ladder snipping the hedges with a large pair of scissors.

The front door swung open, and their elderly butler welcomed her with a warm smile. Abby greeted him, then traversed down the hall toward the salon, reveling in the familiar smell of polished wood. As much as she loved it here, her home was Laurel House, and despite her nostalgia, she preferred it that way.

Stephen and Katherine had resided at Willowstone since their marriage, and Mama had moved into the east wing, but not much else had changed from when Abby used to live here.

Centered on a table at the end of the hall sat the lovely new crystal vase Stephen had gifted Katherine for their anniversary. Abby envied their love. She and Nick had had that same love—once. Last night ignited the spark of hope that maybe they would again.

Nick had been gone before she awoke, but Abby was determined to not let that—or the disappointing way the evening had ended—sway her spirits. Last night, the walls Nick had erected seemed to crack but not crumble. It was just a matter of time before he would tell his secrets, and life would return to how it should be. She needed to be patient.

Abby snorted. *Patience.* It was a necessary virtue—also her least favorite. *It will happen.* God had opened a door, and no one could shut it. She knocked on the ajar salon door before she peeped around it.

"Abby." Katherine rose.

Abby entered, arms extended, to greet her sister-in-law.

"Lady Abigail, how lovely to see you." Melinda's voice caused Abby to pause.

Melinda Cox, dressed in a pale muslin gown, sipped tea on the sofa against the far wall. She fixed her eyes on Abby, and her face brightened with interest, leaving Abby with the inkling something was wrong. Usually, her smiles were contrived. The woman's authentic enthusiasm raised her suspicions.

Abby pushed back her shoulders and pinned her lips up in a smile. "Good morning, Melinda. I hope you and your family are faring well."

"Quite." Melinda scooted to the edge of her wingback chair. "The children are well. I could do with fewer sick people since it keeps my husband so busy, but it's wonderful for his practice."

Melinda's eyes narrowed in on Abby. "The other day a servant interrupted our dinner for an urgent matter. Who was the man who carried you home? My husband assumed it was a hunter who stumbled upon you in the woods, and I heard he was well-built. It's the stuff written about in romance novels. Who was he? Tell me the tale. You had food poisoning—"

"I can't recall much." Abby smoothed her skirt. "I fainted in the woods on my way home. A man found me and brought me home."

"Were you alone with him? Did he try anything?" Melinda's tone sounded worried, but the way she licked her lips appeared like she was ready to devour any morsel of gossip. "Are you unharmed?"

"Polly, my lady's maid was there, and Nick—" Abby gasped. Oh no. She shot a look at her sister-in-law, whose eyes were wide with concern.

"Nick?" Melinda placed a hand over her heart. "You said Nick, as in your husband? He returned? He's alive?"

Abby swallowed and looked to Katherine for assistance.

"She was very ill." Katherine squeezed her hands until her fingers turned white. "It all could have been a dream brought on by the illness."

"Abby," Melinda said, "if I'd had known the gentleman who summoned my husband was Nicholas Emerson, I would have come along too. I can't believe the wonderful news. You must be beside yourself with joy. I want to hear the whole story. Do tell."

Abby sank onto the settee and flashed a heaven-help-me glance at Katherine. Why did her tongue speak without first consulting her head? "It is a long story. My husband miraculously returned a few days ago. As you can imagine, I was delighted to see him."

"Has he aged well? He was always so handsome."

Abby's stomach fluttered, remembering how Nick's eyes had danced as they laughed over dinner. His profile now held a mature, rugged strength that made him even more sensual than what she remembered. His scars were noticeable, but Nick hid them well behind his long hair and his high collars. Somehow they added a mysterious allure. Would Melinda still find him attractive, or would she only see the scars?

Melinda's tongue seconded only Lady Etheridge's in its ability to wound like a saber. From what Abby knew about her, it seemed likely she would focus on the imperfections.

"He'll always be handsome to me," Abby replied.

Melinda peered at her over the rim of her teacup. "Where has he been?"

"At war."

"Yes, but the war ended. Where did he go after?"

Why did she keep answering Melinda's questions? Hadn't she just been taught a lesson on reining in her tongue? "As you can imagine, my husband has been through quite an ordeal, one he's not eager to discuss at this time. I'm sure you understand."

"I do, but why did he let everyone believe he'd died? Why didn't he write you?" Melinda asked. "If you had taken my advice, you'd be married to another right now."

Katherine sucked in a horrified gasp.

Melinda swiped a hand through the air. "Well, thank heaven you didn't listen, but he really should have written.

Surely, he had considered the possibility of your remarrying, especially since everyone presumed he was dead." She leaned in closer. "Did he say *why* he couldn't write?"

Abby had to unclench her teeth behind her smile before answering. "Just that he couldn't."

"Was he in France or Spain or Africa?"

"Melinda!" Katherine's tone reprimanded the woman for her persistence.

"Ah, well, I'm sure you're still coming to terms with his reappearance. It's just"—Melinda's gaze swept back and forth across the room before whispering—"I've heard of soldiers having separate lives with another wife and children in a different country." She sat back and set her teacup aside. "I'm not saying that Mr. Emerson did anything of the sort. I merely find it scandalous that such things could go on."

An awkward silence filled the room.

After a moment, Katherine started to speak, but Melinda cut her off. "We'd love to invite you to dine with us to get reacquainted. So much has happened since Mr. Emerson left. He probably doesn't remember my husband. Simon's practice only started ten years ago. Now it's thriving, and we have little Simon, Jr. and Henry. Perhaps, we could sup one evening next week?"

"Nicholas is not making social calls yet. He wants more time for the two of us to get reacquainted."

"Oh?" Melinda raised her brows with a sly look.

Heat warmed Abby's cheeks. "And, he has work to do."

Melinda's head tilted, and she raised her eyebrows. "You don't say? What is he doing now that his enlistment is over?"

Abby wanted to kick herself. She should have realized the implications. There was no evasive answer she could give that wouldn't be a lie. The truth was, she didn't know what he was doing. He wasn't being forthright with her, and she was his wife. For heaven's sake, she should have some idea of what her husband did during the day.

Katherine's eyes gleamed with sympathy. "I'm certain he has plenty of follow-up projects and correspondence with his Majesties' army, in addition to all the things that have happened in the past ten years with his lands and estates. It must be very time-consuming."

Abby smiled her gratitude to Katherine.

"I must be on my way." Abby stood and inched her way towards the door.

Katherine stood to see her out, but Abby waved her off.

"I can see myself out. My apologies for cutting my visit short, but Lady Etheridge is expecting me."

The women flinched at the mention of Lady Etheridge's name. Funny what a strong impression she made on people. "It was lovely seeing you, Melinda. Katherine, I will call again soon."

"Give Mr. Emerson our regards and welcome him back for us." Melinda called.

Abby scurried out the door.

CHAPTER 14

icholas blinked away his weariness. Could one fall asleep standing upright?

Lady Etheridge stole another glance at the clock on the drawing room wall. Other than her sharp eyes' quick flicks toward the clock, she hadn't moved from the tufted sofa in ten minutes. She adjusted the lavender turban swirled up on the top of her head then re-folded her hands in the lap of her gray day gown.

Never was a woman so adept at appearing calm, but Nicholas wasn't fooled. Her calculated gaze jumped as if sorting and checking off a mental checklist. The meal was prepared, ready to be served.

He ran through his list of suspects. The cook wouldn't have known who the food would have been served to, so Nicholas mentally crossed him off. He'd spoken with the apothecary and discovered the maid had purchased morphine for her ill mother. The young servant was the sole provider for her family, and if she lost her income from working in the Etheridge household, she wouldn't be able to pay for her mother's medication. He struck the maid from the list.

Despite her calm exterior, the corners of Lady Etheridge's mouth twitched with a smile. She'd made it clear how he was to conduct himself as an undercover footman for their guest, Lady Felton.

Would his mother-in-law recognize him? If so, he already had his alias worked out. He was James Emerson a nephew of Aunt Em. His family lived in the States but had sent him to England for work and to meet a wife.

Nicholas shifted his weight to ease the ache of his bad leg.

"I haven't been this excited in years." Her lips curved again. "Not since I coerced my husband into marrying me."

Nicholas was spared from commenting by the butler entering and whispering into Lady Etheridge's ear that her guest had arrived.

"See that the terrace is properly set." She glared at Nicholas.

He'd already inspected the table setting three times, and it wasn't likely that the silver had up and walked away.

She nodded for him to hurry into position to serve the food and smoothed nonexistent wrinkles from her skirt.

She addressed the butler. "Show her in."

A moment later, a familiar voice filled his ears. "Lady Etheridge, how are you faring?"

Abby. His body jolted at the sound of her voice. He ducked into the kitchen and yanked the door shut behind him. She was Lady Etheridge's guest? What happened to Lady Felton? Abby hadn't mentioned visiting last night when they were playing chess.

He cracked the door and glimpsed her shiny, mahogany hair.

Was Lady Etheridge getting confused?

"As well as can be expected." Lady Etheridge rose from her chair, and Abby placed a light kiss on her cheek.

She hitched up her skirts. "Come, my dear. The food should be almost ready, and I do believe I'm famished."

Lady Etheridge led the way to the terrace, where a table had been set for two.

Nicholas stepped back, closing the door. If Abby recognized him, she'd blow his cover. Lady Etheridge knows he's an agent for the Home Office, but she doesn't know he's Nicholas Emerson. He'd initially worried that Lady Etheridge would recognize him, but his hard-earned girth and scars were a far cry from the scrawny young man who left for war and never returned. He'd learned in the spy business that often people see what they expect to see and don't question it.

But if Abby spotted him, there'd be a ruckus. No one would believe a gentleman of means would willingly become a lowly footman unless he'd fallen on hard times. Questions would be asked, and he'd be forced to lie or out himself as a spy. Once his true identity was divulged, he would no longer be able to protect Abby from whomever was attempting to poison her or Lady Etheridge.

Arsenic was colorless and odorless. There was only one way to find out if the food was poisoned before Abby ate any. Nicholas swiped a finger sandwich from each tray and crammed it into his mouth. He turned and poured himself a cup from the teapot to wash it down. He flinched as the hot water burned his throat.

The serving girl gaped, then continued garnishing the tarts while shaking her head. He grabbed one of those and asked the other footman to aid Lady Etheridge and let her know the food would be ready shortly. He yanked a tray of sliced fruit from the man's hands, using it to shield his face from view as the servant opened the door. Nicholas followed him onto the terrace but hid behind a tall potted palm.

Lady Etheridge scowled at the other footman's lateness but sat in the seat he pulled out for her and gestured for Abby to do the same.

Nicholas approached Abby from behind, pulling out her chair.

Lady Etheridge glared at him, and he wasn't surprised. He was out of position. Maybe she'd chalk it up to his being new to the job.

"Are you all right, Lady Etheridge?" Abby asked. "Is something paining you?"

"I'm fine," Lady Etheridge snapped, drawing her attention back to her house guest. With a wave of her hand, she soothed her tone. "I assure you, everything's lovely."

Nicholas ducked back through the door to the kitchen, only to be met by a splash of scalding hot tea down the front of his shirt followed by a maid's stifled scream. The sensitive scar tissue on his chest protested at the hot liquid soaking his shirtfront.

Still clutching the tea tray, the maid stared at the mess. The poor woman looked like she was about to burst into tears. "What are we going to do?"

Ignoring the pain, Nicholas signaled to the other footman and instructed him to stall for time, then turned back to the woman. "Quickly, refill the pot. There's more heating near the fire."

"A spare shirt and jacket hang on a peg in the galley storeroom." She pointed in the direction.

Nicholas dashed through the kitchen, stripped off his wet shirt, and replaced it with the fresh one. All the while, his mind reeled. How long until arsenic had an effect? He'd investigated a case where a high up member of the Tory party had been poisoned by his mistress because he was no longer willing to pay for her apartments. Within thirty minutes of ingesting the poison he was vomiting. In forty, he was dead. Nicholas paused and internally assessed for any reaction.

Nothing.

When he'd questioned Lady Etheridge about which guest she'd invited, she'd specifically stated Lady Felton. If Abby was truly Lady Etheridge's main suspect, she'd want to disclose that information, so he could prepare and keep a sharp eye on her. Did she really believe Abby was behind the poisoning? Her friendly tone, at least for Lady Etheridge, didn't make it seem so. Was she hiding something from him?

He'd have to think more about that one, but in the meantime, he didn't want Abby to see him like this, dressed as a servant, waiting on Lady Etheridge of all people. His cover would be blown along with his reputation and dignity. Nicholas grasped the blue and gold livery uniform, shrugged it on, and buttoned the front.

He couldn't go back out there without a better disguise, and even then, he'd have to stay out of Abby's direct line of sight, or she'd surely recognize him. He scavenged the contents of the galley storeroom.

Underneath a row of jars of pickled beets, he found a white, curly mass—a powdered wig. Lady Etheridge must have at some point required her footman to wear the old formal style of headdress. It looked matted, but Nicholas shook it out and plopped it on top of his head anyway. In a stroke of genius, he lifted the flour barrel lid and grabbed a handful of the soft, white powder. He smeared it over his face and patted the rest into the wig. With a sniff to get the excess powder from his nose, straightened and strode back to the terrace. He wouldn't go down without a fight.

A half smile tugged at the corners of his lips. He couldn't wait to see the expression on Lady Etheridge's face when he served their luncheon looking like a ghost from the past. Though out-of-date, those in some elite circles still required servants to powder their hair.

He grabbed the silver tray covered with fruits of all kinds

and held it close to his face as he approached the table. The thrill of evading discovery heightened his senses. Careful to serve Abby only from behind, his hand deftly arranged the food on the table without the slightest noise. *Please, don't turn around.*

In his mind, he saw her face propped up on her elbow as she lay laughing at him across the pillows.

Lady Etheridge sliced a strawberry. "How are things at the Emerson household?"

"Ah—unbelievable." Abby smiled, but from the view of her profile, it didn't quite reach her eyes.

A polite and ambiguous word. Nicholas's chest swelled. Abby's quick wit had been one of the many reasons he'd fallen in love with her.

"In what way?" Lady Etheridge paused to listen before spearing the piece of fruit.

"Becoming ill and keeping the house in order with Mrs. Smith being away." Abby picked up her fork. "Have you heard from your children?"

"Harrumph," Lady Etheridge grunted. "Of course not. They are busy with their own lives. They have forgotten their poor mother, and I'm afraid I won't hear from them until—"

Lady Etheridge caught sight of her ghostly white footman, and her mouth fell open, but she recovered quickly and pursed her lips.

Nicholas relished her baffled expression.

She cleared her throat. "... until they need something. How about you?" She arched a narrow eyebrow, and her gaze flicked to Nicholas before returning to Abby. "Have you accepted any of the offers for your hand? I know your brother has turned away several suitors, but time passes quickly. You don't want to wind up on the shelf. It's time for you to begin seriously considering your options. You're too pretty a girl for spinsterhood."

Nicholas checked the hall clock. Enough time had passed for him to have started to feel some symptoms, but his stomach didn't cramp, his fingers weren't numb, and he wasn't even perspiring. The food should be safe to serve. He moved to Lady Etheridge's side, purposely keeping his back to Abby as he served her plate.

"I don't believe God intends for me to be a spinster."

"Rightly so. Who has caught your eye, the McAllister lad? He *is* from a good lineage and, you must admit, he's not bad on the eyes either."

"He is distinguished, and his bloodlines are impeccable."

A bitter taste filled Nicholas's mouth. He shoved the empty silver tray into the second footman's hands and moved back into the shadows behind a large potted palm. Out of their line of sight, he relaxed and willed Lady Etheridge to finish without any more requests.

"But I'm not looking to remarry." Abby sipped from her cup.

"You contradict yourself, my dear. You just stated that you don't believe God intends for you to be a spinster." Lady Etheridge scanned the room with narrowed eyes. "James," she bellowed, "bring us more tea. These cups have cooled."

Nicholas headed to the silver service tray. So much for wishful thinking.

"Mine is still warm," Abby said.

Lady Etheridge's smile appeared tight. "Don't be ridiculous. The air is brisk today, and no one cares for lukewarm tea."

Abby leaned forward, inspecting her host. "Are you certain you feel all right? You seem in a dudgeon. Has something upset you?"

"Only that my new footman needs better training," Lady Etheridge grumbled.

Nicholas took no offense to the woman's comment. He was a spy not a footman. He poured the tea and offered sugar, which Abby declined with a wave of her fingers. How could Abby discern the difference between Lady Awfulridge's normal, uptight, embittered expression from her current, dower, Friday-faced expression? He poured tea into the woman's cup, careful to stay out of Abby's direct line of vision. Thankfully, she appeared distracted by Lady Etheridge's odd behavior.

"Mayhap I am a bit out of sorts." Lady Etheridge sighed, and her expression turned sorrowful. "You've probably noticed the absence of Poopsie, my beloved pet."

"Where is she?" Abby peeked under the table and around the floor.

"Sadly, she's been put to bed with a shovel."

Abby's hand flew to her mouth. "Oh, Lady Etheridge, how dreadful. I'm so sorry."

Nicholas couldn't help but cock an *I told you she's innocent* eyebrow at Lady Etheridge. The woman's expression never changed, but he questioned whether the spark that lit her eyes was the glitter of determination.

"She was poisoned." Lady Etheridge's voice rang loud enough to create waves in their water glasses.

Abby jolted forward in her chair. "I beg your pardon?"

"Arsenic. Someone poisoned her. The food had been intended for me, but the dog ate it."

"What? Someone attempted to kill you. Who would want to do that?"

"Who, indeed. It happened a week ago last Saturday. After your visit, Sir Walker Baton escorted you into town for the day, as I recall."

Nicholas clenched his fists at his sides. McAllister, now Baton. What had Abby been doing with those fops? He wanted her to remarry, but McAllister had no spine, and Baton had a nasal drip and cleared his throat incessantly.

Abby stared at Lady Etheridge, her mouth agape.

"You didn't happen to overhear gossip or information that

might explain who would want to hurt me?"

Abby pressed her lips together. "Of course not. Are you certain it wasn't an accident? I can't fathom someone doing such a wretched thing."

"Indeed." Lady Etheridge sliced a piece of melon with her knife. "There are no accidents, my dear. Things happen for a reason."

The conversation moved on to upcoming church events and if the orphans were practicing singing as a choir for Christmas. Nicholas served the finger sandwiches and the ladies conversed in between bites. After they finished eating, he swooped in from behind, collecting the plates.

"Thank you for the delightful lunch." Abby draped her napkin on the table. "My condolences regarding Poopsie. If there is anything I can do, do not hesitate to ask."

"Must you be going so soon?" Lady Etheridge reached out across the table, but Abby was already pushing back her seat.

Standing behind Abby, Nicholas assisted in pulling out her chair.

"The children are expecting me at the orphanage."

"But you haven't eaten dessert."

Nicholas grabbed the dessert tray the second footman passed to him. He stood behind Abby and lowered the tray so she could eye it.

"Thank you, but I must be on my way."

Abby stood and turned in Nicholas's direction. With the adept footwork of a skilled dancer, Nicholas step-turned, spinning the tray around to Lady Etheridge and once again putting his back towards Abby. The older woman waved it away with her hand, and Nick passed it back to the second footman.

"I will see you out." Lady Etheridge replied, and Nicholas assisted her with her chair as Abby moved towards the door.

He retreated to the shadows, but he overheard Abby exclaim on her way out, "Lady Etheridge, I must commend you on your staff. Your new footman is like a ghost. I hardly noticed he was there except for an occasional breeze."

His charade had succeeded, but hiding from Abby lacked the thrill he'd found in other secretive operatives. How could he find enjoyment when he wanted to be in her arms.

CHAPTER 15

*A*bby's time at the orphanage with the innocent and guileless children was a marvelous change after a strained morning of guarding her words with Melinda and Lady Etheridge. How terrible for Lady Etheridge to lose her dog—and to poison. Who would do such a thing?

The morning was forgotten as she engaged them in a raucous game of blind man's bluff. Abby was still laughing as she waved goodbye. She blew the youngest ones kisses before exiting the building and heading down the brick walkway and through the wrought iron gate.

She closed the latch and turned.

"Beg your pardon," a man with a throaty voice croaked.

Abby sucked in a gasp.

The strange man she'd seen in Mr. Kroger's store the other day stood so close she could see the open pores in his skin. Cigar smoke leeched from the fabric of his clothes.

She stepped back to put some distance between them, but her foot struck the rough metal gate behind her.

"May I help you?" she asked, raising her chin. She refused

to cower, even though her skin crawled from the man's sheer presence.

"Most generous of you, I could certainly use your service." His lips curled up into a wicked smile, and his gaze darted about. His long face held a ruddy tint, and greasy hair curled below his collar. He dressed in fine clothes that were well-worn at the elbows and knees.

The man rested a hand on the metal post and leaned toward her. "You're a fine bit of goods. Even more beautiful up close."

"I'm afraid you have me confused with someone else. I haven't made your acquaintance, sir."

"There is no mistake. I've had my eye on you, and I know your secret. I've seen you steal into the woods at night. I know what you're up to—who you're off visiting."

He knows Nick? His greedy gaze set her nerves on edge and warnings rang in her head. Why would Nick associate with such a man of obvious ill repute? Had the man served in battle alongside him? If so, perhaps he could answer her questions.

"Do you know my husband?"

"God rest his soul." One side of the man's lips twisted into a half smile. "Seein' you're a widow, I would like to offer you a proposition." He held a pouch up at eye level. "I have quite a bit of coin saved."

Abby forced a calm breath, but the hair on her arms stood on end. What did being a widow have to do with this man's savings? His gaze strayed down to her bosom.

She gasped. *He thinks she's been visiting a lover.*

"You're mistaken. Now if you'll excuse me." She ducked under his arm and tried to walk away, but he repositioned, blocking her escape.

"Am I not genteel enough for your kind. Are you too high in the instep?" His eyes clouded over. "I'll have you know, I used to run in your circles. I have been a guest of the Duke of

Cumberland. I've had my own table at White's." His lips curled into a sneer. "I was even admitted to the subscription room at Tattersalls until I had a falling out with my wretch of a father."

With a blink, his eyes cleared. He shook the pouch. "A shilling is a shilling no matter whose hand it comes from, and I have plenty more of this stashed away." He leaned closer. "You smell like I imagined."

She pressed her back into the hedge that lined the walkway. Sticks poked her skin.

"I'm not interested in a proposition." The clopping of horses on the street running parallel on the other side of the hedge meant if she screamed someone would most likely come to help. But if the man vocalized his insinuations, it could tarnish her reputation beyond reproach.

"You haunt my thoughts each night. I find myself wondering how soft your skin feels—how silky is your hair?" His hand lifted as if to touch her.

Abby slapped the man with such force that his head snapped sideways. "Don't *ever* come near me again."

The man was a deranged monster. Before he could recover, Abby grabbed her skirts in one hand, pushed around him, and sprinted toward the street. She glanced back to ensure he wasn't following her.

"Lady Abigail, may I be of service?"

Abby gasped as she practically ran headlong into Mr. Barnsby, her groomsman. He dropped the tack he'd been carrying and grasped her upper arms to keep her from falling.

"Oh, thank heaven! Mr. Barnsby. There was a man." How could she describe her encounter?

"Lady Abigail." Lord McAllister stopped in front of her and tipped his hat. "You look pale. Is something the matter?"

She couldn't tell Lord McAllister about the rogue—what he'd said—what he'd insinuated. It was humiliating and shock-

171

ing. The allegation alone could ruin her reputation. Her eyes jumped between her groomsman and Lord McAllister.

Mr. Barnsby saved her. "Most likely a snatch cly out to lighten yer pocket. I'll go have a look-see and alert the constable." He bowed and stalked off in the direction she'd come.

Lord McAllister craned his neck to look around. "Point me in his direction, and I will ring a peel over the chap. Only a blackguard goes around scaring young women."

"I was merely frightened, that's all." Abby threaded her arm through his. "I believe he's gone now. However, I would be grateful if you would escort me home."

"Of course, Lady Abigail, I'd be delighted."

~

*I*n the middle of clearing dishes, the bell rang summoning Nicholas to Lady Ethridge's side. He washed the flour from his face and removed the wig before locating her seated in the salon on the tufted sofa with a pinched expression on her face. After Abby left, Lady Etheridge's mood turned foul. He got the impression that she was disappointed he didn't apprehend Abby on the spot.

"Well?" She folded her arms and frowned at him.

Well, what? He stood at attention facing her but said nothing.

"How do you expect to question my suspect's motives as a footman? Servants don't speak to guests except to say, yes milady. We should have gone with my suggestion of having you be my estate manager, or I could have said you are my visiting nephew."

"Lady Abigail isn't your only suspect. I have other means of gathering information where she is concerned."

"You do?" Lady Etheridge gasped or sniffed. Nicholas

couldn't tell which by the sound or the slight jerk of her upper body. "How, precisely?"

"Spying is the area I know best so please leave that part up to me." He countered her frown with a glare. "What would be helpful is knowing in advance the proper names of your guests so I can prepare. You'd said it was Lady Felton who'd be in attendance."

"Bah." She waved a dismissive hand. "You're mistaken. I might have said Lady Abigail Hartington and you heard Lady Sarah Hartington. It's an easy mistake."

An easy mistake? It wasn't like Lady Etheridge to let anyone get away with any sort of mistake, and her quick protest seemed odd.

"What I cannot abide is the lackadaisical way in which you handled your footman duties." Lady Etheridge rang a peel over him for leaving his post and returning wearing a wig which wasn't part of the required uniform.

His head pounded by the time she dismissed him. Miraculously, he'd survived the encounter unscathed. Well, if one could consider his condition after an hour lecture from Lady Etheridge on decorum and the proper conduct of a servant *unscathed*.

Nicholas chuckled to himself as he strode into Laurel House through the servants' entrance. *Your new footman is like a ghost. I hardly knew he was there except for the occasional breeze.*

In the parlor, he threw a couple of logs into the fireplace. His leg hurt, and he could have summoned the maid to tend to the fire, but he heard her humming in the kitchen and chopping up food when he passed the kitchen. Polly was probably upstairs sewing, and Abby was still at the orphanage, which meant he had some time to himself.

At his next meeting with Lady Etheridge, he'd need to further explain the process of an investigation. Developments were sporadic or came in waves. One couldn't expect to catch an attempted killer immediately. Unfounded hunches were often wrong. And suspecting Abby? *Ludicrous.*

His questioning of the Etheridge kitchen staff progressed better than he'd anticipated. All he'd had to do was act interested, and they'd supplied a plethora of information regarding Lady Etheridge and her staff. Several servants openly disliked their mistress and had spoken of quitting or getting revenge. He would keep an eye on the other footman, who referred to her as the old bat. After a particular set-down, Nicholas overheard the man grumble, *she has it coming.* But the only real crime accounted for was the cook spitting in her soup.

Nicholas stoked the fire until it blazed in the hearth. He inhaled the smell of burning wood and enjoyed the warmth. He should have met with Laurel House's staff this morning. Abby had spoken to them about remaining quiet about his return, but he wanted them to swear an oath and offer them a financial reward once his mission was completed. In the meantime, their stories about him being a relative of Abby's must stay congruent. Between his falling asleep a few hours before dawn, and his rush to not be late for Lady Etheridge, he'd pushed off the meeting.

He set the poker down to use the opportunity to gather them and also ask a few questions regarding who prepares and has access to the food. Afterward he'd update his list of viable suspects and the timeline of their whereabouts on the day of the poisoning. Lady Etheridge's cook and footmen had access to the food, but could they get their hands on arsenic? Were they good blokes with a ratcatcher who could supply them. He'd already spoken to the apothecary, and he had no record of selling arsenic to anyone in Lady Etheridge's employ.

He stood to ring the bell pull. A cushy blur of skirts rounded the corner, then froze in the entry.

The interim housekeeper let out a piercing scream.

The sound stabbed his brain. He pinched the bridge of his nose. *Hounds' teeth.*

Nicholas squeezed his eyes shut to ward off the fear that attacked his mind, filling it with the smell of gunpowder and the racking tremors of shots fired.

"What do you want?" the quaking woman asked, hiding behind her apron. "Who are you?"

Nicholas forced his eyes open. Images of blood and death rattled in his brain as he fought down the panic.

The woman didn't move. Fear and mistrust glared through her narrowed eyes.

"See to your duties," He spit words through clenched teeth. "In twenty minutes, gather the staff for a meeting." He might need every minute to get his mind back in good order.

Her mouth fell into a tight *O,* and she crossed herself before scurrying away.

He leaned against the fireplace mantel for support. His hands were clammy, and beads of perspiration formed on his upper lip. A few deep breaths and thankfully the episode passed. He wiped the sweat from his brow and waited for his body to return to normal. That was a close one.

This attack he'd been able to contain but others swallowed him into a past nightmare, and he was helpless to escape. He retrieved a quill pen, ink, and paper and sat off the writing table to focus on updating his list of suspects.

He crossed off the orphanage staff. Abby's illness had been the result of eating bad soup. The reverend promised to terminate the current chef and hire anew.

Nicholas drew a line through Lady Etheridge's cook and scullery maids for lack of motive and a way of knowing who partook of the tart, but could they have unintentionally poisoned the food by mistaking a bag of white powder for flour? Could the grocer have accidentally combined arsenic in with the sugar? Or the rat catcher left the substance where it could have been spilt and mixed in with the meal. He ruled that out, because others would have displayed symptoms.

On the few occasions the interim housekeeper passed by the doorway, he caught her shaking her head and clucking her tongue.

He dropped the quill back into the ink and leaned back in his chair, raking a hand through his hair. His last operation had been about spoiling an attempt on the life of the Whig party's leader. Now he was solving a canine murder.

He rang for tea.

The housekeeper brought the service tray with enough haste and the proper amount of politeness, but Nicholas squirmed under the woman's disapproving looks.

"If I may, sir?"

He acknowledged her with a nod.

"I don't know what kind of house is being run under Mrs. Smith's nose, but as a God-fearing woman, I cannot partake in it." She slid the tray onto the tea table and pulled off her apron.

Nicholas opened his mouth to explain, to tell her she'd gotten it all wrong, but her eyes were full of loathing. He'd had enough of judgmental, opinionated women today. He'd put up with Lady Etheridge in order to finish his last assignment, but he wouldn't be harassed by a servant.

"Wait here." He left the room, gathered the funds from his pack and returned, holding a pouch full of guineas to pay two months of her salary.

"You're dismissed." He held out the small bag to ensure the woman didn't gossip and Abby's reputation remain intact. "Take this for your trouble, and do not mention your employment here, Lady Abigail's name, or my presence to anyone."

She seized the pouch and peered into it, sucking in a breath. "Bless you, sir."

A few coins turned him from sinner to saint. Nicholas snorted as she skittered away. Under Mrs. Smith's watch, he would never have witnessed such a display of disloyalty. His residing at Laurel House didn't hold up with the original alibi he'd told the staff. He gathered the remaining servants, which, without the housekeeper, consisted of Polly, Abby's lady's maid, a scullery maid, and Barnsby.

"As Lady Abigail has probably already informed you, I'm Nicholas Emerson, her husband. I've returned only temporarily on an assignment for the Home Office and to protect Lady Abigail."

Polly gasped, and her eyes darted around the room as if a killer might jump out at any moment.

"Lady Abigail isn't aware of my position or assignment, and loose tongues could endanger your mistress. My time here is limited, and for Lady Abigail's sake, I pray that you will keep my identity and whereabouts quiet. If the townfolk are alerted to my presence, Lady Abigail could suffer." He explained what they should say if directly questioned. "I appreciate a loyal staff, and once again, it is for Lady Abigail's protection, which is in your best interests. I will award a hefty bonus for your coopera- tion and the trouble." He waited until they nodded and then dismissed them to go about their work.

A peace settled over the house with the housekeeper gone, and Nicholas relaxed until he realized the woman had been responsible for preparing supper. He groaned and got to work.

With the help of Polly and an inept scullery maid named Delia, who only knew how to cut vegetables, he skewered a roast and cooked it over a spit in the fireplace with some pan- baked vegetables. After checking his watch, Nicholas readied the table as he'd been taught as a footman, then stepped back to admire his work.

It was a table set for a king. With the roast and vegetables in the warming tray, Nicholas waited for Abby to return from the orphanage.

Moments later, her chattering voice rang through the open

window. The lovely sound brought a smile to Nicholas's lips. But with whom was she speaking? He pulled back the drape to peer out and saw Abby on the arm of Lord McAllister.

Nicholas's grip crushed the velvet drapery material into a twisted mass of wrinkles.

She grinned and waved goodbye to the pompous aristocrat.

She entered the foyer, a bright cheeriness still on her face.

Nicholas fumed like a hot iron on wet cloth. He leaned against the door frame in the hall, waiting for her to notice his presence. "Enjoying yourself?" He forced a light tone in case the servants were listening.

Her skirts ballooned as she whirled to face him. One hand rested over her heart, and her chest rose and fell with each rapid breath. "Nick, it's you."

"Who else would it be?" He hated the bitterness squeezing his heart.

Her pink lips spread wider, and her eyes shone bright, but Nicholas ground his teeth.

He couldn't stop the involuntary flip of his stomach or how his breath caught when she fixed her dazzling smile on him.

In the past, Lord McAllister would not have posed any threat at all, but now he was a menace. Nicholas couldn't compete. The unsightly scars that marred his body were daily reminders of what he couldn't change. McAllister was a whole man. Nicholas couldn't take Abby on long walks through town, dance a full set with her at balls, or parade her around at social venues. What if he had an attack while in public.

He'd bet McAllister didn't wake up clutching a rifle, his finger about to pull the trigger.

Abby would be happier with McAllister.

"I guess I'm a little jumpy." She let out a weak laugh, and relief crossed her features. "I'm so glad you're here."

She was happy to see him. He wanted to throw that in McAllister's face. "Supper is ready and waiting."

"Wonderful." She strolled into the dining room. He held out a chair for her, and Abby sat. "What did Helena make tonight?"

"Helena didn't make anything." He served her plate, a slice of the roast and vegetables.

She cocked her head to the side. "Then how is dinner ready?"

"I prepared it with help."

"You?" Abby's jaw dropped. "Is Helena ill?"

"She's in fine health."

"Then where is she? I'll need to speak to her about shirking her duties. I pay her to prepare dinner. It's a shame." Her brow furrowed. "She came highly recommended by Mrs. Smith."

"I dismissed her."

"You did what?" Abby half rose from her seat. "You could have consulted me first. Do you realize how difficult it is to find trustworthy help?"

"I did what needed to be done."

"What has she done wrong?"

Nicholas's grip tightened on his fork. He wasn't used to having to explain his actions. "Servants are to not be seen or heard unless needed. The woman was a nuisance."

If the maid-of-all-work jumped to the wrong conclusions, what would the townspeople think? Another reason for him to finish the case and leave quickly.

Abby blinked a couple times. Her mouth opened as if to speak, then she shook her head and closed her lips tightly.

Nicholas was about to eat a bite of meat when Abby asked, "May we pray first?"

Swallowing his chagrin, Nicholas put his utensil down. He bowed his head and waited for the prayer. When nothing happened, he cracked open one eyelid and peeked at Abby. She raised both her eyebrows with a nod of encouragement.

Nicholas closed his eyes and cleared his throat. "Dear Heavenly Father."

What next? It seemed he'd forgotten how to pray. His father had always prayed, and when his father passed, his mother assumed the role. She prayed with the eloquence of a poet. In comparison, Nicholas felt tongue-tied and inadequate. "Bless this food to our bodies ... er—help us to ... to not trespass against our trespassers. Forgive our debts and ... ah ... for your kingdom. Amen."

～

*A*bby slowly raised her head and studied the man seated in front of her. It was obvious Nick hadn't prayed in a long time. The war, it seemed, had robbed him of more than his carefree disposition and a life with her. It had robbed him of his faith, too. What could have been so horrific that he'd turned from God instead of clinging to Him for comfort?

"I saw Melinda Eyre today. She's married now to Dr. Cox." Abby sipped from a glass of water. "She questioned me about the huntsman who rescued me in the woods, and I slipped and mentioned your name."

Nick didn't respond, but his grip tightened around the handle of his spoon.

"They would like us to pay them a visit at some point, but not until you're ready." It had to come out eventually that he was alive and back at home. How angry could he be? Abby speared a carrot and popped it into her mouth, but it tasted like bland mush.

"No." Nick resumed eating.

She bristled at his tone, but maybe he needed a reminder of all the people who love him, no matter what he's done or how he's changed. "I also saw Katherine and thought it might be lovely if we invited her and Stephen to dine with us one evening. Stephen will be delighted to get reacquainted."

Nick stared at her, narrowing his eyes. "I specifically told you not to tell anyone. You are only making this harder."

Abby shrunk back from his harsh words. Was this the same Nick from the night before?

He inhaled a deep breath and leveled her with his gaze. "Listen to me."

His hardhearted tone blasted her like an artic wind.

"This is merely temporary. I'm not staying. This isn't my life anymore. The fewer people who know of my return, the easier it will be for you when I leave."

"Leave?" He'd said it before, but things were different now. Didn't he see how much she still loved him—how much she needed him? Indeed, they'd changed, but there was still the same longing between them. She'd felt it and saw the yearning reflected in his eyes. How could he leave when all she wanted was to be with him every minute of every day for the rest of their lives? "Where would you go?" Abby put down her fork. The roots of her hair lifted, tingling her scalp. "The war is over."

"I have duties." Nick stared at his glass, turning it slowly in his hand, his face strained.

"Duties?" She pointed a finger at her chest. "I'm your wife. You have a duty to me. You vowed on our wedding day to love, protect, and cherish me."

Nick pushed his plate away, the food barely eaten. A blaring silence filled the room.

"Nick, talk to me."

He met her gaze with stony eyes. "The only way I can protect you *is* to leave."

With a painful swallow, Abby fought down a rising scream. "I don't understand."

"There isn't an explanation to be had." Nick rose from the

table, and with a polite bow, he turned to leave. "I have work to do."

"You can't just walk away." Abby jumped up from her seat, overturning her glass in the process. Red wine marred the white tablecloth. She righted the glass but ignored the seeping liquid. "We ... we haven't finished dinner."

Nick stared at the spill before turning and striding from the room, not even acknowledging her plea.

Abby followed him into the hallway. "Why are you shutting me out? Why all the secrets?" Desperation rang in her voice. "What happened to you?" Her last sentence sounded more like an accusation than a question.

Nick turned. In one stride, he towered over her.

Abby arched back.

"War. The war happened, Abby. It's ugly and wretched, and it nearly destroyed me."

Abby shivered at the intensity of his voice. "You need to talk about it."

"It will trigger..." He shook his head, and his brusque tone sliced the air. "I can't."

"Please." She grasped at threads to hold him to her or keep him at bay. "Don't keep secrets from me. D-don't block me out." Her eyes stung with tears. Melinda's words echoed through her mind. *Some returning soldiers have an entire, other family in another country.*

Nick spun on his heel and headed for the door.

Abby's voice was but a broken whisper. "Is there someone else?"

He faltered.

Abby stared at his back through a haze of unshed tears. "Do you have another life? Another f-family somewhere in S-Spain or France or elsewhere?"

Her body tensed. Maddened by the silence. As the seconds ticked by, she petitioned God, *Please, don't let it be so.*

Without turning, Nick voiced a solitary, "No." He pushed through the back door into the night air.

A wave of relief crashed over her body.

The door creaked as it swung back, hitting the frame with a loud bang.

Abby sagged against the wall for support.

Now what, God? Where do we go from here? Inhaling a deep breath, she pushed herself upright and smoothed her skirts.

She trudged back to the dining room, but Delia had already cleaned up the spilt madeira and collected the dishes. All the while, self-doubt nagged Abby.

Why had Nick hesitated? Why had it taken him so long to answer a straightforward question?

Had he lied?

~

*N*icholas inhaled the thick night air. He had to get out of here. When Abby pressed him with questions, her nearness suffocated him. His head pounded, and he could feel his control slipping. Then the blood...

He shook his head. *No*, spilt wine had soaked the white linen. *Get ahold of yourself.* The imaginings had to stop. He couldn't work like this—*live* like this.

Nicholas grabbed a lantern from the barn and lit the wick. The flame ignited and cast distorted shadows on the walls. He needed to calm down, to clear his head and think. Ten years after leaving Abby and he was still doomed to lose his composure around her.

Why hadn't he let her believe he had another family? It would give Abby the perfect reason to let him go. She'd have been upset and angry, but then perhaps she could divorce him. A scandal would be unavoidable, but they'd only been married one night. He'd say whatever was needed to make her seem innocent and him the scallywag. She could then move on with her life and marry someone else Then she could have children like she'd always wanted.

You haven't fooled God.

Nicholas picked up a rock. He tossed it in his palm a couple times then hurled it deep into the woods.

He hadn't been able to hurt her like that. The aching pain in her voice had been his undoing.

Nicholas paced in the garden fighting to keep his self-loathing at bay for having to hurt Abby once again. There were so many things he longed to say. He wanted to scream, *It was all a mistake!* His whole life—a mistake. He shouldn't have enlisted. He shouldn't have married her before being shipped off. And he certainly should never have come back. His fists curled, but he kept them by his side instead of railing at God for not listening to his past prayers each time before he'd stormed onto the battlefield or started a new assignment. *Please, get me back home to Abby.*

He spied an ax in the corner, picked it up, and headed to the wood pile. His muscles flexed and tensed as the ax swooshed through the air, then struck the logs with a resounding crack. His leg pained him, throbbing in tempo with the pulse in his temple, but the monotony and rhythm of the movement soothed his nerves.

He should have been crippled for life, but a young aid made it possible for him to walk. Most of the other burn victims, if they lived, became invalids, their joints solidifying. The horrific events of that night flashed through his memory, and he gripped the ax and swung harder, splitting each piece of wood until it neared mere kindling.

His mind broken, his body marred, his skin twisted, but he could still move. He owed that to Guillaume. God had left him to die, but a young physician's assistant had stepped in and changed his fate.

The truth was ugly. People had suffered all around him, some pleading for mercy, others for death. Their screams haunted him, echoing through his mind day *and* night.

Maybe he should tell Abby what had happened. Part of him wanted to protect her innocence from the ugliness of life, but if she truly wanted to know, maybe he should tell her. Then she'd turn away from him, and his heart could find rest and she could find true happiness with someone whose mind was intact and whose body was whole.

A twig snapped in the woods close by. The hairs on the back of Nicholas's neck stood on end. "Who's there?" The underbrush rustled.

Nicholas grabbed the lantern, held it high, and scanned the woods.

"Barnsby?"

The groomsman emerged from the stables, the opposite direction of the sound.

Nicholas lifted the ax, ready to take on an assailant. The rustling sounded again but distant this time.

Must have been an animal. Probably scared off a deer. They tended to roam this time of night, but he walked the perimeter of the grounds just in case.

Nicholas snorted, thinking about the townsmen and their outrageous ideas about mythical werewolves roaming the area. He glanced towards the house, following the ivy laden trellis to Abby's silhouette. She bent and doused the candle, and her window darkened. She'd soon be asleep.

He'd give his life to protect Abby, even from himself. He'd wanted to offer her the world, but all he'd given her was grief. Several minutes passed and he waited until the familiar night-time sounds resumed before returning inside. Fortunately, he'd bought himself time before having to face Abby again—at least until morning.

CHAPTER 16

"God, please help him."

Get out! Run! Nicholas jolted awake when the French woman from his nightmare wouldn't flee. He was kneeling on the bed, his fingers locked in a tight grip around Abby's upper arms. The creaks and groans of the overhead beams and the snap and pop of the surrounding fire faded until he could only hear Abby's sobs.

He released her and the white marks where his hands were turned red.

Bile rose in his throat. *Dear Lord.* He'd hurt her.

She pushed back the mahogany tresses and peered at him with wide frightened eyes. "Nick?"

"I'm sorry." He pulled her into his embrace. "I never meant to hurt you."

Resting her head on his shoulder, she rubbed her arm and said in a choked whisper, "It's me—Abby."

"I know, darling. I'm awake now." He stroked her hair. "I'm sorry to have frightened you."

She clung to his nightshirt.

Why would she come to him after the way he'd ended their meal last evening?

He held her close, stroking her hair until his racing heartbeat settled and she yawned into his shoulder. He lowered onto the bed, reclining against the pillows, and curled her against his side. Listening to her even breaths and feeling the rise and fall of her chest as her sleep deepened, he hated himself for what he'd put her through. This was why he needed to stay away. She shouldn't come near him while he slept. From now on he'd bar the door at night. He was dangerous and he couldn't bear it if he hurt her further. His duty was to protect her—even from himself.

Her hair stuck to the perspiration on his neck, the stubble on his chin and even wound around his arms. Extricating himself from her silky hair was becoming part of his morning routine.

As he unwrapped the last strand, she spoke. "Shush. Everything's going to be fine. I'm here now."

Nicholas closed his eyes, overcome by this small woman who soothed him with her voice and would forgo a night's rest to ease his nightmares. He lay there listening to her deep even breathing and couldn't resist placing a kiss on top of her head.

Her thick eyelashes fluttered open, and she lifted her head. "Nick, how long did I dose off?"

"Not long, darling."

A shy smile graced the corners of her lips. With her free hand, she swept her heavy mane behind her. "You were in the throes of a horrid dream. Your moaning woke the staff. Polly almost fainted dead away, and Barnsby stormed into the house wielding a pitchfork. He wanted to check each room. I had to order him back to the stables."

She could order the servants back, but she wouldn't be able to send away the sanitarium workers when they came for him.

LORRI DUDLEY

"All I could think to do was pray." She peered up at him, her long lashes like sweeping fans. "It worked."

Prayer. After all the techniques he'd tried to calm his mind, it was naive to think prayer would work. But he swallowed his scoff because her expression reminded him of the small girl he'd once known, his best friend's little sister who'd trailed on his heels, desperately hoping to get in his good graces.

"It appears so."

A shy smile blossomed across her lips, and Nicholas's chest constricted.

She absently drew circles on the coverlet with her fingertip, and her smile faded. "Do you ever have a night without nightmares?"

He folded an arm behind his head and watched shadows dance away from the sunlight on the ceiling. "Every now and then, my body's too exhausted to even dream. Unfortunately, those nights are few."

"Is it the same dream?" Abby's gaze flickered to his face.

"It varies. Sometimes, I'm in the thick of battle, other times, I'm trying to escape. Often, I'm fighting the flames."

"Is that what happened? I mean, how you came to have those scars. Was it fire?"

His jaw tightened. "Yes."

Abby's gaze dropped to the coverlet. "You don't need to speak of it. I'm sorry I asked."

"No, what you said last night was right. I need to talk about it." He owed her an explanation after giving her a fright.

Abby waited for him to elaborate, but he struggled to begin.

"It was supposed to be a simple assignment."

Her eyes found his.

He averted his gaze. "They needed men on the inside, so I was disguised as a French diplomat. There had been rumors that General Sebastiani and Napoleon Bonaparte himself were to be present. We were in position, but something went wrong.

188

Our Royals attacked too soon. The troops set upon us with cannon fire and blazing tar."

Abby folded her hand over his.

"They were supposed to wait for the signal. I thought I could still fulfill my assignment, but within moments, the hall became an inferno. The smoke was so thick I couldn't breathe. People screamed and ran in all directions. I watched helplessly as a man, his clothes on fire, jumped through a glass window to his death."

The muscles in his shoulders tightened, and the memory pounded him like a spray of grapeshot bullets. "I couldn't get out in time. I barely heard the crack of the overhead beams above the screams. One fell and pinned me to the ground. Flames spread to my clothing, burning my skin. I couldn't get the beam off, even pushing with all my strength..." His voice cracked, and he swallowed against the painful memories that tore away a piece of his sanity with each remembrance.

"The impact broke my left leg."

Tears shimmered in Abby's eyes. Pity.

He rubbed his face with his hands.

She didn't jump in to speak or fidget. Silent tears streamed down her cheeks, but she remained still. Perhaps she feared that if she moved, he'd never talk about it again. Maybe she'd be right.

He dropped his gaze. "A man—I never got a look at his face —lifted the beam and pulled me out from underneath. Flames were everywhere, but somehow, he remained calm—unnaturally so. He threw me over his shoulder and carried me out of the building.

What happened next is a blur. I could have blacked out. It was impossible to think past the waves of pain. The man didn't say anything, just placed me on a stretcher, and the next thing I knew, I was being rushed off by the flying ambulance carriers to a French medical post."

He gazed at the ceiling but only saw the fluttering of the aid station's canvas roof and the frenzied movements of the field medic as he sought to ease the pain of the hundreds around him.

Nicholas could feel himself lying on the stretcher. The stench of burnt skin mixed with the smell of body odor and hot wax. Men screamed in pain, begging for water, calling for help, or pleading for God to take them.

He floated in and out of consciousness like scattered clouds shadowing the sun. The burn victims screamed in agony as the surgeon poured hot wax over the charred skin to seal the wounds.

Nicholas needed to get out of there before his identity was discovered. He struggled to sit up.

A boy, around fourteen years old, appeared by Nicholas's side and pushed him back down into the stretcher.

Nicholas grabbed the boy's hand and said in what he hoped was fluent French, "No wax. Don't let them pour that stuff on me."

The boy's eyes locked with his own. He must have read Nicholas's desperation, because when the surgeon appeared, the boy swiped his hand over Nicholas's face to close his eyes. "Don't waste the wax on this one," he said. "He's already dead."

The surgeon passed to the next patient.

Nicholas grasped the boy's sleeve. "*Merci*," he whispered as blackness took him.

Later, Nicholas awoke to find himself in another unit. The boy, Guillen, stood by his side and spoke about some experimental treatments.

Guillen said he'd witnessed the ineffectiveness of the wax and oil treatments. If they didn't die, the victims lost all mobility. Their muscles often contracted and appeared to freeze up. Despite being a young lad, Guillen's notions for treating burns seemed more logical than the surgeons' ideas. Nicholas allowed the boy to test out his treatments on him.

The lad cleaned his wounds with drops of colloidal silver in water and then wrapped him in cloth bandages that were changed periodically. As Nicholas regained his strength, Guillen encouraged him to move and stretch his skin and joints. It was painful, but Nicholas was a dead man if he didn't get out of the French holdings. With sheer determination, he recovered. It was slow, and his leg pained him to the point that some days he couldn't even stand. But unlike the other surviving burn victims, he'd regained most of his ability to move and walk.

"Once I was past the threat of death and my broken leg had healed enough for me to walk, I overheard that the Royal army was close. That night, I snuck out of camp on a mission to get to the British brigade or die in the process. Which I almost did. I was mistaken for a French soldier and evaded two shots before I convinced them I was on their side. The commander of the brigade had me transported to a field hospital in an old monastery. After six months of more healing, I was told my services were required for a special operative only I had the inside connections to do."

Nicholas closed his eyes and exhaled a deep breath. As much as it pained him to relive the past, his body tingled with a sense of lightness. The retelling was cathartic. He opened his eyes to tell Abby she'd been right.

Her eyes were red and swollen, and she choked back sobs. Her sorrow scarred him in the few places left untouched by the war.

"Abby," he whispered.

"God spared you," her hoarse voice held a reverent note. "He answered my prayers and brought you back to me. I wasn't even sure God was listening, but He was."

She rose onto her knees. "I pleaded and pleaded in my

prayers. When all I got in return was silence, I thought God was ignoring me, but He was working. He heard me and sent people to help you."

Tears spilled down her cheeks. "Oh, Nick. I'm so ashamed I ever doubted Him. I will be forever grateful that God sent that unknown man to pull you out of the fire and the boy, Guillen, to heal your wounds."

He itched to pull her into his arms and kiss the tears away, but neither God nor Guillen's methods had healed him entirely. The scars still marred his skin, easily discernible through the lightweight fabric of his shirt. He couldn't find it within him to give God credit for his survival. If God truly loved him, there wouldn't have been a fire. He wouldn't be scarred from neck to knee and relive that battle every night in his nightmares.

Silence wedged its way between.

Nicholas ignored the flash of disappointment in Abby's eyes. He stood and grabbed an overshirt from the nightstand. "Enough depressing talk for today. How about we break our fast?"

An overly bright smile spread across her face. She jumped up and began to ramble, words spilling out of her mouth as she smoothed the bed covers. "Wonderful, I'm famished. I despised the late breakfast hour kept in London. I was always starving and had to restrain myself from devouring everything in sight. It's one of the reason's I never felt compelled to attend a London season and one of the many benefits of residing in the country along with—"

"After they believed me killed in action, why didn't you go to London and enjoy the season?" He interrupted. "You love balls and dancing." He moved behind a screen before tugging off his nightshirt and pulling the fresh one over his head.

"For one, I wanted to be near you. Even though you were gone, I felt closer to you being in your house, sleeping in your bed, touching your clothes. You know..." Her words drifted off.

He stepped out from behind the screen and saw her run her hand over his pillow. Her cheeks deepened in color. "I inhaled all the scent out of your clothes."

Nicholas raised an eyebrow. She'd missed him that much?

"Your mother used to always find me standing in your wardrobe, breathing in the cedar fragrance from your shirts. Eventually, your scent faded and disappeared."

"I smell like trees?" He flashed a crooked grin.

She hurled a pillow at him. "Yes, you do."

"And your other reason?"

"London didn't sparkle anymore."

"Sparkle?"

"I still love balls and dancing, but it wouldn't have been the same. I couldn't go without you. The Quality reminded me of beautiful dolls that I'd somehow outgrown. I needed a purpose, something more than the mere frivolity of the *ton*."

He admired her singular devotion. She sacrificed as much for him as he had the crown, but it hadn't been necessary. Once he'd been declared dead, she'd had opportunities—she *still* had options. "But you love the social scene. You took to it as a flame to a candle. People flocked to you as—"

"Only to use me for an introduction to Stephen or to you." She laughed. "*Not* because they wanted to talk to me."

"That's absurd."

She drifted out the door, and he followed.

"It doesn't make sense. The *ton* adored you. Did you not go because of Melinda? She married and stayed in the country, so logically you wanted to remain close to your friends."

They walked into the adjoining room and sat at the dining table. Polly brought a tray with bread and jam and two cups of steaming chocolate.

"Melinda has changed, and we're no longer close. After you disappeared, she found my situation rather awkward. Most of my friends didn't know what to say, so they avoided me."

She slathered butter and raspberry jam on a slice and handed him the plate before making one for herself.

"Thankfully, Katherine met Stephen, and she rescued me from my isolation."

"So that's why you didn't venture to London?"

"I still could have gone. They were newly married, and because of our close friendship, I knew they needed time to settle in."

"So, why didn't you?"

"I told you."

"Right. But it doesn't make sense."

Abby chuckled.

A sound clinked against the window like a pebble hitting the glass.

~

"*W*hat was that?" Abby gripped her dressing robe's collar. Her strange encounter the day before with the ruddy-faced man streaked through her mind. If he had dared to approach her in broad daylight outside the orphanage, what would stop him from following her here? She turned toward the sound.

Nick's expression darkened, and he rose from the table. "Stay here. I'll find out." He marched into the kitchen. She heard the latch of the back door to the courtyard lift, but he hollered before exiting. "Don't move. I'll be right back."

She nodded. The fine hairs on her arms stood on end, and she rubbed them with her hands. Thank God, she wasn't alone. Nick would protect her. But what if the man was armed? She twisted her napkin. Sitting idly by would be her undoing. Flinging her napkin aside, she crept to the window.

She crouched low and peered over the sill.

A young lad stepped out of the shadows, and Abby released

a breath. It wasn't the man who'd attacked her, but neither was it anyone she recognized.

Nick glanced back at the house, and Abby ducked lower.

Her curiosity overrode her guilt, and she peeked again.

The boy passed a letter to Nick.

Was the child a paid messenger? Who else knew Nick was here?

He used his thumb to break the seal, then flipped it open to read. When he was finished, he stuffed the note into his pocket and tossed the boy a coin. In a flash, the child was gone.

Nick glanced around the courtyard once more, then strode back into the house.

Abby scrambled to return to her chair and fumbled to find her napkin. As Nick entered the room, she bit into her bread and jam, trying to appear casual. Swallowing practically without chewing, she asked in a measured tone, "Who was it?"

"It was nothing. A bird must have struck the glass."

Nick lied to her.

She smothered a gasp and fought to keep her face neutral. What was in that note, and who'd sent it? The weight of his secrets pressed in on her like rocks being piled on her body, pushing the air from her lungs and crushing the life out of her.

She opened her mouth to dispute him, but his hazel eyes grew distant.

He'd already withdrawn. Pressing him further would give him cause to leave.

After their talk this morning, she'd believed he was finally letting her into his life again. In one instant, all that had changed.

How could they ever restore their relationship with so many walls between them?

Nick flipped open his watch and pushed his plate aside. "I must change. I have work to do."

She bit into the bread, hoping he wouldn't notice the tears forming in her eyes.

He paused halfway across the room and turned. "My work involves some travel. I may not be back tonight. Don't wait up for me."

Crumbs caught in her throat. Abby coughed and reached for her cup.

Oblivious to her reaction, Nick bounded up the stairs.

She sipped chocolate and continued to nibble at the bread slowly as if the mundane action might somehow bring stability to her shattering world. Would her life ever have a sense of normalcy? Would she ever again know the man she'd been married to for ten years? She heard him descend the stairs, and the front door closed with a thud.

Nick was gone, again, but for how long?

After finishing her toast and jam, she went upstairs to change. As she passed the guest chamber Nick occupied, she paused and peered in.

The scent of cedar lingered in the room. Inhaling a deep breath, the woodsy aroma drew her in.

At any moment, she expected Mama Em to walk in and tease her. A lump formed in her throat. Mama Em never learned Nick was still alive. She died thinking her son had been cheated by life and sent to an early grave. He never came back to tell her otherwise. Mama Em should have had the chance to see her son again.

Where did he go after his injury? Why hadn't he come home?

The injustice of it burned like hot acid in Abby's belly. She spied the jacket he'd been wearing earlier strewn over the bed. The same one she'd watched him stuff the missive into.

She searched his pocket and retrieved the paper.

Her fingers shook as she unfolded it, but whether they shook from anger or from fear, she wasn't certain.

Leaving London now. Meet me at half past seven at the Mad Monk Tavern. I'd like for you to return to France, after you've finished your task.

Melinda's suggestion that he had another family rang in Abby's head, but now her words held an edge of truth, especially after Nick had hesitated in denying her accusations.

He was meeting another woman, the one who'd obviously caused him to forget he was married.

Abby sank onto the thick rug, her legs unable to support her any longer. Her skirt puddled around her. She peered at the ceiling and blinked away tears, resolving to harden her heart.

The scripture Katherine had quoted rang in her head, *If God opens a door no one can shut it.* God brought him back for a reason. She must figure out who she was up against, and the reason why Nick would consider returning to France.

Then she would give him a bigger reason to stay.

CHAPTER 17

*I*n a stunned daze, Abby set about the rest of her day. Even Reverend Cantor's kind words didn't cheer her. Playing with the children distracted her for a time, but she couldn't shake the thick fog of gloom surrounding her.

If Nick had a French wife, what would that mean for her? What if he had children? It was one thing to lose him to death. Another to know he chose another life and was out there living it without her. Bitter bile rose in her throat.

One of the older orphans, Lydia, sat by herself on a fallen log near a clump of trees on the far side of the courtyard. Her head was down, and her hands were stiff by her sides as she drew circles in the dirt with her toe.

Abby wandered over and sat next to her with a deep sigh.

Lydia echoed with a heavy exhale of her own.

"Look at us," Abby said. "We make quite a pair." She glanced at the tree above them. "I wouldn't be surprised if this tree drooped its branches and became a weeping willow merely from being near us."

Lydia's lips twitched, but Abby couldn't coax a smile.

"What has you so Friday-faced?"

Lydia's chin sank deeper into her chest. "I turn four and ten in a month, and when that happens ..." She broke off and wiped away tears with her sleeve.

Abby finished for her. "You will be sent away from the orphanage."

She nodded. "I'll be sent to a workhouse"—her voice cracked—"doomed to crush bones for fertilizer or pick oakum until I die."

"Lydia, do not give up hope." Abby put her arm around the girl's shoulders. "It's scary when we don't know what to expect from our future. One minute it seems bright and full of promise, and the next a dark void. I don't know what to tell you except that thankfully, God is in control. He made the earth and all who are in it, so surely, He can see to your future. We are much more important to God than the birds in the trees, but He makes certain they don't go hungry. So too with the flowers in the fields—they mean less to God than we do, but He dresses them in the best of clothes. Just continue to tell yourself whenever you're afraid, 'I will trust in my Heavenly Father.' You'll be amazed at how God will turn things around."

"Truly?" She looked at Abby through lowered brows. "God would care for an unwanted orphan?"

"He especially has a heart for orphans."

Lydia shrugged. "If you say so, but it's hard not to fret."

"I know." She patted Lydia's arm. "I struggle with worry, too, but my mama always told me, 'God gives us the strength for each day, so don't borrow worry from tomorrow. If we do, we'll exhaust ourselves before it has come.'"

"Then why are you so sad, Lady Abigail?"

"Because sometimes I forget to heed Mama's advice."

"It's hard to believe you struggle with anything."

"Well, believe it. I'm human. I've made plenty of mistakes and shall make plenty more. And not because I intend to."

"Are you sad because you miss your husband still?" Lydia peered at her through eyes too mature for someone so young.

"Yes and no." Should she tell Lydia about Nick? Who would a young orphan mention it to? Perhaps the other girls, but no one who'd report it back to adults. And if they did, it wasn't likely an adult would believe them since Nick refuses to appear in public. Lydia peered at her, waiting, and the pressure to bare all pressed against Abby's breastplate. Abby straightened. "Miraculously, my husband has returned."

Lydia let out a gleeful squeak. "That is splendid news."

"It is, and I'm *very* grateful." Abby closed her eyes to ward off the tears that choked her. "But quite a bit of time has passed. Ten years—almost your entire life—and I'm not certain he loves me anymore."

Abby watched the kids playing in the tall grass of the field, laughing and running carefree.

Lydia jolted upright and exclaimed. "I have it. You must bring him here. We shall tell him what a delightful person you are, and he shall see how good you are with children. Certainly, he must want children. Why else would someone marry?"

Abby chuckled at the girl's innocence.

"He shall fall in love all over again. You must bring him, you must. You'll see. Just leave it to us."

"Lydia, I don't think—"

"It will work. It must work. And in the meantime, you are not to worry. Leave it all in God's hands. And mine." Lydia laughed and stood, eyes sparkling.

Abby didn't want to douse the girl's spirits, especially when she'd repeated Abby's own advice. "I shall try my best, but I can't guarantee he'll come."

"He will. At morning and evening prayer, I'm going to pray for him until he appears. You'll see."

Abby rose and shook out her skirts.

Lydia flung her arms around Abby then ran off to play with her friends.

"I'll be praying, too," Abby whispered.

~

*N*icholas eyed the physician as he packed up his bag and left after his regular visit with Lady Etheridge. The butler opened the door and bid the man good afternoon.

The countless hours each day Nicholas spent secretly questioning each of Lady Etheridge's staff had only led to dead ends. The footman he'd suspected had the day of the poisoning off, and Nicholas confirmed his alibi. He'd been fishing with a friend and caught a memorable trout that day in Lower Slaughter. The friend also confirmed the footman was all bluster—expressing his frustration with little intent to do anything about it. Lady Etheridge's servants may not like her, but not one of them had the backbone or spite to pull off such a stunt. He still had one inquiry out on the housekeeper and had to request Lieutenant Sparks to check into the death of a prior employer. Could the housekeeper be a serial killer? He'd been keeping a close eye on the woman, but if that lead turned into another dead end, then the poisoning had to have been from a source outside of Lady Etheridge's employ.

The physician had moved higher on his list of suspects, especially since he'd visited Lady Etheridge the same morning that her food had been poisoned, and he had access to arsenic. He could have sprinkled the powder on Lady Etheridge's food on his way out. Still, the motive was an issue. Why would the physician want Lady Etheridge or Abby dead? Why did he regularly visit Lady Etheridge when the woman seemed perfectly healthy? Could his wife have put him up to it? He'd always suspected Melinda of being jealous toward Abby, and

Abby had said Melinda had changed. Could her spite have grown to the point of murder?

The clock in the hall chimed the hour, and Nicholas resisted the urge to let out an expletive. His shift had ended some time ago, but he'd wanted to observe the physician's behavior, so he'd lingered.

Unfortunately, now he was late leaving for his rendezvous. He threaded his fingers through his hair and glanced down at the pastel blue livery. There was still enough time to change his clothes before Abby would return from the orphanage, but there would be no time to waste. He didn't want her to question where he was going.

Nicholas pulled open the door and had one foot out when Lady Etheridge's voice bellowed his name. He groaned as he turned back to his employer.

"Have you made any headway with the investigation, Agent Scar?"

She sat in a tufted chair, her back ramrod straight, her hands crossed and resting on her lap.

"I have some leads, my lady."

Her chin lifted even higher in the air than normal. "Oh, who is of interest?"

"There's your housekeeper who was hired before the incident."

"Yes, yes, who else?"

"I'm also inclined to suspect your physician. I'm still waiting to hear back from the department regarding the doctor and maid's histories."

"Doctor Cox?" Her brows rose. "That is preposterous. I give him a small fortune in business. The man would have to close shop if not for me."

The woman held herself in too high of regard if she believed that, but Nicholas bit back his remark.

"What about the Hartington woman?" Lady Etheridge

asked.

"Lady Felton, the dowager countess?"

"Her daughter, Abigail Hartington."

"You mean Abigail Emerson?"

"Yes, yes. She was married for such a short time." Lady Etheridge waved her hand in a dismissive manner. "I barely remember the name change."

"There is nothing suspicious in her background."

"But she has motive. She's jealous. I would like you to put her under closer surveillance."

Nicholas clasped his hands behind his back so she wouldn't notice his fingers twitch, itching to strangle her.

"Jealous?" How ridiculous. He forced his voice to remain calm, but his jaw clenched. Should he make Lady Etheridge a suspect? Maybe she tried to poison Abby and Abby shared her food with the dog. Lady Etheridge could be covering her own tracks by implicating the person she was trying to rid herself of. The woman had certainly been acting suspiciously.

"Her family has an Earldom, and my husband was merely a Viscount. However, her family has remained quiet and secluded whereas the Etheridges have forged themselves to a new level of respect within the community. I have demanded excellence among myself and my children and have gained the esteem and admiration of the people of this small town. I did my moral duty by constantly reminding the poor chit of how she must conduct herself as a lady, but she refused to listen. Now she suffers for it. She especially lost her clout when she married a man of no consequence. Lady Abigail is jealous the Etheridges have usurped her position within society."

Nicholas barely restrained his tongue. The gall of this woman had no end. His carefully held composure cracked like an over-stressed dam, but he forced a neutral tone. "I will look into it. Please excuse me. I have an appointment."

She nodded her dismissal and turned back to some papers

she had laid beside her. Her lips twitched. Was she hiding a smile?

Nicholas's jaw tightened until it pained him. Boiling heat surged through his veins reaching frightfully dangerous levels. He stomped his way back towards Laurel House.

A fallen tree branch blocked his path.

Nicholas snapped it off with a resounding crack, then hurled it through the woods. Its hollow echo filled the forest as it bounced off one tree trunk and then another.

When the house came into view, Nicholas still hadn't fully regained his composure.

Abby shouldn't have returned yet. The last thing he needed was for her to witness his foul mood, slamming doors and muttering under his breath. He certainly didn't want her plaguing him with questions.

He moved quickly, changing into a dark pair of breeches, top boots, driving coat, and cape.

~

A slammed door reverberated throughout Laurel House as Abby entered.

She paused at the side door, muscles taut. She tiptoed into the hall. Her ears strained for sounds.

Nick's baritone voice grumbled upstairs, and she relaxed against the wall. It was merely her husband. The clock read quarter till six.

Was he preparing to meet the mysterious person who'd sent the note? Could he be paying a visit to his secret love or his second family? She squeezed her eyes shut, trying to dismiss the horrid thoughts, but they plagued her.

How long would her doubts torment her? Would her suspicions subside over time? How could she rid herself of this fear?

She felt that there was no place to take shelter from a storm.

Would it ever ease? His secrets were maddening. If she had answers, then maybe she could find peace, even if it meant her undoing.

Abby needed to act. If she discovered whom he was meeting, at least then she would find resolution.

A plan began to form. She would secretly follow him. See for herself. Then she could confront Nick with the facts. Ten years she'd lived with the unknown, but tonight she would have the full truth of it.

CHAPTER 18

*W*afts of unbathed maleness and spilt ale assaulted Nicholas's senses as he stepped into the *Mad Monk* Tavern. The dimly lit room was sparsely filled. A few customers clustered near the bar, and a couple of single individuals slumped over their drinks at the corner tables.

The barkeep let out a boisterous guffaw as a half-sprung man dressed in farmer's clothes enlivened everyone with his tale.

In his enthusiasm, the storyteller missed his stool and crashed onto the dank floor, and ear-splitting laughter filled the air.

Nicholas selected a table in a dark unoccupied corner and sat with his arms crossed over his chest. He scanned the room for Agent Sparks, but it appeared he hadn't yet arrived. The ride should have cooled Nicholas's ire, but Lady Etheridge had pushed him too far.

He wrestled with walking away from the assignment. His presence was only giving her false hope—him too. But it was a matter of time before one of his episodes endangered Abby. Why couldn't she see he must go for her good. He disliked quitting an assignment and going back on his word, but his inquiries hadn't turned up any culprits. If there was one thing war taught him, it was that life required sacrifices. He must sacrifice himself for Abby's future.

Lady Etheridge's staff's loyalty was nothing short of miraculous. Interview after interview, the people in Lady Etheridge's employ often stated she was demanding and strict, but in the next sentence, mentioned how she was understanding—compassionate even. Nicholas, who struggled with controlling his own aversion toward Lady Etheridge, was more bewildered than ever about who would have attempted to poison her.

A bell above the door jingled. A small, cloaked woman entered, her face hidden in the dim tavern light by the shadow of her hood. With hurried steps, she crossed the room and occupied a table next to an individual drooped over his tankard of ale.

The man lifted his head, and a slow smile spread across his face.

She must have uttered something because the man straightened and leaned towards her.

Nicholas shook his head. This was not a place for a woman. He felt sorry for such a soul, one whose lot in life had brought her to visit places as seedy as this.

The bell jingled again. Nicholas recognized the large build of the lieutenant, and the man's loud hacking cough confirmed his identity. Making eye contact, Nicholas nodded.

Sparks weaved through the maze of tables and sunk into the chair across from Nicholas.

Nicholas leaned forward. "I hope you have some information for me."

"The files on the housekeeper and physician. Not much there. I do have something new developing with another case I'd like to share. I was hoping to convince you to take on one more project, but it's in France."

The lieutenant's eyes darted to the left, and he leaned in closer to Nicholas. "Before we start"—his gaze leveled with Nicholas's own—"did you know you were followed?"

Nicholas's jaw clenched. "Who?" His gaze traced the direction of the lieutenant's glance.

"The woman being harassed by the elbow crooker already in his cups. I think you'll recognize her."

His eyes snapped to the hooded woman.

She drew her cloak tighter around her face and leaned farther from the inebriated man.

The man scooted closer and reached for her hood, but she turned away, scooting to the edge of her seat.

Heavens above. It was Abby. It had to be.

He honed in on the man who dared touch his wife. Nicholas stood, his chair clattered to the floor. In two strides, he closed the distance between them.

The besotted man was about to place his greasy fingers on her when Nicholas grabbed him by the collar and hauled him out of his seat.

With a growl, Nicholas shoved him away, rolling him over a table. The crack of splitting wood rang through the tavern.

Abby screamed, and the sound drew the attention of the barkeep and the other foxed patrons.

The inebriated man stumbled to regain his balance, toppling chairs in his attempt to stand. He released a stream of profanities as he struggled to rise.

Lieutenant Sparks moved to Nicholas's side as the men at the bar slid off their stools, their angry faces eager to fight.

"Get her out of here." Nicholas thrust Abby in the lieutenant's direction.

Sparks heaved her over his shoulder and bounded for the exit.

*E*mbarrassed by her unladylike position and determined to stay and help Nick, Abby struggled to get down, but Nick's friend's hold was firm.

Someone grabbed her cloak from behind.

She screamed, and her captor turned and elbowed a bearded man in the nose with a sickening smack. Her cloak flopped back down, but not before she caught a flash of the blood that poured over the man's lips and into his beard. She needed to find Nick. She twisted her body and pushed up with her hands to get a glimpse of the fighting.

Nick stood alone, feet braced, as an angry mob approached him from all sides.

The sight was enough to suck the wind out of her lungs. "They're going to kill him!" She struggled all the harder.

"Quiet down before you get yourself hurt." The stranger bolted outside into the cool night air.

"We have to go back. We have to help him." Desperation rang in her voice.

The stranger kept moving until they reached the horses. Dusk illuminated the sky in a orange-yellow glow. He tossed Abby unceremoniously into Duchess's saddle and grabbed the reins.

Abby attempted to jump down, but the man detained her with one hand.

"I have to help him. He's my husband. Please, let me go."

"You will only make matters worse. Stay still, or you'll spook the horse."

Abby's gaze darted to the horse's ears and face. The man couldn't have said anything more effective. She held a healthy fear of horses. Did he know that about her? Who was this man?

Abby gritted her teeth and fixed her eyes on the stranger. She was livid at him for not aiding Nick and furious with herself for letting her fears get in the way. She stared the man squarely in the eyes, strengthening her resolve. "I demand that you take me back to the tavern, or else I will scream at the top of my lungs until everyone for miles around comes running."

The man shifted to scan up and down the road in each direction.

There were no nearby cottages, no farms, not a single lantern light from a window in any direction.

Abby swallowed and tried to squelch the sickening feeling of despair.

"Please," she begged him. "Please help him. I can't lose him again."

The stranger dropped his gaze to the grass. He let out a long sigh before he met her gaze. "Scar can handle himself just fine."

How insensitive to call Nick that. She knew from experience with her own brother that men often jested about things women would take issue with. It was done in good fun, but Abby burned to defend her husband's name.

The man eyed the tavern. "You must let him go and handle things his way. He will do better on his own. You'll just be a liability."

Abby blinked twice and stared at the stranger. A distant voice from the past echoed in her memory. *You must let your husband go and pray that God will return him to you.* Ten years ago, a man dressed in all black, a younger version of the man standing in front of her, had come to collect her husband and take him off to war.

Abby's voice shook as she whispered, "You—it's you." She slid down from her horse. "You're with his Majesty's army. You took my husband off to war."

Abby gasped as a new revelation struck her. "Nicholas is still working for you. He's still enlisted. Isn't he?"

The man pushed back a step.

They wouldn't let me contact you, Nick had said.

Her vision blurred with rage. She stepped toward the stranger and poked one finger against his chest.

"You don't want me to see my husband? You don't want me communicating with him?" She moved her hands to hips. "He's still working for you? Isn't he?"

The man crossed his arms. "I provide opportunities for the crown, but he agrees to the missions."

Abby's world spun, and she feared she might faint. Just as quickly as the feeling came, it passed, and everything came into focus. Nick was a spy. Her husband has been part of the crown's cloak-and-dagger operations.

He never meant to be discovered. He never meant to come back. Her mind rang with accusations, each one a nail driven into her heart. *He never planned to stay with me.*

She closed her eyes against the pain. Her hopes of happily-ever-were snuffed out as easily as if the man had licked his fingers and pinched a candlewick.

Abby's skin flushed with heat. She grabbed the strange man by the wrist, and with a strength she didn't know she possessed, yanked him in the direction of the tavern.

"You are going to help me save my husband so that *I* can kill him!"

~

Something moved in Nicholas's periphery, but there wasn't enough time for him to react. His hands were occupied by a bearded man who didn't know when to stop swinging.

Another man barreled in his direction.

Nicholas ducked to the left, but not far enough. The man's head crashed into the wall, but not before his shoulder bumped Nicholas's jaw.

The man sagged, crumpling to the floor. The impact had knocked him unconscious.

The metallic tang of blood seeped into Nicholas's mouth, and he wiped his jaw, holding back a snarl. Red smeared the back of his hand. Blasted man split his lip.

From behind the bar, the barkeep defended his liquor supply.

The other men were a blur of activity. Punches flew. Chairs were smashed. Some men shouted angry slurs, others groaned in pain. In the chaos, Nicholas was forgotten.

He'd been in bigger skirmishes than this with even worse odds. The key difference here was that the drunkards didn't particularly care whom they fought. A few dodged punches and a couple fakes to the left, and chaos ensued. They turned on each other like animals.

The paperwork Sparks had brought Nicholas lay on the floor. He scooped it up and slipped out the back door to seek the lieutenant and Abby. Poor Abby. She was probably shaking in fear and begging to be escorted home.

Nicholas rounded the corner and stopped short. He should have known better. She stood halfway between the stables and the tavern, her jaw set in a hard line and her eyes blazing.

She dragged the lieutenant behind her like an errant child.

An unexplainable wave of pride washed over him.

Rosy cheeks contrasted against her alabaster skin, and her eyes flashed a deep sapphire blue. Her hood rested on her shoulders, revealing the mass of glossy hair blowing behind her and carelessly tumbling down her back. When she spotted him, she paused and yanked on the lieutenant with renewed vigor.

Nicholas's lips twitched with laughter.

Sparks, the hulking man who been his superior for ten years, who intimidated recruits and was known for scattering

French forces with one quelling look, appeared confused and contrite as this slender beauty hauled him forward.

Nicholas forced his feet to keep moving toward them, despite the notion that he might be safer inside the tavern.

"Nicholas Emerson, you're a spy!" Abby's accusation pierced through the air like an arrow intent upon its target.

Ten years he'd kept his secret even through the toughest of interrogations. How did she know? Nicholas hid his surprise as his gaze flicked to Sparks.

"We will discuss this later, Abigail." Nicholas leveled his eyes on hers, compelling her into silence.

She wasn't deterred. "When were you going to tell me?" Abby stepped closer until her head tipped back to peer up at him. Hands on her hips, the edge in her voice demanded answers. "Or were you planning on disappearing again without a trace?"

Nicholas pushed his words through clenched teeth. "This isn't a good time." A loud crash against the exterior tavern wall emphasized his point.

She opened her mouth, but Nicholas grabbed her by the elbow and hauled her against his side.

He half carried her back toward the horses, her legs running to keep up with his long strides. The sun dipped below the horizon. He needed to get Abby to safety before darkness fell. Bandits, highwaymen, and thieves prowled the roads at night. Nicholas's leg pained him, but it didn't slow him down. He hoisted Abby into the saddle, then he and the lieutenant mounted their horses. Nicholas took the lead, and Sparks flanked Abby. They spured their horses to a gallop, leaving the tavern far behind.

They only made it ten minutes up the road before the sky turned from pink to purple to dark indigo. Nicholas signaled for them to slow the pace, and Sparks reined up next to Nicholas.

"Even though we only have less than an hour's ride ahead of us," Nicholas said, "this road is too dangerous at night for a lady. I don't want to risk it."

He pointed left, where a small dirt path led deep into the woods. "There's a cabin about two hundred yards that way. It's neglected and rustic, but it's safe. We can settle there for the night and ride out at first light." He nodded to the lieutenant. "Are you headed back or staying with us?"

"We still have business to attend to."

Nicholas nodded, and the trio filed down the overgrown path.

~

Rustic was a kind way of phrasing it. Abby slowed her mount as she approached the dwelling. A tree had grown into what remained of the moss-covered wooden shingled roof. The front door was off its hinges, lying flat in the overgrown weeds. Fireflies glowed within the dense brush, and the crickets' chirps seemed almost deafening. Moisture hung in the night air and dampened her skirts, causing her petticoats to cling to her legs. With the sun now set, a cool breeze sent a shiver across Abby's skin.

Nick dismounted and tied his horse's reins to a nearby branch. He eyed the cabin and then Abby. "Stay here," he commanded with a stern look.

Abby wasn't about to oppose him. A shudder ran through her at the thought of what might be residing in the abandoned shell of a home. She itched to get off her mount—needing to walk, to pace and think things through. The ride had subdued her anger but hadn't quenched it. There were answers she needed to hear from Nick, but shelter for the night took priority.

The lieutenant hopped down and collected wood for a fire.

Nick tore a strip of the lining from his cloak and wrapped it around a large stick to create a makeshift torch. He pulled a flint rock out of his pocket, ignited some kindling he'd gathered, and lit the end of the torch. The flickering light cast eerie shadows across the rickety siding. He entered the house with caution, holding the torch in front and stomping his feet to scare off any critters. After a few moments, he reappeared and assisted Abby out of the saddle.

She kept her hands clasped together in front of her so Nick couldn't see them tremble. Her nerves were frayed. The spooky appearance of the dilapidated cabin, with its unknown residents, didn't help matters.

The smell of wet moss and rotting wood combined with the smoke of the fire Nick had started inside the stone hearth. Lieutenant Sparks carried in firewood, and soon a cheery blaze lit the dank space.

Additional light helped to calm her imagination, and the cabin now resembled more of a home than a bear cave. Abby settled in front of the fire to offset the chill.

The lieutenant followed her lead.

Nick brought in his pack and a couple of blankets from off the horses to use for bedding. Afterward, he pulled the front door out of the weeds and propped it up in the entranceway to keep out critters. Once he'd seen to everything, he crouched down near the fire opposite Abby. For a long moment, he stared into the mesmeric flames.

Abby studied his taut face and the deep crease between his brows. It still felt surreal to know he was alive and next to her.

He still resembled the man she'd fallen in love with, but now a savage ruggedness hardened his features. War had stolen his youth and robbed him of the twinkle in his eyes. In the firelight, he looked dangerous and unpredictable.

Abby lifted her chin. No more secrets. No more disillusionment. She wasn't going to waste another minute hoping their lives could pick up where they'd left off when that had never been his intention. She wasn't going to leave until she had answers. Even if the outcome crushed her. She'd survived devastation before.

As if he'd known she was about to strike, Nick rose and took the offensive. "What in the devil were you thinking, following me?" He faced her. His eyes reflected the flames as they pierced her own. "Do you have no regard for your own life?"

Yes, she may have been foolish in following him, but he wasn't going to turn this around on her. She leveled him with her own glare. "I have no regard for carefully kept secrets. How long were you going to keep your double life from me? Am I supposed to lie around thinking everything is sunshine and roses when you keep an entire alternate life hidden from me?"

Her voice cracked, and she fought against the tears clogging her throat. "I followed you because I believed you were meeting another woman."

"That's ludicrous."

"What else could I have thought, when you took so long in answering such a simple question? What was there to consider?" She crossed her arms over her chest. "*Do* you have another family?"

"No!" Nicholas's bellowed answer reverberated off the cramped cabin walls. His eyes flicked to the lieutenant, who stoked the fire as if it was his sole purpose in life.

Abby had grown tired of excuses. The truth must come out. Tonight. She lifted her chin higher. "You know, for a moment, I was actually relieved to discover you were a spy."

"I'm contracted by the Home Office for specialized intelligence-gathering missions."

"You're a spy."

"I don't need this right now, Abby." Nick stared into the fire and dragged his fingers through his thick hair.

She continued to watch him, using silence to demand the truth.

He let out an exasperated sigh. "Very well, I'm a spy. The lieutenant is my liaison. He can confirm I have no other family." Cynicism tinged his voice. "Since my word isn't enough."

A single nod from the lieutenant verified Nick's statement. Once again a hush fell over the room, interrupted only by the popping and hissing of the fire.

Lieutenant Spark's gaze shifted between her and Nick before he slowly stood, faking a yawn. "It's been a trying day. I'm going to turn in for the night."

Abby followed him with her gaze and used it as a chance to blink away tears.

Lieutenant Sparks grabbed a blanket from his saddlebag and curled up in the farthest corner facing the wall.

Nick snapped a twig in his hands and threw it into the flames one piece at a time. The fire crackled in response.

"You never meant to come back home, did you?" Abby demanded in a hoarse whisper. "I discovered you by accident. You planned to sneak back in to grab your bow and arrows while I slept."

"Don't do this, Abby."

Abby stood. "I waited for you for ten years. I prayed and prayed and prayed until I thought God had forgotten me, but you were alive."

Her arms hugged her midsection. "Did you ever plan on telling me?"

Silence screamed between them.

She shook her head. "No, of course not. That's why you suggested I remarry. You wanted to continue to play dead so you could spy for the crown."

The truth tightened her chest making it hard to breathe. "You would prefer that life over being with me."

"I wanted you to remarry," he hissed in a rough whisper, "so you could have a chance at happiness."

Abby crouched beside him, her tone lethal. "I'm already married."

"That is of no consequence. I'm not the boy you wed. I was giving you an out."

"I never wanted an out. I wanted you. I wanted a life and a family of our own. You never gave our marriage a chance."

"Don't turn this around on me," he roared. Nick's gaze flicked to the lieutenant's still form who could only be pretending to sleep amid the noise and lowered his voice. "Everything I did was for you."

"What do you think you did? Save me from heartache? My heart shattered into a million pieces ten years ago."

His hands were clenched into tight fists. "You've made up your mind. I'm a scoundrel. I can't reason with you if you're not going to listen."

"So, you're not even going to try? Am I so easy to give up on?" Hot tears flowed down her cheeks.

Nick chucked a large stick into the fire and stood. "I have to go." In three long strides, he stalked to the exit. The wooden door crashed into the weeds as he departed, leaving a gaping hole.

CHAPTER 19

A sob tore from Abby's throat. Nick didn't care enough about their marriage to fight for it. He didn't care enough about her to stay. That thought cut through her like a cavalry saber down to the very marrow.

Lord, what am I going to do? Nick doesn't love me. Maybe he never loved me. I always believed my love would get us through. My love could bring him back from the dead. My life's been a big lie. She buried her face in her hands and sank to her knees.

She kneeled hunched over in the center of the dilapidated old house, and her tears splashed on the weathered floorboards. Nick left her. She was alone in an abandoned cabin with a strange man. Nick may never come back. She may never see him again. It was too much to bear.

No. She couldn't lose him again. She needed to try harder to make him love her.

She jumped up and raced out of the cabin. Her damp skirts slowed her steps, but she didn't stumble. She would find him, make him see reason. She would fight for her marriage.

A horse whinnied, and she peered through her tear-drenched lashes to see Nick mounting his stallion. He glanced over his shoulder, and their eyes locked. Abby held her breath, but Nick snapped the reins. His horse sprinted down the overgrown path.

"Wait."

He held a hand up warding her off, and his pace never slowed.

Abby ran to Duchess and fumbled with untying the reins from the tree branch. Once she'd freed her horse, she searched frantically for a step up to mount the mare, but it was difficult to see in the darkness.

There was nothing, not even a low-lying branch or tree log. She attempted to pull herself up with her arms, but Duchess's back was a good hand above Abby's chest. What could she use to stand on? Yanking the reins, she pulled Duchess down the path until she finally found a broken branch to leverage herself into the saddle. She dug in with all her might, and Duchess darted down the lane.

At the main road, Abby searched up and down, but there was no sign of Nick. She cantered a few yards in each direction, circling to find any indicator for which route he'd taken. Nothing.

Nick's words from earlier sounded a warning in her head. *These roads are unsafe at night for a woman.*

"God, please help me." The words were a broken whisper she repeated over and over. Her body ached as if physically ill. She stayed in the middle of the moonlit road for a prolonged moment, knowing her only option was to turn back. The stillness of the night seemed to stretch out in all directions. It was then that a still small voice spoke to her.

My love is patient, it is kind, it doesn't keep record of wrongs...and it never fails.

Abby sucked in a breath. She hadn't shown Nick patience. Instead, she'd thrown his wrongs back in his face. "But God," she cried, "his secrets continue to tear us apart."

Do you want to be right, or do you want him? The words were spoken into her heart. Moisture filled her eyes, but these tears were different. They were tears of gratitude. He'd heard her plea. Once again, she had jumped to conclusions. She hadn't prayed for God's direction, and things had gone poorly, but God had been patient with her misdeeds, and now she needed to be patient with Nick. She might have messed things up, but she wasn't alone. God loved her, and His love didn't fail. He had a plan, and He was in control.

"God," she whispered into the night air, "change my heart. Grow me to be a better wife. Bring Nick back. I prayed for the physical, but now I'm asking for You to bring him back entirely—mentally, emotionally, spiritually. Shine your light on all the dark secrets and wipe them away. Only you can reach him."

She stared up into the night sky. All the stars had been placed there by God. He'd painted them with broad brush strokes. If He could make the earth, sun, and moon and still take a moment to give her a word of encouragement, then God would get her through this. Her life and her marriage were in His hands.

She closed her eyes. Her heart still ached, but the warmth of God's presence spread through her bones. The only reason she remained upright was because He was there beside her. She would lean on Him. With a flick of the reins, she headed back to the cabin.

~

*N*icholas flew down the road not caring where he went. He needed to get away, to reason things through. He couldn't think while Abby hurled accusations at him. Was he really a wretched scoundrel? All he wanted was for Abby to be safe, but her words rang with truth when she said all he'd done was break her heart. That had never been his intent. He'd wanted to give her the world, but he'd failed.

He slowed his horse to a walk and sunk his hand into his hair.

Why did everything go so wrong? He'd merely wanted to do the right thing. He was trying to save Abby the embarrassment of having a madman for a husband and from the sadness his mother had carried with her, pining away for the life she could no longer have among the *haute ton* after marrying a country gent. More times than he could count he had come home to find his mother tucked away in her room reading letters from family members about all the wonderful balls she would no longer attend.

The memories surfaced before he could push them away.

"Nicholas, is that you?" his mother called from above.

He winced, having woken her up. A golden glow fanned out from under the crack of her bedroom door. He gently pushed it open.

Candlelight flooded the far corner of the room, where she sat behind her writing desk in her dressing robe. Her graying hair peeked out from beneath the ruffles of her nightcap. Her reading glasses perched on the bridge of her nose. She peered through her spectacles, down her arm, to the letter held in her hand.

Nicholas folded his arms and leaned against the door frame. "Who's the letter from now?"

"Oh, Cousin Margaret." She wiped a stray tear from the corner of her eye with her knuckle. "She loves to keep me abreast of all the latest family happenings and gossip from the *ton*." Her voice held a wistful note.

She set the letter aside. "Tell me about the party? Who was there? Who did you dance with? What did they wear?"

He chuckled at her questions. "It was pretty much the same people doing the same old things."

Her eyes filled with exasperation. She wanted every detail, but it was late. Other than a few small local parties, it had become too awkward for her to try to run in the same circles she used to before she married his father, a poor estate manager. The *ton* wasn't an accepting lot, especially for those who married beneath them. Too often, Nicholas watched his mother's expression of excitement quickly change to sadness when she heard of a grand ball or some social soiree.

"You could have come. I obtained an invitation for you."

"No, no. I had my day, and I wouldn't trade the time I had with your father for anything. I merely wanted to hear how you enjoyed yourself." She pretended to be happy, as if it didn't matter, but Nicholas knew she felt the weight of being an interloper, part of the crowd, but not completely accepted.

"Did you have a good time, darling?"

"I, uh ..." Nicholas fought for the right word. He didn't want to worry his mother with his problems. "It was ... ah ... unbelievable." He smiled a crooked grin.

"Oh, splendid."

Leaning over, he placed a kiss on the top of her head. "I'm exhausted. I'll tell you all about it tomorrow."

Nicholas lay in bed, but sleep had eluded him. Images of his mother living her life through letters haunted him. He loved Abby, but how could he put her through the same thing? She was the daughter of an earl, and he was untitled, but that didn't change his feelings. True, he wasn't a poor shop owner. He'd worked hard to better himself and establish his wealth, but was it enough?

As viscounts and barons had attempted to woo Abby during the party, he'd found himself hawking her even more than her own brother.

He'd tried to convince himself Abby wouldn't care that he didn't hold a title or that his family tree didn't measure up. Their love would conquer the impediments, especially since he'd returned from Eton. Perhaps he could impress her with his suave sophistication, maybe then ... *Maybe then?* Nothing would have changed. He didn't hold, and would never hold, a title.

He tossed and turned in bed, unable to shake the hopeless feeling, before giving up and staring wide-eyed into the darkness. *God,* he cried, *what can I do?*

A Bible verse he'd read earlier ran through his mind: Psalm 27:14. *"Wait on the Lord: be of good courage, and he shall strengthen thine heart."*

Nicholas rolled onto his back and squeezed his eyes shut. *Wait.* It seemed impossible. He needed God's help now. Waiting wasn't going to get him Abby. Some other dandy would come along, and Abby would be even further out of his reach. Thoughts stormed his mind, rumbling like thunder until he couldn't bear it anymore.

An idea struck him. He threw the covers off and sprang out of bed. *Major Ruggles.* They'd met in London and instantly established a rapport. The man was well connected and had an answer for everything. He'd pay his old friend a visit. If there were a way, Major Ruggles could find it. Lying in bed and sulking wouldn't get Nicholas anywhere. He needed to fight for Abby and for his dreams.

He'd been so naive back then. Look where his fighting had landed him. His enlistment with the War Department nearly destroyed him. He'd fought bravely and used his intelligence to achieve his goal, but at a high cost. Now, what good were his achievements? Officially he was a viscount with land and a respectable income, but he'd lost Abby, the only person he wanted to please.

The handsome, fun-loving man she had married died in France, replaced with a marred, cynical shell. His soul cried out to show her all his scars. Tell her of his experiences so she'd know the horror of it all, the monster she was bound to on earth. Then he could beg and plead for her to love him despite his broken mind and body. He'd dared to let hope flare when she'd stayed even after witnessing his nightmares, but when would she no longer be able to stand the torment? Even if she could manage that, the isolation of being married to a social outcast would eventually cause her to despise him. He squeezed his eyes closed and leaned his head into his horse's mane.

And what if he hurt her? What about the times he'd awoken with a gun in his fingers or gripped her so tightly he'd bruised her arms?

Fear kept him from throwing himself at her feet, pride from begging forgiveness. He'd prefer to be alone than be rejected. His greatest dread was that he'd frighten her away.

Alone and untouchable.

He'd had an assignment in India and witnessed firsthand their caste system. The untouchables were the lowest of the low, a class of degraded people who weren't allowed to even cast their shadows near the upper classes. Their plight had struck a chord with Nicholas.

Britain had its own caste system, even though it might not appear as ridged as India's. Nicholas knew his place. Despite his title and land, he would never be accepted in the upper crust. As a young man, he'd already bent the rules in an attempt to force himself into their ranks, but they would never accept him now. They would scoff, if not to his face then, even worse, behind his back. He wasn't sure he could bear it. Not while Abby stood by, trying hard to keep a cheerful demeanor. Society would reject her, too, because of him.

He hadn't realized how much he craved human touch until he had become like an untouchable. Handshakes, loving caresses, intimate touches—they had been a thing of the distant past. People didn't casually touch him anymore. Now they shrink away in fear.

He cherished the memory of Abby absently drawing circles with her finger on his palm. It used to drive him wild with desire. A deep sadness reverberated through him like an echo down an empty well. He may never again feel Abby touch him out of love.

Nicholas tilted his face toward the night sky. He could still feel her embrace. When he'd appeared in her kitchen, she'd thrown herself into his arms. He would have to live off that memory, to cherish the feeling of her smooth skin against his cheek, her soft lips moving on his. That was before she saw the traces of his scars above his collar. She'd hadn't touched him since witnessing his last nightmare, and he couldn't blame her after he'd gripped her tight enough to leave a mark.

As much as he wanted her, leaving was the right thing. He had to protect her from himself. Nicholas sighed and sagged in the saddle. His head pounded to the same throbbing rhythm of his pained leg. His energy was all but sapped.

He never should have come back. He turned his horse and headed toward the cabin. Questions pressed in on him from all sides. What was he to do? How could he stay when he was a danger to her? But how could he leave her alone? Because of his return—now that she knows he's alive—she no longer could marry and have children. He'd ruined not only his life but now hers. She'd be forced to live her life alone, suffering his same fate of isolation, and he'd have to live with that guilt forever.

～

*A*bby awoke to Nick's groan from the pallet on the opposite side of the fireplace. The reddish embers cast the room with a faint glow.

Another nightmare? How could he withstand this torture every night?

Lieutenant Sparks jolted awake and fumbled his hands along the floorboards and under his makeshift pillow. He leapt into a fighting stance as if still ready for battle. His head shifted, turning toward the sound in the dark room. "Who goes there?"

Nick's eerie growl sounded again, loud and low, with a desperate edge to it.

In the dim light of the dwindling fire, Abby saw a flash of polished steel in the lieutenant's hands.

Nick rustled a few feet away, and the lieutenant pointed the object in his direction. Lieutenant Spark's hand shook, and he raised his other to steady it.

Abby snapped out of the haze of sleep.

A gun!

"No, lieutenant!" Abby darted in Nick's direction, blocking his body with her own.

"Get back, madame, before it attacks. I'm going to shoot it dead."

Abby waved her hands. "It's Nicholas. He's having a nightmare."

The haggard shadows in the lieutenant's face softened. His arms sagged, and he lowered the gun, exhaling a whoosh of air. "Lud, I thought some wild beast was attacking."

Nick thrashed, flailing his arms and legs.

"Should we wake him?"

She shook her head. "It's best to let him sleep."

"There must be something we can do for the poor bloke."

Abby peered at Nick's stiff form and untied the ribbon holding back her hair, letting it spill over him. Was he battling ghosts or flames? "We can pray."

A strangled laugh escaped the lieutenant's lip, but he covered it by clearing his throat. "Of course." He followed her lead, folding his hands and bowing his head.

She waited to see if he might begin the prayer..

He shifted on his knees before whispering, "Please, do me the honor."

"Dear Father." Abby began the prayer and mentally asked God to forgive her for her dual intensions. "Please take away the fear and pain Nicholas is feeling."

Nick let out a whimper, but turned toward her hair, pressing it to his face with his hand and began to settle.

"Help him to feel the peace of Your presence. Release Nicholas from the past that continues to haunt him and deliver him from the demons that plague him night and day. Your word says that we can boldly approach Your throne and, God, we come before You, asking for grace for Nicholas. Strengthen his being and subdue his thoughts and dreams. He has been through so much. Offer him the safe haven of Your peace that surpasses all understanding. Father, pull him through this trial and leave him with a stronger faith for it. Amen."

"Amen." Lieutenant Sparks pulled at his collar and stared at Nick. He'd quieted. "Are his dreams always this bad?"

Abby nodded. "Most nights."

"I didn't know. Scar always seemed so collected and in control. I never would have suspected nightmares tormented him." The lieutenant swallowed hard.

"I convinced him to stay on with the Home Office even after he was injured, but he never complained. He remained on long after his enlistment was over."

Sparks shook his head. "I should have known, watched for the signs. I shouldn't have begged him to complete one more assignment, then another, then another."

He tucked his gun into the buckle of his pants. "The average length of service for a foreign intelligence gatherer is two years. Scar served five years with the Foreign Office and another five with the Home Office, with no sabbaticals and very few days off. He's the best in his field. He performed his duty to the crown better and faster than any of his contemporaries, but the strain has obviously taken its toll. I had no idea he'd been affected like this. He hid it well."

Abby narrowed her gaze. "Why do you call him that?"

"What? Scar?"

"It's rather cruel, don't you think?"

"It's fitting. He didn't get the nickname for the burns on his body. His nickname was awarded because of his holdings."

"Oh. I see." Abby had no idea what the lieutenant was talking about. Nick had no holdings other than Laurel House.

But he'd joined the service to earn a title, one she'd never cared about. Apparently, he'd succeeded.

"So Scar is short for...?"

"Scarcliffe, after his land holdings, of course. He received the title, Earl of Scarcliffe, for the special services he rendered to his King. Our troops might not have defeated Napoleon at Waterloo if he hadn't obtained crucial information. If not for Scar, we might be speaking French right now."

"I didn't realize. He doesn't talk much about it."

The lieutenant's brow furrowed. "It sounds like he hasn't spoken of it at all."

She shook her head and lowered her gaze. These were things a wife would know, but she was learning Nick was a man of full of secrets. Her heart clenched. Nick had gotten the title he's sought after, but at a terrible cost. Had it been worth it? "You told me once that I needed to let my husband go and pray that God would return him." The air quivered as she inhaled a shaky breath. "God has brought him back."

She stomped a foot stirring up dust from off the dirt covered floorboard. "Now, lieutenant, I must ask that *you* let him go."

"He told me this would be his last assignment, but I didn't believe it. I figured I could convince him to keep at it. I already told the King I'd put his best man back in France, but now...."

He turned back toward his makeshift pallet. "Scar's one of

my best men, and he's needed by the crown. I must think on it."
He lay back down. Pulling the thick wool blanket over his
shoulder, he turned and faced the wall.

Abby curled up closer to Nick so she could sooth him with
her hair in case he had another nightmare. Lieutenant Sparks
could go ahead and think on it. She would pray on it.

~

*A*bby awoke the next morning to the sound of horse
hooves galloping away.

Was Nick leaving? Disappearing once again, this time
forever? She flung back the rough horse blanket she'd used as
covers and raced to the front entrance, where the propped door
had been slid aside. The horse and rider turned onto the main
road out of sight.

"He said to give you his regards."

Abby Jumped. *Nick. Thank God.*

"He told me to apologize for not bidding you a proper
farewell. He needed to get back to his duties. As do I."

What did that mean? She paused to get her emotions under
control before turning.

Nick stood in front of the fire. He appeared lost in thought,
his expression subdued.

She set about folding her cloak and the horse blanket to
keep her hands occupied. Occasionally, she glanced at Nick.
What were his plans? Had he made up his mind to stay?

The events of last night changed her view. Abby had been
expecting Nick to be the carefree husband of her past. She tried
to force a mature man, one who'd spent ten years as a spy, into
aligning with her prior newlywed expectations. Now, she
acknowledged the permanent changes in him.

His playful boyishness had been replaced with a focused
intentionality. Even as he lounged by the fire, he exuded power,

like a panther who casually flicked its tail before suddenly pouncing on its prey.

Her heart fluttered, but was it a result of a new healthy respect of her husband, or fear of the unknown?

They rode back to Laurel House in silence. After dismounting, Barnsby took the reins and stabled the horses while Nick and Abby filed into the house.

A hundred questions plagued her. She concentrated on not blurting them all out at once, so much so that she tripped over the threshold.

Nick grabbed her hand and slid an arm around her waist.

Her breath caught at the dizzying current that raced through her. Flashbacks of Nick's passionate kisses filled her senses. She trembled, and it took all her willpower not to throw herself into his arms. Needing a clear head, she jumped back and yanked her fingers from his grasp.

A shadow passed over his face, and his eyes darkened. He fisted his hand.

Something was wrong.

She cleared her throat. "We have a lot to discuss."

"I have business I must attend to." He spoke through a tight jaw.

"Can't it wait? We have been through an ordeal. I need to know where you and I stand."

"Nothing has changed, Abby."

"Everything has changed." Her voice pitched two octaves higher than she'd intended. She sucked in a deep breath. "I need to know what our future holds."

The ice in his gaze chilled her more than a winter wind. "It's simple. I continue being a spy, and you continue being a widow unless you decide to marry some poor bloke whose touch you *can* abide."

"What?" Abby couldn't hide her confusion. "That's absurd."

He put one hand against the wall and leaned in until their

faces were within inches. "It. Was. A. Mistake." The muscles in his jaw twitched. "We should never have married. Fortunately for you, the crown considers me dead, and be thankful, darling, because it's your ticket to freedom, away from a loveless marriage to a crazed man."

With that, he pushed off the wall and turned on his heel. The door slammed behind him.

The shock hit Abby like a strike to the face.

CHAPTER 20

*T*ears rolled off Abby's chin as she climbed Willowstone Manor's front steps. She paused to wipe her face and rub the water stains from the bodice of her day dress before knocking.

Weston, the butler, opened the front door and ushered her in. He whisked his crisp white handkerchief out of his front pocket and passed it to her. Lines of concern creased his brow. "Lady Felton is in the breakfast room, and Lady Katherine took Master Benjamin to the stream to sail his new toy boat. Would you like me to send someone for them?"

"I'll show myself to the breakfast room."

Abby's mother sat at the table still laden with plates of pastries. Her Bible stood open, and she traced the lines she read with her finger.

A fresh wave of tears burned the back of Abby's eyes at the familiar sight and the vacant chair next to the window that her papa used to occupy. Mama peered up from her Bible. "Why, Abby." She closed the Bible and stood. "It's about time you visited. I've been dying to know how your re-acquaintance with Nicholas is ..."

She broke off as Abby moved closer. "Oh, darling. Something is wrong. Come here, dear."

Abby dove into her mother's embrace and held on tightly to her soft, warm frame. As her mother stroked her back, Abby released a torrent of tears.

"There, there, darling. There were bound to be a few hiccups. If you count the days you've spent together, you're still a newly married couple. Being a husband and wife takes some getting used to."

Abby snorted at the understatement. She wiped her eyes and blew her nose. "But what if it was a mistake? What if I married the wrong person? I don't think Nicholas loves me anymore."

"Pshaw." Mama pushed a chair out for Abby and sat across from her. She clasped Abby's hands. "My dear, marriage isn't an emotional thing. People don't merely fall in and out of love. You make a decision to love, for better or worse. Sometimes you have to make that decision daily—sometimes it's hourly. I can tell you, with your father and me, it got easier over time, but there were days when I wanted to give up on that man. Especially after his accident. The pain turned him wretched."

Her brother had told about when their father had tried to save his sister-in-law from taking her own life and instead fell twenty feet off a cliff onto a ledge, injuring his leg so he barely could walk. He remained in constant pain for years until the Lord took him home.

"He didn't like having to depend on me," her mother continued. "But we got through it because we made a decision to love each other, and we were committed to that love."

In those days, her papa *had* been awful at times, but she had never guessed Mama was suffering too. She'd served her husband without complaint or hesitation.

"What got me though was God's word. It says specifically, *Love bears all things, believes all things, hopes all things, endures all things. Love never fails.* I didn't merely marry your father. I made a covenant to love him, like the covenant God made with us. God brought you and Nicholas together. The problem is that the right person can seem wrong when life throws change your way. Circumstances can make love seem hard."

Her mother heaved a heavy sigh, but a soft smile tugged the corners of her lips. "After your father and I had you and your brother, we didn't get much sleep even with a nursemaid. Because we'd waited so long for the blessing of children, we didn't want to merely pass you both off to your nurse, but twins are hard work. We wore ourselves out keeping up with the two of you. I remember looking at your father and thinking, *he'd better not even touch me.*"

"Mama!" Abby stared at her mother in shock. It wasn't like her to be so blunt.

She chuckled. "I'm becoming forthright in my old age. No use in flittering around a topic." She patted Abby's hand. "I've never told you this, but that was when your father started pursuing other means to heal the wounds caused by my rejection. He started spending his evenings at the local pub and caught the eye of a young widow. She granted him the attention I didn't."

Abby felt the color drain from her face.

"Oh, darling." She clasped Abby's hand in her own. Her paper-thin skin was cool to the touch. "Thankfully, it never came to that. I daresay, we owe it to Lady Etheridge, who had the wisdom to realize the situation that was unfolding. She barged in one day and lectured us both."

Mama smiled and shook her head at the memory. "I'll never forget. She poked your father in the chest and said 'the Baker widow may be appealing right now, and you may be starting to think you married the wrong woman, but that's because you're blinded by your circumstances. I'm telling you, Sarah Hartington is the woman for you."

"She didn't!" Abby could imagine the woman doing just that. Lady Etheridge had wielded her saber-like tongue to save Abby's parents' marriage. The stern woman continued to surprise Abby.

"Indeed. She told your father that the pretty young widow wouldn't be half as appealing after she stayed up the entire night caring for her children. Without giving us the opportunity to refuse, she snatched you both up, one in each arm and said, 'I'm taking the children with me until you remember just how right Sarah Hartington is for you.' Then, she stormed out the front door with the nursemaid in tow."

Abby chuckled and shook her head.

"We spent the weekend refreshing ourselves and our marriage and remembering how a husband and wife should act towards each other." Mama held Abby's gaze and patted her hand.

She leaned closer. "Don't make the same mistake I did. Ask yourself if you're loving him the way you would want to be loved. I know it's tough to do, especially when your feelings are still raw, but ask yourself, are you behaving like the person Nicholas wants as a wife?"

"But ..." She wanted to tell Mama everything, that Nick had lied to her and kept secrets. But was she being the wife Nick needed? Since his return, she'd argued with him over cleaning the cottage, dismissing Helena, and refusing Melinda's dinner invitation. All trivial things. Also, she hadn't believed him when he told her there wasn't someone else. Instead, she'd followed him and unintentionally involved him in a brush with some tavern Jerry-wags who were already three sheets to the wind.

Argumentative and distrustful. Were those the qualities that Nick wanted in a wife? She hung her head. Earlier that morning, she'd seen anger in his eyes, but it wasn't merely anger. It was hurt. Why?

She replayed the scene in her mind. He'd caught her from

falling, and she'd snatched her hands away. Did he take her withdrawal as rejection? When was the last time she'd shown him affection? Yes, she'd soothed him while he slept, but when he was awake, he intimidated her. She couldn't remember holding his hand or stroking his cheek other than the first day when she'd sewn up his arm.

Before Nick's disappearance, she used to hold his hand, flirtatiously swat his shoulder, rest her head on his chest, and draw little circles in his palm with her index finger. Abby's breath caught. She hadn't truly touched her husband since the first day he returned. He'd acted reserved and sensitive about his scars. She'd worried he'd disappear. Or had she feared he'd reject her?

"Don't give up, dear. A great marriage doesn't happen overnight. There are mountains and valleys, and the journey is lifelong, but it's better together."

"Mama, you're right. I haven't been loving him the way that I should." Abby rose out of her chair. "I need to go."

She pecked a kiss on her mother's cheek and hurried home. It was past time she threw herself into her husband's arms and kissed him like a wife should kiss her husband. Yes, things were different between them, but that was no reason to give up. Her parents hadn't, and neither would she. She'd fight for this marriage with everything in her.

Out of breath from her haste, Abby threw open the front door and dashed up the stairs. She scanned his empty room, then slumped against the doorframe. Somewhere in the whirling clutter of her thoughts, she remembered he'd mentioned having business to attend to. "He'll come back." She spoke firmly to the still room, then whispered, "Please, God, have him come back."

The wind blew the curtains, and birds twittered outside the window. Her chest rose and fell with each breath.

It was in God's hands. She'd hurt Nick by pulling away from him, but she could make amends.

Abby strode into her room and, with Polly's assistance, donned her best day gown, a dark pink chiffon dress that cinched her waist and heightened her coloring. She dabbed some lilac water behind both her ears and brushed her hair until it shined. She'd been afraid, but no longer. She would move on from the past and focus on what was possible for the future. She would seduce her husband and show him love the way a wife should. With a burst of inspiration, she grabbed a basket and her shears and headed to the garden, where asters, mums, and some late roses still bloomed. She returned and filled every vase in the house with beautiful bouquets.

When she was done, the fragrant house was filled with vibrant bursts of color. She sat in her favorite chair and stared at the clock. It was almost noon. Unable to subdue her restlessness, she laid out the best china and brought out every candle and votive she could find for a romantic dinner. Once everything was laid out perfectly, she sat and peered at the clock.

Only half past. Nick wouldn't be back until early evening. She sat in silence for a minute, the only sound being that of her tapping foot. The chimes on the hall clock struck one. It was going to be a long wait. Usually, she would be at the orphanage at this time. Abby's foot tapped in rhythm with the clock's pendulum. She jumped to her feet. It would be better for her to keep busy. She would spend a few hours with the children and still be back before Nick returned.

⁓

*I*n Dr. Cox's exam room off the back of the physician's home, Nicholas sat on a whitewashed table. He focused on scanning articles of the various books lying open on the table for any indicators he may have been involved in the attempted poisoning of Lady Etheridge. When the good physician entered, Nicholas described his pain and rolled up his pantleg as instructed. He tried to ignore the doctor's cold hands as he probed Nicholas's knee and resisted the urge to knock Dr. Cox's arms away. He had a job to do, so he observed the physician's every movement.

The doctor kneeled for a closer look and peered through his thick-rimmed glasses. His delicate fingers lifted and bent Nicholas's leg.

"Was this injury sustained during the war?"

"Indeed." Nicholas's solitary answer punctured the air.

The physician kept his gaze on Nicholas's knee. "That's quite an injury. I imagine it still pains you a great deal. The bone was broken in several places. What happened?"

Nicholas tried not to flinch as the doctor's cold fingers slid along the scarred leg and lifted his knee until it bent to a forty-five-degree angle. "A burning beam collapsed, and I was unfortunate to be standing beneath it."

Dr. Cox nodded. "I see. I have no idea who patched you up, but they did a bang-up job. You're lucky to have movement in your knee at all. In the few cases I've seen, the joints freeze up like rusted metal, and the skin tightens with contracture."

Nicholas was done appeasing the man's curiosity. "Lady Etheridge said you might be able to give me something for the pain?"

"Ah, yes. She was concerned you might not be able to keep up with her demands, especially with your limp." He looked Nicholas in the eye. "She can be a demanding employer. I must say, all that time on your feet is surely contributing to your leg pain. Will you consider other employment?"

Nicholas shook his head. "It's all I know how to do, and Lady Etheridge's pay is the best."

Dr. Cox gave a curt nod. "Yes, she is demanding, but it's well known she pays a good wage for it. If that is the case, I can give you some laudanum, but I want you to be aware of some of the side effects." He rolled down Nicholas's pant leg and settled in a chair, crossing one leg over the other and lacing his fingers together in his lap.

"You seem well acquainted with Lady Etheridge," Nicholas probed.

"She is a client and"—he hesitated a brief moment—"I daresay, a friend."

"She calls upon you frequently. You don't find her a bit infuriating?"

The doctor shrugged. "She will drive a person daft if you let her. Lady Etheridge and I have come to an understanding. I will only make house calls if I'm not needed elsewhere, and she indulges me in a quick hand of piquet. She's a proficient card player. One would think she were an ivory turner if one didn't really know her."

"So your frequent visits are to play cards?"

Dr. Cox chuckled, his shoulders shaking. "Yes, Lady Etheridge uses the ruse of different ailments to keep up appearances. The old goat's as healthy as they come. She's merely lonely and looking for someone to keep her company. When I'm inclined, I humor her. It's much better than having her march down here and interrupt my practice, as she often used to do."

This lead, too, was turning out to be a dead end. Nicholas forced a sympathetic half-smile. Unfortunately, nothing the doctor said could be seen as a motive to harm the woman. "Was it the same with Lord Etheridge? Did you visit him frequently?"

"No, no. I never had the privilege of meeting Lord Etheridge. I started my practice here shortly after his passing."

"Shame." If the doctor had never known Lord Etheridge, then he couldn't have poisoned him. Granted, Lady Etheridge only speculated that her husband's death was related to the dog's.

This simple assignment turned out to be anything but simple. He'd had more luck in uncovering the weaknesses in Napoleon's defenses.

"Well now," the physician said, "let me explain your options. I can give you some laudanum for the pain and to help you sleep, but many people begin to crave the drug and have ill effects if they go without it."

"I'd rather not."

"I could also try leeches and get some of the bad blood out—"

"No."

"Then I recommend a poultice to reduce the swelling, but to warn you, it can be messy and smelly."

"What about stretching or moving about?"

The doctor cocked his head and rubbed his chin. "I recently read an article from the *British Medical Journal* on such. I keep a copy in my library. Let me see if I can retrieve it for you. I'd be interested in documenting your progress if you decide that's the course you want to take."

With the physician temporarily gone, Nicholas could look around his office. He nodded.

Dr. Cox's eyes brightened, and he scurried from the room to retrieve the article.

Nicholas stood and, keeping an eye on the door, pulled open the medicine bag and scanned its contents. Hartshorn, laudanum, Hungary water, *white arsenic.* There it was.

The good doctor had arsenic on hand.

It made Nicholas suspicious, but why would the doctor try to kill Lady Etheridge? Or Abby?

A door closed down the hallway. "I've found it," the physician shouted. Nicholas shut the bag and slid back into position.

CHAPTER 21

$\mathcal{L}$ydia's embrace restricted air flow from Abby's lungs.

"Truly you mean it?" Lydia's eyes were bright with excitement. "You'll hire me?"

"Of course." Abby smiled and pulled the girl's arms down. "I wouldn't say it if I didn't mean it. You can start the day after your birthday. I will show you around and get you settled in. Then when Mrs. Smith returns, she'll show you your new duties."

"Bless you, Lady Abigail. Truly, you have no idea how much this means to me."

Abby laughed at the girl's enthusiasm. She didn't know why the idea hadn't occurred to her earlier. It was perfect. Mrs. Smith was getting older, and eventually she'd want to be with her family. This way Abby would have a trained assistant who could take over when Mrs. Smith retired.

Lydia was still beaming as Abby said goodbye to all the children.

They pleaded with her to stay longer, but she wanted to beat Nick home.

"Don't worry, I'll be back to visit soon." Abby turned to

Lydia. "Keep praying and who knows? Maybe Mr. Emerson will love me again. God is a God of miracles."

"Oh, I most certainly will."

It had been a wonderful day. Miss Quiller let the children have an extra half hour of free time, and the children's enthusiasm had been contagious. With a final wave, Abby headed out the door with a spring in her step. Her biggest adventure awaited her. The tingle of excitement ran over her skin. This time, she would be the wife Nick needed. She would show him how much she loved him.

She tried not to run, but her feet couldn't contain themselves.

The church bells tolled the four o'clock hour from the gothic tower that rose above the church's steep-pitched shingled roof and high arched stain glass windows.

Her lips parted into a wide grin that she couldn't subdue and didn't want to. In a couple of hours, Nick would return to Laurel House. That gave her plenty of time to freshen up before his arrival.

She opened the front door, and the fragrance of fresh cut flowers surrounded her. She unpinned her hat and peeled off her gloves, handing them to Polly.

"Polly, I need you to see to dinner. I'd like you to make roasted goose with chestnut stuffing. It's Mr. Emerson's favorite."

Polly blanched but bobbed a curtsy. "Yes, milady."

"Mrs. Kroger will recite you the recipe. Take Delia with you to get what supplies you need from Mr. Kroger."

As Polly dashed out the servant's entrance to do her bidding, Abby's stomach fluttered as if she'd swallowed a live goldfish. She bit her lip to keep from bursting into a fit of giggles like a school girl. *Tonight,* she was going to rewind the clock and start new with her husband. *Tonight* would be the start of their new life together, the beginning of a new beginning.

The front door creaked behind her.

"You're home." Abby spun around with a bright smile, but it wasn't Nick.

A man stood in the entrance.

She gasped.

He closed the door behind him, and the click of the latch resounded in her ears.

"May I help you?" Her voice was unnaturally loud.

Abby recognized him as the ruddy-faced man who'd approached her outside the orphanage. The stench of imbibed spirits surrounded him.

"I knew you'd welcome me." He pulled his hat off his head and held it against his belly. A lock of greasy hair fell over his forehead. "Have you considered my proposal?"

"I'm not that kind of woman." Her blood turned to ice, but she resisted the urge to cower. "You, sir, are not welcome."

"Too high in the instep for the likes of me?" His nostrils flared. "I'll pay an entire month's wages." His breath reeked of cigars and gin, contrasting with the sweet fragrance of roses in the bouquet behind her. His shifty eyes roved over her face, neck, and then lower. "I may not be some titled dandy"—his voice was rough metal on a grinding wheel—"but I have other things to offer you."

"You need to leave." She pointed to the door.

He greedily strode forward. "I struggle to work because I find myself waiting for a glimpse of you to pass by. I just need a taste of you to put an end to my misery." He slid a finger down the inside of her arm.

She snatched her arm away and stepped back, colliding with the foyer pedestal table in the center of the room. A large crystal vase filled with flowers teetered.

He gripped her arms. "I can't sleep at night. I can only lie there, thinking of you."

Abby screamed, but his gloved hand covered her mouth, muffling the sound.

"No one needs to know. Nobody will hear us." His face lowered to within inches of her own. "It's your groomsman's day off. Your maids just left, and you terminated the maid-of-all-work. Your regular male guest doesn't arrive for two hours. If you've scheduled another appointment, he'll have to wait."

Her eyes widened. He knew all her comings and goings and that of her staff. The man was mad as a hatter and should be in Bedlam.

She tried to slide away from him, but he trapped her with his body and his arms.

This isn't happening. Her neck and back ached from leaning back so far. *I'm at home. Home is safe.*

He traced her jawline with gloved fingers. "I've become appallingly disagreeable. I can't work. I can't take this suffering. You've done this to me, and you're the only one who can end it."

She tried to turn her face away and pushed at his chest with her hands.

"I was willing to pay for your services—handsomely, I might add—but you've driven me to this."

His whiskers scratched her face and neck.

Abby's stomach turned sour. She let out a whimper against his hand. *This can't be happening.* He weighed too much to shove him off, so she pounded blows against his ribs and back, but he captured her wrists and pinned them to her side.

She screamed until there was barely any air left in her lungs, but he gripped her jaw with his thumb and index finger. "Go ahead. No one can hear you."

He nuzzled her neck and reached for the hem of her skirts.

The severity of her situation sunk in.

Panicked tears clogged her throat, suffocating her, and her

scream faded into a whimper. She closed her eyes and squeezed them tight.

He inhaled. "You smell how I knew you would." His thumb rubbed against her cheek. "I can't stop dreaming about you, when I'm awake, when I'm asleep. My wife worries I've contracted cholera. Only you can end my suffering."

He's deranged! Ice permeated deep into her bones, leaving her paralyzed. Her body quivered uncontrollably. *God,* she prayed, *don't let this happen. Tonight is my new beginning with Nick. Save me!*

"You are gravely mistaken." She opened her eyes to face him. "My husband will—"

He laughed a bitter hiss. Leaning back, he studied her expression. His face cracked into a vicious smile. "Enough with the games. I know you're a widow."

"No." Abby struggled harder and let out a whimper. *Think, Abby, think!* She wanted to feel nothing, to distance herself from this wretched man. She wanted out of her body so she wouldn't feel his filthy hands on her. *Oh, God!*

I did not give you a spirit of fear, but of power, love, and sound mind.

The verse she'd memorized to overcome her fear of horses shouted through the recesses of her mind. Her fear became a righteous anger that exploded through her being. *You have a sound mind, Abby, use it. Think!*

He let go of her arm, reaching up to yank back on her hair.

She groped for the vase behind her, finally touching it with her fingertips and wrapping her hand around the base. With her forearm she pressed against his neck, shoving him away so she could get enough torque. She lifted the vase high and slammed it on top of his head. It shattered into pieces, drenching them both with water and littering them with broken glass and flowers. For a moment, he stood there, dazed. Then, he bellowed in pain, curses spewing from his lips like vomit. His hands flew to his head, feeling the shards of glass that stuck out of his forehead like crystal thorns. Crimson blood oozed over his eye.

Pushing him away, she shouted, "Get out! Get out! Get out!" She dashed down the hall to the kitchen and grabbed a knife from the butcher's block.

He bellowed curses, and she heard him stumble out the door. From the window, Abby watched him stagger across the grounds into the woods.

On shaky legs, she moved into the next room and sagged onto the arm of a nearby chair. Her entire body quaked. She hugged her midsection and tried to erase the mental traces of the man's vulgar touches.

~

*T*ears burned but she refused to let them fall or any feelings escape as she sat in the tub of lukewarm water. She needed to get the filth off and couldn't wait for the water to heat any longer. The memory of that man's hands on her body made bile rise in her throat. She scrubbed her face and neck raw where the man's whiskers had brushed her skin.

What would she tell Nick? How would she explain that a strange man had invaded her home because he'd mistaken her for a whore? What would he think? Their relationship hung on a tentative thread as it was. A sob escaped her throat, and she stuffed the rest back down until her eyes hurt and her body felt as weak as a wilted flower.

Abby delved into her energy reserve to step out of the bath and wrap herself in her robe. Her feet padded down the hall and into the solarium. The sweet, fragrant perfume of fresh flowers brought back comforting memories of Mama Em. She'd always said she felt closer to God when she was among her flowers. Abby busied herself watering the precious plants.

"God, why? Why did this happen? What do I tell Nick?"

Abby waited and listened intently for an answer. Nothing.

"Father, I don't understand. You were with me. You gave me the strength to fight. I know you were there. I felt you. Why do you stay silent? I still need you."

She squeezed her eyes closed to block the tears burning for release. The watering can slipped from her fingers and made a hollow metallic sound against the wooden floor. Cool water splashed around her ankles, but she didn't move.

Polly and Delia had returned from the market. They'd entered through the back and by the smell of it had started cooking the evening meal.

Nick would be home any moment. What would she tell him?

"God, please tell me what to do?" She waited for an answer as a battle of tug-of-war fought to keep her spirit, her life, her joy from being dragged down into a dark pit of fear.

I knitted you together in your mother's womb. Impressions filled her heart. *My child, I have numbered the hairs on your head. Your name is carved in the palms of My hand. I died that you may have life and be with me for eternity. I promised never to leave you or forsake you. I am with you always.*

Abby opened her eyes. "But when you're silent, I get frightened and begin to doubt."

Even in the silence, I am working. Open your eyes, and you will see Me in everything. Open your eyes, and I will show you.

Abby dragged in a ragged breath that shuttered her body.

The front door opened and closed. Abby's heart stuttered, and her eyes shot open.

"I came to collect my things," came Nick's voice from the front hall.

Her body relaxed.

"Abby?"

"In here."

His boots crunched over the shards of broken glass and crushed flowers. "What happened?"

Abby's eyes filled with tears. She'd forgotten about the mess in the front entry.

He strode into the solarium, looked at her standing there in her dressing robe, and froze. He studied her expression, his brows drawing together. Awkward and unsure, his eyes searched hers. He approached her with slow steps, concern lining his face.

God was showing her His love through her husband.

Nick shifted his weight and scanned the room as if searching for context clues. He didn't question her, but neither did he back away. He hesitantly opened his arms.

She rushed to him half blinded with tears. "I love you." She slid her arms inside his unbuttoned jacket and wrapped them tightly around his torso. She leaned her head against his chest and listened to his beating heart.

～

*N*icholas was undone. He couldn't control the rush of emotions that erupted when he saw Abby standing there barefoot, wet hair hanging loosely about her shoulders.

She wore nothing but a thin robe.

He couldn't breathe.

Abby was upset, and instinctively he'd opened his arms to her.

He'd expected her to turn away, but when she ran to him and slid her hands over the thin material of his cambric shirt, his body shook. He flinched at her touch and waited for her to draw back when she felt his scars.

She didn't. Instead, she rested her head on his chest.

"Did you cut all these flowers for me?" The heady blossoms overwhelmed his senses.

She nodded and sniffed into his shirt front. He could feel the moisture of her tears.

"Are you crying over the broken vase?"

She tensed. He felt like a cad for putting such a strain on her emotions. He should have stayed and talked things out instead of running like a coward.

"It's merely a vase." He stroked the back of her head. "I'll have it replaced tomorrow. I'll trade it for a thousand vases. Please don't cry."

The heat of her body permeated his shirt, flooding him with a warmth he hadn't felt in ten years. He wasn't sure how long they stood there and held each other, whether it was a minute or an hour, but when she lifted her head and stared at him with longing, Nicholas's last thread of restraint unraveled.

Her lips parted as if to ask a question, but then she hesitated. Her mouth began to tremble.

"What is it?" He stroked her damp hair. "Tell me."

"Kiss me, Nick. Remind me that I am loved and cherished." She rested her palm gently against his cheek and pleaded with her eyes.

Despite the warnings of his mind, his heart knew he would grant her anything she asked. He released a groan as his lips molded over hers.

Nicholas didn't hold back. His mouth moved with urgent passion. The heady taste of her reminded him of berries and cream. A shudder ran through his body. He kissed her lips, her cheeks, her neck, trying to atone for ten years. Her soft moan sent his pulse leaping. He lifted her and carried her upstairs, where they wouldn't be happened upon by servants. Kissing her soundly, he meant to answer her demand to feel cherished by pouring his heart into each caress. He set her on the bed and hesitated from the cool air that now separated them. If he didn't leave now, he wouldn't have the willpower to do so later.

Abby needed him.

Was it wrong for him to love his wife? Could he ever atone for his mistakes? Must he love her from afar, or could her love heal his broken and lost soul?

She slid her hands around his neck and leaned back onto the pillows, pulling him. His body followed hers, their arms entangled.

When her hands moved to the buttons on his shirt, he froze. He jerked back, but Abby persisted until he grabbed her hands to still them.

"No." His command echoed louder than he'd intended.

Abby's eyes widened. He could see she was startled, but a glint of determination lit their depths.

"Nick, you are my husband, and I love you. Let me do this."

"Abby, it's not something you should see."

"Nothing can change my love for you." She gazed at him with such tenderness that his heart physically ached.

He wanted to pull away, to refuse her, but he needed to know if she could love him, even as a deformed monster. Nicholas dropped his hands to his sides, but he couldn't watch. He closed his eyes against the repulsion he'd see when she opened his shirt.

Nicholas felt her fingers deftly unbutton his shirt and the breeze of cool air as it parted. He tensed, not daring to breathe. His jaw ached from clenching his teeth as he waited for her reaction.

She hesitated, and he lifted his hands, ready to close his shirt.

Her gentle fingertips touched his scarred skin.

He gasped, and his eyes flew open.

She was staring at his scars, touching them gently.

He melted into the sweet tenderness of her caress. Like dry

ground receiving a drop of rain, he craved the feeling of skin touching skin and wanted more. His toes curled as her fingers traveled along his gnarled skin.

Her hand lifted and her mouth lowered, leaving a trail of kisses.

His breathing stilled, and he didn't dare move. He feared the moment would end, that Abby would run away in horror.

Droplets landed on his skin, cooling in the evening air, and he realized she was crying. His heart shattered.

"Abby don't ..." But he couldn't finish. He could no longer find his voice.

Her featherlike touch on his cheek beckoned for him to look at her. Tears glistened in her eyes. "Nick, I love your scars. They remind me that God heard my prayers. He kept you alive, He brought you back to me. He was listening to me the entire time. Even though all I heard was silence, God was working. He was saving you—for me."

Nicholas moaned low. His hands moved into her hair, crushing her to him as he kissed her with unrestrained passion.

She was his wife, and he was never going to let her go.

It was his last thought before he stopped thinking entirely and made love to his wife. He had ten long years to make up to her.

CHAPTER 22

*N*icholas awoke not to a nightmare but to a rare, good dream. The delicious traces of it still clung to him like the scent of lilac soap on his skin. He squeezed his eyes tight not wanting his dream of returning to Abby and living as man and wife to end.

Abby stirred beside him, turning her face toward him, and her eyelids fluttered open. A warm smile touched her lips, and a lock of hair fell over one eye.

He tucked the tendril behind her ear and trailed his knuckles down the soft skin of her neck and round the curve of her shoulder. This wasn't a dream.

The ugliness and shame he'd expected to feel after allowing her to see the full extent of physical damage the war had cost him didn't shadow their love making. Even in the morning light, Abby didn't turn away from him, squirm with regret, or appear embarrassed. She met his gaze with unswerving affection and said, "I love you."

"I love you more." He kissed her shoulder and pulled her closer. She rested her cheek on his chest and splayed her fingers across his taut and scarred muscles. He stared up at the ceiling savoring the moment and pushing back the plaguing thought that this wouldn't last. It was only a matter of time before his mind would slip and he would lose her.

Right now he would savor her sweetness and closeness and be grateful.

I prayed for God to return you to me.

Abby's words echoed in his mind. Was this God's doing? Could He restore their marriage? Could God restore him? Yesterday, Nicholas had come back to say goodbye but found Abby distraught.

He wrapped his arm tighter around her. "You never told me what happened last evening to make you so upset. It couldn't have been the broken vase."

Abby hesitated, but he couldn't tell whether it was to gather her thoughts or to debate whether she should broach the topic. "A man came to the house and accosted me."

Nicholas jolted into a seated position and Abby would have rolled off if he hadn't held her tight and brought her up with him. "Who? What happened?"

He'd had survived severe burns and a broken leg, but the strength he had to muster to remain calm as Abby revealed that she'd been attacked by that blackguard, Lester, had him seething and his insides quaking. He told her he had some work to do for Lieutenant Sparks but only for a couple hours.

"You haven't yet told me about your assignment." Abby smoothed the wrinkles out of the bedclothes. "Where do you go? What do you do?"

"I cannot speak of my missions by decree of the Home Office. If I did, I could be hung for treason."

"Oh." Her eyes widened.

"I appreciate your understanding." He kissed the top of her head. "Go back to sleep, especially since I kept you up half the night."

Abby yawned and snuggled deeper under the covers with a content smile.

He dressed and put the groom on alert to watch for any housebreakers because one was spotted in the area. Nicholas didn't bother to open the front gate, merely put a hand on the rail and leapt over it. His determination overrode any pain in his leg.

"Agent Scar."

He pretended not to hear Lady Etheridge's call and continued to march down the street.

"I daresay, Agent Scar." Her open carriage rolled to a stop beside him. "I'm pleased to see you investigating my suspect."

He stared at the woman ready to strangle her for delaying him. She looked past him at Laurel House. *Abby.*

He cleared his throat. "Indeed." Perhaps Lady Etheridge could help. "Do you happen to know where a Lester Shue resides, and has he been at your home in the past couple months?"

"I employ Mrs. Shue as a seamstress. I've never met her husband, but wagging tongues say he's a drunk and a laggard."

"He attacked Lady Abigail." His fingers curled into fists.

Lady Etheridge's eyes widened.

"I intend to pay him a visit."

She swung the carriage door open. "Get in, Agent Scar."

He considered refusing. He needed to move, to plan. But if she could help him find the rogue, he'd tolerate her. He stepped up and sat beside her.

"Driver, take us to Letch Hill." She tapped the end of her parasol on the side of the carriage then addressed Nicholas. "Tell me what happened."

Nicholas's body shook as he recapped what Abby had told him with as few details as possible. Her coach wove down the narrow streets of the less fortunate section of town, and Lady Etheridge, the same woman who flew up into the boughs over a crooked seam sewn into a gown, watched the scenery pass with cool detachment.

Whereas Nicholas rolled his shoulders, cracked his neck, ready to see justice done.

Lady Etheridge rapped her parasol once more on the side of the carriage, and the driver pulled to a stop in front of a small, thatched cottage on the edge of town. Smoke poured out of the chimney, and a child's screams could be heard within. A young woman carrying a bundle of neatly mended clothing exited the house, adeptly dodging the puddle in the street where a chamber pot had been emptied.

"I realize you want to hunt down the wretch and challenge him to a duel." Lady Etheridge blocked his way with her parasol. "But I have a better plan."

"It better involve Lester lying dead in a ditch or hanging from the rafters." Nicholas forced his hands to relax. He'd find a way for justice to be exacted.

"My plan has it so that you don't wind up at Newgate for murder." She pursed her lips. "I intend for you to finish my case."

He wouldn't rest until Lester Shue no longer posed a threat to Abby. "Do you even know if Mr. Shue is at home?"

"He isn't."

Nicholas rounded Lady Etheridge. "What?"

"We are merely here to confirm the dependence of his family upon the sluggard. And I am to do all the talking. Understood?"

Nicholas snorted and didn't answer. *We shall see.*

Holding her parasol despite the overcast day, Lady Etheridge allowed Nicholas to aid her in crossing the street. She thumped on the door with the butt of her umbrella.

The top half of the Dutch door opened, and a thick woman with sewing needles still in her hand peered up at her. Her hair was tucked under a frilled cap that framed her round, blotchy face set with a pair of speculative eyes that had creases in the corners as if she squinted a lot.

"Lady Etheridge, goner." The woman reached back and placed her sewing things on a nearby shelf. She straightened her cap and smoothed her skirts. "Do you 'ave some clothes in need of mendin'?"

"Mrs. Shue." Lady Etheridge exhaled as if she hadn't all day. "May I have a word with you regarding your husband?"

The woman raised her chin, and her lips thinned into a tight, defiant line, but Lady Etheridge held her gaze until a flash of defeat flickered across her face. Mrs. Shue unlocked the bottom door. As it swung inward, she said, "I'm afraid my husband has stepped out."

Lady Etheridge swept into the room and assessed its contents down the bridge of her nose.

Nicholas ducked under the low framed door to stand beside Lady Etheridge. Pairs of curious eyes peeked out from behind curtains, and small hands curled around corners.

Lady Etheridge's demeanor softened as she sat in the cleanest looking chair. Nicholas remained standing. *Blast*, precious time was being wasted.

"Mrs. Shue." Lady Etheridge raised her chin. "You are a skilled seamstress, and an industrious worker whom I'm sure provides the food to fill the bellies of your children."

"Yes, milady, six hungry mouths, but good little 'uns, all of 'em."

"You have provided excellent service for myself and others, which is why I'm coming to you privately and not going to the magistrate."

"Thank you, ma'am." She twisted her apron between her red-knuckled fingers. "About what, milady?"

"What I have to say is not pleasant. Please, bend your ear."

Mrs. Shue leaned forward, and Nicholas leaned his ear as

did other curious faces, but he didn't catch a word. Lady Etheridge was wise to whisper so the children wouldn't hear.

The seamstress's gaze dropped to the floor, and with a curt nod, she acknowledged the accusation.

Despite her obvious embarrassment, her voice remained strong. "Isn't the first time. When Lester gets in his cups, he loses his mind, he does. I hoped a new town might change his ways."

Nicholas's jaw tightened until his teeth ached.

Lady Etheridge reached out her gloved fingers and tilted Mrs. Shue's head to the right, revealing ugly bruising along her neck. "Did he do this the last time he dipped too deep?"

She nodded.

Nicholas shifted his weight to relieve the pressure building in his chest.

"Is that where he is now, at a tavern getting foxed?" Lady Etheridge asked.

She nodded again.

His foot angled toward the door ready to find the bloke and plant a facer.

"Has he ever hurt the children?"

Mrs. Shue crumpled into her apron and cried, "I protect them. I do, but I can't always be around."

Lady Etheridge waited for the crying to subside. When Mrs. Shue regained her composure, Lady Etheridge handed her a card. "This is the name of a relative of mine who owns a dressmaker shop. She is always seeking good seamstresses and will hire you upon my recommendation. Pack up your things and go there tomorrow with the children."

A spark of hope illuminated Mrs. Shue's eyes.

Lady Etheridge rose, and Mrs. Shue did the same, following Lady Etheridge.

Nicholas moved to the door and opened it.

"Your husband will be sent on an errand to Portsmouth

tomorrow," Lady Etheridge said. "A press gang actively seeking able-bodied men has been spotted in the area. Your husband will be on the next Navy vessel."

Would that punishment be enough? He'd reach out to Lieutenant Sparks and ensure Lester Shue was impressed into Naval service on the worst and farthest-traveling ship possible, one not likely to return. Preferably to the Artic Circle.

Mrs. Shue stood motionless. A faint whisper escaped her lips. "God bless you."

Lady Etheridge stepped onto the street.

Nicholas nodded to the woman before he crossed the threshold. He patted his hat back on his head and strode to the carriage with Lady Etheridge.

Before Lady Etheridge placed her hand into the footman's and stepped into the carriage, she turned. "Maybe falling into trials will build the man's character. Best of luck to you, Mrs. Shue."

Nicholas stared at his companion. Since when had Lady Awfulridge grown a heart?

~

*A*bby spent the next few weeks in a blissful state, as if she were cocooned in a warm blanket. Love was wonderful. She'd finally breached the fortress walls of Nick's heart, and he slowly allowed her back into his life.

During the day when he wasn't working, he relayed stories of how he came to be a spy and of things that transpired in the ten years he was away—at least those he could speak of. He talked about building her their dream manor—one with a conservatory and fields of strawberries just because they were her favorite fruit, and more and more, she believed in her heart one day they would build it and raise a family together. They spent passionate nights snuggled tightly in each other's arms, and she cherished and thanked God for every minute.

This morning, the honking of geese headed south for the winter woke her. She snuggled deeper in Nick's embrace and relished his closeness before climbing out of bed. After dressing, she made her way to the kitchen to oversee Delia preparing their food and heating their morning chocolate.

The stairs creaked, and the heavier footfalls meant Nick had awakened. "I'll take over the toast and cups of chocolate," she said to Delia. "You continue making the eggs." Abby carried the tray to the breakfast room, where Nick would read the morning paper. She hadn't yet replaced the maid of all work, but Mrs. Smith was expected to return by the end of the month, and Lydia would be coming to assist with the duties. Abby was growing fond of her domestic tasks. There was a quaint appeal to serving her husband. In a way, she would miss it when the Mrs. Smith returned. However, if her assumption was correct, she was going to be busy in the next nine months and would need assistance.

Abby hummed a lullaby.

She set the tray down and leaned over to plant a kiss on Nick's cheek.

He set aside the paper and surprised her by turning his face and kissing her lips so passionately that she melted against him. When he pulled away, a familiar spark glimmered in his hazel eyes, and an irresistibly disarming smile played on the corner of his lips.

"Good morning." His voice was warm and husky.

"It's a beautiful day." She sat beside him.

Nick chuckled. "It's overcast and chilly."

"It's going to clear up." Famished, she chose a scone and took a big bite.

"So what topic is it this morning?" he asked. "Is it going to be Thomas Moore's radical concepts or the upping of the newspaper tax to a fourpence? Or something more light-hearted for my day off work, like the works of Wordsworth and Byron?"

His kindness overwhelmed her. "Thank you." She smiled. "Thank you, for being willing to discuss anything with me." She placed a hand over his warm one. He turned his palm over and wrapped his fingers around hers.

Anything except where you're working, what your assignment is, and why you're still opposed to appearing publicly together, she amended.

"The pleasure is all mine." His eyes twinkled. "You have an insatiable mind."

They enjoyed their morning meal together, talking about everything from the weather to the latest happenings in the House of Lords.

She glanced down at their entwined fingers. "I was planning on visiting Mama today if you want to come." Abby held her breath and peeked up at him.

Nick withdrew his hand and cut a piece of ham. "You know I can't do that."

"But Mama and Stephen wouldn't tell a soul. They will keep quiet about your return. I've told you. They already know." She used a napkin to wipe imaginary crumbs off the table into her hand. "Plus, I need them to know I'm not imagining you. They're going to start believing I'm nicked in the nob and halfway to Bedlam."

"You're not mad." His eyes flared and expression darkened. "Don't ever let anyone say that about you."

Had she touched a nerve? Had someone believed his mind was slipping? Because of his nightmares? "I won't."

His features softened, and he tugged on her hand, pulling her onto his lap. "Why leave when heaven is here, and I can keep you all to myself." He trailed light kisses down her neck to the pulsing hollow of her throat.

She squirmed at the heady, tickling, sensation. "Stop." She giggled. "I'm serious. Please come and visit them."

He responded a muffled "no" as he nuzzled the back of her neck.

"Eventually they're going to come calling. I can't keep making excuses and pushing them off to a later date. Stephen has come by twice, and I had Polly tell him I was out because I can't hide secrets from my brother. He'd bombard me with questions I couldn't answer."

"You'll need to keep sending him away for the time being."

"For how long?" Abby's spine stiffened, and she pushed off his lap. Nick reached for her again, but she wouldn't be distracted. "Stephen was your truest friend. Can you imagine how hurt you'd be if he returned to town and waited several months to call upon you?"

Nick lowered his gaze but not before she caught a glimpse of regret clouding his eyes. He shrugged as if their life-long friendship didn't matter and stood.

"You can't hide forever," she half shouted, swallowing her nausea. "Chins are wagging, and word has spread. We've received calling cards and invitations by the dozens, and I've had to turn them all down."

"Once my assignment is over, we can discuss plans for me to be re-introduced to society, but for now I need to keep my reappearance secret."

"For how long?"

"I don't know." He waved his hand near the side of his head. It could be two days, or it could be six months—maybe more."

But that was too long. She may not have that kind of time. "People want to see you. I want to be seen with you."

He stepped towards her with a heavy-lidded gaze, reaching to pull her into his arms.

She stepped back, needing to convince him.

He stiffened as if she'd rejected him.

Tension hummed in her ears, but she pressed the matter. "You said you'd planned to leave once your assignment was over, but that was before. At some point, you'll need to come out of hiding. We can start with just my family."

"Abby." His tone communicated he was done discussing the topic.

"But how can you stay a recluse? What are we going to do if the baby starts to show?"

Nick's face blanched, his eyes widening.

Abby groaned. She'd ruined the surprise. Once again, her lips had spoken without consulting her brain.

"What? Y-you're with child?"

She nodded. "I believe so."

Nick didn't move. The air crackled with tension. She'd expected him to be happy, even if a little stunned. She hadn't anticipated the sheer terror in his eyes. She blinked, and it was gone, his emotions masked like they'd been when he'd first returned. After a moment, he reached for her and hugged her to his chest.

"That's wonderful, Abby. Everything is going to be fine. We'll figure this out together."

It was not the response she'd hoped for, but she clung to Nick and managed a weak smile. At least he'd used the word *together*.

~

*N*icholas held Abby tight against his chest and gently stroked her spine while his stomach rolled. He squeezed his eyes closed to ward off the inky, black cloud that closed in around him. The dream they'd been living in these past few weeks would eventually end, but he hadn't wanted to acknowledge it. This was his fault. He'd known the risks, but he'd convinced himself he had more time. Abby would occasionally call upon friends and family, and he could stay hidden away in Laurel House until his assignment was over and until he knew for certain his spells were on the decline and he was no longer a danger.

Now, a baby was involved. Nicholas's return would have to be exposed or Abby's reputation would be in beyond recovery. He needed to solve who tried to poison Lady Etheridge before he was forced to blow his own cover.

He wasn't afraid of being a father, he was afraid of being seen. What if he had an episode in public? Any sound could set him off. He couldn't predict it, nor could he control it despite his attempts. But if he hid from the world, everyone would think Abby was some doxy and their child baseborn. They would be scorned, but all it would take was one public attack. The citizens of Altonwood would lock him up in Bedlam like he'd witnessed other soldiers in their own hometowns whose night terrors also infiltrated their days—like they'd done to Aaron. He'd witnessed Aaron have an attack in public, tried to calm him to no avail. The local constable arrested him, and he was thrown in Bedlam. Nicholas visited Aaron on a couple occasions. The remembrance of how they'd locked away Aaron, who'd served his country honorably, into a humiliating spectacle burned Nicholas's insides, leaving scars to match the ones on his outside.

One episode and he too would be ridiculed, maliciously slandered, and taunted. Then because of his disgrace, the town would turn their backs on Abby and their child.

Trapped like a snared rabbit, he saw no other choice. When Abby started to show, he'd have to come out of hiding. He held her closer. "I love you, and we will love this child."

She relaxed in his arms, and they continued to hold each other.

He pressed a kiss on the top of Abby's head. "I need to go to work, but I can escort you to your mother's gate."

She leaned her head on his shoulder. "Nick, I'm so happy. If I'm dreaming, I don't ever want to wake up." She stepped away and looked up at him with those wide, trusting eyes, laying a hand on her flat stomach. "I have everything I ever wanted."

After she walked away, he stared out the window at the barren trees, at the few leaves still clinging to life before the harsh winter. He didn't want to wake from this dream either. He was scared he'd awaken to another nightmare where he was bound, restrained, and hauled off to a madhouse, while Abby and their child wept.

CHAPTER 23

*A*bby heard giggling and paused instead of knocking on Willownstone's library door. Was that Katherine?

"Your sister will come calling at any moment."

"Then we'll tell her to come back later."

Definitely Katherine and Stephen. His seductive baritone voice and the telling silence that followed hinted for Abby to follow her brother's advice. She turned to leave.

"Seriously, Stephen. I want to hear more about Mr. Emerson's return."

Stephen snorted.

Did he not believe her? Abby backed up and leaned her ear toward the door.

"What was that for?" Katherine's tone rang with warning.

"You are a loyal friend through and through, but my sister has a remarkable imagination."

"Stephen, she wouldn't gull her own family."

"Not to fool us, but she's fanciful. She probably mistook a dream she had while ill as reality."

Stephen cleared his throat. "If Nick were alive, why haven't we seen or heard from him? He'd make himself known, especially to me."

"What if there is a good reason?"

God bless, Katherine for standing up for her. If only Abby knew the reason—other than it would interfere with his assignment.

"What reason could there be other than she hallucinated?" Stephen had always been the doubting-Thomas type, needing to understand the logic before he believed. "Now she's too embarrassed to admit the truth. It's not the first time she's said something before thinking it through and regretting it later. Besides, Nick was like a brother to me. If I wasn't a firstborn male with the responsibilities to Willowstone Farm, I would have enlisted with him because we've always had each other's backs. If he was alive and at home, I would know."

Should she let them believe she's some whimsical peagoose? Nick wanted to remain unknown, and this perception would allow him more time. Abby placed a hand on her stomach. How much time before she began to show? A few weeks? A month? Hadn't Katherine's middle already rounded when she announced the news of Benjamin being on the way?

This was her family. They didn't deserve to have such momentous occurrences kept from them and she needed her family on her side, especially Stephen, to help Nick to see reason. Together they would pray and battle off the demons that plagued him each night. Nick had only instructed her to stay silent before he'd learned of the baby. Surely he didn't expect her to stay quiet now?

Katherine sighed. "Let's say Abby did dream up his return. Then maybe she needs your guidance. When was the last time you visited her?"

"Twice I called upon her,"—defensiveness crept into Stephen's voice—"but she hadn't been at home, and then horses arrived to be trained, and life turned hectic." He paused. "Perhaps I haven't paid my sister the attention she required.".

Touched by his sentiments, Abby tapped lightly at the door and poked her head into the room. "I beg your pardon. Am I interrupting something?"

"No." Katherine jumped up from Stephen's lap. "Please, come in." She shot a look at Stephen.

"Of course." His words came out cordial, but Abby saw the desire for his wife still lingering in his eyes.

"I can come back."

"No, no, do come in and have a seat. Stephen and I were merely talking."

Stephen raised a single eyebrow at his wife, and a blush heated her cheeks.

"Tea should be delivered any moment," Katherine said. "It's been ages since you've come to visit. How go things at Laurel House?"

"Lovely." She lowered onto the sofa. "I think."

Stephen crossed his arms. "What's there to think about?"

"It's complicated." Abby twisted the thumb of her glove second-guessing her resolve to tell the news.

Weston carried in the tea service tray along with a plate of scones.

"Do I smell cook's delicious scones?" Mother swept into the room with a warm smile.

"Mama." Abby rose and kissed their mother's cheek.

"Darling, how delightful for you to pay us a visit. How are you faring?"

Abby pressed her lips together but couldn't hold back her surprise news. "I believe I may have a surprise coming seven or eight months hence."

"You're with child." Katherine jumped up and clapped her hands.

Mama leaned over and hugged her daughter, tears filling the corners of her eyes.

Stephen's fingers gripped the arms of his chair tighter. Was he shocked? He had to believe Nick had returned after such an announcement. He nodded and told her congratulations, but his face appeared pale and his voice tight.

"How delightful." Katherine reclaimed her seat. "How are you feeling?"

"Starving. I think I could eat an entire tray of scones, but other than that, I'm hale."

Mama laughed. "Katherine, ring for two plates of scones, immediately."

"Of course." Katherine rang the bell pull.

Stephen rose. "I'll let you ladies talk of the private matter. I must attend to a new stallion."

Abby swallowed, her gaze trailing his retreating form. His phrasing her news as a private matter stole her appetite.

"How did Nicholas take the news?" Mama asked.

Abby tried not to squirm. "As well as could be expected."

"You don't have to pretend with us." Katherine took her hands. "I can already tell you're upset by something. Tell us the truth."

"I don't know what to do. Nick's afraid to go out in public. He doesn't want to call upon anyone or receive any callers. Not even family." Abby exhaled the tightness that had wound in her chest. "Stephen was his dearest friend, but he won't yet come out of hiding. And now with the baby..."

"What is he afraid of?" Katherine's mouth twisted into a grim line.

"He says it's for work but I think he's ashamed of the scars he obtained during the war and his nightmares. I thought his emotional wounds were on the mend, but they're not. I believe he's fearful people will see his scars and disdain him."

"Are they that noticeable?" Katherine asked.

Abby let out a faint sigh. "He was badly burned." Her voice faded as if she felt his pain, then rose again. "But he hides them well. He keeps his hair long and his collar points high. I daresay people wouldn't notice right away. He walks with a slight limp but moves about remarkably well, and He doesn't do anything to draw unwanted attention, so people won't recognize him."

"Perhaps he could assist you at the orphanage," Katherine suggested. "No one would recognize him there. Perhaps it's like getting into cold water? He merely needs to go slowly and let himself adapt."

"I reckon it may run deeper than that," Mama said.

"What do you mean?" Abby scooted forward in her seat.

"What you said"—Mama nodded—"is consistent with his past."

"Consistent? How?" Abby asked.

"Do you remember when Stephen and Nicholas wore eye patches?"

Katherine's eyebrows rose.

A memory of Stephen and Nicholas fighting with wooden swords on a long plank flashed through Abby's mind. "I remember them pretending to be pirates."

"Nicholas wasn't merely playing pirate. He wore the eye patch because he was cross-eyed. The patch was put over his good eye to force his other eye to become stronger. It worked, but children can be cruel. Nicholas had become the object of their malice. For years, the older kids taunted him with cruel names. If he ignored their jokes, they bullied him, often leaving him bloodied and bruised. They were merciless."

Hazy memories of kids chasing them and calling him names seeped out of the recesses of her memory. He and Nick used to climb trees to hide.

Mama continued. "One day, I rode into town and saw a circle of kids gathered around laughing. I tapped the roof for the driver to pull over and discovered Nicholas beaten unconscious. The kids scattered, and the footman helped me bring him here, where I sent for the physician. Nicholas woke up, and after a thorough examination, the doctor suggested he wear a patch."

"Stephen offered to wear one, too, and from that moment on, the two of them were inseparable." Mama frowned. "Unfortunately, the emotional damage didn't heal as quickly. Nicholas was a tough and exceptional young man. He buried the hurt and hid his insecurities through a gregarious nature. It eventually became part of his charm. Above all else, he desired to be well liked. It was obvious to those who knew his history that he wanted to be all things to all people."

"But Mama, why don't I remember any of that?" How had she not known something so personal about her own husband?

"You were an energetic and optimistic child"—Mama smiled fondly at her—"too busy running in the meadow chasing butterflies to notice such things."

"I didn't know... I wasn't aware. I shouldn't have pressed him to be in public if he wasn't ready."

"I know, dear. You have a soft heart." Mama stirred her tea. "Give Nicholas time. He needs to realize the good things he has sacrificed in order to pacify his fears. It's those fears that keep him imprisoned in a jail of his own making. At some point, he will fight to be free, and with God's help, he can. Only then can he have life to the full as Jesus intended. I must warn you, though. Things could get worse before they get better. Your grandmother often said, 'The success of one's turnaround depends upon the depths of one's desperation.' Pray for your husband, my dear. Katherine, Stephen, and I will do the same."

CHAPTER 24

A week later, Abby lay abed snuggled in Nick's arms. Her mother's insight into his history had helped her see him differently. Propping her head up with one elbow, she laid her other hand gently on his arm, careful not to wake him. He needed his rest even though thankfully he'd been spared from his nightmares as of late.

Abby pictured him as a boy surrounded by a circle of taunting children, attempting to keep his chin high as their words pierced his little heart. She saw him older, handsome and charming with a beautiful lady on each arm, nodding to a group of acquaintances, the same ones who used to taunt him but now longed to be like him.

Nick had proved them wrong, and she couldn't be prouder of him. He'd fought back the only way he could, by beating them at their own game. Nick had been well respected in Altonwood and the surrounding towns, a sought-after match for unmarried ladies all around.

If someone told him he couldn't do something, he tried even harder. He was willing to take risks, to work hard, to rise above his station. It was no wonder he'd enlisted in the army to obtain the title he'd thought she desired. He'd been biting and clawing his way through life since he was a child.

But the battle was still to be won. These scars couldn't be fixed with a patch. He still struggled with the same childhood anxieties, only now they were mixed with the horrors of war. Nick's fear of rejection had resurfaced.

It was her fault. If she hadn't been so thoughtless, if she'd only kept her tongue in check and hadn't spouted out that he needed a silly title, none of it would have happened.

God, please redeem and restore Nick. Deliver him from his past. Renew his mind and change the way he thinks. Help him to see himself the way You see him, uniquely and wonderfully made. Help him to see his worth through Your eyes, Lord.

Nick shifted and she saw the scars on his neck in the pale moonlight. They whispered to her the pain and suffering he dealt with each day.

She traced a scar with her finger. To her, the marks were beautiful. They reminded her how precious life was and how God had blessed them with a second chance.

Nick viewed them as ugly and debilitating. Yet the real impairments were the mental scars that had cut deep and rooted in the fears of a young cross-eyed boy.

Abby gently brushed back a thick lock of his hair and ran her fingers down the side of his face. She would no longer push him to come out in public. If Nick wanted a solitary life without anyone but his immediate family, then she would grant it to him. It was the least she could do.

God, she prayed, *let Your will be done, not mine own.* Abby couldn't resist kissing Nick's brow. She snuggled deeper into his arms and fell asleep.

*A*bby sat across from Nick in the dining room, scooping a fork full of eggs and eyeing the last bacon strip. She was still hungry.

"I have the day off today," Nick said while scanning the *Morning Gazette.*

She pried her gaze from the bacon dish. "Oh?"

"I was thinking I could join you on your trip to the orphanage." He snapped the paper so a corner folded and glanced at her.

"Really? You want to join me?" Wasn't that exactly what Katherine and Lydia said could help ease him back into the public?

Thank you, God.

Abby wasn't going to keep insisting he go out in public if he wasn't ready. "You don't have to if you don't want to. I don't want to push you into anything."

With a half-smile, he raised a hand to still her tongue. "Do you not want me to come."

She grabbed his hands. "No, no, no, I would love for you to come. I'm delighted you want to come. I just want you to know that you don't have to. I'm not going to force you."

"We're going to be a family now, and you're right. It's time I let a few people know I'm alive. Perhaps tomorrow night we can call upon your mother and Stephen."

"Oh, Nick." She threw her arms around him and kissed him soundly.

Thank you, God. Please, let him love the children, and the children love him in return. Help things go smoothly.

～

*A*bby leaned back on her palms and refolded her legs beneath her skirts. A blanket had been spread out in the courtyard for her and the children to listen to Nick's tale. Her heart swelled with pride at Nick's bravery to speak to the orphans.

The air held a chill, but boys and girls didn't seem to mind as they sat cross-legged in the grass, listening to Nick re-enacting a battle.

When the children had first asked him to tell them a story, he'd hesitated. And after he relented and began, he kept reaching up to adjust his collar, pulling it higher to hide the scars. But as the story progressed, the scars were forgotten.

The children sat wide-eyed, captivated by his facial expressions and quick wit.

Nick's imitation of Napoleon Bonaparte was similar to the caricatures depicted of the French military commander in the papers. When Nick kneeled, pretending to be standing, and placed one hand inside his jacket, she laughed so hard it brought tears to her eyes.

Nick made a surprise attack jabbing at an invisible foe with an invisible sword, the children jumped, and Abby swallowed another fit of laughter.

The story was about a *friend* who'd spied for the crown and had to steal an important document from the desk of Napoleon Bonaparte himself. As the tale progressed, Nick was crouching, jumping, and ducking behind the makeshift log-bench.

The children barely blinked, hanging on his every word.

Abby savored the moment and wished she could capture this feeling in her heart forever. Her hand strayed to her stomach and rested there. She couldn't wait for the future. It was going to be everything that she had dreamed. Nick's response to the children, and their reactions to him, were better than she could have ever imagined.

When Nick was finished, the children jumped to their feet and applauded. The boys bombarded him with questions about the war while the girls moved into their own circles, chattering about the amazing Mr. Emerson, the fun, mysterious man who was married to Lady Abigail.

Lydia scooted next to Abby.

"I'm delighted that Mr. Emerson is here. God has answered all my prayers. First, I prayed for work, and starting next week, I'll be in your employ. Then, I prayed Mr. Emerson to come to the orphanage and fall in love with you all over again, and it is happening."

As if on cue, Nick glanced at Abby with a twinkle in his eye that heated her cheeks.

Lydia sighed. "I hope someday a man will look at me like that."

Abby bit her lower lip to keep from laughing at her dreamy expression. "Someday, Lydia. Keep praying."

Miss Quiller rang the bell, signaling the end of playtime and to return to their studies.

Abby clapped her hands to get the children's attention. "It's time to line up. I want everyone to thank Mr. Emerson for his visit."

Disappointed cries from the children split the air before they gathered to express their appreciation.

The smallest girl in the group, Hannah, held a daisy chain of flowers in one hand and tugged on Nick's trousers to get his attention. When he looked down, she held up the necklace with a shy smile.

"I made it for you," she whispered.

Nick squatted on his heels and examined the necklace. "You made that? All by yourself?"

Hannah nodded then whispered in his ear.

"Of course, you may." Nick ducked his head, and Hannah

circled it with the flowers and pulled the daisy chain down around his neck.

"Snakes!" Hannah screeched like a banshee. "Snakes!"

The girls started screaming and running in all directions, some jumping up on benches and wailing.

Abby rushed to quiet Hannah and calm Nick who turned white and covered his ears.

The boys almost knocked Abby over to scan the ground for the slithering creatures. They elbowed their way in, rustling the grass and overturning rocks. Some of the aggressive boys knocked girls over in the process.

Abby caught one falling child and passed her off to Lydia.

Nick had begun to visibly shake and held out a palm as if to ward off an unseen enemy.

"Hannah, shush. There are no snakes. Go to Lydia." She handed the child to the elder orphan and turned to Nick, cupping his face in her hands. "It's me, Abby. Everything is fine." She reached back and frantically pulled pins from her hair to allow it down.

"Get out of here!" He grasped her forearms in a painful grip causing Abby to wince. "The building's going to collapse. Run!" He spun her around and shoved her toward the children.

She tripped over a boy bent over and hunting for snakes and fell. Her hand grazed the top of the bench as she tried to catch her fall, but instead her stomach took the brunt of the hit on the hard, wooden backrest. The impact knocked the air from her lungs and pain seared her midsection. She stumbled off the bench still hunched over and holding her stomach.

Lord, please protect the baby.

She raised her head to find Nick, but he wasn't there. Straightening as best she could, she scanned the courtyard, but Nick was nowhere to be found.

Where had Nick gone?

"Hannah, shush." Lydia cradled the child. "It's all right, there aren't any snakes."

"B-b-but I saw them crawling under his skin. They were all over his neck."

Oh no. Abby covered her gasp and lowered to meet Hannah's gaze. "Darling, those were scars. Mr. Emerson was badly hurt, and what you saw was how his skin has healed itself, mending itself back together."

"Not snakes?" Her big blue eyes met Abby's, uncertainty still lurking in their depths. "Are you sure?"

Abby nodded. "Yes, I'm very certain. I've seen them myself."

"Were you afraid?"

"I think I was more sad than afraid. Mr. Emerson had to go through so much pain, but now I'm happy that he is alive, and God is restoring him."

"Oh." Hannah's lips formed a small circle.

"Children!" Miss Quiller's voice boomed. "Stand at attention."

The children stood straight as boards with their arms at their sides.

Abby put Hannah down and turned to face Miss Quiller.

"Lady Abigail, it appears things have gone awry in my absence. I do not understand the meaning of this chaotic outbreak, but these children need to learn to conduct themselves in a sensible manner, not run around like a bunch of heathens."

She peered over her spectacles with a frosty look meant to put Abby in her place. "Line up single file and quietly move to the classroom. Once you take your seats, open your primer, and prepare to do your sums and equations."

Abby's heart sank as the last child exited the courtyard.

Nick had vanished.

～

*N*icholas couldn't breathe. His heart writhed in his chest.

The children's screams rang in his head, blurring with the horrific echoes of war. Crouching down in the dark corner of an alley, he held his hands over his ears to block out the sounds and memories. He refused to close his eyes, tried not even to blink.

When his eyes shut, he saw it all again—the fire, the blood, the bodies—and now Abby doubled over in pain and holding her stomach. He didn't remember hurting her, but he knew his episode had caused it. Cold sweat trickled down his back. He wasn't certain how long he stayed like that, minutes or hours. Eventually, his breathing slowed, and his heartbeat thumped back to a regular rhythm.

Nicholas turned into the wall and rested his forehead on the cold stone. What a fool. How had he ever thought he was healing?

His nightmares and episodes had subsided the past few weeks, and he'd gotten cocky.

Why had he thought he could go in public and act normally? He was cursed to hide in the shadows, steal about unnoticed, stay isolated and alone so he couldn't hurt anyone.

His episodes were becoming more debilitating. If an attack came on while he was in action, he would be a dead man. He couldn't continue with the Home Office, even if he wanted to, and he couldn't resume his old life. He was a boat adrift with no place to dock and no shore to welcome him.

And now he was going to be a father.

The image of Abby doubled over gripped him. Had he hurt the baby? He rose needing to get back to Abby and make sure she was all right.

He stumbled in the direction of Laurel House, staying in the back alleys. What triggered him? Where did he go wrong? The afternoon with the children had gone swimmingly until —*snakes.*

In the chaos of his wide-awake nightmare, he'd hurt Abby, but he wouldn't hurt her again. He needed to stay far away from her, leave Altonwood. But if he left, Abby would face ridicule and their child would be raised fatherless.

He was trapped between two terrible alternatives.

Perhaps it would have been better if he'd just died in the fire.

~

*A*bby paced the foyer. Other than the orphanage and home, she hadn't known where else to search for Nick. When she caught a glimpse of him unlocking the gate, she almost collapsed in relief.

She opened the front door and met him on the stoop. "Nick. Are you all right?" She wrapped him in an embrace.

"I'm fine. It's you I'm worried about." He pulled her arms away and guided her inside into the drawing room. "Are you well? And the baby?" He crossed to the opposite side, creating a wide gap between them.

Obviously, he was not fine. She drew up alongside him and rested her hand gently on the arm of his jacket. "I'm fine and the baby is fine. It was an accident."

"It was an episode, and I can't stop them, nor can I control them." The words came through clenched teeth, and he sank onto the sofa as if his legs could no longer hold him. "I'm gunpowder that can explode by the tiniest spark. I'm dangerous —to you—to our child. The best thing for us all is for me to leave so you can be safe and live your life."

She knelt beside him. Her fingers curled around the lapel of his coat. "Don't you understand? I won't move on. You are my husband. I love you. We will get through this together."

Nick stood, brushing off her hands, and stepped out of her reach. "All that's left of me is a bitter deformed beast of a man who frightens children. If I stay, you will suffer for my sins— physically and emotionally. I cannot bear the thought of hurting you or our child. If I injured or accidentally killed our child during an episode, you can't tell me that you'd still look upon me with love, that you'd still want me in your bed."

She gasped, not having considered those implications. Could she still love him if his actions resulted in the death of their child?

"I'm an outcast, an untouchable who will forever pay a penance for my arrogance."

Abby rose. "It's not like that—"

"You don't know," he yelled. "You don't know what it's like to be tormented every night. Eaten by guilt for what you've done and for what you didn't do. Terriorized by shame and helpless for what you couldn't prevent. You've never suffered a day in your life."

"Haven't suffered? How dare you! I suffered endlessly when you didn't return from the war. All the tears, the worry, the sleepless nights, the anguish I endured when I thought you were dead. Guilt ate at me for believing I'd driven you to your death chasing after a meaningless title. And all the while, you were alive. Alive, but you couldn't bother to let me know.

"I know the pain of awkward silences. I know the pain of being abandoned by my friends because they didn't know how to handle my grief. I don't belong with the married couples or the single women. For ten years, I've been married with no husband. My friends have started families and forgotten about me." She heaved in a breath. "The difference between my suffering and yours is that mine could have been prevented, if you'd cared more about me than about yourself. If you leave, I will suffer even more. I carry your child, but everyone believes you dead." She remembered Stephen's words, she hallucinated about her husband being alive. "Not even my brother believes me. He thinks I'm fanciful and dreamt you into being." She crossed her arms. "The town will label me a harlot. I'll be scorned, shunned and so will your child."

"Don't you think I know that! It's why I had planned to stay for you for our child, but today changed my thinking."

"An incident with screaming children and you'll leave me in disgrace?"

"I'm trying to protect you!" His words were low, seething.

"You're trying to protect *you.*"

"You don't understand." He paced the room, raking his fingers through his hair. "If I stay not only could you get hurt, you'll wind up shamed anyway. All it takes is one public incident and I'll be carted off to Bedlam. I've seen the sanitarium workers come and take away good soldiers for less than what I've exhibited. Then you'll be mocked as the poor woman married to a madman."

Finally, they were getting to the truth of it. She inhaled for patience, exhaled a prayer, and softened her tone. "I won't let them take you. Stephen won't either."

"You won't be able to stop them." He gripped the sides of his head.

Her frustration spiked. "What about these last weeks? Your nightmares were lessening. We can pray for God to take them away. If you stay, you'll have me, and the baby, our love can strengthen you."

"My love can make you dead."

Abby stood stiff-armed, hands clenched at her sides. "You're so blinded by your fear you can't see your future. I know it's not going to be easy, but without going through trials, you won't experience any of the joys that life can give you."

"And what joys will there be when our child is teased and ridiculed? Where is the joy when the other kids are afraid to play with him because his father is the town freak?"

"That won't happen, and if it does, God will see us through."

"Believe me, it will happen. People, especially children, can be merciless when someone is different. I won't stand back and watch my son or daughter endure it, knowing it was on my account. How are you going to feel when all of your friends and family shun you? Well, it's not going to be joy, that's for certain. It will only be a matter of time before you resent me. Our future is not a pretty one, Abby. Stop believing life is some fairy tale."

Nick turned his back and pounded his fist on the wall. "Blast it all, Abby. Why can't you understand?"

She didn't know how to convince him. He had a rebuttal for her every argument. She couldn't keep fighting for them both.

"I would never resent you. I love you." Abby meant the words with all her heart, but they came out as a desperate, whispered plea. A dull pounding ached in her head. Their arguing left her body weak, and she needed to sit. Her hips hurt and her legs wobbled. She slid into a chair before she collapsed. The room spun. She didn't feel right.

Something is wrong.

Her stomach cramped, and a stabbing pain gripped her midsection. She tried to call out to Nick but couldn't find her voice.

$\sim$

*N*icholas forced himself to say the words. He didn't have the courage to look Abby in the face when he told her the only alternative, so he addressed the wall. "The only option I see is for me to leave. You can tell everyone that I was sent on a mission in Africa where it's too dangerous to bring a wife and child. I'll write you daily letters. You can use them as proof that I'm alive and the baby's father.."

He turned. Abby was seated, her face pale and drawn.

He had known she would be shocked, but her pained expression pierced his heart. She winced, and her hand moved to cradle her stomach as if to protect the baby.

This wasn't a reaction to his words.

He rushed to her side and knelt beside her chair, taking her cold hand in his. "What's the matter?"

"Somethings amiss. I don't feel right." Her whisper was barely audible.

"Darling, it's going to be fine." He felt no truth behind his words. "Everything's going to be all right."

Nicholas gently scooped her up in his arms and carried her up the stairs to her bed. He swallowed a wave of panic at the smell of blood.

CHAPTER 25

*D*r. Cox closed the bedchamber door with a soft click.
"How is she?" Nicholas cleared his throat, but his
voice still sounded strained and hoarse.

"Lady Abigail is resting. She was having pains, but they
appear to have subsided."

"A-and the baby?"

The physician's eyes dipped low for a moment, then met
Nicholas's square. "I'm afraid she has miscarried."

Nicholas gripped the wall and closed his eyes. It was his
fault. All of it. He'd ruined her chances to remarry by returning.
His episodes had caused her to miscarry. And his leaving would
break her heart again. He'd lost their child and they'd never
have a chance at another. He hadn't intended to have a baby,
but it was a glimmer of hope amidst all his confusion and
uncertainty. A spark he hadn't realized he wanted until it was
gone. This baby was his one chance at leaving a legacy.

His throat closed, and hot tears formed in the back of his
eyes, but he held them at bay.

"There may still be more pain and hemorrhaging," the
physician continued. "Send someone for me right away if the

bleeding begins again. Otherwise, I'll check back tomorrow. She is to stay on bed rest for the next few days."

Nicholas gave a terse nod, and Dr. Cox headed to the door.

The physician's hand rested on the knob as he turned back to Nicholas. "I will not inform Lady Etheridge of your transgressions. I've taken an oath to protect your right to privacy, but sir, I do hope you plan to do what is right by this woman."

He'd made so many bad choices. No matter how hard he'd tried, he'd caused Abby pain. Had he done what was right where Abby was concerned? His heart wasn't so sure, but that wasn't the answer the physician was looking for. "I've pledged my life to her."

"If word gets out, she'll be ruined. Is that what you want?"

Nicholas's jaw tensed. "I appreciate your silence."

"I suggest you end this and find a woman within your station."

It was on the tip of Nicholas's tongue to tell him he was Abby's husband, but he couldn't while the man was still a suspect. He watched the physician until he exited the gate, then turned and went upstairs to check on Abby. The sounds of soft weeping emanated from her room. Nicholas opened the door, sending a soft crack of light into the darkness.

"Abby?"

"Oh, Nick." She reached toward him.

He pulled back the covers and crawled in. His arms encircled her, and he cradled her body with his.

Her entire being shook with deep, pitiful sobs. "The b-baby, the baby is-is ..."

"Shh, I know, darling. I'm sorry, so sorry."

She cried until his shirt was damp and soggy. Eventually, her breathing evened out, and the tears subsided. Only the occasional shuddered intake of breath remained. Once she'd drifted off to sleep, Nicholas slid out from under the covers. Kneeling beside the bed, he watched her peaceful slumber. He wanted to tell her it was going to be all right. That they would have more children, an entire quiver full. But he couldn't. If he was declining into madness, he didn't want to drag her down with him.

How could he accept this future, now that he'd had a glimpse of what could have been? Even in the midst of their sorrow, his body still ached to touch her.

Abby's eyes fluttered open. She saw him there, and her lips tipped up the slightest. "If it had been a girl, I thought it would be nice to name her after your mother."

"And if it was a boy?"

"Nicholas Emerson the second."

"No. Give our son a fresh chance. I think a strong name, like David or Daniel."

Abby smiled weakly, and her eyes fluttered shut, but he heard her mumble, "I like those names."

~

*H*is arrows sliced through the air, each hitting their desired target. Nicholas didn't pause or rest, merely reached back and notched another, never breaking rhythm. Sweat beaded on his brow, and his arms hurt from maintaining his form, but he kept going until every arrow had sunk deep into the bark of the tree. He reached back into his quiver but grasped only air.

He strode to the tree. Placing one hand on the trunk for leverage, he pulled out each arrow and dropped it back into its container. The deeper ones he dug out with his pocketknife.

After freeing the last tip, he turned and leaned against the tree. He sank to the ground with his knees up. The rough bark cut into his flesh through his thin cambric shirt. He rubbed his temples. His nightmares had returned with a vengeance. The peaceful lull had ceased, and now he once again awoke every morning in a cold sweat, struggling to determine where he was, what was real, and if he was among friends or foes.

The past few days he'd spent seeing to Abby's comfort and rest while doing his best to be wary of any attack and keep his distance. She slept most of the day, and Nicholas did everything he could to ease her grief. When she finally asked for a tray of food to be brought up, Nicholas had almost leapt for joy.

On the heels of her healing came another struggle. The time had come for him to leave. The threat of Lester Shue was gone, and the more he dug into the arsenic poisoning, the more he got the notion that Lady Etheridge had concocted the entire thing out of a need for attention.

When the initial angst of losing their child faded into a resigned, deep-set sorrow, another emotion arose that fed his self-hatred—relief. He tried to deny it, but the feeling was there.

It was as if he'd been released from a smaller cage to find himself in a slightly larger one.

He continued to ask himself, *would staying really be so bad?* But, his pride roared a fearful, *yes!* If he stayed, he'd never be able to keep his hands off her. It wouldn't be long before he found himself back in the same predicament. Abby would once again be with child, and he would be forced to uproot her from her family and all the people she loved. The adoration he'd witnessed in the eyes of the children in the orphanage was all he needed to see. They needed her. Only a selfish blackguard would stash her away for himself.

Nicholas closed his eyes in shame. He was that awful cad. He wanted her all to himself, but he knew Abby would wither in isolation. How could he ask it of her? How could he expect it of his child?

He could still see the horror in the little girl's eyes as she shouted.

Snakes!

Between the scars and the nightmares, his own child would fear him, and if he didn't, then surely he would come to loathe his father for being a social outcast. The miscarriage had granted Nicholas an out. He would be the greatest of fools if he didn't take it.

But the thought of leaving Abby sucked the air from his lungs. His body trembled.

She would hate him for all eternity.

If he stayed, her resentment would be subtle, slowly infiltrating and dissembling their love the same way he'd helped the crown permeate the French defenses, bringing them down from the inside. He couldn't leave now, not so soon after her recent heartbreak, but the sooner he left, the better. A clean slice heals better than a ragged wound.

Her family would comfort her. After a couple of years, he'd use his contacts to fake his death certificate. It was the only way she would move on and have the life she deserved. He would go find a hole in the northern wilds to live out his days—alone.

Nicholas lowered his head in his hands. Part of him felt like he'd been given the gift of freedom, but the other felt like a handful of dirt had been thrown on his grave.

"Pardon me, sir?"

He turned to find a woman barely out of adolescence from the orphanage standing before him. She wore basic sturdy clothing and her hair was pulled back into a kerchief.

"Good day, Mr. Emerson."

Nicholas stood and dusted himself off. "Good day, Miss ..."

"Lydia O'Donnell." She bobbed a formal curtsy. "I'm here to begin my employment."

"I see," he said, but he didn't see. He hadn't the slightest clue what the chit was talking about. "Why don't we go inside, shall we?"

He opened the door and had her take a seat while he climbed the stairs to Abby's room.

~

*A*bby scooted to a sitting position and called out for Nick to enter. He opened the door and paused in the doorway, his face thin and drawn, still haggard from the ordeal of losing the baby.

Her heart rose into her throat, but she swallowed it back down and patted the bed for him to come and sit.

He moved to her side but remained standing. "Your color is back. You're feeling better this morning?"

She tilted her head to the side. "It's odd, but besides being sad, I don't feel physically any different than I did before the baby was"—she faltered but forced the word past her lips—"lost."

"Miss Lydia O'Donnell is downstairs. She claims she's to begin employment today."

"I completely forgot. She is to start training under Mrs. Smith, who's supposed to return in a few days. The time got away from me." Abby tried to stand up, but Nick restrained her with a hand.

Abby met his gaze. "I've thrown my temper tantrum in front of God. He's shown me that the baby was His to give or take away. I'm not happy, but He keeps giving me the impression He's going to doubly bless us in other ways. I've learned to trust Him. It's time for me to get out of bed."

"You may feel ready, but the physician said you should take it easy." He gently pushed her shoulders back onto the pillows.

"I thought you didn't like doctors?"

"Quite right."

"Then why do I need to listen to his advice?"

"Because it's the same advice I would have given."

Abby huffed out a sigh.

"I will send Miss O'Donnell up. If you are feeling well, then this afternoon you can move to the solarium and check on your flowers. They were looking droopy, so I watered them. I hope I didn't kill any of them."

She squeezed his hand, hoping the gesture would show her appreciation. "Thank you."

A well of giggles bubbled up inside Abby, and she tried to cover it with a cough.

"What is so funny?"

She snorted, still trying to smother laughter. "I pictured you with an apron on and watering can in hand."

A smile cracked Nick's lips, and Abby couldn't contain herself any longer. Her laughter filled the room with a melodious sound, and Nick joined in. One minute she was laughing, and the next tears sprang to her eyes.

Nick's laughter died. He sat next to her and encircled her in his arms, cradling her head under his chin. Nick held her tight until the tears subsided and then held her some more.

Her fingers toyed with the ends of his hair. "Thank you for understanding."

"I'll give you a moment, then I'll send up Miss O'Donnell."

Abby nodded and wiped her tears with the back of her hand. "I don't know why I get this way."

Nick kissed her softly on the temple and rose from the bed, but he paused at the door. A love, almost tangible enough for her to reach out and touch, shown in his eyes. Her heart quickened its pace. His fingers patted the door frame twice, and with a weak smile, he ducked out of the room.

Abby stared at the open door. Now that Nick had returned, she couldn't imagine how she'd survived without him. How did she live ten years without her heart beating?

*M*iss O'Donnell's presence was the final piece that fell into place.

Now Nicholas could leave.

Over the past few days, Lydia had doted on Abby, allowing him to remove himself more and more, knowing his wife was well cared for. He'd already sent a missive to the Home Office informing them he could not finish his assignment at Lady Etheridge's estate. Now, he needed to inform Lady Etheridge. After that, the task he dreaded the most—he had to tell Abby.

Two weeks after Abby's miscarriage, Nicholas stood in front of Lady Etheridge's assessing gaze and tried hard not to shuffle his feet like a schoolboy being chastised. He'd prefer to be forced to clean chalkboard erasers than suffer any longer in her presence. Despite the oversized drawing room, the heavy furniture and elaborately fringed upholsteries suffocated him.

"I'm extremely disappointed, Agent Scar." She pulled off her spectacles and peered at him over her writing desk. "The Home Office assured me you were the best of the best."

"You have my sincerest apologies. I will ensure the department sends another highly qualified agent, and I am—"

"Please explain why *you* can't finish what you started?" Lady Etheridge leaned forward. Her astute eyes scrutinized him as if to determine the truth.

"I'm not at liberty to say."

She leaned back in her chair and adjusted her spectacles. "The truth is, you do not *wish* to tell me."

His jaw clenched. "I will detail all of my findings in my report. There doesn't appear to be any malice among your staff. Despite the high demands placed upon them, they're loyal to you. The likeliest scenario is that you made the entire thing up to get attention."

Her eyes widened. "How dare you." She drew back and placed a hand over her heart as if affronted.

He pulled a black book out of his pocket and flipped it open to scan his written observations. "I found nothing to link the physician. The local ratcatcher hasn't been out since last winter, and your staff is loyal—even the housekeeper who takes the brunt of your set-downs, needs the money for a sick relative and can't afford to lose her employment if something happened to you."

"You've thought of everything." As she slid on her spectacles, she muttered, "If only you'd spent more time researching my suspect."

Keeping his temper in check, he said, "You and I both know Lady Abigail is a dead end. However, if you wish me to add your suspicions to the list for the next agent, then I—"

"No!" She came out of her chair. It took a moment before she regained her composure and continued in a calmer voice. "No need, Agent Scar, no need."

Her reaction furthered his suspicions, but he didn't question her further. Whatever got him out of Lady Etheridge's presence the fastest. "Very well, then. Good day."

Nicholas bowed and turned on his heel. He was about to see himself out when she spoke again.

"Are you certain you are making the right decision, Agent Scar?"

The infuriating woman couldn't leave things be. Peering over his left shoulder, he replied, "I believe it to be the best course of action considering the circumstances, Madame. The best for *all* parties involved."

She let out an exasperated sigh. "Have it your way."

Nicholas strode out the door and didn't look back.

LORRI DUDLEY

*A*bby sat under the willow tree near the stream in front of Laurel House. She drew her wool wrap tighter around her shoulders. The air held a chill, but the sun warmed her face and danced through the bare branches as they swayed with the wind. It felt nice to be outside. It had been a dark few days, but her strength was returning.

Lydia was a blessing. She cheered Abby's spirits and took her mind off the miscarriage. There was still hope. She'd been given a second chance with Nick. God would surely grace them with a second chance at children.

Abby let out a loud yawn. She'd hoped the fresh air would give her more energy, but the weariness stayed deep in her bones. It was taking longer to return to a normal life than Abby had anticipated. She closed her eyes and lay back on the quilt Lydia had spread on the ground for her.

A noise awoke her. She sat up straight and rubbed her eyes to wipe away the drowsy feeling. How long had she'd dosed? The leaves rustled, and Abby blinked to focus better.

Nick turned down the lane towards her. The sun was still high in the sky, and it was odd to find him coming home at midday. Her heart did a little flip.

She stood and shook her dress to dislodge some of the wrinkles. When he spotted her, she smiled and waved.

"You're home early. To what do I owe this delightful occasion?"

Nick's face remained impassive. "I need to have a word with you."

At his tone and lack of smile, Abby swallowed a sense of foreboding and nodded. "Would you like to take a turn about the lawn?"

Instead of offering her his arm, he clasped his hands behind his back.

She fell into step beside him and watched his profile. His

294

eyes were veiled, and lines of tension creased his brow. She waited for him to speak, but he appeared lost in thought. Just when she believed he'd forgotten her presence, he began.

"Abby, I have to go away."

Her heart sank, and her legs felt weighted, but she tried not to let her hurt show. She counted her steps and waited for him to explain further. *Three, four, five ...* She couldn't wait any longer.

"For how long?"

He continued to stare straight ahead. "Forever."

Abby stopped. The wind blew tendrils of her hair loose, and they whipped her face. *Forever.* It sounded so final, so absolute, so—devastating.

"You wouldn't. You mustn't."

Nick turned on his heel, his body poised as if for battle. His face softened when he noticed the tears spilling from her eyes.

She made no move to wipe them away. "Is it because I couldn't keep the baby?"

He pulled her to him and wrapped her in a tight embrace.

Abby leaned into him for strength. His scent left her heady and disoriented. Within the warmth of his arms, his announcement seemed surreal, like a distant storm brewing, not a current reality.

"No, darling. This is not your fault. It has never been your fault." His hand stroked the curve of her spine. "I've put you through more than you can bear. It is my fault, and I know your troubles will only get worse if I stay. Tell people that I'm a spy for the War Department and was sent to a place where it was too dangerous for you to come. I will write to you and you can use the letters to prove my existence and my return. It's time I left so you can go on with your life in whatever manner you choose."

"I choose you. Don't leave me. I don't want to live my life without you." She leaned back to study his face for a reaction.

It remained stony.

A new thought occurred to her. "Couldn't I go with you?"

"Not with my mind slipping. I love you too deeply to risk hurting you, nor can I bind you to a madman. You'd be a constant temptation, and I wouldn't be able to keep my hands off you."

"It's not true."

He ran a hand through the top of his hair. "Inevitably you would end up with child again."

She'd meant his mental state, but he continued before she could explain.

"I've calculated the risks, and they're too great." He shook his head. "I don't want to bring a child into this world. I can't be a father."

Abby recoiled as if he'd slapped her. He'd never wanted their baby?

The miscarriage was a blessing for him?

He continued. "You have your family and friends, the children at the orphanage. You need them, and they need you. I see that now. It would be selfish of me to take you away."

Abby jabbed her index finger into his chest. "You said on our wedding day that all that was important were you, me, and God. The rest were frills and fluff. You wanted to proclaim I was your wife in front of the whole world, but you said if you had to settle for merely a priest, you would, because you loved me, and nothing else mattered, not rain or dresses or flowers ... Just you, me, and God. That's what you said, and I believed you. So now ... I don't understand." She held her palms up. "What has changed?"

"I was naïve. I believed all we needed was each other, that love could heal all wounds, but I've learned otherwise." He lifted her chin with his forefinger. "Abby, you sparkle around others. They excite and energize you. I can't sit back and watch you wither away in the recesses of some God-forsaken land.

You would eventually come to resent me for it. I would die watching the spark diminish in your eyes."

"Stop telling me what I would do. You don't know..."

He cupped her face in his hands. "I can't stay here, and you can't come with me."

"You're wrong." She stepped back and shook her head. "I'm not going to give up. I won't lose you again."

"This is the only way. If there were another choice, I would take it. You have my heart, Abigail Emerson, and you always will."

His lips took hers, and she responded. Her arms slid around his neck, and she kissed him with all the pent-up emotion she needed to shed. Maybe she could show him how much she loved him. Maybe if he understood...

Nick slowly pulled away and, after disentangling her arms, drew back. "Abby, *this* is why I must go." His voice was a ragged whisper as they both fought to catch their breath. He pressed his lips to her forehead. He then released her and turned to leave.

She wanted to scream and fight. The man needed to see reason, but she'd fought too long holding the reins of a horse that wanted to run free. She felt God nudging at her to let go. She watched in silence as he walked away. Nick didn't bother to collect his spare clothes from the house. He just grabbed his bow and arrows.

Abby followed him into the stable, where he mounted his horse.

"Wait!" She grabbed a pair of shears, pushed back her bonnet, and undid the ribbon tying back her hair. With a steady hand, Abby lopped off a lock of hair from the underside. She crouched down, using her thigh as a table, and tied the ribbon in a tight knot around the strands to hold the hair in place.

"Here, take this." She stood and held out the parting gift towards him.

Nick's eyes questioned hers as he took the lock of hair.

"For your nightmares," she explained. "It seems to help. You aren't responsible for your injuries, but you can be accountable for your own healing."

She put a hand on his pant leg. "Nick, my vows to you are a covenant I will not break. There will never be anyone else. I will always love you. I will be here praying for you. Praying you'll come back to me."

Tenderness shown in his eyes, but his expression was pained as he rubbed the silken hair between his fingers. He nodded, pulled open his jacket, and stashed the lock in the inside pocket, closest to his heart.

He turned his horse but held her gaze steady. "I love you, Abby." With one last backward glance, he snapped the reins.

"I love you more!" Abby shouted at his retreating form blurred by unshed tears. "I love you more, Nicholas Emerson."

CHAPTER 26

*S*tumbling back into the house, Abby climbed the steps to her room in a daze and tumbled onto the bedcovers face first. She cried so hard she became sick, barely making it to the chamber pot in time. Day settled into night, and the nausea didn't stop. As she finished emptying the contents of what had been her supper, she leaned her head back and mentally screamed at the whitewashed ceiling. *Why, God, why did I lose him? Why would you bring Nick back into my life only to take him away again?*

Abby let loose the loud sobs she'd held back most of the day, but now she meant to have it out with God. She crawled to the window and lifted the sash. The cold night air cooled her heated skin. Leaning out on the sill, she raised her eyes to the heavens. For hours, she questioned, argued, and pleaded with God. After her tears were spent, she lay on the floor, completely drained. She was destined to be alone, truly and utterly alone.

As the tears and nausea subsided, Abby realized she had a choice. She could blame God and remain bitter, or she could beg Him to pull her out of the dark pit she'd fallen into. *Just keep breathing.* Mama Em's voice floated through her memory. With what little energy Abby had left, she crawled onto her knees.

"Father, there is nothing I can do to bring Nick back. Your ways and thoughts are higher than my own. Align my will with Yours. If this is what You intend for my life, then help me to live it according to Your purpose. I've been trying to force my own way, but I realize now I need to pray for Your will and my surrender. I have been putting my desires first. I need You. I need You now more than ever. Forgive me, Father."

Abby sat up and stared out the window. The sweet night air rustled the branches and leaves remaining in the trees, and familiar night sounds surrounded her. Life was continuing. It didn't stop because Nick left. Dawn slowly yawned and considered waking. The chatter of birds filled the air.

A little sparrow appeared on a branch near her window. Its energetic body hopped down the limb towards the window and cocked its head at Abby.

A verse her mother used to say from the book of Luke popped into her head. "Are not five sparrows sold for two pennies? Yet, not one of them is forgotten by God." A small smile formed on her lips, and a fresh bout of tears filled her eyes. But these tears were different. The pain and anguish had lifted.

My precious daughter. A still, small voice spoke to her spirit. *I will never leave you nor forsake you. I have been beside you the entire time, quieting your spirit from all the noise you have stirred up in your mind. I know how you're hurting but put your concerns in My hands. Trust in me. My love will not fail you.*

~

*a*bby awoke before noon feeling refreshed, despite her sporadic sleep, and starving. She descended the stairs to the kitchen and Lydia dished out the morning meal. A wave of nausea threatened to overtake her, but she fought it down and finished the plate of eggs and ham Lydia brought her. To her amazement, she felt much better and even asked for another helping. Over the next few days, she found the only thing that kept the nausea at bay was to nibble on food at all times.

"If this illness doesn't pass, I'm going to become quite fat," she said to Lydia.

A knock sounded on the back door, and a gray-haired woman poked her head into the kitchen.

"I'm hoping to find my kitchen all in order and just the way I left it."

"Mrs. Smith." Abby jumped up to greet the housekeeper.

"Milady, you are a welcome sight. The crisp air has brought color to your cheeks and has put a glow to your skin. You look splendid, my dear. How fare things at Laurel House?"

Abby wasn't sure how to answer her question. So much had happened in a few short months. "Unbelievable." She touched Mrs. Smith's arm. "You have been greatly missed. How is your precious grandbaby?"

Mrs. Smith puffed up like a proud peacock. "He's a strong boy, very alert. Has his mama's eyes but his pa's nose and chin. He's a Smith through and through. Came out weighing a stone. His mama was sore for a couple weeks. Goin' to be a healthy child." She glanced at Lydia, who had begun clearing the dishes. "And who have we here?"

"Mrs. Smith, this is Lydia O'Donnell. I met her at the orphanage. She came of age and sought employment, so I figured she could work under your tutelage. She has been a tremendous help this past fortnight."

Lydia and Mrs. Smith got along famously. Mrs. Smith appreciated the extra pair of hands, especially since her own were beginning to ache from old age. Lydia was a quick study. They both chided Abby for snitching rolls straight from the oven and asking for second helpings. One day, however, Mrs. Smith's smile wasn't quite as bright.

Abby plucked another scone off the tea tray, and Mrs. Smith frowned.

Abby spied her grimace. "Is something amiss?"

"It's not my place."

"Don't be silly. You've been with the Emerson family longer than I."

Her eyes lowered to examine the floor. "You see, there are wagging tongues in town. At first, I wasn't having any of it. I reminded them you are a respected woman of good breeding. But you've been acting so strangely. I've been watching all the signs, and I know 'em when I see 'em."

Abby's brow furrowed. "I'm not following."

"Yer with child. You can't deny it. Even though Polly helps you with yer dressing, it's obvious yer middle is thickening already."

Abby's hand flew to her belly. She had been feeling swollen, but she'd figured it had something to do with the miscarriage or all the eating she'd been doing. Hope, like the coals of a dead fire, reignited in her chest.

"I wish it were true, Mrs. Smith, but you don't understand. I had a miscarriage—"

Her gasp stopped Abby mid-sentence.

"It's not what you think."

"You up and got married since I've been gone?"

"Well, no. I've been married."

"God rest his soul. With all due respect, milady, I love your family, and it breaks my heart that you would tarnish their name by letting a man into your bed. I know it's not my place, but it's not right."

Abby didn't know whether to be touched by her devotion to the family or miffed at her accusation. "You are mistaken. Nick is not dead. He returned."

"Glory be." Mrs. Smith sank into the chair behind her, and then, remembering her station, shot back up. "Master Nicholas. Where is he?" Tears of joy sprang to her eyes. "I used to bounce that boy on my knee. He's alive. I knew I smelled him when I first returned. The scent was so strong, I was beginning to believe his spirit was haunting the place. It's a miracle. When will he return?"

"He's not coming back."

Some of the woman's joy faded. "I don't understand."

"He didn't want to have children, so he left."

"Well, that's not right. Mr. Emerson is an honorable man. He wouldn't have left you to raise his child on your own."

"I'd miscarried, or so we thought. When he left, he believed the child gone. I never considered..."

Abby couldn't finish her sentence. Suddenly, her nausea, her exhaustion, her increased appetite, her curved belly. They all made sense. The physician had been wrong.

She was still pregnant.

Thank You, God.

Mrs. Smith prattled on in the background, but Abby focused on the precious gift God had granted her.

"Master Nicholas is alive. Glory be. I think a celebration is in order, some plum pudding, I do believe." Mrs. Smith bobbed another curtsy. "Ring for me if you need anything, milady. I'll be in the kitchen."

Abby nodded in return, her heart filling with possibility.

*N*icholas rose from behind his desk as Lieutenant Sparks strolled into his study.

"Well, Scar, you certainly have accomplished a lot in a short period of time. This land was a pile of rocks a year ago."

Nicholas couldn't help but smile. Everything was progressing nicely. The main portion of the house was complete, and the workers would begin on the west and east wings next week. The fields had been properly irrigated and prepared to produce crops in the spring, and without a day to spare before the winter winds froze the ground solid. Nicholas had met with countless designers and architects to get everything perfect. He had chosen this specific spot because of similarities to the topography of his own hometown. Not far down the road, he'd recently broken ground on the building of a new children's orphanage so Abby would feel right at home.

"So you plan to reside in the lap of luxury and live out the rest of your days in comfort?"

Nicholas gestured for him to have a seat. "I don't intend to live here." He absently rubbed the silky locket of hair Abby had given him. He had kept it hidden in a drawer in his bedside table, but recently he'd felt he needed it during the day for extra strength.

"What is that thing?"

Nicholas glanced down at the lock clutched between his thumb and forefinger. "Merely a luck charm."

"Has it helped?"

Nicholas thought of the recent nights when he'd awakened deep in the throes of a ghastly nightmare. He'd grab the lock of hair, but it didn't chase away the demons that plagued him. The lock wasn't what had soothed him, as Abby had guessed. His mind summoned the familiar images of Abby kneeling by his bed and praying over him. He could still remember the words he'd overheard one night. *God help him to feel the peace of Your presence. Deliver him from the demons that plague him night and day. Pull him through this trial and leave him with a stronger faith for it.*

"The luck was on the other end," Nicholas said.

"Isn't that always the way of things?"

Nicholas let the question go. "What brings you out to these parts?"

"Just checking in. I wanted to see how you'd taken to a life of leisure."

"You were looking to convince me to come back."

Lieutenant Sparks drew back, looking affronted. "Egad, can't a man check in on a friend without accusations?"

"I've been in the business too long. I'm trained to look for angles and read into things."

"That's what made you the best."

Nicholas offered him a drink, but Sparks declined with a wave of his hand.

"How fairs Mrs. Emerson?"

An image of Abby's effervescent blue eyes, fringed in long dark lashes, passed through his mind, a teasing smile tugging at her lips. "Why do you ask? Is something amiss?"

"She isn't here with you?" Sparks crossed an ankle over his knee and leaned back in his chair.

"No."

"I see. You plan to remain living as a bachelor?"

Nicholas fiddled with the paperwork on his desk. "What are you getting at, my friend?"

Sparks shrugged. "Nothing really. There have been a few inquiries regarding your whereabouts."

His head snapped up. "From Abby?"

"I'm not at liberty to say."

Nicholas scowled. "Did you tell them my location?"

"Of course not, but they put up quite a stink about it."

"You're not going to tell me who?"

"No. I needed to see for myself how you were faring."

"Rest assured, I am quite well."

Sparks stood. "Well then, I must be heading back." He donned his gloves and propped his hat on his head.

"So soon?"

"Yes, yes. Other assignments call. It doesn't appear like you've been relaxing much."

Nicholas chuckled as he pushed his chair out and stood to walk the lieutenant to the door. Halfway there, Lieutenant Sparks stopped. His head cocked to the side as he studied Nicholas. "There is someone I think you should meet."

"I'm living a bachelor's life, but I'm still married."

"No, my friend. My matchmaking days are behind me. He's an old war chap of yours. I think he could help you with your nightmares."

The lieutenant had mentioned he'd witnessed one of Nicholas nightmares the morning he rode away leaving him with Abby in the dilapidated cottage. "Who?"

"Aaron Cooke."

Nicholas jolted. "I thought he was locked up in Bedlam."

"Not anymore." He tipped his hat. "I must be going, but I'll bring him with me next visit."

"If you can get away from the department for a holiday, there's a lake less than a mile from here where the fish practically jump into your boat."

The man's face lit up, and he rubbed his chin. "I might take you up on that. I'm due for some time off." He clapped Nicholas on the shoulder. "Stay well, my friend."

"You do the same."

Lieutenant Sparks dipped his head then turned and trotted down the steps to where a footman held the door to his carriage open.

As the carriage rolled down the lane, Nicholas couldn't

dispel the unsettled feeling in his stomach. There had been more to this visit than the lieutenant had let on.

$\sim$

*a*bby's nephew dug his hands in the dirt as he helped her re-pot a growing hibiscus.

Seeing the mess, Katherine picked up the boy's discarded rag and ran over to him. "Benjamin, don't wipe your dirty hands on your breeches. Use the rag Aunt Abby has for you. He gets into everything nowadays. It's nearly impossible to keep him clean. He's driving his nanny to perdition."

Abby chuckled, watching her eager nephew as he squished the damp dirt between his fingers.

"How are you feeling?"

Abby rubbed a hand over her stomach. "Like I swallowed a horse." Her belly was huge, stretched beyond what she'd thought was even possible. Surely the baby would arrive any day now. "Or maybe an octopus. I swear the baby has eight legs. It kicks me in every direction."

Katherine laughed. "Benjamin used to wedge his foot right here." She pointed to her lower rib cage. "It would hurt so bad that I would have to stop and take deep breaths."

Abby's head lifted, "Did it work?"

"No, he'd merely kick more."

"Thanks for the tip." After sending a wink her sister-in-law's way, Abby dusted her hands together and waddled to the basin to wash off the remaining dirt. "That's enough for me today. Even the slightest activity leaves me winded. I need to rest."

"Here, let me help." Katherine took Abby's arm and led her to the nearby chaise lounge. After helping her get comfortable, Katherine hovered nearby. Her eyes darkened, and creases formed on her brow.

"Tell me," Abby said. "I know something is bothering you. What's amiss?"

"Nothing's amiss ..."

Abby cut her off with a stern look.

"I don't want to upset you, especially in your condition. Stephen is handling it, and I'm sure everything will be right as rain."

Abby crossed her arms. "What is Stephen handling?"

"You're in a fragile state right now. The news could upset you."

"Not any more than not telling me will," Abby said, voice rising.

"All right. It's probably nothing, but there are some people in town who have stirred up gossip. There is a gathering tonight to discuss the matter."

"What matter?"

"Your condition."

Dread filled her stomach, but it was quickly overruled by anger. "What are they saying?"

Katherine chewed on her bottom lip. "It's the most ridiculous thing you've ever heard."

Abby's brow drew together, and she clutched the sides of the chair to brace herself for the accusations she knew were coming.

"There is a rumor going around that your baby was conceived with a werewolf and is part human, part beast."

Abby threw back her head and laughed out loud. She laughed so hard that she had to hold her stomach to keep it from shaking. Wiping the tear from the corner of her eye, she glanced at Katherine, who still held a nervous smile. "That *is* the most absurd thing I've ever heard."

"I know it's completely ludicrous, but some folks in town are superstitious. Others don't understand why Mr. Emerson never showed himself around town. They've drawn the conclusion that you are a"—her cheeks pinked—"a wanton woman who is pitching gammon about Nicholas to save yourself from disgrace."

"Truly? I wouldn't be able to come up with a better lie? Who would believe that someone's husband came back from the dead to give her children?" But as she heard her own words, the truth formed a knot in her stomach. "I have his letters to prove he's alive."

"And an old letter to compare his signature and handwriting?"

"How ridiculous." Of course she had old letters from when he was a youth, but he hadn't written to her during the war, which she now knew was due to him being a spy. Was his handwriting still the same after ten years and war injuries? "Is there something wrong with my word?"

Katherine winced. "I know they're being unreasonable and got carried away by all this fanciful talk of werewolves."

"But the servants have seen him and so have the children from the orphanage."

"People in your employ and children."

Dr. Cox had seen Nick, but did he tell the doctor he was her husband? If he didn't, what must the good doctor think of her? She sobered and stared at Katherine. "No one believes me. Do they?"

"I do." Katherine moved to her friend's side. "I believe you." She clasped Abby's hand.

"Thank you." Abby squeezed Katherine's fingers. "I don't know what I would do without you."

"I've been on my knees every day praying. God will change their hearts, you'll see."

Abby let out a deep breath, "I know. God will take care of everything. In the meantime, you need to sneak me into the meeting."

"But you're in your confinement period. If you're seen, people will talk."

"More than they already are?"

"We don't need to give them more cause."

Abby grabbed Katherine's hands. "We can be discreet. I can sit in the bell tower. No one will know I'm there. Please help. I can't lie here fretting about what they're saying. I need to know what to defend myself from."

Closing her eyes, Katherine frowned but nodded.

CHAPTER 27

*A*bby wiped her sweaty palms on her skirt and shifted for a better position on the hard stairs. Getting comfortable was difficult no matter where she was, thanks to her swollen belly, but being hidden in a cramped stairwell between the church's balcony and bell tower made it nearly impossible.

The baby's kicking only added to the nervous quaking of her stomach. She didn't have a good feeling about this. The town loved to gossip and grew overly excited about nothing. The grocer, Mr. Kroger, was the worst of the lot. If their imaginations got the best of them, it would undoubtedly mean trouble for her. Honest townsfolk could be misled if compelling individuals started lashing out accusations.

Abby clasped her hands to keep them from shaking. The significance of this meeting wasn't lost on her. Her fate and the fate of her unborn child would be determined. She prayed God would use Stephen to bring sense and order to the room.

She glanced at Katherine. "Why don't you go into the meeting."

"I should stay here with you."

"No." Abby flashed her friend a wobbly smile. "It's better for appearances if you're seated next to Stephen. We don't need to give them any more gossip to feed upon."

Stephen had a speech prepared to defend her, and Katherine needed to be next to her husband in a joint show of support. With a nod and a quick hug, Katherine left to take her seat below.

The chattering of the crowd began to settle.

Thanks to the thin walls Abby's hiding spot allowed her to hear the discussions without being seen. A cool breeze occasionally drifted down from the bell tower, causing the heavy rope to sway and allowing a reprieve from the heat rising from the crowd below. The last order of business was announced, and her heart jumped at the sound of her name.

"It grieves me to present an accusation against the widow Abigail Hartington-Emerson." Abby recognized the voice of the barrister. "Lord Stephen Hartington, the Earl of Felton, and his family are pillars in our small community, held in the highest regard."

He paused, and Abby could hear the rustle of his clothes as he paced the room below. "The Emersons, God rest their souls, lived respectable lives, and though not part of the peerage, they were noteworthy within our small community. Nicholas Emerson died serving the crown, further honoring our town and our beloved country."

His voice grew grave. "It is with great regret that I must confront our parish with the allegations against the widow Emerson. Allegations that state she has been keeping a disorderly house—a bawdy house."

The gasps from the crowd echoed throughout the church and reverberated in her mind. She forgot to breathe. *They thought she was running a whore house?*

Stephen's voice boomed. "I object to these ludicrous accusations, and I am offended on my family's behalf and on behalf of my sister that such insinuations have been unjustly made."

"We understand your objections, my lord," stated the magistrate, sitting as judge. "Does anyone have any proof for such strong claims?"

She heard a low rumble, and seconds passed before a woman spoke out. "Lady Abigail—ur—I mean—the widow Emerson, is in a family way, your worship. I've seen her with my own eyes, and she paid me to let out some of her gowns around the middle."

It was the voice of the seamstress Abby had hired to alter her dresses. Abby wouldn't retain her services in the future. And to think, she'd paid the woman an extra sixpence for her time."

"I, too, can confirm that Abigail Hartington is expecting." A shrill female voice rose above the chatter. Melinda. "My husband, her physician, confided in me that—"

"Melinda." Her husband's disapproving voice attempted to quiet her but to no avail.

"He was wrong in thinking she'd miscarried."

Stephen's voice spoke over the rumble of stunned whispers. "There is no question that my sister is in a family way. However, she asserts that her husband, Nicholas Emerson, is alive, and the child she is carrying is his."

She asserts?

Stephen's words hit her like a musket ball. Did he not believe her?

She'd felt the distance growing between them, but she hadn't realized it had come to this. If her own twin doubted her, then the town will have already condemned her. *Lord, help me.*

"'Twas the werewolf!" shouted Mr. Kroger. He couldn't keep the excitement out of his voice. "Remember less than a year ago when the strange howling noises kept the entire town awake at night. We had to post men to watch the graveyard to keep our dead safe. Well, the werewolf wasn't hungry. It was seeking a mate. Poor Lady Abigail became its victim. The werewolf transformed itself into the image of the late Mr. Emerson, and I guarantee the baby she's carrying is only half human. She's either still fooled or trying to protect her baby by claiming her husband's alive."

Whispers rumbled throughout the meeting house, increasing in volume as they tried to talk over one another.

"This is absurd talk!" Stephen yelled over the crowd. "I thought the citizens of Altonwood had more sense than to believe in mythical beasts and fairy tales."

An unknown man spoke, "Lester had a brush with the werewolf near Lady Abigail's home, and he had the scars to prove it."

The magistrate sitting as judge let out a frustrated sigh. "Where is Lester now?"

"Vanished a couple days after the attack." There were several sharp intakes of breath. "I think the werewolf finished him off. He'd told me, before he disappeared, he'd been walking back from work right past the widow's house, and a werewolf jumped out and pitched it to him. Left its claw marks over Lester's right eye and down his cheek. He's lucky his eye was still intact. Claimed he fought the beast off with his own two hands and escaped after wounding the creature."

Attacked near her house? Abby leaned forward and put her ear to the vent. Was Lester the man who'd assaulted her? The man whom she hit over the head with the glass vase. The glass shards had been sticking out of the right side of his face.

"Mitchy, the barkeep at the *Swan and Plough*, and me saw the scars. He was scratched up something fierce."

Despite the heat, a cold sweat broke over Abby's body. She bit her lip to keep in her scream of *Liar!* Her hands trembled with fury and betrayal. Who would believe her? It was Lester's word against hers now that Nick was gone. Would a town that gave credence to such ridiculous allegations take her side over a man's?

Below, roars broke, angry voices drowning out all reason.

"Order! Order!" shouted the magistrate. Someone let out a piercing whistle, and the crowd settled.

The barrister spoke, "We can easily get to the bottom of this. Has anyone seen or come in contact with Nicholas Emerson since his disappearance?"

There was a shuffling, and Miss Quiller spoke, her no-nonsense voice stern. "Mr. Emerson paid the orphanage a visit and told stories to the children this fall."

"You saw Mr. Emerson?" asked the barrister.

There was a pregnant pause. "I didn't lay eyes on him. I was busy preparing a lesson. But Lady Abigail told me he would be coming, and the children spoke often of his visit. One of them became frightened, and Mr. Emerson disappeared."

"Became frightened? By what Miss Quiller?"

"A snake, I believe."

"Indeed. And then Mr. Emerson disappeared? Would anyone else have seen him?"

"Only the children and Lady Abigail."

"I see," said the barrister in a low voice. "So he was only seen by children, who have vivid imaginations, and the woman in question."

Miss Quiller spoke as if reprimanding a child. "Lady Abigail is a God-fearing woman who is charitable to a fault. I will vouch for her character, and this town needs to reconsider its accusations. The crown no longer condones witch hunts, your worship."

A burst of hope filled Abby's chest. She was flabbergasted. Of all people, Miss Quiller had just defended her publicly.

"I agree, Miss Quiller," the magistrate said. "We are here to bring out the facts. Has anyone else come into contact with the returned Mr. Emerson?"

A chair scraped across the floor as someone stood. Abby recognized the deadpan voice of Dr. Cox. "I've spoken with the father of the child."

"You've spoken with Mr. Emerson?"

"The gentleman didn't give me his name, and I never held the acquaintance of Mr. Emerson. I arrived in the area shortly after his disappearance."

"Can you describe him to us?"

"Certainly. He was above average height, almost six feet, and had black hair and broad shoulders. He was gruff when he spoke and to the point. His eyes, I think, were brown or maybe hazel. He also had a slight limp and scars on his leg and neck."

Abby couldn't make out the whispered words that followed. Then the magistrate spoke and confirmed her fears. "Nicholas Emerson was above average height, but if I recall, his hair was light brown."

She wanted to scream. *Nick was in disguise. He was dying his hair for his mission.*

"Besides, Mr. Emerson was never gruff. In fact, he was the opposite, known for his charm and wit. He also didn't have a limp or scars, but those could have been the result of a war injury. Unfortunately, this is not enough tangible information to confirm the man you met was, in fact, Nicholas Emerson."

"Tall and dark. Scares children," shouted Mr. Kroger from the crowd. "Was he hairy? Sounds to me like a werewolf in human form."

"Enough, Mr. Kroger!" The bellow came from Lady Etheridge.

Not surprising, a hush fell over the room.

The click of her shoes on the tile floor echoed in the silence. Abby held her breath, knowing the influence Lady Etheridge had over the community.

"Before you gullible simpletons believe this poppycock, I

will enlighten you. Not only have I seen Mr. Nicholas Emerson, he was in my employ fewer than nine months ago."

A gasp escaped Abby's lips, and her hand flew over her mouth. Nicholas's assignment had been for Lady Etheridge? Why? And why hadn't Lady Etheridge bothered to mention it?

"Any of my staff can serve as witness to his employment," she continued.

"Where is Mr. Nicholas Emerson presently?" the barrister asked.

"I cannot say."

"And, why is that, Lady Etheridge?"

Her voice assumed in an even haughtier tone. "Because he did not feel the need to inform me."

"Do you know when he will be returning?"

"No."

"Well then, how are we to question him?"

"Did I not say that he was within my employ less than nine months ago?"

The barrister stuttered, "I-Indeed. You did."

"Let me help your understanding." The direction of her voice changed as if she were calling over her shoulder. "Dr. Cox, can you tell me approximately how many months Mrs. Emerson has been in a family way?"

"By my calculations, she would be coming into her ninth month," the doctor replied.

Lady Etheridge continued. "And I just stated that Nicholas Emerson was in my employ nine months ago. It appears obvious to me that the baby's father is Nicholas Emerson, Abigail Emerson's husband."

Abby gasped. Ten years ago, she would have laughed if someone had told her Lady Etheridge would someday be her white knight, coming to her defense.

"My sister also has letters written by her husband to her

since his departure." Stephen's voice rang out and murmurs filled the room.

"Order!" shouted the magistrate.

Sharp pain cramped Abby's stomach as all her abdominal muscles tightened, enough to steal her breath. She grabbed the arm of her chair with one hand, her nails digging into the wood. Her other hand massaged her lower back. Peering down at her massive bulge, she whispered, "Don't start that, little one. I'm not ready for any more surprises tonight."

CHAPTER 28

*A*bby bore down with all her strength. Her hands twisted the sheets into knots. Waves of pain ripped through her with no reprieve. She clenched her teeth so tightly that she feared one would crack. Hot, wet drips of perspiration ran down the sides of her face and back but did little to cool the fire in her belly. Her vision blurred as her muscles seized, twisting harder and tighter until she couldn't breathe. Finally, the contraction subsided, leaving her wrung out like a dish rag.

The midwife watched for signs of progress. "That's it. Brilliant. Now, when you feel the next birthing pain coming on, I want you to bear down with all your might."

Before she'd even finished the sentence, the next wave hit, and her body tensed.

"Push now."

"I *am* pushing," Abby said through clenched teeth, wishing she had something to throw at the woman.

"You need to bear down harder with the next contraction."

"I can't."

"You must, Abby." Her mother's soothing voice floated to

her like a life raft. Mama mopped her forehead with a damp cloth. "You can do this. God shall give you the strength."

Abby fumbled to grab her mother's hand as the next contraction overtook her body. Abby couldn't contain the scream that tore from her lips.

"That's it. Now push, Abby, push."

Her mother helped her lean forward. Abby closed her eyes, scrunched up her face, and pushed with all her might.

"I see the head. Keep pushing."

Abby bore down, determined to put an end to the pain.

The midwife guided the baby out.

"You have a son," the woman declared as her hands deftly wiped the baby off and gave him a pat on the bottom.

The baby's cry rang out, and Abby's heart leapt at the sound. The midwife swaddled him up tight and held him out to her.

Abby took her son and cradled him to her chest, her eyes never leaving the little pink face she'd waited nine months to see. Her fingers brushed his soft skin, and he squirmed in his blanket, so small, so perfect.

"He's beautiful." She blinked away tears. The two women clustered around with smiles on their faces.

Suddenly, searing pain shot through Abby's stomach, and she cried out again. The midwife snatched the baby and passed him to his grandmother.

"No, not again. Why are the pains starting again?"

The midwife lifted the sheet and popped her head under. Abby arched her back as another contraction ravaged her body.

"There's another head," the midwife called. "It must be twins."

Twins? Another violent contraction consumed her. "I can't go through this again." She gripped her mama's skirt. "I can't."

"You need to push," Mama said. "The second will go easier than the first. Now push, Abby, push!"

Abby put her chin down to her chest and pushed. Her own scream rang in her head like an echo, but she squeezed until she felt the last of her strength wane.

"One more time."

Tears slid down her cheeks, and she shook her head, but the next contraction hit, and she once again pushed with all her might. She just hoped it was enough.

Another baby's wail filled the room, and Abby fell back against the pillows.

"Blessed Jesus," announced the midwife. "You, my dear, have a set of boys."

Abby looked to her mother, who smiled as broad as the morning sky.

"I thought you were carrying a bit large, but I didn't want to excite you."

The midwife finished cleaning and wrapping the second baby, then passed him to Abby. She stared in awe at the little fingers and nose. Her mother propped her hip on the side of the bed and held the first born up for her to see. Tears of joy brimmed in Abby's eyes as she beheld the two little miracles God had given her. They were beautiful and perfect. She'd never thought this moment possible, but God had blessed her with two of Nick's children.

"I wish Nick were here," Abby whispered.

Her mother brushed the damp hair from Abby's forehead. "I know, darling. Me too."

Abby pulled her eyes from her precious newborns and peered up at her mother. "You believe me then—that Nicholas is alive?"

"Of course."

"Others don't." Her voice trailed off as a lump clogged her throat. *Stephen doesn't even believe me.*

"Why wouldn't I, Abby? I know your character, so I will take you at your word."

Abby bit her bottom lip to keep it from quivering. Heavy tear drops splattered onto the baby's blanket. "Thank you, Mama. I love you."

"I love you too, darling, but stop your crying before you soak the baby."

She and Mama each stared at the bundles snuggled in their arms. Disappointment in Stephen pestered Abby's thoughts. In the past, she would have blurted out her accusation, jumping to her own conclusions, but she was wiser now. "Why doesn't Stephen believe me?"

Her mama let out a loud sigh. "Stephen does believe you, but he's hurt that Nicholas remains hidden, and he's struggling to deal with it in his own way. He grieved for his friend when he went missing. We forget how close they were. As kids, they were inseparable. Stephen idolized Nicholas, and now he's confused about what to think. If he believes you, then his heart is crushed thinking Nicholas's friendship wasn't true. If he believes Nicholas to be dead, then he has to believe you deceived him. Neither option is pleasant." She brushed her finger over the baby's face. "Give him time, Abby. Stephen is coming to terms with it in his own way."

~

Nicholas oversaw the finishing touches to the main house. Everything was progressing nicely. He just wished he could witness the shock on Abby's face when his lawyers explained that the house and lands belonged to her.

He wandered into the conservatory. Bright sunlight streamed in through the walls of glass, filling the room with warmth. He'd designed this room to be twice as large as his mother's solarium. Plants ordered from all over the world were to be delivered at the completion of the project. He'd even hired a full-time gardener and grounds crew. He imagined Abby's face when she arrived to find a hundred cut glass vases with flowers in full bloom.

It would take a couple more days of detail work before the main living areas were finished, then probably another three months for the east and west wings to be completed. After that, he would notify Abby of the title and property he'd gifted her. The manor had been eight years in the making, but it was worth it. He broke ground after receiving payment from his first espionage assignment, and the project offered him a reason to continue on after his life had been destroyed by the fire. This was the reason he'd accepted the risky assignments no one else wanted. He'd reaped the rewards, including several titles. Finally, he would give Abby the home they'd talked about and dreamed of before the war.

His throat tightened. If only ...

No! He pushed the thought from his mind. He wouldn't wreak havoc upon Abby's life any further. He'd ruined her chance to remarry by revealing to her that he was still alive. Of course, Abby felt morally bound to honor their marriage. She was faithful to a fault. He couldn't ask her to sacrifice more. A palatial estate would never account for the price of spinsterhood, but at least it was a start.

Abby probably wouldn't live here. Why would she want to leave her family, friends, and community? But even if she visited it occasionally, it was still worth it to him. Nicholas would be content to know he had done everything in his capacity to allow for his wife's happiness and in some small way atone for his absence.

Finishing Abigail Manor, as he'd begun to refer to it, was bittersweet. For eight years, this house had been his motivation. The builders had witnessed one of his episodes and now hurried to be done with the job. They avoided him and kept their distance as if his madness was contagious. It was past time he made plans to leave. The wilds of Scotland would allow him to be a recluse, or he could become a pioneer and farm the isolated American plains.

His butler cleared his throat. "Pardon me, my lord. Lieutenant Sparks has arrived with another gentleman.

Aaron.

"Show them in."

The butler bowed and retreated the way he came.

Moments later, the hacking cough of Lieutenant Sparks could be heard. Nicholas met him with a bow. "Good to see you, lieutenant." His gaze turned to the man behind the lieutenant dressed in a bottle green coat, breeches, and top boots. Instead of the strained, peaked, expression he'd remembered on the soldier's face, Aaron's eyes glowed with warmth. The corners of his eyes crinkled with smile lines hinting at a new maturity. He looked well—healthy—whole.

Nicholas issued him a broad smile and clapped a hand on his shoulder. "Aaron, good to see you, my friend."

"And you. It's been a long time."

"Too long." He gestured for the men to enter the drawing room and to be seated on the sofa. Nicholas pulled up a chair and sat. "We have some catching up to do."

Aaron glanced at the lieutenant who nodded the go ahead. Aaron inhaled a deep breath. "Last time we saw each other I wasn't in a good state."

"Nor a good place. The only person I'd wish to Bedlam was Napoleon himself."

"Indeed. Bedlam was a disturbing place to say the least and I appreciate you visiting me those few occasions."

Nicholas swallowed. "I wish I could have visited more."

"I understand. The conditions were harsh, the noise hard to bear, and the startling laughter.... It could set a man off. I had numerous episodes while locked up."

"Then how did you get released?" Nicholas laced his fingers and leaned forward resting his forearms on his thighs. What did Aaron do to save himself? What was the secret? Could it help him too?

"There was a local church parishioner who came in and prayed for the inmates. He took a special interest in me, asking me questions about what I'd seen during the war and then prayed for healing and forgiveness of each event." Aaron glanced at the ceiling as if reviewing the past, but instead of cringing or wincing, he chuckled. "At first, I didn't tell him much. I feared it would set off another attack and the sanitarium workers would put me in solitary confinement. But the God-fearing man was a persistent bugger. The more I spoke of the horrors the more relieved I began to feel, and then he'd pray and ask God to come into those dark places and fill it with Himself." Aaron's voice cracked.

Lieutenant Sparks nodded to him to take a moment.

An image of Abby kneeling by his bedside flashed through his mind. Hadn't she said it was her hair and her prayers that soothed him? The lock of hair she'd given him had done nothing to ease his nightmares since he left. Was it the prayers that had eased his torment?

Aaron cleared his throat. "The parishioner came faithfully every day, and my nightmares slowly eased. He asked me to give my life to Jesus and I dropped to my knees, repented, and asked Him to come into my heart and take over my life. He taught me how to pray and spiritually battle for my mind. Eventually my nightmares stopped, and the parishioner convinced the administrators to let me out of Bedlam."

"Your nightmares stopped completely?" Disbelief laced Nicholas's voice.

"I'll still have a bad dream now and again, but I immediately start praying and asking God for protection."

Lieutenant Sparks met Nicholas's gaze. "I thought he could help you overcome your nightmares."

Would prayer work? Hadn't he prayed in the past to no

avail? He didn't want to get his hopes up, but Aaron seemed filled with the peace that Nicholas desired. Talking about his experience with Abby had helped, but wouldn't reliving those moments cause another episode? Even if it did, Aaron would understand, and the lieutenant had already witnessed him in the throws on an attack. Both men peered at him with encouragement in their eyes.

"All right then." Nicholas sighed. "Let's give it a go."

Aaron grinned. "Bow your heads. We'll begin with a prayer for God's guidance."

~

"*A*ll right, where are they? It's about time I was introduced to the heirs of Laurel House."

Lady Etheridge brushed past Mrs. Smith, who held the door for her in the foyer, and marched into the salon where Abby rocked the twins. In the past, Abby would have cringed at the sound of Lady Etheridge's cutting commands, but now she stood with a smile and passed one of the twins into her open arms.

They chatted, but the older woman's heart was not in the conversation. Holding little Daniel, the supercilious woman goo-gooed and gaa-gaaed, making faces and doting on the tyke.

Abby pretended to be checking on little David to hide her laugh at Lady Etheridge's playful antics. Eventually, they exchanged babies, and Lady Etheridge did the same routine for his twin, David.

Abby's spirits buoyed. Besides her own staff, her only other visitors were her mother and Katherine. At first, she'd thought everyone was giving her time to adjust to newborns, but as the weeks passed, she realized no one intended to visit. The community she had been born and raised in had judged her and now ostracized her. At times she wanted to run out in the streets and scream at the injustice of it all. Other times, she wanted to crawl into bed and bawl like a babe. However, neither of those options were viable with infant twins to care for. Her children came first. She would deal with the town later.

Abby cleared her throat. "Lady Etheridge, I want to thank you for what you said at the parish meeting. I appreciate you siding with me."

Lady Etheridge snorted. "All I stated were the facts. If this town wants to go on believing in foolish ghost stories and such, so be it. Better not to associate with ignorant folks."

David cooed and wiggled his hand free from the blanket. Lady Etheridge looked down at the bundle in her arms. "Anyone with half a brain can see these two are the spitting image of their papa."

Abby peered down at her sons. They had Nick's nose and eyes. Even the gray-blue eye color they were born with had started to hint more towards a warm greenish-brown.

Curiosity flickered. Cocking her head to the side, Abby asked, "Why was Nicholas working for you?"

The corner of Lady Etheridge's mouth curved slightly as if she'd been waiting for this question. "I requested it."

Abby blinked. "Pardon me?"

"Indeed." Lady Etheridge settled into a nearby chair. David had drifted off into slumber in the crook of her arm, and so she relaxed and sipped from her teacup. "Most folks aren't as observant as I, but there is not much that happens in this town without my knowledge. I caught a glimpse of a man sneaking into Emma Emerson's funeral."

So many had come to give their sympathies, but she had a hazy recollection of a man with his face hidden. He had entered and sat in the back among the shadows. She'd seen him again as he hovered on the outskirts of the cemetery. That had been Nicholas?

Lady Etheridge smiled. "For your sake, I was curious as to

why he didn't make himself known. I have a relative within the Home Office and thought it would be best to contact him to see what he knew about a missing person who suddenly reappeared. It took him a week, but eventually, he informed me that the Nicholas Emerson I was referring to worked within their department. 'Agent Scar,' they called him."

"Why didn't you tell me?"

"My dear, you had been through so much, and God bless you, despite it all, you never gave up. I needed to know for certain. I didn't want to give you false hope. So I harassed the higher-ups within the Home Office until they agreed to let a fake case be investigated. They assigned Agent Scar the mission."

She leaned in closer to Abby with a heavy-lidded stare. "He thought he could fool me by dying his hair. He thinks his looks have altered enough to make him unrecognizable, and yes, his appearance has changed: he limps, he has scars, and the boyishness of his youth is long gone. But that mischievous glint is *still* in his eyes. It doesn't surface as often, but whenever I mentioned your name, which I did often, it surfaced."

Abby's heart warmed. It was nice to hear Lady Etheridge speak of Nick in the present tense. Everyone else referred to him in the past. "So during the days, he was with you? Working on your fake case?"

"Yes, he was in my employ, so to speak, undercover as a footman."

Abby's eyebrows shot up. "As a footman."

"I wanted him to go undercover as my steward, but he thought a footman would gain better confidences from my staff."

"A footman," Abby whispered to herself. "It was Nicholas who served us that day at lunch."

One side of her lips drew up in a half smile. "Indeed, I was attempting to force his hand. You see, I thought you didn't know he was alive, and I figured you'd recognize him. He'd then have to explain why he'd stayed away for so long. I daresay, I'd hoped you two would rekindle your love for each other."

Abby shook her head in disbelief. "Lady Etheridge, you were playing cupid. I didn't know you had such a romantic side to you."

Abby watched as two rosy spots grew on the apples of her cheeks. "For all the good it did me. That blasted man was adept at keeping himself hidden." She leveled her gaze, and Abby thought she detected a shimmering of tears in their depths.

"My meddling had good intent. I didn't mean to cause you more harm. If I had known he would disappear again, perhaps..." She let out a loud sigh. "Perhaps, I wouldn't have interfered."

Abby shook her head. "If you hadn't interfered, then I wouldn't have David and Daniel. They are a blessing."

"I want to locate him and knock some sense into that man. How dare he leave you with two children to raise."

"He doesn't know he has children. He believes I miscarried."

"Well, maybe it's time you told him."

Abby let out a sigh. "I wouldn't know how to reach him, and the look of relief on his face when he discovered I had miscarried told me he didn't want children. That's the reason he said he had to leave."

Lady Etheridge pursed her lips. "I still don't think it's right."

"I shall never lose hope that one day, God will heal Nick's heart, and he will come home, and we can be a family." The all too familiar sting of tears threatened, but Abby blinked them away.

Daniel let out a small cry. Abby shifted him in her arms and bounced. She glanced at Lady Etheridge. "What was the case he was trying to solve?"

"Who poisoned my dog."

Abby blinked. "Poopsie wasn't poisoned?"

"Died of old age, but Agent Scar was led to believe otherwise. I told him the dog ate a tart meant for me. Agent Scar easily believed there were individuals who'd want to do me in."

Abby squelched the urge to giggle. "Who was his prime suspect?"

Lady Etheridge's face folded into a puzzled frown. "I'm not certain why, but Dr. Cox was top of his list."

Abby hooted with laughter. "I should have known. He doesn't like doctors."

CHAPTER 29

*A*bby blew return kisses to her boys. Their little pudgy hands smacked their lips with loud *mmmmaaaahs* before they waved goodbye.

Lydia had Daniel by the hand. He'd used the door frame to pull himself into a standing position, and David excitedly bopped up and down on Mrs. Smith's hip as he waved. It was past time she visited the orphanage to check in on the children. As much as she hated leaving her babies, she missed the orphans, and it felt good to venture outside after a long winter.

A few dark clouds rolled by, and the wind whipped up the corners of Abby's bonnet. She placed a restraining hand on top in case it suddenly decided to take flight. The breeze chilled her skin, but now and then, the sun would peer out between the clouds, warming the earth with its rays.

As she rounded the corner to Mr. Kroger's store, she spotted Melinda strolling arm in arm with Emily Hendricks, another old friend, giggling and chattering on. Abby's steps slowed.

There was a flash of recognition before Melinda looked through her. Their only acknowledgment was to move aside and physically step around her like they would a dead rat lying in the gutter.

Funny how, of all people, Lady Etheridge and Miss Quiller had become her biggest champions. She asked Miss Quiller, who came to visit a few days after Lady Etheridge, why she did it and she said, "It was completely out of line with your character. Just because the town wants gossip doesn't make it right."

Her eyes shined overly bright as she said it, leaving Abby with the impression Miss Quiller had a similar story. Abby's heart broke for her. The reproachful spinster knew Abby's pain, but God had used Miss Quiller's trials for His good. Despite her stern exterior, she was devoted to helping those who couldn't help themselves. Like the orphans. Like Abby.

That revelation filled Abby with a fresh peace. With her new perspective, she now considered people as works in progress. God shaped and molded people into His image. He chiseled away at Lady Etheridge and Miss Quiller's hardened shells to reveal their kind hearts.

Her perception of Nick had transformed too. She still loved him. She always would. His departure hurt her deeply, but she could forgive him. Despite his leaving, despite his fears. She had thought her love could heal his wounds, but she was wrong. Only God could heal scars that deep. Nick's leaving hurt worse than any rejection he could have saved her from, and despite his sacrifice, she had been rejected anyway. Pity replaced her anger, not for Nick's injuries, but because he lived in bondage. Until he stood up and faced his fears, he would never be whole.

The bell on the door to Mr. Kroger's store jingled, and the man's bushy eyebrows raised.

"Lady Abigail, good day to you."

"It's Mrs. Emerson, and good day to you, Mr. Kroger." Abby nodded to the elderly man.

"What can I get you on this fine spring day?"

"Twenty licorice whips for my visit to the orphanage."

"Ah, you are kindhearted to still offer your services. I'm certain the children will be eager to see you, and for their treats." He counted out the licorice and placed them in her basket. "How fair your little ones?"

She smiled at the opportunity to talk about her boys. "They're getting along splendidly. Already crawling. How kind of you to ask."

Mr. Kroger put a restraining hand on her arm. "The full moon is coming up. I reckon you tie up those young'uns in their crib and lock the nursery door. I don't want anything unsightly to happen to you."

Jerking her arm away, she replaced her smile with a mama-bear scowl. "Nothing unsightly will happen to my children, myself, or anyone else, Mr. Kroger. Good day." She snatched up her purchase and slammed the shop's front door behind her.

Mr. Kroger's comment tainted Abby's visit to the orphanage. She was still dwelling on it as she trudged home. Large drops of rain splattered on her bonnet and shoulders. She picked up the pace. Through the blur of raindrops, she caught sight of her brother, who was also running to take cover.

Stephen met her at the gate to Laurel House, lifted the latch, and followed her through.

～

*T*he rain poured down in sheets. Abby held her bonnet tight to her face and glanced back to see if Stephen was behind her. Stephen stood by the gate, hooking the latch with utmost care despite the deluge as if hoping to delay their inevitable confrontation for as long as possible. A pit opened in her stomach. When had he started dreading seeing his sister? The rumors in town had been slow to diminish, but Mama had said he believed her and just needed time to understand why Nicholas refused to see him.

She'd been anticipating his visit. It was past time Stephen brought his thoughts out in the open.

Warmth and light met her inside. A cheery fire blazed in the hearth of the drawing room, and Mrs. Smith helped her out of her wet coat as she untied and removed her bonnet.

"Welcome, Lord Hartington. It's lovely to see you." Mrs. Smith took his overcoat. "I merely wish the weather was better."

Stephen settled into a chair, and Abby placed a steamy cup of tea in his hands that Mrs. Smith had prepared for her return.

"The boys should be up from their nap any minute now." Pride rang in her voice, and she couldn't diminish the grin that stretched her lips. It was long overdue for the twins to meet their uncle.

"Wait until you see what fine boys they are, m'lord." Mrs. Smith brought over a tray of scones, set it on the tea table, along with a cup for Abby's tea.

Stephen returned a strained smile.

"It's good to see you, Stephen." Abby poured the hot tea into her cup. If only she could restore the familiar teasing between them, but so much time and accusations had flowed, she didn't know where to start. "I've missed you."

He cleared his throat. "And I, you. It's been an age, and the blame for that lies at my door. I hope you will someday be able to forgive me for my neglect and for my actions."

Abby tilted her head. "You're my brother. I love you. I will always forgive you."

"I hope you'll continue to do so."

Abby hesitated at the ominous nature of his words and seated herself across from him. She stared into her tea, cupping it in both hands to draw the heat into her chilled fingers, and waited for him to speak.

"Listen, Abby." He set his cup down and rose to pace in front of the fire. "I've been putting off this confrontation, hoping you'd come to your senses on your own, but I'm tired of waking up in the middle of the night playing out this meeting in my head." He raked a hand through his damp hair. "I want you to move back home to Willowstone where we can help you."

Help sounded lovely but leaving Laurel House felt final as if she'd given up on Nick. There was no reason to think that he would someday return to her and have a desire to be a family, but God kept a spark of hope alive inside her.

"No, thank you."

Stephen blinked.

As the earl, Stephen had grown accustomed to people doing as he said. Abby sipped her tea.

"Abby, as your eldest brother—"

"By a mere five minutes."

"I am the head of our family. With that role comes responsibility. Sometimes it requires me to make unpopular but necessary decisions. Ones that will benefit, even though they may not be viewed that way at first. I feel it is in your best interest that you and your children move back to Willowstone Manor."

Abby didn't move, didn't rage at him, didn't fidget, just peered at him.

He peered at her and rubbed his chin as if something about her was off but he couldn't place it. "Logic dictates what must be done." His stiffness screamed that he was trying to convey something more but couldn't spit it out. "You value your independence, but it's past time you came back home under our protection. There, surrounded by those who know what is best for you, you'll get the help you need."

"Protection from what exactly?"

"Lady Etheridge told Mother about the man who attacked you, and he's still unaccounted for out there somewhere. With

Nick off, God knows where, neglecting his duties, I can't have you living alone."

Was that all? She exhaled. "I'm already interviewing more staff, a footman and butler who could defend me and the boys if needed. Thank you for your offer, but I must decline."

Stephen stiffened. "It was not a request. I will send servants to collect your things—this afternoon."

"Why? What has you in such a dudgeon?" She remained still and calm, having learned it worked best in the handling of small boys—not that Stephen was a child, but he was a male. "I won't be living alone. Mrs. Smith and Lydia are here."

He shifted his weight and his voice lowered. "The rumors aren't dying down. If anything, they're growing more outrageous. The townspeople are feeding on gossip as a means of entertainment at your expense. Your living alone isn't helping the situation. It's best for you to reside with your family who can shield you from the sordid rumors."

"I have nothing to hide and doing so will only make me look guilty."

"But—"

"God will protect me, and His truth will prevail."

Stephen furrowed his brow. "Something's changed in you."

Indeed. She looked up. God made her a mother. She rested her teacup on the side table and folded her hands in her lap.

He studied her with a frown. "You're not fidgeting."

She chuckled. God had also given her His peace. Her past inability to sit still must have been more noticeable than she realized. The unrest and constant whirling of her thoughts had calmed with the acceptance that God's ways were higher than her ways. The image of the twins snuggled in their crib flashed through her mind. She could fight and work for her own means, but in the end God's will was best.

A child's cry rang out, and a young maid hurried up the

stairs. Stephen pulled his gaze back to Abby. "Think of the children. The boys would be safeguarded against vicious slander."

"Laurel House is their home—their birthright. The picture of their father and their grandfather hangs in the drawing room. I want them to grow up knowing whose child they are."

"Even though he left you to scorn and mockery? You forgive him?"

"I have."

Stephen blinked, his mouth curving into a frown.

Lydia carried down the twins, but David wiggled as soon as he glimpsed his mama. A warm smile stretched across Abby's face, and she held her arms out.

Stephen turned and froze.

Daniel snuggled up on Lydia's shoulder, proving slower to wake than his brother who struggled to get free from her arms. Lydia put the wiggling form down and passed the other sleepy boy to his mother. Abby nodded to excuse their young maid, and Lydia turned and exited the room in the direction of the kitchen.

Daniel curled into his mother's chest and nestled his face into her neck.

Always curious, David crawled over to the new company and placed a pudgy hand on the top of Stephen's shoe. Stephen bent down to pick up the baby. As he crouched low, he gently rubbed the smooth skin on his nephew's pudgy arm, the child lifted his head, and a pair of big round hazel eyes locked with Stephen's.

He paled, obviously unprepared for the sight that Abby observed daily. She bit back a smile. Before Stephen sat a younger version of Nicholas Emerson. His eyes, his nose, and his coloring were the exact same as Nick's. The child smiled, and even though toothless, his grin was that of Nick. The toddler peered down at Stephen's bootlace, then back up at him. A familiar glimmer of mischief flashed in the child's eyes before he tugged and untied the bootlaces. It was the same mischievous look Nick had often held.

"David." Abby gently scolded.

"No, it's all right."

"He loves to go after laces. I should have warned you."

David held his arms up towards his uncle. Stephen pulled the child into his embrace and stood. He was still staring when the boy's twin, Daniel, turned out of curiosity. Stephen's chin jerked back, met with the second pair of hazel eyes. He blinked several times and opened his mouth as if to speak but said nothing.

David grabbed Stephen's nose with one hand and the side of his face with the other and pressed his little forehead against Stephen's cheek in what resembled a hug. Stephen let out a choked laugh and sank onto his chair. He screwed up his face and made a silly noise. David gurgled with laughter. Soon his brother wanted in on the play and Abby set him down on the floor.

Tiny hands smacked the floor as he sped-crawled up into Stephen's lap. Stephen glanced at Abby, who watched the exchange with a warm smile. When the clock struck the hour, the young maid reappeared again, gathering the boys for their noontime meal.

Stephen followed them with his gaze, and tears glistened in his eyes. When they disappeared around the corner, he said in a hoarse voice, "Nick's alive."

Abby nodded and smiled at her brother.

"I believed you, but seeing them..." He rubbed the lower half of his face and exhaled a shaky breath. "One look at these boys and the town will have to accept the truth."

He peered at Abby and his jaw tightened. "Where is the slippery bloke? I have words for him."

The door burst open startling Abby. In trounced Lady Etheridge followed by Katherine and Mama.

"We were in an open carriage and surprised by the storm."
Mama handed her pelisse to Mrs. Smith who also took Lady
Etheridge's dripping parasol.

"We needed shelter because the rain is coming down hard."

Abby beckoned them over. "Come and warm yourself by
the fire."

Stephen greeted the women and pressed a kiss to Katherine's cheek.

"I see you had the same idea." She shivered in her wet coat
and Stephen aided her in sliding out of it, hanging it on a hook
next to the fire to dry.

Mrs. Smith passed the women towels who dried their faces
and removed their bonnets. Abby took their bonnets and also
hung them to dry. They huddled near the fire until steam rose
from their clothes and chattered about the storm.

Stephen stared out the window.

"What's the matter, darling?" Katherine's face lined with
concern. "You look like you've seen a ghost."

He glanced over his shoulder, discovering all eyes on him.
His eyes flicked to Katherine, his mother, and then to Abby. "I
have seen a ghost." He snorted. "I saw one ghost in two little
bodies."

"Ha!" A loud cackle erupted from Lady Etheridge's mouth.
She slapped a hand on her wet skirt where her knee was. "It's
about time he visited his nephews. They resemble their father,
don't they? This whole town can gossip all they want, but the
truth is as plain as their little faces."

Mrs. Smith brought in the tea service and Abby steeped the
leaves. Stephen settled onto the sofa and draped his arm over
the back. Katherine sat next to her husband, and Mama on her
other side. Lady Etheridge sat in the chair opposite Abby and
Abby handed her a cup of tea the way she liked it—two lumps
of sugar. Lady Etheridge's gaze returned to Stephen as if
waiting for more details while Abby offered cups to her family.

"There are things my mind can't wrap around." Stephen crossed one leg over the other. "Why didn't Nick make his arrival known? I was his closest friend, and he didn't even bother to see me."

"It was never his intention to come back." Lady Etheridge stirred her tea.

Abby winced at her words. It still hurt even though they were true. Mama and Katherine both flashed her sympathetic looks.

"Through my connection at the War Department,"—Lady Etheridge sipped her tea—"I discovered Nicholas Emerson became part of a special intelligence-gathering unit during the war."

Stephen snorted. "Of course Lady Etheridge could make the War Department reveal their secrets."

She pursed her lips. "I recognized him at his mother's funeral and did some digging. Abigail's faithfulness to her missing husband, broke my heart." She nodded at Abby before telling about how she'd fabricated a mystery in hopes of reunited the husband and wife. When finished she studied the faces that stared back at her in stunned silence.

Stephen finally leaned over and whispered into his wife's ear but loud enough for Abby to hear, "I'm not certain whether she's a mastermind genius or a crazed lunatic, but I'm leaning towards mastermind."

Lady Etheridge issued him a stern sideways glance, but Abby noticed the corners of her lips twitch. With a smug grin, Lady Etheridge picked up her cup, but before taking a sip, she said, "It worked, didn't it?"

"No. He left, and now my sister bears the burden of raising his children alone." Stephen uncrossed his leg and stamped his foot down, jostling the tea service and sloshing liquid over the edge of the pot. "What about all the gossip he subjected Abby to? I don't care if he's afraid of public humiliation."

"Stephen, it's all right." Abby attempted to reassure him she was fine.

Katherine placed a hand on his arm, but Stephen rose. "By Jove, I will hunt that coward down and drag him back here."

Lady Etheridge's voice stopped him. "He doesn't know he has children."

"What?" Stephen jerked around to stare at Lady Etheridge.

Katherine and Mama gasped.

"You need a plan before you break down the man's door." Lady Etheridge sipped once more from her tea. "The irony is that he left to save her from humiliation, but by doing so, he left her to face something far worse—scorn."

CHAPTER 30

*A*bby's screams echoed through Nicholas's dream and jolted him awake. The nightmare began with Abby crying and reaching towards him for help, but he was frozen, helpless to do anything as bombs and chaos broke out everywhere around her. He was paralyzed, and the beating of his heart thundered in his ears louder and louder until it drowned out her screams.

He woke drenched in sweat and shaking. He snatched the oil lamp from his nightstand and turned up the flame. The small light chased the shadows to their corners.

He flipped open his pocket watch. Half past eleven. He'd slept for less than an hour before the nightmare woke him. Frustration burned hot behind his eyelids. He grabbed the lock of hair and slid his thumb over the strands to calm himself.

Each time he closed his eyes, he saw Abby's face and heard her sobs. His fingers moved faster and faster until he'd turned the lock of hair into a tangled mess.

Nicholas stood and hurled the lock of hair across the room, unsatisfied with the light plop as it hit the wall and slid down. The hair didn't work. Why had he ever set foot back in Altonwood? Spending time with Abby had only made his heart ache more. After the war, he'd gone blissfully numb, but she'd awakened something within him, a part that had died resurrected, and now he was dying a slow, painful death.

Despite the pain, he relived those precious moments with her minute after minute, day after day. Why? Why couldn't he be whole? Why had God forsaken him?

The days spent with Aaron exchanging war traumas and what they'd done and encountered spying for the crown had lessened the frequency of his episodes. He'd gone over a month since his last one. Aaron also encouraged him to pray, but each time he bowed his head he felt like a nervous greenhorn. He lacked the words to approach God's throne and ask for forgiveness and protection. The prayer Abby had prayed while she believed he was sleeping rang through his mind as clear as if she were kneeling by his bedside once more.

He sank to his knees. Her prayer said it all. It was exactly what he needed. Desperate, Nicholas spoke to God on his own, from his heart. *Release me from my past. Help me to feel Your presence, strengthen my faith. Protect me.* He prayed that someday, he could live with himself for the torment he'd put Abby through.

~

*L*ight poured through the crack in the heavy velvet drapes. Nicholas rolled onto his back and stretched his arms above his head. He'd fallen asleep on the floor. His body was stiff and his leg ached. He pulled out his pocket watch, flipped it open, and smiled. Half past eight.

"God, thank You." He hadn't had a full night's sleep since the day he'd left Abby, but last night he'd slept a full six hours.

Something had changed.

A shift in his heart. Or weight lifted from his shoulders. Not only did his body relax, but his mind did too. For a year, he'd been lost, struggling through a dense forest, but last night he'd tumbled into an open clearing. He'd poured his heart out to God, cried out to Him with everything he had. Then, completely spent, he fell into a peaceful sleep.

Nicholas pushed off the floor and slid into a chair. Leaning back into the soft cushions, he kicked his feet up, laced his fingers behind his head, and stared at the ceiling. He blinked, awed by the feeling of peace he felt for the first time since he'd left Abby.

God hasn't forgotten me after all. He prayed for rest, and he rested, but why? Why would God pay him any heed after all this time? *Help me to understand,* Nicholas prayed. *Abby believes in You—that You are always there working, guiding. She has always trusted You.*

Abby knew God, and she believed God loved him too. But, if God truly loved him, why would He allow him to undergo such trauma, sustain burns, let his mind slip?

Abby's words played in his head. *"It sounds like God rescued you."*

Had God saved him? Nick had known the risks when he'd taken the assignment. He'd blatantly ignored all the warnings of his conscience when he'd purchased a commission in His Majesty's army. Nicholas had known he didn't need a title to please Abby. He'd seen the regret etched on her face after she'd said those rash words. She hadn't meant it, but his pride had gotten the best of him. It was his unwise decision that had caused him to be injured. God had saved him despite his mistakes.

Had God sent an angel to carry him out of the building? Had God sent Guillen to heal his burns? If so, then, God had given him a second chance at life, and what had he done with it?

He'd hidden in fear, afraid of having an episode. He'd been daring as a spy because no one knew him, but he was cowardly when it came to being vulnerable in front of those who did.

God, I'm sorry. Please forgive me. Take control of my life. Guide me on a better path. Tell me what I should do, how I should change. Give me a sign.

~

*L*ater that afternoon, at his weekly meeting with Aaron, he explained the events of the prior evening. Toward the end of their conversation, a horseman riding up the lane distracted Nicholas from his meeting. He shifted in his desk chair for a better look through the large window of his office, which faced the drive. He recognized the lieutenant's dark cape flapping.

"Humph." Nicholas grunted, surprised to see him back so soon. "Either Lieutenant Sparks is coming to check on our progress or he's taking me up on my fishing invitation."

Aaron pushed up from the chair across the desk from Nicholas. "I'd say he'll be impressed by the progress you've made. To God be the glory."

"Amen." Nicholas stood. "Last night was a breaking point. I feel different. Lighter."

"That's what Jesus's peace will do to you, brother." He flashed Nicholas a wide smile folding the fan of creases on the sides of his eyes. "I must go. The misses is waiting on my return." He waved to Nicholas to sit. "I can see myself out. I'll give the lieutenant my regards and tell him the great news."

Nicholas nodded, and Aaron exited into the hall.

"Aaron." He paused and turned back. "Thank you, for your help and for pushing me."

"I just gave you a nudge." He winked. "The rest was God." He turned and left.

Nicholas heard the rap of the knocker, and the front door

swung open. The new butler informed their visitor the viscount was not receiving callers at the present.

"It's all right, Rupert," Nicholas called out. "I'll make an exception." He leaned back in his desk chair and listened to Aaron update their lieutenant on his progress.

The lieutenant hacked out a deep cough as he entered the study, and Nicholas gestured for his friend to take a seat.

"Shall I ring for tea," Nicholas asked, "or would you prefer something stiffer?"

Lieutenant Sparks sat and wacked himself hard on the chest as the cough subsided. "No, no, this blasted cough comes and goes. It's that wretched air down at headquarters. The war didn't kill me but sitting in that drafty building might just end me."

"So, you needed an excuse to get away and decided to pay me a visit?"

"Something like that." The lieutenant glanced around. "The place has come along nicely since my last visit. I think your wife will be well pleased."

Nicholas furrowed his brow as he eyed the lieutenant. It wasn't like him to start with small talk.

"I must say, she'll be awestruck when she arrives."

Nicholas crossed his arms. "What are you getting at, my friend?"

"Deuced woman," Sparks muttered under his breath.

"Pardon?" He better not speak of Abby.

"My apologies. Not Lady Abigail. It's been a trying day." He rubbed the lower half of his face. "Every time this woman barges into my office, vetted agents run for cover. My secretary hides under his desk, and I found one of my operatives trembling in a broom closet. That same man faced combat and capture during the war and held up under interrogations by Napoleon Bonaparte himself only to cower in her presence.

She's shaming the entire Home Office, and now she has me running errands for her."

Who would treat the Home Office in such disregard? Only one woman came to mind.

He sighed. "I'm here to give you a message."

"What's the message?" Nicholas couldn't swallow the unease that something was wrong with Abby.

The lieutenant's jaw tightened, and his eyes jumped about the room. "Your wife needs you," he said flatly.

The hairs on the back of Nicholas's neck prickled.

Sparks shifted in his seat. "That's all the information I have."

Nicholas bolted upright. "Who gave you this information?"

"I, ah—I don't know if I'm at liberty to say," the lieutenant sputtered.

"Is she hurt? Is she upset? Is it her health?"

"I'm certain it's nothing—"

A commotion broke out in the front hall. Nicholas's gaze jerked to the door, and Sparks's head whipped around.

"Tell him I'm not a visitor," a familiar voice from his past said. "I'm family, and blast it all, he's going to receive me whether he likes it or not."

Who in—Stephen?

Lieutenant Sparks jumped from his seat, drawing his weapon.

Nicholas stayed him with a hand and cracked open the study door, peeking into the front foyer.

Indeed. It was his brother-in-law and old time friend. Stephen stood facing Nicholas's young, stiff-looking butler, who tilted his chin up and looked down his nose at Stephen as if to intimidate him. He stepped left but the butler moved to block his way. Stephen grabbed the man by the lapel and tossed him aside. Undeterred the butler clung to his arm like a leach.

Rupert was worth every shilling.

A small scuffle ensued, but Stephen had him in strength and size. A head start, too, at least until the butler grabbed hold of Stephen's coattails. The butler dug his heels into the slick, polished floor to get traction. Despite the resistance, Stephen marched through the foyer with Rupert dragging behind.

"Show yourself, Nicholas Emerson," Stephen shouted.

Nicholas crossed his arms and leaned against the study door frame. "Welcome, my friend. I'm not hiding."

Stephen's gaze snapped to Nicholas's. "You're coming back to Altonwood with me."

Nicholas dismissed his butler with a nod, and without the added weight Stephen straightened and jerked down on the bottom of his waistcoat which had bunched up.

"Why don't you sit in my office, and we can discuss the matter first." Nicholas stepped inside and resumed his seat behind his desk.

Stephen halted in the doorway.

"Lieutenant," Nicholas's voice boomed. "Put the pistol away before you shoot my brother-in-law."

Stephen eyed the man warily while he holstered his weapon.

"Introductions are in order." Nicholas gestured to his brother-in-law. "Lord Felton, may I introduce to you Lieutenant Sparks my superior. Lieutenant Sparks, this is Stephen Hartington, Earl of Felton, and my brother-in-law."

Instead of bowing the lieutenant's gaze narrowed. "You followed me."

Stephen adjusted his cravat with a contrite expression.

"You know each other?"

The lieutenant shook his head. "I told you I couldn't reveal an agent's position. It's against protocol." He sat in a low-backed chair next to the fireplace and murmured again about a blasted woman and losing his touch for espionage.

"We need to talk." Stephen's eyes flicked to the lieutenant

and then back. "In private."

"It's Abby, isn't it?" Nicholas gripped the edge of his desk. His voice, as tight as a wound spring, desperate to know of his wife. "Is she ill? Hurt?" His fingers gripped the corner of his desk. "Is Abby all right?" When Stephen didn't answer fast enough, Nicholas slammed his palms on his desk and yelled, "Answer me, blast it! Is Abby well or not!"

"That depends on your definition of well." He turned to Lieutenant Sparks. "If you will."

The man pushed off from the chair. "I won't be far, if you need me." He closed the door behind him.

Nicholas's fingertips turned white.

Stephen widened his stance and crossed his arms. "If you think being shunned by her community, scorned by her friends, and doubted by her family is all right, then she's faring very well."

"I sent letters in case anyone questioned." Nicholas shook his head, as full understanding that his plan hadn't worked dawned.

"Letters didn't substitute for a real person. They didn't quash the rumors or the doubts."

His nightmare of Abby crying with overwhelming anguish had come true. He pictured the light leaving her eyes, snuffing out the joy in her heart—because of him.

"I left because I was a danger to her. I left so that she wouldn't..."

Silence filled the room.

Lord, I need to go back, but what if my nightmares return? What if I hurt her?

"There's one way to rectify the situation." Stephen eyed him with a hard gaze.

Nicholas straightened steeling his resolve and trusting that God, who changed him on the inside over these past six months of meeting with Aaron, would guide him in doing the right thing.

"You must return to Abby."

The words hit Nicholas's heart and sank in like a direct command from the Lord himself.

"You won't be able to hide anymore. The public will need to see you with Abby as a married couple." Stephen dropped his arms back to his sides. "You will have a lot of explaining to do. Someone saw you coming and going from Laurel House, and rumors spread that Abby was running a brothel."

Heat rose, burning around his collar.

"Others believe you are some sort of werewolf who takes on human form and whom Abby is secretly protecting." Stephen raised his brows. "You will face ridicule and suspicions. It could be your biggest nightmare."

Nicholas raked a hand through his hair and rounded his desk, stopping in front of Stephen. "It's worse than my nightmares, and Abby is living it. This is my fault, but believe me, I shall rectify it."

"That's the Nicholas Emerson I remember." Stephen clapped him on the shoulder. "Good to see you, my friend. It's been a long time."

Nicholas sighed. "It's good to be seen." He peered into the warm eyes of his childhood friend. "I owe you an apology."

"You're forgiven." Stephen flashed a smile. "But I will ask for a full explanation at a later date."

Nicholas eyed the door eager to get to Abby. "When do we leave?"

Scuffling sounded again from the entrance way, along with the butler's shout of pain.

Nicholas yanked open the door to see what was amiss now, and spied Lady Etheridge dragging the poor butler along by the ear.

Lieutenant Sparks trailed them, grumbling about Lady Etheridge being a beastly woman.

"Now, are you going to announce my arrival, or do I need to do that too?" Lady Etheridge stopped in front of Nicholas.

The servant sent a pleading look to his employer before wincing as Lady Etheridge tugged harder. "M-may I present Lady Amelia Sudham, Viscountess of Etheridge."

She released her grip on his ear and smoothed the wrinkles from her coat. "Lord Scarcliffe, it is good to see you again."

Lady Etheridge nodded to the other two men. "Lieutenant Sparks, Lord Felton." She locked gazes with Stephen. "My instructions were to wait for my arrival."

Stephen shrank back towards the office door under Lady Etheridge's deadly glare.

"What have I missed?" She shifted to face Nicholas, who held her gaze.

With a snort, she glanced at the lieutenant, who was quick to study the tips of his Hessian boots.

Stephen cleared his throat. "Lord Scarcliffe"—he glanced at Nicholas as if testing out the new title—"has decided to return with us."

"Well, of course he has." She tapped the end of her parasol on the marble floor in emphasis. "What are we waiting for then? My carriage is out front and ready to depart posthaste. I didn't come all this way to miss Lady Scarcliffe being vindicated."

Lady Etheridge watched Nicholas with an amused smile as if waiting for the title to register.

Nicholas turned to a curious footman who listened from a safe distance in the background. "Have my horse readied." He slid his arms into the jacket his butler held for him in the foyer.

Lady Etheridge yanked on Stephen's arm as he tried to follow. "If you ever leave me out of the excitement again, I will make it my personal duty to pay daily calls upon you and your wife." Her voice lowered, "And you better not have mentioned the surprise."

Nicholas stilled. What could be more surprising than what he'd undergone this morning?

"I thought it best not to discuss that subject yet."

"How very astute of you." She straightened and released his arm.

Stephen blinked.

Praise from Lady Etheridge would stun any man, but Nicholas had no time for trivial matters. He needed to get to Abby, so he signaled to the lieutenant, and they exited through the front door.

"Stop basking in the compliment, and hurry or you'll miss it." Lady Etheridge followed right behind them. "No need for your horse. We can take my carriage."

He eyed the lieutenant who turned ashen. They'd both rather run all the way to Altonwood than ride in an enclosed carriage with Lady Awfulridge.

CHAPTER 31

*a*bby placed her hands on her lower back and arched in a much-needed stretch. Her stiff backside ached from being jostled around in Lady Etheridge's carriage. She didn't care how plush and luxurious her town coach was, after six hours of sitting in it with two active toddlers, the most patient of people would need a long stretch and a breath of fresh air.

Grassy moors spread out as far as the eye could see. Sprinkles of wild daisies, thistles, and purple gromwells dotted one side of the drive while the other side held green hills staggered with limestone outcroppings that rimmed a large, placid pond.

Lydia escorted the boys to the water's edge, where they were diligently grabbing every available rock and tossing them in. Squeals of delight followed each plop.

Small rings of waves rippled the reflection of a proud Elizabethan manor house less than a furlong away. *Where in heaven's name had Lady Etheridge brought them?*

She had arrived early on their front doorstep and asked— but in Lady Etheridge's tone it had sounded like more of a demand—that she and the children accompany her today to call upon an old friend.

At first, Abby thought it would be wonderful to take the boys on an outing, but after a long waylaid stop at London's Home Office, of all places, where she was told to remain in the carriage, and a trek north to Lord-knows-where, Abby started to question Lady Etheridge's sanity. Two toddlers, determined to walk around and get into everything, trapped in a carriage with herself, a frazzled Lydia, and a reproving Lady Etheridge, had Abby's nerves worn thin. Thank heaven for the brief reprieve when David and Daniel napped.

When they finally arrived at their destination, Lady Etheridge had the gall to tell them to stay put while she went inside the manor.

Abby'd had to bite her tongue, but thankfully the carriage door had slammed shut before she pulled caps with the older woman, giving her a scathing lecture. She didn't have the slightest bit of remorse for not remaining in the carriage, despite Lady Etheridge's instructions.

Activity at the house drew Abby's attention. Two men, one of above average height with broad shoulders, the other an older stocky fellow, exited the front door.

The larger of the two shouted something to the nearby footman, who scurried towards the stables.

Abby waited for Lady Etheridge to appear and signal her, but when she didn't exit the building, she decided she'd better make her presence known. This day was turning out to be completely dreadful. The last thing she needed was to be discovered wandering the grounds of a stranger's property without permission. Certainly, the owners would see them as they rode by.

She called to Lydia. "Keep an eye on the boys. I'm going up to the main house to see what's keeping Lady Etheridge."

"Take your time. The boys are happy here."

Turning, Abby lifted the hem of her skirt and headed in the direction of the manor.

∽

*N*icholas slapped his gloves against the side of his leg. He wanted to rail at his groomsmen to pick up the pace. He ached to get to Abby, to end her torment. Emotions and thoughts clashed as he fought to process the drastic change to his future.

All of his carefully laid plans were flipped upside down, but it didn't matter. He concentrated on Abby. Would she forgive him for all he'd put her through? Would she give him a second chance—no, a *third* chance—to right the wrongs he'd committed? He ached to see her again, to touch her, to hold her. If he had another opportunity to redeem himself, he would not let her down.

He closed his eyes.

God, please help me to rectify my offenses. Continue to renew and heal my mind so that I can be the husband my wife needs. Please let only the biggest threat to her be our not being together. And, please, please, help Abby to forgive me.

Nicholas sucked in a deep breath and let his spirit settle. God heard his prayers. His hand was on all this.

The groomsman finally saddled Nicholas's horse and had him ready to ride.

Sparks rode the other groom's heels to ready his mount.

Nicholas grabbed the reigns and hoisted himself into the saddle. If he rode hard, he could get to Abby before nightfall and end her torment.

"You're making a mistake." Lady Etheridge jabbed her parasol in the air toward him as she approached the stable entrance.

The wind shifted, and the sound of children's laughter drifted to his ears. He trotted his mount out of the stable and bent low, ready to nudge his horse into a gallop. He turned his horse toward the lane and froze.

As if she'd miraculously appeared out of the mist of the moors, Abby walked towards him.

He yanked back on the reins, halting his mount. Blinking several times, he half expected the vision to disappear. Was he hallucinating? He flicked his gaze to the lieutenant for clarity.

With a gruff nod, Sparks said, "I see her too."

Abby.

"I told you that you didn't need a horse." Lady Etheridge's reprimanding tone ensured he wasn't dreaming.

"You had Abby in your carriage the entire time?" Stephen jogged over.

"Obviously. That's why I told you to wait for me."

Nicholas lowered himself from the saddle.

"What was your backup plan if things didn't go well?" Stephen asked of Lady Ethridge.

Nicholas passed the reins to Stephen.

Lady Etheridge snorted. "Where is your faith? There was no backup plan, only God's plan. He merely allowed me to help put the pieces together."

Nicholas's hands shook, so he linked them behind his back and strode toward Abby. He barely breathed, believing she'd vanish with the next gust of wind.

Many a night he'd lain awake rehearsing what he would say to Abby if he could ever see her again, but now as she strolled towards him with a purposeful stride, his carefully prepared speech eluded him.

She faltered a step in the gravel lane and stopped, her eyes widening. He drank in her porcelain skin and the shiny dark hair tumbling over her shoulders. His heart clenched at the dark smudges under her eyes. *Lord, I've been such a fool. I should have trusted You.*

He dared not move, fearing his knees would crumble.

Abby hesitantly stepped forward. "Nick?"

Shock laced her voice. And then, a smile lit her face.

His body responded with a jolt of pure joy.

"Nick!" Abby raced towards him, but his legs covered the remaining ground in a sprint. She threw herself into his arms, and he crushed her to his chest.

His nostrils filled with the scent of lilac soap, and he reveled in the softness of her skin, roving his hands over her back and shoulders.

"Abby, my darling, my love." He whispered the words over and over into the silky texture of her hair. His lips brushed kisses onto her temple, her forehead, her cheeks. "I'm sorry, so very sorry. Please forgive me. I've been a fool."

"I forgive you." She clung to him. "I love you."

"Heaven help me, I love you more. I haven't slept. I can't work. I tried to put you out of my thoughts, but I couldn't. I tried. I tried for half my life, but I can't. I love you too much." He released a strained laugh.

"I started praying again," he said. "I thought God had forgotten me, but He hadn't. He was listening. He heard my prayers. I prayed for a sign." Nicholas squeezed her tighter and chuckled into the curve of her neck. "And He sent three messengers to my doorstep."

They both glanced in the direction of the house, where Stephen, Lady Etheridge, and the lieutenant stood with goofy smiles on their faces.

Nicholas cupped Abby's face between the palms of his hands. "I needed God to tell me I should come back, that I wasn't being selfish by wanting you so badly. I was afraid I'd ruin your life."

Abby shook her head. "You are my love and my heart." Tears glistened in her over-bright eyes. "What God has joined together shouldn't be separated."

Nicholas claimed her lips in a searing kiss, sealing her vow into their hearts forever. He didn't pull away until they were both panting and breathless. Nicholas rested his forehead on hers and whispered to heaven, "Thank You, God, thank You."

He slowly drew back, and his eyes sought hers. "Abby." He nodded in the direction of the manor house. "This house is yours. I built it for you. This whole time, I've been here, doing this, but it doesn't make up for the wrongs I've done to you." His voice trembled. "Stephen told me about the wretched gossip."

Nicholas ran his hands down her shoulders and gently held her upper arms. "I will go back and prove to them I'm alive. I'll make everyone who has aggrieved you apologize, and then you can make your haven here. You won't ever need to be subjected to them again."

She glanced at the manor house. "All I want is to be with you. Wherever you go, I will go."

"I'm not hiding anymore. God rescued me for a reason, and I can't let my fears keep me from living out His plans any longer. No more hiding, no more secrets. I promise."

Abby bit her lip. "Nick, there is something I need to tell you."

He linked her hand with his. "Anything, sweetheart. You can tell me anything. You can yell at me and curse me for all the things I did. Just keep me by your side."

Her eyes searched his. "I shall ask the same of you." She pulled him in the direction of the pond.

Nicholas allowed her to lead him, not caring where they went, as long as they were together. Halfway down the lane, he tore his gaze from her and followed her line of vision. There on the bank were two identical toddlers.

He lost all ability to breathe.

The servant girl, Lydia, scooped up the children, placing one on each hip, and strolled toward them. The world faded away until all he could see was their precious faces.

Lydia stopped a few feet from them and lowered the children to the ground. One of them let out a peal of laughter and clapped his dimpled hands together. The other took off running with wobbly steps towards the open arms of his mother.

The child laughed and hugged Abby's skirts, then peered at Nicholas with green-gold eyes. *My green-gold eyes.*

Nicholas fell to his knees unable to stand. "I'm a father?" he whispered. "You didn't miscarry. You had twins. *We have twins?*"

"Nick." Abby's soft voice flowed with tenderness. "I would like you to meet your sons, David and Daniel."

Water splattered on his overcoat, and Nicholas realized they were his tears, tears of gratitude. With shaking hands, he gathered one of his sons into his arms, and Abby passed him the other.

One curled into Nicholas's chest while the other gripped Nicholas's shirt.

He placed a kiss on the fine hairs on the tops of their heads. "Daniel, David," he said in a choked voice. "I'm your papa."

He grinned at their mother, who watched the exchange with tears dripping down her cheeks and with so much love in her eyes that Nicholas tangibly ached from it.

Abby bit her bottom lip. Was she worried over his response?

"I will never truly understand why God would want to bless a man like me." He leaned close and kissed her on the forehead. "But He's blessed me with abundance."

"I love you." She choked on a sob.

"I love you more."

EPILOGUE

*A*bby sat next to her mother and Katherine in the small church box listening to the reverend's preaching. She had returned from spending over a fortnight at Abby Manor, where Nick proudly showed her the house he'd built for her.

The thought and detail he'd put into its construction swelled her heart, but when she had stepped into the conservatory he'd built for her, in his mother's honor, Abby had wept tears of joy.

A cloud passed and a ray of sunshine filled the room like God's countenance smiling down upon them. With all the secrets gone and the walls crumbled to dust, their rekindled love surpassed her dreams.

It was Nick who suggested they return home to Laurel House.

Abby explained that there was no need to rush back. They could wait until he was ready, but Nick was adamant.

Her mother, thrilled by their arrival, fawned over Nick and the boys like a mother hen.

Nick and Stephen's friendship resumed, as did their teasing and chiding as if nothing had changed in eleven years.

Someone coughed, and Abby used the distraction to glance back for what must have been the hundredth time. It seemed the whole town had gathered today in the old stone church. The pews were filled to overflowing.

The reverend stood in front of the podium, preaching to his congregation.

Abby sighed, hoping to release the weight that pressed on her heart.

Nick told her he would be late to Sunday's service, but now it was drawing to a close, and there was still no sign of him.

She fought to keep her spirits high, even though they teetered with every passing minute.

Nick still struggled with public appearances.

She noticed his slight hesitation before he entered a room. His smile appeared strained when he was re-introduced to people from his past. She admired his strength as he dutifully reacquainted himself, but he usually remained aloof. Whenever possible, he stood to a person's left, keeping his *good side* in plain view, and he always wore his collar points high.

Abby had tried to convince him these public appearances weren't necessary, but Nick was adamant. He'd let the entire town know he was alive and proved it by accompanying Abby everywhere—the orphanage, the candle makers, the grocer.

Only Mr. Kroger kept a wary eye on Nick as they did their shopping. Nick hadn't made things any better when he growled at the fanciful man before they left.

Abby had shaken her head.

Nick chuckled. "The man needs to learn a lesson. He'd better be afraid to start another rumor about my family."

Most of the town now claimed they'd believed Mr. Emerson, now Lord Scarcliffe, was alive the whole time and that, of course, they'd always known the children were his.

Abby merely smiled and let them say what they wanted. In the end, she was grateful for the miracles God had worked in her life. All of her dreams had come true. Her husband was alive. They were together. The boys adored their father, and they were a family.

Katherine squeezed Abby's hand. "Stephen and Nicholas will be here soon," she whispered.

Nick wasn't going to want to make a spectacle of himself by walking up the center aisle to sit with his family. Abby chewed her bottom lip.

"I wish we had sat in the back instead of so close to the front," Abby whispered.

Katherine patted her hand and whispered, "He'll be fine. Don't fret."

Abby smiled at her faithful friend. She thanked God again for the people He'd put into her life, like Katherine, who was such a blessing. He'd also brought Mama Em, Mrs. Smith, Lydia, and—she giggled at the thought—even Lady Etheridge and Miss Quiller. They'd come to Abby's side at just the right times and helped to sustain her when her world had fallen apart.

Katherine leaned over and whispered, "They're here."

Abby twisted in the pew, and her heart did a flip-flop as she gazed upon the handsome duo so close to her heart.

Nicholas and Stephen stood like sentinels, tall and erect in the back of the church. Each was dressed in his Sunday best, complete with dark cambric jackets, matching trousers, snowy white shirts with contrasting black cravats, and well-polished Hessian boots.

Nick scanned the crowd until his gaze locked upon hers. The deep love that lit his warm hazel eyes wrapped around her like an encouraging hug.

Her vision blurred with tears. Even though this was difficult for him, he'd come anyway. He'd faced his biggest fear for her, and she couldn't wait to get him back home so she could show him how much she appreciated his sacrifice.

Nick passed her with a nod and strode to the front of the chapel.

She blinked. What was happening?

Mother pulled a sleeping Daniel out of Abby's arms.

Katherine reached underneath their pew and procured a small bouquet of flowers that she stuffed in Abby's hands.

Stunned, Abby stared at the red roses and pure white lilies until Stephen cleared his throat. She glanced up at her brother, expecting him to ask her to scoot over so he could sit with his wife. Instead, he held out a hand to her.

Suddenly, everything registered, and Abby's gaze flew to Nick, who stood proudly next to the reverend with the hint of a mischievous smile at the corners of his lips. She placed her trembling hand in Stephen's and rose in one fluid motion. She floated down the aisle, her eyes never leaving Nick's.

At the front of the church, Stephen handed her to her husband and returned to sit next to Katherine.

Nick peered down at Abby, and the heat of a blush warmed her cheeks. She felt more beautiful and more in love than the first time he'd stood with her in the front of a church. Here he was, after all they'd been through, smiling at her with laughter in his eyes and an awed expression on his face. Despite standing in front of the entire town, she itched to pull him into her arms and kiss him with all the love she felt.

The reverend's voice interrupted her thoughts as he addressed the crowd.

"We have a special service today. The honorable Lord and Lady Nicholas and Abigail Emerson, the Viscount and Countess of Scarcliffe, are renewing their vows of eleven years of marriage in front of God and witnesses."

Abby's skin tingled all over, and her heart burst with joy. The wedding service proceeded, and they promised, in front of an entire town of witnesses and before God, to once again honor and cherish one another until death.

By the time the reverend announced them man and wife for the second time, there wasn't a dry eye in the house.

Nick hauled her into his arms and planted a searing kiss on her lips, taking her breath away.

Hoots and hollers followed.

When Abby finally pulled back, her cheeks blazed.

"I love you, Nicholas Emerson."

Nick lowered his head until their noses touched. "I love you more." He looked about to pull her in for another kiss, but he shook his head. "In fact, I love you with all my heart, and I would give my life for you."

He cupped her face in his hands and captured her gaze with his own.

The rest of the room melted away until all she saw was him.

"Abigail Emerson." His voice was a whisper in her hair, deep and warm. "You have shown me a love that goes far beyond human capabilities. You never gave up on me despite all that I put you through. Your love believed in me, it never relinquished hope, and it endured every trial. You have shown me the same love Jesus showed his church, a love that I did not deserve."

His lips tenderly kissed hers before his warm arms encircled her body. "You've reclaimed my soul and shown me a better life because of a love that never failed."

Abby rose onto her toes. Not caring what spectators might think, she wound her arms around her husband's neck and kissed him back, thanking God for rewriting their tragedy into a happily-ever-after.

Did you enjoy this book? We hope so!
Would you take a quick minute to leave a review where you purchased the book?
It doesn't have to be long. Just a sentence or two telling what you liked about the story!

Receive a FREE ebook and get updates when new Wild Heart books release: https://wildheartbooks.org/newsletter

Don't miss the next book in the Agents of Espionage Series!

Redeeming the Rake
By Lorri Dudly
Releasing December 1st, 2024!

FROM THE AUTHOR

Dear Readers,

I'm so blessed by you. Thank you for reading my latest series. God had a bigger plan for me when writing *Reclaiming the Spy*. In researching the beginning scene with Mama Em, I read *Glimpses of Heaven* by Trudy Harris, RN. Ms. Harris was a hospice nurse who tells of her clients' stories in their final days. I've never sobbed through a book quite like I have this one, but at the same time, it was encouraging to hear how many of her patients heard glorious music, observed beautiful scenes, recognized past friends or family members, witnessed angels, or even saw their Savior, Jesus Christ.

I didn't know that God was preparing me through my research for my dad to go into hospice care. My dad spoke of seeing his mom and dad in vivid dreams, and I know they were waiting to welcome him into heaven. I've drawn comfort in seeing how God blurs the lines of this realm and the next to make for an easier transition, and I've felt God's presence beside me the entire way.

God is good all the time.

I'm so grateful to my publisher, Wild Heart Books, for how understanding they've been and touched by their prayers and encouragement. Thank you for bringing another one of my creations to life. To my editor and friend, Robin Patchen, thank you for refining my books and me in the process. I've grown so much in my writing because of you.

And to my freelance editor and friend, my other Robyn,

Robyn Hook, thank you for your significant input and for helping me in a crunch, even emailing me back my manuscript at one a.m. I owe a special thanks to my launch team for spreading the word and posting reviews and to my beta readers for catching my inconsistent name spellings and missing conjunctions. Thank you to my mom, husband, boys, and extended family for being there and encouraging me all the way.

And most of all, to my Heavenly Father.

I love you.

If you love historical romance, check out the other Wild Heart books!

The Pirate's Purchase by Elva Cobb Martin

Escaping to the New World is her only option...Rescuing her will wrap the chains of the Inquisition around his neck.

Marisol Valentin flees Spain after murdering the nobleman who molested her. She ends up for sale on the indentured servants' block at Charles Town harbor—dirty, angry, and with child. Her hopes are shattered, but she must find a refuge for herself and the child she carries. Can this new land offer her the grace, love, and security she craves? Or must she escape again to her only living relative in Cartagena?

Captain Ethan Becket, once a Charles Town minister, now sails the seas as a privateer, grieving his deceased wife. But when he takes captive a ship full of indentured servants, he's intrigued by the woman whose manners seem much more refined than the average Spanish serving girl. Perfect to become governess for his young son. But when he sets out on a quest to find his captured sister, said to be in Cartagena, little does he expect his new Spanish governess to stow away on his ship with her six-month-old son. Yet her offer of help to free his sister is too tempting to pass up. And her beauty, both inside and out, is too attractive for his heart to protect itself against—until he learns she is a wanted murderess.

As their paths intertwine on a journey filled with danger, intrigue, and romance, only love and the grace of God can overcome the past and ignite a new beginning for Marisol and Ethan.

~

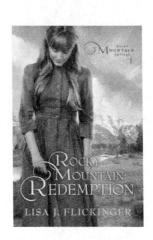

Rocky Mountain Redemption by Lisa J. Flickinger

A Rocky Mountain logging camp may be just the place to find herself.

To escape the devastation caused by the breaking of her wedding engagement, Isabelle Franklin joins her aunt in the

Rocky Mountains to feed a camp of lumberjacks cutting on the slopes of Cougar Ridge. If only she could out run the lingering nightmares.

Charles Bailey, camp foreman and Stony Creek's itinerant pastor, develops a reputation to match his new nickname — Preach. However, an inner battle ensues when the details of his rough history threaten to overcome the beliefs of his young faith.

Amid the hazards of camp life, the unlikely friendship growing between the two surprises Isabelle. She's drawn to Preach's brute strength and gentle nature as he leads the ragtag crew toiling for Pollitt's Lumber. But when the ghosts from her past return to haunt her, the choices she will make change the course of her life forever—and that of the man she's come to love.

~

Lone Star Ranger by Renae Brumbaugh Green

Elizabeth Covington will get her man.

And she has just a week to prove her brother isn't the murderer Texas Ranger Rett Smith accuses him of being. She'll show the good-looking lawman he's wrong, even if it means setting out on a risky race across Texas to catch the real killer.

Rett doesn't want to convict an innocent man. But he can't let the Boston beauty sway his senses to set a guilty man free. When Elizabeth follows him on a dangerous trek, the Ranger vows to keep her safe. But who will protect him from the woman whose conviction and courage leave him doubting everything—even his heart?

Made in the USA
Coppell, TX
27 March 2025

47600666R00213